d 12
20

CAROL
BRUNEAU

GLASS VOICES

A Novel

Cormorant Books

Canada Council   Conseil des Arts
for the Arts   du Canada

The publisher gratefully acknowledges the support of the
Canada Council for the Arts and the Ontario Arts Council
for its publishing program. We acknowledge the financial support
of the Government of Canada through the Book Publishing
Industry Development Program (BPIDP) for our publishing activities.

Printed and bound in Canada

Library and Archives Canada Cataloguing in Publication

Bruneau, Carol, 1956 –
Glass voices/Carol Bruneau.

ISBN 978-1-897151-12-9

I. Title.

PS8553.R854G53 2007   C813'.54   C2007-902750-4

This is a work of fiction; names and characters are products of
the author's imagination, and any resemblance to persons
living or dead is coincidental.

Editor: Marc Côté
Cover design & image: Angel Guerra/Archetype
Text design: Tannice Goddard/Soul Oasis Networking
Printer: Marquis

CORMORANT BOOKS INC.
215 SPADINA AVENUE, STUDIO 230, TORONTO, ONTARIO, CANADA M5T 2C7
www.cormorantbooks.com

For my dad, John Bruneau.

And what can this sorrow be? It is brewed by the earth itself. It comes from the houses on the coast. We start transparent, and then the cloud thickens. All history backs our pane of glass. To escape is vain.

— VIRGINIA WOOLF, JACOB'S ROOM

One

STICKY AS GRASSHOPPER MOLASSES, this is the last, the frigging *last* day (put that in your glass and guzzle it, Harry Caines!) anyone *or* their dog should be slaving over a stove. Easy for him, though, upstairs lollygagging as per usual. Rules for one aren't always rules for another. But there it is: make hay — make pickles — while the sun shines. Make whoopee, Harry would say, yes he would, shame, shame, and at his age. But what else is new? Here she is, knuckled down on all fours, searching for the right pot. At least the linoleum's a friend: its coolness, never mind the pain like a spike through each knee! Lordie, she can almost picture the *Herald* headline: Lady found petrified in Armview kitchen, while hubby shaves.

Like Lot's wife in the Bible, how about that? Turned into a pillar of salt — enough to do up ten batches of dills. But first things first: she's got to find that canner. It could be animal husbandry, digging inside the cupboards; what *was* Harry thinking when he installed everything lock, stock, and barrel? It's as if something's curled up and died: the dust!

What the heck's he doing up there? "Harry?" Is he alive? "Better get moving, if you're planning to —"

A burst of song burbles through the ceiling, that quavery tenor, "Oh Danny ... oh *cranky* Boy," through how many layers?

Mopping her brow, she cannot help herself. "Get a move on, mister!"

Typical, so typical. "The pipes, the pipes are ..."

And what does he have against Bick's, anyway? They're just as good. But try telling him, waltzing in the other day with ten pounds of cukes. Baby peckers, Rebecca, her daughter-in-law, called them, making even Harry blush. Well. He's not the one on his knees, is he? And his aren't full of arthritis, not like hers, stiff and blue as the day she almost died but didn't.

"Hurry up! If you hope to get there any time soon ..." Trained on the trickling inside the wall, her voice bounces off the plaster.

"... are ca-a-alling." The words get sliced in two, then drowned out by the lawn mower starting outside. Harry's no Charlie Chamberlain, and he's certainly no Mel Tormé.

"Harrry? You'll want to catch the boy before —" She has to scream above the noise, and yet, isn't it true? There's always something to be grateful for. The fact that that old bird next door has finally replaced her push mower with a gas one: *que-ching que-ching que-ching* all the livelong day, for how many years? Still, the high-powered roar rocks the jars lined up on the counter. Short term pain for long term gain? Well, at least it's not winter; it could be snowing, and pickling beats pushing up weeds, or daisies.

"Robert's going to wonder where on earth you're at — Harry?"

"From glentoglen, and ..."

"He'll think you got lost."

"Dooooown the mouuuntain ..."

"If you're giving him that talking-to, better get your London-derriere over there —" A tower of pots gives, and, lo and behold, with a crash of lids, the canner wiggles free. Something small and cool grazes her fingers, too perfectly round to be a pea. A marble.

"Harry, for heaven's sake ..."

Neither a cat's eye nor a pretty, neither a doughboy nor a peewee, it's somewhere in between. If she stuck it under their son's and Rebecca's queen-size mattress, well, that princess would feel it; on that Lucy would place money. In her palm it's the colour of bathwater, a murky crystal ball, an iris-less eye. The memory that oozes from nowhere is as golden as cod liver oil: Robert, their grandson, rigging a slingshot when he was little, firing marbles for cannonballs.

"You tell him, Harry," she mutters above the mower, "stay in school, or else."

Then, just as unbidden, a parable springs to mind, a bit of Scripture: a woman turning her hovel upside down looking for one measly coin. Well, she and Robert searched high and low that day for a lost glassy, Robert bawling his eyes out. Imagine him bawling now — into a glass of beer, maybe.

Weren't marbles the prime thing for little kids to choke on?

The trickling in the wall piddles out. Heaving the canner up and onto the counter like a medicine ball, she rocks back to rest. Smoothing her hem over her knees, she rolls the marble in the valley of her skirt; it clouds a printed violet. Sunday best, this dress was once; it's still her favourite. The colour, robin's egg blue, makes her think of early summer when she was small, and the world more tender, maybe, and softer on the eyes. Clingy and damp, the filmy polyester keeps riding up: those knees of hers look as if she's kneeled in grease.

Do they go to this much trouble at Heinz? Dragging herself up, she drops the marble into a glass of geranium slips. Safekeeping, a keepsake. Now she'll get down to business: rinsing cukes, nipping off stems like cords. Pouring vinegar, measuring salt. The concoction coming to a boil sounds like a distant train.

Never mind what Robert's dad says about him staying out all hours, sleeping till noon — as if Rebecca doesn't. Bucky, she calls him. His own mother. That nickname as bad as gum stuck to your shoe. "Harry? You don't catch him now, no telling what he'll choose," she yells, half to herself, half to the ceiling. "Go on, while Jewel's at work and her majesty's putting on her face."

The trouble is, she can already picture it, Harry raising his hands like Festus on *Gunsmoke*: "I'm not interfering. Just offering advice." The trouble with Robert, with kids today, as far as she can see, is the parents, all the pussyfooting and kid-gloves handling. When Jewel, their son, was a boy ...

Packed into clean jars, the cukes wink back: specimen frog princes. Sweat tickles her sides as she ladles in liquid. Harry loves garlic, so at the last minute she minces some and throws it in; wouldn't have bothered, once. Nasty, that smell on her fingers, as the princes swim in their brine.

The sun and the burbling roar pour in, but not a twitch of a breeze.

Next step, the boiling bath. The water on a roll, she roots out tongs to lower in the jars. Steam curls up like the girl on *I Dream of Jeannie* leaving her magic bottle, and the flowers on Lucy's dress shimmy. What'll she do with all these pickles, anyway? Palm them off on Rebecca, after Harry's had his fill — or the women's league; they're always after donations. God willing, Robert'll be around to make short work of some, though lately he's talking about going west — that's after he's moved out, quit school, bought a car, got a job: security at the yacht club, watching boats. Like watching paint dry, it would seem. Though not to Harry, who loves making reason play second fiddle, just to get her goat: "What've you got against a kid making money? Okay, okay, so I'll talk to him."

All the same, since retiring Harry's slowly begun waking up to the future, what's left of it. Never mind his bad eye and the bad leg that's plagued him since the shipyards — with Robert he has, or should have, a project, when there's nothing on TV and he's bored with his accordion. "Pardon me, Lucy. It's a Don Noble, not just any old 'cordine."

Never mind. *We live in hope*, the pale, greeny blue of her dress still whispers, from the swish of its slippery weave. But what is keeping the man? Today's Harry's day for watching wrestling, enjoying a sandwich and his weekly Keith's in front of the tube; playing along with the ads keeps him in practice. "Practice, Lucy, practice," he's always saying. Funny how cradling the instrument doesn't remind him of cradling a child, or anything else for that matter. It reminds her.

The first batch of jars jiggles in the canner; the rest wait, lined up on the counter. "Harry?" Trudging to the stairs, out of patience, she hollers up: the last straw. "If you don't get moving NOW, you'll miss your show."

Next door, the lawn mower scrapes something and cuts out. In the sticky silence just before it restarts, something prods her — like a hand — at first gentle, tapping her shoulder, then gripping her. She has the presence to turn off the stove, letting whatever it is propel her back to the stairs without stopping to drop the tongs. Knees and all, her body reacts, climbing, flying past the landing, the way a car remembers driving. It's "automic," as Rebecca calls her washing machine. Despite its stickiness, the air prickles her arms, bringing things back: air thick as lava, but icy too. Harry's name in her throat, wedged there like a picket. Drawn upwards, her feet barely touch the plastic treads. The flash in her skull almost like lightning as the walls virtually dissolve.

Harry's sprawled on the bathroom floor, eyes open, his good one pale and frozen. The shock is like a clap of wind. Something leaks from his blue pajamas. The instant of seeing, she launches a prayer. His cheeks glow as if he's been on the worst tear ever. A dribble of spit, a thread of blood where he's nicked himself. One hand — his left? — jumps like a mouse on the tiles. Slowly, slowly, rising, falling: his chest works like the Don Noble's bellows, and in a blink, she sees herself young once more: her mouth open in a scream, gums pink as the felt edging the accordion's keys.

"HARRY!" Her cry flies off the fixtures, bleaching the room of light and sound. She's kneeling, the tongs splayed like forceps. Her fingertips stuck to his pulse; the hint of garlic a memory, stinky-sweet as kerosene.

His lips squirm: nothing more than a gurgle comes out.

Downstairs, she hears herself dialing, giving the address. The voice inside her is like her son's, ordering: *Start the car.* Foolish, since she's never learned to drive. She should call Jewel at work, or even Rebecca. But she can't think, racing upstairs again, ripping the spread off the bed. Blue, it's been washed almost white. She tucks it around him, right up to his chin. Wild with panic, that eye gobbles her up. Suddenly she's freezing, the house is freezing, her dress clammy, wet. His cheek burns beneath her kisses. Another lightning memory: sheets dropped like moths on a harder floor.

Below, in the kitchen, the lids on the jars pop, one by one. Each sound is like a period dropped from space. Just this summer, didn't those crazy Yanks put men on the moon? Mr. Armstrong, Mr. Aldrin. The pickles seem as alien. Then, at last, the wail of a siren, and the doorbell chimes, the bell which Harry just got around to replacing last year.

The men climb the stairs like plumbers, that unhurried and businesslike, murmuring as they probe and poke. It's as if they don't see her, as if she's been vaporized, beamed upwards or drawn inside somewhere dark and airless, lured by crumbs. Prayer. A voice louder than theirs: hers. *Our Father who art in Heaven, hallowed be thy Name. In the name of the Father, Son and Holy ...* As he's lifted onto the stretcher, the crumbs form Harry's name.

"Please don't hurt him!" the same voice begs. The ambulance throws light the colour of marigolds up the stairs, and all around her goes quiet again, so quiet there's only the maple breathing out front. The men load Harry like a loaf into an oven. Doors slam shut.

Only as they scream away does she realize she's been left behind, leaning against the fence in her old dress and apron, the fence Robert keeps promising to paint. In a second, it too could collapse, disappear, pickets and rails blown all over creation. For now, its splintery sag is a comfort.

She should phone Jewel, but can't think of the number. Remembering, though, to check the stove — still there, yes, the burner cool — she peels off the apron, steps into the nearest shoes, ancient espadrilles caked with dirt. The number for the taxi's right there, though, from all the times Harry's been off someplace, unavailable. She even remembers her purse and to lock up, going out to wait on the veranda. Clutching her bag, though all that's there is the five for Robert's down payment. "I'll do it whenever," he's fond of saying.

As the cab cruises up, she can't help imagining a huge, greasy cloud filling the sky, and her legs feel weak, as if every single bone has been wrenched, then slammed against dirt. Yet, there are her shins mapped with veins, otherwise pale and smooth as a baby's arse, Harry would say. When she blinks, looking up, the sky is blue, of course.

SQUEAKY, AVOCADO-COLOURED SEATS, ashtrays and germ-ridden magazines. The waiting room's packed: everything feels contagious. Someone offers a chocolate bar, even a cigarette, but she can barely reply, sinking there, anchored by her purse, her calves freezing. To pray — earnestly — would mean hitting bottom: kneeling on the speckled linoleum, certain tears amid pacing feet. *For thine is the kingdom, the power and the glory, for ever and ever and ever ...* Limping to a phone, she rummages for change. There's something reassuring about the dime's tiny Bluenose as she inserts it, something almost portentous. Like the feel of the marble. The first boat had sunk, but then been replaced, as if nothing bad had ever happened.

Rebecca answers, music blaring behind her. A noise like screeching tires: Robert's music, a racket that makes her want to hang up.

"Is Jewel home?" She has to shout.

"That you, Ma? You don't have to take my ear off. He can't come to the phone right now, he's just got in and he's ..." A snicker. "Can he call you back?" That voice burns her ears. "Everything okay?"

Someplace in her imagination, the sky oozes. "I'm all right," she says resolutely, almost ashamed, "but Harry isn't."

When Jewel finally comes on, he grills her with a barbed gruffness. Then, "Hang tight — you hear me?" As if she's a little girl. "I'm on my way."

Putting down the receiver, she trembles, anger a slow but sudden pulse inside. There's a rawness she hasn't felt in years, not since Jewel was a boy, when, on occasion, truthfully, she could've slipped Comet into Harry's beer, for pity's sake. Chopped up a dumb cane plant and put it in his salad. All those times she'd ridden out, done her best, of course, and now look.

Dumb, dumb as dirt. Dumber than the little white numbers peeling off the phone ...

Someone touches her arm: a nurse. She can go in. The corridor clatters and hums. *Hurry hard*, the voice inside her croaks, like the curlers Harry watches on TV when there's absolutely nothing else.

Lucy barely recognizes the body in the railed bed, a tube taped to its mouth, a string of saliva like a cobweb.

Harry's eyes are closed, mercifully, sparing her that stricken look, and his chest moves gently up and down under the sheet, though who can tell if he's asleep or awake? Sporting a tartan cap, the doctor speaks through a spreading fog, and in the back of her head an alarm sounds. A foghorn, its moan not a warning but a reminder, always a reminder. And suddenly it's no longer summer, not even summer's close or the cusp of fall, but winter, as if cold, wet snow is veiling everything.

"Left hemisphere. Fairly major. Right side paralysis. Three to five days. Ab-so-lutely critical."

"Is it very bad?" is all she can ask. The tube in Harry's mouth makes her look away; it's as if he's been invaded by a large plastic snake. Useless, his hands are pale gloves lying on the snowy sheet.

"Too early to tell," the doctor says, much too succinctly. "Possibly a clot ... The brain swells ... Survival depends, Mrs. ..."

Survival? She gazes at the ramparts of Harry's knees, the steep slope of his belly: like a gull's view of Citadel Hill in the middle of town, just after a blizzard.

"All depends on how he comes through the next four or five days."

That measurement of words: a louder blast. "Is he in pain?"

The doctor smiles, the brackets around his mouth matching those around his eyes.

"He seems to be resting comfortably, Mrs. Caines."

Another curl of memory, neither golden nor white: Rebecca's mother slurring at her husband's wake: "He's up there resting where no more shuffering can give him grief," when anything that fellow'd suffered had been his own doing, and those two not properly married. Others suffered: women losing children, people with horrible diseases and any number of wounds — Jewel, for instance, suffering the daily insult of his wife.

"Can he hear us?" Her whisper is almost babyish, blotted up by the cubicle's green curtains. "Harry?" she croaks, stroking a limp wrist.

"He's aware of what's happening," the doctor murmurs. "His hearing doesn't seem affected. A good sign. Though, as I said, the next few days ..."

Watching Harry's face, she slides her fingers over his. They jerk at her touch, but they're warm. The feeblest squeeze, it feels like the first time a child twitched inside her.

"His injuries?" the doctor interrupts, and to her embarrassment her face is wet. There's the tiny cut on Harry's jaw from the razor.

"His eye." The doctor pats the breast pocket of his greens. "His chest?"

The blue crescent above Harry's nipple.

"Your husband's a vet? First or Second World War?"

Fixing on the snake — Harry's breathing tube — she's confused. How can anyone, especially a doctor, not know?

"How did he lose it?" His mildly curious look. "The eye?"

"It was an accident," she manages. "That's what they say."

"Well. He's a trooper then. As I said, the next few days will determine — wish I could tell you more, Mrs. Caines, but ..."

How does he know her name?

A nurse appears; apparently the family's outside — what family? Whose? It's as if the room's an aquarium and she's swimming through greenish water as someone guides her out into the hall, and, oh yes, there they are. *Her* family. Their faces bob like pale buoys, three of them. Jewel, Rebecca, and oh Lord, it must be dire because even Robert's here. Jewel drapes his arm around her; it feels warm and heavy, clammy in this watery atmosphere. Rebecca looks scared, her thin little brows arched in a way that makes her appear to be holding her breath; they're all holding their breath, even Robert, who watches a spot on the floor as if it's a sculpin.

"This is all of you?" a voice interjects, a kindly voice, the doctor's.

"Yup," Jewel replies tersely, as if to say what did you expect, a little league team?

Lucy nods, nods in time to their pale bobbing faces, an old feeling swarming round her, settling in. A regret she's had for most of her life now, like a phantom pain, the ghost of a missing limb.

"This is us, our little clan." All of us, but ... Instinctively, as if this regret might be the thing that pulls her under, that fills her lungs finally so that she *can't* breathe, Lucy reaches for a hand. Robert's. For once he doesn't pull it away, staring at the windowless door that's like a hatch between this side of the fish bowl, and the other, off-limits one where Harry is.

"So granddad makes five," the doctor says and she nods weakly, because it's easier than having to explain: Yes, all but ...

"One visitor at a time, sorry," says a nurse whisking by, then to Lucy, more gently: "Why don't you go home now, Mrs.? Try to relax, rest." She'll need it, in other words. It's the same as being told not to worry.

When they finally leave, all together, a tiny pack, shadows stretch across the hospital grounds, the sun a dusky bloom over the buildings. People scurry past as Jewel helps her into the car, Rebecca leaning to buckle her up before sliding in. She's hemmed between them, Robert alone in the back. But who has the energy to object? Creased with dread, Jewel's face looks old, as old as his father's. How can it be? The boy she nursed and bounced on her hip. Thinking back to his birth, no hospital then, only the cold and a nursing sister's touch. For most of the drive nobody speaks. It's gotten chilly and, shivering, she tugs her skirt over her knees. Her whole body feels icy now, the way she would after an ocean dip; cramped and trapped there on the seat that's as hard as a berm and feeling every bump, she might as well be dragged along the pavement.

Finally, Rebecca breaks the silence. "All we can do is hope, Ma."

Her throat tightens, and all she can say is the obvious, which sounds mawkish, trite: "And pray, I guess. Jewel. Rebecca, you too. And Robert." Under any other circumstances they'd laugh and make jokes, and when they don't it sinks in how bad this is. Jewel flicks at his nose. Robert's voice is halting, a shaky hum behind her so low she asks him to repeat himself, a request she instantly wishes could be sucked back like toothpaste up a tube.

"My girlfriend? When her grandpa nearly croaked?" Why, why do kids speak in questions? The more so when all that's asked, and offered, is a simple declaration. "Well, they brung him back, and he seen angels, and they had feathers."

"Bucky!" Rebecca's tongue is like one of those fancy choppers advertised on TV. Still, he doesn't have the sense, poor little bugger, to just leave it; in that respect, Lucy supposes, he rather does take after his mother.

"But he seen them, white feathers." As if the colour is proof. His sigh a swallowed cuss.

"It's all right, dear," Lucy says through the brick in her throat, eyes fixed on the cardboard pine tree swinging from the mirror. A deodorizer, Rebecca's idea no doubt, since to Rebecca's nose everything stinks. Try as she might, Lucy can't detect a single odour, except maybe the smell of Robert's hair, the smell of unwashed jeans.

"It's all right," she hears herself murmur again, clearing her throat. It's expected of her, of course. "I almost lost him once, you know," and as she twists toward Jewel a little despairing laugh escapes. "Well, more than once."

Rushing by, buildings, trees and pedestrians make a lush, greenish blur, and with a shock she's picturing herself alone in the house. Preparing herself, sort of, the way Mr. Armstrong must've for his first giant steps. Jewel must sense it; maybe he can smell it off her the way she can pick up the scent of teenage trouble no matter how many showers a kid takes a day.

"Come home with us," he says. "Becky'll rustle something up for us — won't you, Beck?" As usual, next comes the buttering-up, never mind that it's as though Rebecca's deaf. "She made meatloaf the other day. From scratch."

"Congratulations," Lucy volunteers; what else can she say? The poor darling, as if housekeeping's an Olympian feat.

But Rebecca stares stubbornly ahead, her lip twitching slightly. Better to say nothing, nothing at all, so Lucy closes her eyes, the better to hear the tires hissing, a sound like summer rain. Oh please God, *let* it rain, she thinks wildly, longing for its softness, the way it has of blurring edges. Rain makes it easier to stay inside and concentrate, which she'll need to do. Her work is cut out now; it digs in sharply, like a little knife poking into her stomach. Nothing for it but to start her vigil, petitioning God, or somebody, to give Harry back. She's had some practice, and the thought tightens her hope a notch or two, never mind its slippery hold. She might even call the priest as well as the women's league, have Harry added to the prayer chain. *Right*, she can just imagine his voice, imagine him rising up, sitting in that chilly chrome bed: *Now you've got me where you want me, on a frigging chain gang.*

Never mind that Father Whasisname doesn't look old enough to shave. *Wherever two or more are gathered*, he says ...

As she thinks it, her hope floats, and Jewel pulls up the street slowly, turning in.

"You're sure you won't come over't the house?" Rebecca peers at her, and is that a glint of tears?

"Becky'll have my head later for droppin' you off." *Heeead*, Jewel says, a word halfway between *hid* and *heed*. Instead of glowering, Rebecca strokes Lucy's arm. Now she really can't wait to get out of the car; they mustn't see *her* cry, any of them.

"Another time, my dears." She's careful to add the *s*. Always this game of including; sometimes she feels like the president of America, keeping the peace.

Jewel tugs on her arm, walking her up to the door. "Come on, Ma." But she knows what she's up against, needing to be alone. It'll take all her wits, every ounce of concentration, to retrieve Harry this time, to pluck him back from wherever he's slipped to. Jewel must know. His eyes swim, that blue a mirror of his father's good one, a blue so familiar it's a pearl inside her, no, a sapphire. Her little Jewel, her gem. People aged, of course; the world changed by the minute, they said on TV, but people didn't, not themselves, not deep inside.

Hunkered there in back, Robert looks up at her through his mop of hair and setting his jaw, nods. A man-to-man sort of nod that under any other circumstance would touch her funny bone.

"Well. Don't forget to eat," Jewel was bossing her, tender now but cocky, always cocky, towering over her; or was it Rebecca talking through him? "The old man," he hesitates, "he's gonna pull through."

But that's the thing with hope, part of her wants to argue: no one can presume.

"Jeez, Ma ... that bloody fence." Unlocking the door, he doesn't look at her. "Listen, I'll get that kid over here if it kills him. Even if I gotta drag his arse out of bed."

"It's okay," she murmurs, sick of saying so, as an image flits through her head of Robert the last time he let himself be photographed: a school picture, his gawky smile at, what, thirteen? He has Harry's looks, too, though Jewel denies it. Kid's got Marryatt written all over him, he's always insisted, and Rebecca would say amen to that, if amen were in her vocabulary. But she knows different: there's the bridge of his nose, that grin, and Harry's build. Harry when she first met him. That loose, loping tautness, though Harry'd been on the short side, lacking the boy's height. Something about their movement, though — body language, Rebecca calls it — makes it impossible to picture one without seeing the other. Which will make it harder, banish the thought; or easier, she realizes, glimpsing Jewel in the hall mirror. Depending on whether the glass ends up empty, or full.

He can't seem to leave, lingering as if she'll change her mind and come home with them after all, then finally saying he'll be by first thing, and they'll go in. "Early. Unless something ..." His voice trails off; then that brusqueness again, so much closer to what she's used to. "You call me, okay? You need anything, gimme a shout." As if she would do that: stand on the verandah and bellow till the neighbours phoned the cops, the pigs as Robert calls them. So little respect ...

His breath is sour as he pecks her cheek, and then he's getting back in and they're driving off. The shapes of their heads the last thing she sees as the car purrs down the little street. Three: such an odd, awkward number, but with a symmetry all its own, a rightness, she supposes, if one likes triangles.

Two

THE HOUSE SMELLS STALE, as if she's been away a lot longer. On stove and counter sit the pots and withered cukes, the first round of jars standing in their dingy water. Harry would be disappointed; at least, unlike her, he wouldn't fret over the waste. All her industry feels like it happened weeks ago now; it's like turning on the TV at the end of a show.

Upstairs, the bedspread lies balled up on the floor. In their room, the sheets are rumpled. The only signs of orderly cheer: the small varnished cross above her dresser, her candy dish full of earrings. A vanity. At sixty-eight, at Rebecca's urging, she'd got her ears pierced. "Ma, if Harry can have his accordion ..." The girl at the beauty parlour had promised it wouldn't hurt, and it hadn't. But still she felt silly, as if the holes were some sort of pampered stigmata, and Harry's teasing hadn't helped: "My wife the Christmas tree; look at the dingle balls on her, wouldja." But for their fiftieth wedding anniversary he'd handed her a bag from Consumers Distributing: a pair of teeny diamond studs. Harry Caines!

Removing them, carefully replacing the backs, she sets them in the dish, then slips to his side of the bed, where the Don Noble takes up a chair. Shiny as foil Christmas wrap, its red veneer feels sticky-smooth to the touch. Harry's scent is all over the pillow: the smell of Old Spice and cigarettes and something else, just *him*, as she stretches out, closes her eyes. God will excuse her lying down for this; he should, knowing all about her knees. A chill breathes through the screen, the evening's coolness tinged with fall, and with each wisp of air she tries to imagine him, or someone, listening.

But it's hard to concentrate on prayer: her mind keeps lurching back to Harry, not lying on the bathroom floor or in the sterile white bed, but perched on a kitchen chair chugalugging beer and squeezing out tunes one after another, laughing till his molars showed, including the one he'd ended up having pulled. And suddenly there's his eye, the artificial one, which she can almost picture now, a relic, like a kewpie doll's, rolling among her earrings, its flat blue lacking the gleam of his right one; and she can even hear him joking, coming home from cleanings and fittings at the doctor's. How next time he'd pick brown and be like a mutt with a mismatched pair: "How'd you like them peepers? Put that in your cup and drink it, dolly!"

Better, safer, to imagine the marble, Robert's marble and his baby voice: "Nanny, I waaant it." Until in her mind it clouds and grows oblong and opaque as a Scotch mint — a mint rolling in a film of blood. Much as she resists, as fast as the mantra of prayer puts up a wall, the memories topple it. And when she glances up at the dark panes, she can almost see them shattering — over and over and over, a wave of diamonds breaking inwards — and Harry holding the razor to his cheek, turning, both of his eyes blazed wide open.

Oh Danny Boy: if she clamps her teeth and forces air into both ears she can summon his voice and let it fill her head — enough to squeeze out the blackness. Like driving out the enemy, bolting doors — enough to let herself drift off, anyway. Dozing through darkness takes practice, but she has an arsenal of that. Arse-nal, the syllables swagger through her brain, another round of Harry's voice, as if he's yelling *arsehole*, insulting somebody from inside his hospital sleep ...

But sometime in the night she's shaken awake by crying: her own. *Harry?* Flinging out an arm, reaching for him ... But there's only the chilly sheet. Her head pounding. The emptiness of the bed a burden, after fifty-five years of sharing it. Somewhere in the dark a truck throttles downhill. By no means is it the first time she's felt so alone, but now the quiet is like a body falling through space. Or a snowball trundling downhill, gathering weight.

The little Ben at the bedside says 4:30; in its greenish glow her mind grows tentacles, like the tubes that she pictures trailing from Harry in his cold white bed. Choking off his voice and her reason, they latch on to rubble best left buried, snowed or grassed over. But like rocks growing in the garden, the rubble leaches upwards through dust and cobwebs the colours of dawn, if dawn ever comes. There are worse things than dying, *way* worse, and knowing it knocks her down, it no longer matters if she's waking or sleeping, all but defenceless against memory's wave.

Good thoughts, good thoughts: her will bubbles at first in protest, a fierce effervescence. And so it floods back: a flash of light at first, for the only way to begin her freefall is with white. A snowy hill in the background, whiteness solid as a drumlin, Citadel Hill an upside-down bowl ...

FOR SNOW HAD FLOWN the night she gave birth; covering the hill and everything else, it pushed and stung and drifted. Tent walls flapped, men shouted, sweeping them off. The wind yowling like a cat as she'd laboured. A goddamned tomcat, someone said, as God white-washed the wreckage. He was present when the baby came, and only he had known how the jesus she'd got there, because she didn't, shunted through piles of matchsticks to a forest of tents.

Canvas shifted like sand near her face, its smell a comfort as hands worked over her. Freezing hands. Dubbin and the stink of kerosene, a thread of warmth; and in her mind she'd been a schoolgirl again. Grade two, Richmond school, the kid beside her crawling with cooties. Next she'd been home stoking the stove, in the flat on Campbell Road, cracking eggs ...

"Breathe!" the dove had cooed, tending her. A nursing sister veiled in grey. "Push!"

Breath chugging out like a screaming locomotive's plume. Mama? MAMA? There'd been no Mama. But her body'd remembered what to do, no trouble at all jerking up those bloodied knees till the cold had nipped her backside. Push! And quickly, too quickly, the baby'd come.

"Some fast for a first. A boy," somebody said. A *boy? Her first?* A mistake, surely, wrought by the wind's caterwauling, and weeping from the other tents. Her lungs like slob ice; for an instant, she'd quit breathing.

"Poor little critter — it'll freeze to death, we don't get 'em moved."

But before she could argue, before she could explain the difference, they were swaddled in filthy blankets, madonna and child, and moved.

The whisk of runners carving tracks away from the hill and the tent village resembling a sea of Christmas trees huddled at its foot.

But that was as far as whiteness went.

The sky had rained tar earlier, what, a morning before? A lifetime? Tar and blood and needles of glass. It'd wept chunks of earth and flaming metal when she came to on a hill: another, smaller one way across town from the overturned bowl. One boot on, one boot off, she'd found herself lying there arse over teakettle, limbs splayed. Barelegged, knees big as softballs oozing purple.

No sign at all of the itchy grey stockings she'd just pulled on, slouching over her cannonball belly. Gut in her throat, as Harry'd yelled -

"Cufflinks. You seen my —?"

Her shirtwaist wrung like a dishrag, every last button gone. Toes facing uphill, hands and feet the points of a compass rose. Blood drummed her ears as a mushroom grew in the sky, a giant, spreading fungus that crowded out the sun. The spiky grass grazed her cheek: an inch from her eye a bedspring, and something else, unspeakable, purple, with suckers trailing from it like a jellyfish's. A hand?

Pinning her there, a buoy, the baby's weight on her back had made her pant.

Mama? Dad? *Harry?* she'd screamed and screamed, till no sound came out.

AS THE AIR LIGHTENED — gruel thinned with water — its stillness seared her. Not a breath of wind, not a wisp. In the mushroom's shadow, the view was like a pot left on the stove, the bottom burnt right out. Somewhere far below lay the greasy gleam of water. Blood from a gash stained her vision pink, the vision of a cellar dredged clean to China; trees smoking gallows. Curled like a snail, she groped for her name, the day. Limbs starfished, the baby pressing her spine, she flailed for a location.

Harry was getting his tooth out, wasn't he, the appointment booked for the sixth ...?

Rag dolls dangled from wires, wires like skipping ropes: a cock-eyed game of double dutch? Washing stuck in a trapeze. Voices yelling in her head: *Liar, liar, pants on fire, couldn't get over the telephone wire ...*

Dolly, you must've put 'em somewhere. When you washed my shirts?
Our Father. Our fa-ther. Dad?
Mama?
Sis? *Ethel?*
Her big round belly a buoy.

A front-room radiator, a stove pipe, a piano's keyboard lay there too: a junkyard trail. If she followed the pieces they'd lead her home? Thoughts ricocheted. A war zone! A newsreel had spun, like the box office hit that might even come to the Strand, *The Battle of the Somme*, and dumped her into its mud. The Huns. The work of the Kaiser — the Krauts!

Oh sweet Jesus and all that's good, they'd been bombed, and why would the devil give a goddamn if it was Wednesday or Thursday?

Something squirmed: a fish inside her?
Harry? Harry Caines?!

FOUR FORTY-FIVE IN THE morning, there's nothing for it but to get up. Useless, lying here in this black bog.

Downstairs, glancing off the cupboards her voice is as artificially bright and jarring as the overhead light. "I'm calling about my husband?"

It takes fewer muscles to smile than to frown, she's heard somewhere — maybe it's the priest who's said it — therefore it takes less energy. The new fellow at St. Columba's. That earnest voice of his seems to coax from inside her as the nurse, or whoever, answers, puts down the phone. *Believe,* he's always saying, *because believing makes it so.*

"No change. I'm sorry." The nurse's news is a scalpel wiped in compassion. Officious enough that Lucy listens, foolishly, for Harry's voice. But all she hears is

Have you seen my. Shaving brush. My. Cufflinks ...?

The pickles wait on the counter; they haven't gone anywhere. Just as well. A desperate energy fills her: like the "zest" she used to get when her period started, and then when it finally ceased. Keep busy, busy: if she buckles down, the dills might be saved yet. A treat for Harry, when he gets out. The little frogs are wizened, yellowed, but firm enough to justify starting over.

There's just enough vinegar to try again. "Square one, Harry," she declares, as if he's there. A clean slate — if only. If only troubles could be sucked like water up a hose.

ON THAT BARE SLOPE her unborn baby had kicked and jabbed her back to life. Her eyes jammed open like a shutter: roofs ripped off like box tops. Clothes spilled from open-eyed windows, laundry that should've billowed, would have, hung out that morning. Early, early. The pulse of *early* had beat in her neck as she vomited.

The only one in the entire world spared.

Harry, eyeing that tooth in the mirror ...

The air had tasted of roasted iron. As it cleared, in the starless, backwards black, bonfires had sprouted. Boy Scouts? The whiff of scorched meat. But like a genie, like a scent released from a porcelain bottle, it had enveloped and pulled her to her feet. Her face felt sunburned, one ankle like a pincushion, a gash where her boot would've buttoned, and her knees ... It was as if a leg, an arm, a foot, a hand, something had been amputated, and yet, she counted, she could see, none were missing. Her tears were soot: of course she was dreaming. She'd wake, and find herself back on Campbell Road, poaching eggs.

Knife-sharp, the rising wind had shoved her downhill to what remained of the street. A house flagging like cardboard, gusts playing the staircase that dangled by a nail. Turning a corner marked by a picket, she'd passed a cow: an upside-down bathtub, its feet like hoofs. Her ears rang, a dull whining drone, and as she tripped past what looked like a drawer, the wind wailed just like a baby. Picking her way round a horse's fetlocks, she'd heard it again, a whimper. But then a foghorn moaned, and something had staggered out of the darkness towards her. A man, buck naked, skin curling from his bones like wood from an awl. His eyes were holes, his hands pawing at nothing. His cries a rattle of blood: *Help me.*

The wind had pushed harder, and she'd limped and wallowed faster. The moon had appeared, a hazy eye atop a swaying wall. Tiny heels pummelled her lungs, and squatting, she'd dreamed, no, heard, a miracle. Voices. Angels, faint at first, then shouting. Men. Shimmying wheels.

She'd no longer felt her knees; even her belly had grown weightless. Almost airborne ... missing, missing ...

Words. That homey, lazy drawl: Haligonian *not* Deutsch: "Keep yer jesus shirt on. Can't do nothin' for that poor bastard; leave him."

Here. Her voice a croak, the crackle of a tiny flame. Then louder. Loud enough to quicken the dead. *Please.*

The soldiers had loaded her into a cart with a woman clutching something in a towel. The poor creature could have been a Hun, for her lack of expression. Someone wrapped Lucy in his coat, held a flask. Brushfire had ripped down her gullet; she could've kissed each finger of his bloody glove. Her neck snapping to the horse's lope, eyes pinned on the blue of its flanks, she'd given herself up, and been hauled from the lip of hell up Agricola Street ...

DAWN BREAKS AS SHE ladles in fresh brine the colour of the liquid that'd been dripping into Harry's vein. Drip drip drip: she can almost feel a stinging yet invigorating chill entering her own body. As she seals the jars, re-boils them. That sound again: her voice, praying. One long looping *Our Father*. He has to pull through; he can't not.

The pop of each cooling lid buoys her, buoys her more than she might've hoped. He'll make it, says each tiny burst, each lagging beat marking the fridge's melodious drone with a cockeyed percussion. *Believe*, it yells, and dawn sweats through the curtains, a pale flush. Humbled, blushingly optimistic as the sun begins to scale the wall, she digs out her biggest bowl and mixes porridge bread: Harry's absolute fave. Criminy, she hasn't made it in years.

"It'll be all right," she murmurs, kneading. Her hands are stubby as driftwood punching the dough; but the motion of her fists sinking into it suddenly, with no warning at all, pulls down tears. It's the ghost of loss. "I could kick your arse, Harry," she'd like to blame him, "your Londonderriere." Sticky fists in her eyes, her choking laugh graces the air's shadowy, yellowing blue. *O Danny Boy!* Luckily only God can hear. Think white, *think snow*, he shouts back, at least the voice inside her does, the voice that she'd like to consider his. So she obeys. But then there's no stopping it, the whiteness of snow on canvas melting to a dismal grey ...

A SHIP'S ON FIRE, somebody'd hollered first thing that deadly bright cold morning — the fellow in the flat downstairs? And she'd thought, Good, that's as good a place as they could get for a fire, on water. And that had been it for a warning ...

"Lucy, wha'd you do with my goddamn cufflinks?" Harry'd bellowed.

No time to answer, or even to back from the stove ...

Pieces of sky like smelts, a blackened silvery red streaming down ...

And then the tent, the flapping cold, a frozen confusion. *Some fast for a firstborn, wha? Jesus, Mary and Joseph, a small mercy, nope, a miracle she went the way she did, not a hitch.* Loaded onto the sleigh, this boy creature bundled to her like a foundling, yet both her hands, if not sliced right off, then utterly, utterly empty.

Three

TWELVE FRESH JARS SHELVED in the cellar and dough on the rise, she's upstairs rinsing her eyes with cold water when the ruckus erupts. Jewel already, this early? A chill zippers her spine. Her eyes throb, then tingle, and something inside her shrivels. There's news?

Footsteps below on the porch. Banging. A voice explodes: "Scissors? Knives? Anyt'ing youse need sharpened?" The shout cracks around that last word. She forgets and leaves the tap running, creeping across the hallway to the sewing room, Jewel's old bedroom. Peering down, she sees. There's a wagon, of all blessed things, not much bigger than the kind Robert had when he was small, piled high with junk and some sort of machinery. A sign perched on top says *Saints O' Knives*.

God of mercy — of all bloody times! It's that wing nut from the cove, the one who seems to come and go with the tide — or the wind, like birds of the air: crows that is, scavengers. "Take a hike, bud," that was Harry, the last time the fellow had the gall to come around here. "Last thing you want is that frigging traveller in your face." Hard not to feel sorry for him, though; she's always pitied people like Benny. Just Benny, people call him, as if his last name's a secret. "Classified information," as Harry would snort.

Try next door. Mrs. Chaddock'll give you something to sharpen, she almost hollers down. But he's stopped yelling, scenting her perhaps, like a fox or raccoon would. The bell's long, endless *brrring* practically wires her jaw shut. *G'way! Vamoose!* she screams silently.

Still, it's hard to resist peeking down again at his gear, a jumble of shiny things heaped in a dishpan — blades? Just as she looks, he scowls up from the walk, his plaid hunting jacket seedily jaunty. Remembering the tap, its impatient hiss, she shrinks back, though not fully out of sight. There *are* her old sewing scissors and the garden shears, dull as cloth, and the lilac does need pruning. *Now don't encourage the guy*, an inner voice like Harry's warns. And hadn't she done him a favour once, hiring him to fix something? "It's your fault buddy comes around."

"Get lost, Benny — or I'll sharpen you!" The bite of Harry's tongue that day brings a smile even now as she creeps downstairs, uncertain what to do. For half a second, it's as if Harry's not even sick, but right here being pestered in the middle of a tune. "Don't you get it? That's how fellas like him operate. Make you feel so guilty you go, 'Here, take the goddamn shirt off my back, oh, and my boxers too,' just to be rid of 'em." It's true, on top of everything else, she does feel bad for deciding to play dead, pretending not to be home. The frigger, Harry would say. Too late to go blithely answering the door; but now she feels like a hostage trapped inside.

The sound of tires chewing gravel and the tick-tick-tick of an engine save her.

"Not today, bud. Go home to Foxy — your girlfriend?" she hears Jewel joking. "Oh, no, sorry, it's Boxy isn't it, Boxy Lady? Listen, Ma's got a lot on her plate right now. You gotta pick your spots." They could almost be old pals, it seems, until Jewel's voice gets gruff: "C'mon, shake a leg. Get a move on, I'm serious." A few grunts of protest, but the fellow saunters off, his cart clattering behind him. Then dread rushes in: behind the little lace curtain she feels suddenly faint, faintly disgruntled, then dizzy. She wants to lie down.

"They called *you*?" The first thing she says. "There's a change?"

Patting her arm, smiling grimly, Jewel just hands her a paper bag. Baking? "Thought we'd go in early. Becky says — here, she sent these over." His nose wrinkles. "What's that smell?" and she remembers, almost with embarrassment, the dough rising under its tea towel like a belly, a belly with a bun in the oven.

Jewel slides a doughnut onto a plate. "How 'bout a bite, first?" Its middle puckered, the thing's as hard as a puck. Enough to pick off a crow if someone chucked it, Robert might say.

"I'm not too hungry just now, my darling."

He eyes the bowl with its gingham-covered mound. "Jeez, you been busy. Don't knock yourself out now." Sucking his teeth, he shakes Rebecca's treat back into the bag.

"It's just that ... I like having things ready. In all respects ready." That last bit's so officious it even makes her blink.

"Ma —?" His look is searching, incredulous.

Having to explain is like stabbing a balloon with a safety pin. "For when your father comes home, dear. There was that other time, you know. When I almost ... when it seemed for good. That time before," she says, those words quite sufficient.

AFTER THE BIRTH, A spot had come up in a church basement, a shelter full of strangers wearing turbans of gauze. A nurse whisked her and the strange infant behind a curtain and washed them down. Dabbing at her kneecaps, the woman's brisk hands bound Lucy's belly, stopping just short of binding her breasts. Go ahead, she'd wanted to say, staring at the blue-lipped creature fussing between them. Its crib was a munitions box: Ah, so this foundling had come by sea? "But he's not mine," she insisted. "I don't know how *he* got here." The nurse gave her a pitiful look and the infant's face a lick and a promise with her cloth. That look was like the grit on Lucy's scalp, sand? But her fingers came away nicked: it was ground glass.

And who would've guessed Harry was there? A whole day passed before she found him; no wonder. He was unrecognizable at first, lying on a stretcher at the far end of the cellar. All bandaged up, just his right eye staring out, his head cocooned. A pail sat beside him, something round and red and grisly lolling in it. He cried out when she grasped his toe: "Oh my Jesus — is it you, dolly?" He made a choking sound as she clawed at his hand. His one eye roving over her. "What's this? My Jesus, you *had* it?" Clasped to her shoulder was the swaddled babe, which she was minding for someone, she said. Then his eye, the one in his head, glazed over, and his breath was a wave curling, breaking. "But where's my pumpkin? *Lucy?* Where's Helena?"

Then a nurse, the one who'd bathed her, gripped her shoulder. There was news, she said, of both their families. Already caked, Lucy's breasts throbbed; the heat, the tightness worming through her at the same instant a blade fell. *Helena —?*

"Your parents, your sister, gone. Their remains found under a house. A fire." But she was barely listening, the nurse's whisper barely audible above the blood rumbling inside her head. Harry's people, too, she heard vaguely.

But it wasn't his mother or his brothers or his uncles and aunts he keened for. "Hush hush hush, *stop*," they told him, "or you'll open the wound in your chest."

IT'S A SATURDAY, BARELY ten o'clock in the morning. Their footsteps echo down the bright, empty corridors, the hospital so quiet it's as if it's been evacuated. She feels a pang of guilt, the smell of the place dragging her back to those terse yet deadened hours the day before: she should've stayed the night, kept her vigil here, nearby, where her presence might've been felt, might've in some tiny, invisible way helped. She could've curled up on an orange chair, her cheek pressed to the vinyl, and no, not slept, but watched. The way one watches over a newborn, to ensure that it doesn't stop breathing or choke or get strangled by the sheet. The same, but different; and a watched pot never boils, she reminds herself, but it's not quite enough to loosen her guilt, the sudden feeling that, oh dear, by leaving Harry she's let him down. Remorse arcs through her, and she has to take Jewel's arm to keep up. He presses the button and they ride the elevator upwards, swiftly, too swiftly, since there are no other stops.

In a way she wishes she could just keep going, rocketing up the last few floors through the roof.

The nurse at the desk is talking on the phone, and points the way with her pen. Jewel marches ahead, to Lucy's dismay: she'd prefer to pace herself with small, measured steps, as one would walk into the ocean, even on a perfect day. But that's just how Jewel is, the sort who runs up, jiggling, maybe pausing for a split second before pitching himself in.

Harry lies there unconscious, unchanged, the mound of his stomach barely moving under the blanket. Unchanged, except that instead of being florid, his face looks grey. He doesn't so much as stir when they come in, not even when she leans close, her downy lip brushing his ear.

"We're here, Harry. Jewel and me."

The octopus tubes and wires seem to have multiplied overnight. A machine rather like a TV beeps and hums. A nurse slips in behind them, holding her finger to her lips. "He's as comfy as we can make him," she says. "Please, if you don't mind, I have to say it. Rules. One at a time." So Jewel quickly excuses himself, and says he's going downstairs for coffee.

AS SOON AS THE baby could safely go outside, Lucy launched her search. Forgetting her knees and the wrench of giving birth, forgetting Harry, she started with the hospitals, the makeshift wards thrown up all over the city. She huddled in corners to nurse the baby, scouring the aisles and galleries of churches whose pews provided berths for the injured and dying.

She stood through her parents' and her sister's makeshift funerals, clutching the baby the way others clutched relics: a melted watch, a scorched scrap of lace, lockets holding wisps of hair. She watched as they were lowered down, a single casket for the three of them.

Trudging through her daily rounds she ended up, eventually, in the queue outside the schoolhouse morgue for the unclaimed and unidentified. She barely felt the freezing wind, holding the baby close. The murmurs of attendants drifted up through the cellar doors, muffled by the endless sound of boots scuffing stairs. Horses, carts and automobiles came and went with their deliveries and removals.

Inside the cellar, it was as if snow had drifted in banks between the pillars, covering the sooty floor. Pipes snaked overhead, emptied of steam: it was so cold she could see her breath. The windows were boarded over, but there was light, just enough, from bulbs that dangled, haloed and fuzzy as the moon that hellish night. The bodies beneath the sheets were stones, bare and blue as the slate in Dad and Mama's backyard. Many were headless, limbless as squared timber. Others mere assortments, knobs of flesh, tagged. Meticulously, too, with numbers, locations. *Family of five, remains found near Rector Street, brought to mortuary in galvanized bucket.*

Daily she made herself look. The attendants were gentle, pulling back sheets from the smallest stones. Sometimes they held her elbow; once a fellow with scrubbed eyes offered to take the baby. Her heart pounded, arms turning to rubber so it was easy to forget the bundle against her chest. Her feet, swimming in donated boots two sizes too big, wanted to fly her upstairs. But she held together, picturing her innards, all those female parts slowly knitting, tightening, healing.

From the number of teeth she knew this one or that could not be her daughter.

"Well?" Harry would ask from his cot. But the wind just shook what remained of the maples outside the school, and the lineups grew shorter. They celebrated Christmas in the church shelter, and Harry's bandages came off, all but the dressing on that left socket and another below his collarbone. Feeding himself soup cooked by someone from Massachusetts, he dropped the spoon. Laying the baby down, she picked it up, then he let the baby suck his finger. So what would they call him? He needed a name.

She thought of a hand she'd seen, a ring swollen into a finger. The stone missing, but the gold still shiny. Like the ring she'd had, a sapphire that had belonged to her grandmother. She'd shown it once to the baby — her real baby, her little girl. Helena's eyes had the same fierce sparkle: the sun on a hard, autumn ocean. She'd thrown a holy-rolling fit when Lucy'd put it away. Who knew now but that the ring was lying like a filling on the harbour floor, or was part of the clouds, a spangling of dust.

"Jewel," she declared without a second thought, despite Harry's gasps about pansy this and pansy that. Touching the baby's scalp, stunned by its peachy feel and the soft pulsing triangle where the bones hadn't yet knit, she spoke dizzily, as if perched on high and looking down, repeating "Jewel August Caines." Harry just covered his face and made a disgusted sound.

SLIPPING FROM HARRY'S ROOM, she finds Jewel waiting for her in the corridor. He's pacing back and forth, breaking bits off a Styrofoam cup. The squeaky snap hurts her ears, sharpened as they are for the sound, any sound, of life besides the respirator's, that bullish, mechanical breathing: as if each inhalation is hope and each exhalation despair. Approaching quietly, she takes the cup from him, then reaches for his hand, squeezing it so hard he grimaces and tries to make a joke.

"Well, he's still with us, at least." As if his father's down in the basement, tinkering. That boyish brightness belies his age, of course, his experience. He knows as well as anybody, how, in the flick of a cat's wet paw, things can change, and not necessarily for the better. The same way bad can worm its way through the good, and surface like a splinter or even a sliver of bone. What could she do but nod?

He lights up the second they reach the car; never mind that she hates his smoking. She worries about his chest. He should take better care of himself; if Rebecca had more sense, she'd see that he did. His eyes glitter as he starts the engine, and instead of pulling out right away, he just sits for a minute tapping the wheel.

"Stop it, dear." His misspent energy only salts her anxiety. "I know you think it's foolish, but ... maybe if you'd concentrate, you know." Say a prayer, she means: to comfort or prepare himself? Thinking it makes her swallow. If one believes ...

"He's a tough old crank." He stares at the bumper ahead, and it's clear he wants her to say something, a motherly something: *Yes, yes, your father surely is.* But her heart's slipped back to that cool, medicinal room, and guilt floods in, filling the cavity. They've stolen away from the hospital so quickly, so quietly, as if lingering would've only invited, hastened, defeat. It's the watched pot theory. Or maybe Harry's like a geranium: left to his own devices he might pull through, a watched plant not unlike a canner!

"That's right, son," she concurs after a bit, her sentiment an echo of his, bold if weary: "Your father never would do anything without a fuss."

"Cripes, Ma. Look at that — lunchtime already." A distant thunder, the noon gun goes off on the Hill. For the first time in a while, she's glad when he invites her back to his and Rebecca's. Rebecca will be waiting, he says.

"Well," she hesitates all the same; even under the circumstances, it wouldn't do to appear too eager. "I suppose that dough will keep. It'll be a while before your father can eat, anyhow."

BOUNCING THE BABY BETWEEN them, she and Harry stood waiting five hours to place the ad in the newspaper. The lineup had snaked right around the block.

> Girl, 16 months, last seen Young Street and Campbell Road; light brown hair, grey-blue eyes; pale green flannelette nightdress with smocking.

Her description might have gone on and on; dreadful, having to whittle it down, but such a mob, everyone frantic to find their missing, and only so many pages, so many column inches. Always the chance someone had found her, carted her off, Harry'd pointed out after Lucy's final trip to the morgue. As she nursed the baby, a feeble hope had flared.

For weeks she lined up at the Relief Commission, the Red Cross and all the other shelters, posting a plea: *If you have her, please return her*. As if her little girl were a watch or diamond ring. It felt doubly futile, listing her own name in care of St. Luke's shelter. But somebody must know something, she pleaded to anyone who'd listen: ministers, orderlies, filing clerks. Smiles faded when she gave the flat's location.

Once, the paper ran an article about a baby found alive under a tea chest, another under a washtub, not a scratch. Neighbours had kept him as their own till the mother turned up, the father missing and all twelve siblings gone. Inside the Relief Office, Harry at her side, Lucy rattled the page before the man at the counter. You heard things like that, he told her, shrugging. That one had gone to an orphanage: no one left to claim him.

"What about trains?" Harry stepped up. Relief trains had come that black day and the next, blizzard and all.

"Surgical cases," the fellow volunteered, what couldn't be handled here. Some to the Valley, Truro. Some taken as far as Toronto. "Traunno," he dragged it out.

"Children?" Harry twisted his cap. The baby's scent was like smelling salts.

The fellow nodded and someone in the lineup coughed. "No records. In all the confusion ... The name, again?"

"Hel-en-a," Harry enunciated. "But she doesn't talk so good, you know, not two yet." The baby voice inside Lucy's head repeated *Ewinno*. The man had ticked something off a list. "I'm sorry," he said.

Outside, they'd passed a man on the sidewalk — part of a man, eyes bandaged, no limbs, a stump of a body on a board with wheels mired in the slush. A cup of pencils dangled from a hook. She'd stared at some pigeons holed up in the eaves overhead as Harry dropped in a nickel. "Hope you get what's owing ya," Harry'd piped up.

"Means frig-all to me, mack. You been to Ypres?"

It was like being asked if he'd been to Purcell's Cove, and no, Harry hadn't enlisted, barred from service by a weakness in his left eye, the one he'd ended up losing. What if he had gone to fight? It hadn't borne thinking of as they'd hurried away, losing themselves amidst the storefronts' shabby elegance. But after that, even sleep turned cruel: in her dreams Lucy stood in endless lineups, faceless people offering her a choice.

Pointing at Jewel. *You can have your daughter, in exchange for him.* Harry saying, *Collateral?* Waking in a sweat, she'd find herself about to hand her son over.

AS JEWEL TURNS DOWN the lane past the yacht club, past the boatyard full of cradles, Lucy starts having second thoughts; dread is more like it. Already she pictures the kitchen cluttered with Rebecca's magazines, the sink full of dishes, and, heaven forbid, more doughnuts. That's just the half of it; something about their chaos, the mess, always makes her feel like she's forgotten something, neglected some important chore of her own. Maybe it has to do with her habit of watching, minding things: "Jesus Murphy, Ma," Jewel once said, "it's like you're everyone's guardian angel." There's just something about their house, packed as it is with Rebecca's knick-knacks and efforts at keeping up-to-date, that makes a person feel like they're in a pink and orange swamp, sinking in a quicksand of lizard green. Oh, it's nasty to think this way, and she really doesn't mean to judge. It's easy to be critical, she's found herself at times defending both his parents to Robert. Let them that live in glass houses throw rocks, she's even said. But at the moment that's neither here nor there: what she needs suddenly, urgently, is order, the reassuring calm of home and of every item small or large having its own, albeit dusty, place.

And then, who knows, maybe some invisible order exists beneath Rebecca's clutter and her *Better Homes and Gardens*-gone-wrong approach to decorating, a wacky order born all the same of an urge to manage things? Eyeing Jewel, Lucy finds this possibility reassuring, enough at least to get out of the car. Anxious not to offend anybody, at the doorstep she waits politely listening for Robert's music. But it's unusually quiet; after noon, and he's still asleep?

"That kid would slough till suppertime, you let him." Jewel starts in, and she elbows him, another little habit of hers.

"Watch your tongue!"

"Coffee, Ma?" is the first thing he says once they've made it through the minefield of shoes and purses in the hallway, all of them Rebecca's. Her majesty must have overslept too; in she staggers wearing a yellow robe, thick and fuzzy like the mauve one they gave Lucy last Christmas. Except for her reddish hair Rebecca could almost pass for a chick.

"Ma," she murmurs sullenly, reaching for Lucy's hand.

No one even mentions lunch, a relief, really, for who could think of food with Harry in such a state? But, ever the hostess, Rebecca takes over spooning instant coffee into mugs, while Jewel goes downstairs to rouse Robert. It can't be healthy sleeping below ground, especially for someone who must be still growing, someone whose head sometimes seems less than clear. No wonder the boy gets ideas. Maybe he doesn't get enough light? But if she mentioned it, Rebecca'd be all over her like a shirt, an itchy one. Well, if he were hers, he'd sleep upstairs like any civilized person. Like one's child, not a pet.

A few minutes later Jewel comes slouching back, clearly peeved; he makes a slurping sound sipping his coffee. On top of their new green fridge sits a Tupperware container full of doughnuts; mercifully, no one mentions these either.

"Dunno what to do about him." He wipes something off the rim of his mug: lipstick? "I told him, look, 'Your gran's here. You *saw* your grampa — the least you could do ...'"

Rolling her eyes, Rebecca rubs Lucy's wrist; her fingers feel sticky. "Oh, give it a rest, huh? Not like you weren't a kid, once." She pauses, drumming her fingertips on the plastic placemat, which has big lime-green flowers on it, the colour not unlike a pair of those shoes in the entry. "Don't you think you should call?"

"The hospital? We were just there." As he lights a cigarette, the flick of his lighter is a reproof.

"You're always so quick to rip him up," Rebecca harps half under her breath.

The coffee doesn't even taste like coffee, so bitter it's sweet — but who is she to comment?

"Dear?" she murmurs, more to smooth feathers than to ruffle what's on everyone's mind. "Well, Harry's ... hanging on." For dear life, she means, and that murkiness crowds round her heart. Yet such a stupid expression, as if he's in a closet somewhere, waiting to be pressed. "We've just come from the hospital," she repeats, but neither seems to hear as Rebecca hauls herself up, her bulky robe catching on a corner as she squeezes by. Gaping, it shows a slash of pink nightie. Her fluffy slippers look like dusters as she tramps to the stairs.

"Bucky? Get up here, now!"

It's as if she's screaming down to a monster, the basement the oozing depths of the swamp, a kind of underworld beneath the up-stairs clutter. Rebecca disappears. The coffee seems to burn a hole in Lucy's stomach, that and her nerves, and the thought of quicksand bubbling and settling reminds her of the dough rising at home. It'll be useless now, the yeast spent. She was stupid to make it, the time better spent ... on what, dusting? Never mind: suddenly all she wants is to be alone in her own digs, where the appliances are white and the floors no-nonsense lino and fir. None of this overwhelming carpet that Rebecca so favours.

"It's okay — let him be. I'll catch up with him next time," she tells Jewel, but too late. Soundlessly Rebecca reappears, rolling her eyes. She picks up Jewel's cigarette and lights one of her own off it.

"He's wanting you to come down, Ma." She coughs into her lapel; against the cheery yellow her face is sallow. But there's an eagerness there, that look in her eyes that's like a leash or lasso, has been since the first time Lucy glimpsed it.

"If you don't come back in ten we'll send somebody down," Jewel quips, and clutching at her robe, Rebecca holds the red end of her cigarette near his shirt, and goes *Hsssst.*

Trudging stiffly to the stairs, Lucy watches her shoes sink into the dark brown shag. A dust trap, that carpet, but Rebecca's fixation on fashion overrules sense, any day. Even if she were the most fastidious housekeeper in the cove, which she is not.

Panelled in wood to match the rug, the rec room and hallway to Robert's lair are like a tunnel, the gloom broken by a single light fixture, bubbled amber glass that makes her think of an insect's abdomen. The music starts as she steps over a heap of laundry, a keening that makes her ears sting. The singer shrieks as if in pain; good grief, what passes for entertainment!

Robert's door is open, but she knocks anyway. He's doubled over on the side of his bed, as if he's ill. But then she sees he's listening raptly, though he barely looks awake enough to have put the needle on the record. He nods to her, which must mean welcome. The music is fuzzy now and slightly less high-pitched, like an air-raid signal piercing a dirty day, the sound dampened by wind and rain. Like the practice sirens that used to flatten her to the cellar floor during the war, when Jewel was overseas. But then the wails grow muddled and eerie, like a foghorn at the ends of the earth — or on the moon, yes, the moon, she thinks, but not soon enough. Not before the sound pulls at the strings inside her, memories like a marionette, motionless, grey and faceless but ever-present.

Robert's hair falls across his eyes as he nods along listlessly, as if he's mental. Next comes a series of squawks like those of crows caught in barbed wire; if Harry'd been there, he'd have dragged the needle across the vinyl, making everybody jump. And she wouldn't blame him. Out of the noise she can half make out some words, the singer complaining about working every day to bring home his pay, and on the heels of this, a sound like wood being tortured on a nail, swinging back and forth in a slow, hot wind. That inner marionette grins now, still faceless yet baring teeth, ghostly fingers waving while spinning her inside a cocoon that makes it hard enough to breathe, let alone move. Her worry about Harry only part of it.

When the song's finally over, Robert rises to flip the record, but then — in a fit of sympathy? — slides it into its case. "What's wrong, Gran?" His smirk is playful, despite that unwashed doziness. "You don' like 'Dazed and Confused'?"

"Oh. Well, that explains it," she comments, the kindest thing that comes to mind, though isn't music supposed to make a person gay? Happy, that is; not as if one's body is enshrouded. Part of her could just lie down now on his filthy, matted rug and never get up again.

"I got something here for you," he says, rooting through a drawer. "Something you might be in'erested in, Gran. Somethin' I done, I mean, it could be for Grampa." To her bafflement, he's blushing; or maybe it's just the room's stuffiness. He hands her a crumpled sheet of loose-leaf, wiping his mouth on his hand. "It's, um, a pome."

"A poem," she says gently, trying not to laugh out loud at what Harry would think.

"That's right," and shyly he pushes it at her, and studies his album cover as if he's never seen it before. Swallowing, he saunters back to the stereo and puts the record back on. Glory. But this time it's quite pleasant, a slow, almost sedate organ solo that, after that last selection, is like dying and ending up in church. "Your time gonna come," he moans along, when, naturally, like most nice things, the organ ends, giving way to more shrieking. It makes it awfully hard to concentrate. "So. D'you like it? I think it's pretty far out, myself, if I don't mind braggin'..." *Frout*, he's always saying, which sounds to her like some all-purpose word, an all-purpose comment. Like one-size-fits-all gloves or stockings, or, heaven forbid, unisex. *Eunuch-sex*, as Harry never failed to point out.

"It's grand, dear. Grand." But the thought of Harry's laugh clouds her vision, blurring the boy's difficult scrawl. The weight in her chest is like cement, and there's a dreadful frog in her throat that makes her cough. "About my fence, now, Robert." He's still smiling,

smiling the way he had as a tiny kid shooting marbles, and it reminds her how at times the deepness of his voice still startles her. "Your father's getting the paint."

"Frout," he says. Which she takes to mean, yes, yeah, okay, some-day, when I get around to it. "The pome, though. I wanna give it to Grampa, right. I mean, in honour ... As long as he don't think I'm some fruity little weasel or nothing."

"My darling, your grampa would never think that," she lies, tucking the paper inside her sleeve like a Kleenex, for safekeeping. To prove it, speaking for Harry, speaking for both of them, she leans down, never mind her back and her knees, and kisses his cheek. The rough-ness of a tiny patch of stubble startles her too. And before she can stop herself, out it comes, "Now don't be sleeping your life away, young fella." Which brings back the image of Harry sleeping that grey sleep so pale and bleached of light, and she coughs again before something makes her blurt out: "What I'm saying, dear, is don't just drift."

He eyes her with that smirk again. "Oh. Like an astronaut, you mean." The click of his teeth: whose habit is that? "Doubt it." That mumble also like a foghorn. And then the pounding drums, and a drone like a plane flying low overhead, something heavy and hot plying the air. "Oh," he says, almost yelling. "You mean like buddy?"

Buddy?

"Benny. Down the cove, you know. Livin' the life of Riley, like Ma says, right? Wine women an' song. That old broad he got livin' with him?"

"Stop right there," she has to shout, "I take it you mean a pregnant cow."

He shakes his head indulgently, too indulgently. He could get away with being cute when he was ten, maybe, but not any more. "She's loaded, you know that?"

Loaded? Good heavens; the image comes of a drunk barrelling around a tiny listing deck.

"I heard all about it. My friends over the Grounds? Benny told them she got, like, found under a leaf or something when she was a kid, and got raised up by some rich guy down the valley, then went nuts and started cleanin'. Cause she *likes* it, right? Ma keeps threatenin' to have her do my room."

"Right," she says, covering her ears. Out of the mouths of babes. Those friends of his would live in hollow trees if they could, Harry says. Then she tells herself, it's now or never. "So, what's this I hear about you leaving school, gallivanting out west?"

"Gotta get a job first," he says, looking at her, perhaps a bit peevishly. "A real job, I mean. Not like Benny, don't worry," and he laughs. "You worry too much, Gran. Gotta learn to take 'er cool and that. I mean," it seems he's forever explaining himself, "it ain't for a while."

"Not," she can't help herself.

"I mean, I'm not going nowheres till Grampa's. Well. Back on his feet." The resolute way he says it warms her, more than she might've expected, and makes her grateful, suddenly, for his loping, lazy energy. As if he has his whole life, plus everybody else's, to "get his shit together," as he's been heard so unappealingly to say.

Upstairs, Rebecca's already rinsed out her mug: how odd, how unusual, the picture of efficiency all of a sudden. Jewel slides his chair in, eyeing her curiously. "You all right, Ma?" As if she might not be.

Rebecca has gotten dressed, her hair teased into a kind of dome, and she's wearing those green patent pumps. "Don't be a stranger now, Ma. Keep us posted, right? You know, anything happens, holler."

Jewel looks as anxious and weary as she suddenly feels. "How 'bout I run you home? Say the word when you want to go back in."

To the hospital, he means. The very thought conjures the sickly sweetness of disinfected flannelette, and buzzing, hovering sameness — loss? What she needs most right now is air. "Stay put. The walk'll do me good." But it's as if she's being difficult. Rebecca nudges Jewel.

"Call us!"

"For chrissake," she hears, fleeing — and just in time, perhaps, as a whine like a dentist's drill squeals from the basement. That godawful guitar, someone's excuse for a melody.

Four

POOR HARRY. HE'D CRIED, weeks or was it months later, when they'd returned to their old neighbourhood, the levelled grid where the flat had been. Glass from the train station's roof glinted in the patchy snow. Picking through frozen rubble, he'd kicked at a slab of bent metal, scraped off the soot. The oven door from the Fawcett, the name etched into the handle. Hugging Jewel, Lucy'd uncovered part of a comb and a little pink china cup without so much as a chip in it. Even without the saucer it looked as pretty as it had when she'd unwrapped it, a baby gift from her sister Ethel. Hoping to find his father's pocket watch — his only "hairloom" — Harry found under a brick a nub of gold the size of a raisin. Staring at the ice-blue Basin, he'd covered his eye patch as if it alone couldn't block out the sting. But they'd kept going, trudging past rows of foundations, places poking through the snow where the ground looked scorched. Above the rail yards they discovered a wall still smoking — all that was left of the foundry. Forty-one fellows had died there, some of them Harry's buddies. Something had cooked and melted to the coal bins, black as lava. She touched a pebble in the concrete, and the heat singed her finger.

Not far from there, they stumbled across a small, bent wheel, like one from Helena's pram with its big, swooping fenders, a gift, not so long before, from Mama and Dad. Handing over Jewel, she scoured the spot for other remnants. Nothing. But closing her eyes she could almost summon a smell like apple juice, its sweetish dampness warming knitted rugs.

"Could use something like that pram now," Harry groused, giving her the baby, and it came back in a rush: that first birth, like Vimy. Harry inspecting the tiny fingers afterwards, and Mama holding the newborn girl up to the sunny window, to cure what Mama'd called the yellow jaundice. "Lucy? Dolly? I didn't mean to —" What? Biting down on her cheek, she'd hugged Jewel all the way back to the shelter. Given their lack of privacy, the chance never arose to ask what exactly he'd meant by glossing over her hurt.

She celebrated her twenty-first birthday in that basement, cheered by the other homeless. A horrible prank, surely, that baby cup surviving and no little girl to drink from it! Never mind no pot to piss in, as Harry said, regaining his strength. Flicking a dead fly from the font, the minister christened Jewel; no one batted an eye. The next morning, lining up at the sink, Harry shaved as if for work, as if the sugar refinery had risen suddenly from its ruins like a sparkly white bird.

He started disappearing, making his rounds. Rounds which she learned took him in a spreading radius. They needed *some*where to start over. They qualified for relief housing, places built of blocks of fabricated stone, with laneways and postage-stamp gardens. But he wanted space, and found it three miles west. In cottage country, he called it. She was hardly convinced. Jutting into an arm of the harbour, the Grounds was a stony peninsula dotted with shacks.

That June they moved and Harry found work rebuilding the shipyards an hour's walk away. The cabin had an oil stove and electricity but no running water, a well and a privy out back. Hovering on the brackish wind, gulls cracked mussels on the doorstep. "Hillbilly land," the postmaster joked when she gave her address. As if she were some hayseed Wendy hiding out in the woods with one of the lost boys.

"Too risky," Harry'd said, when she broached building in the old neighbourhood. Who could argue, looking at him? Like her knees, the scar on his chest stayed a midnight blue, a tattoo, a *memento mori* that defied scrubbing. The Grounds's only memento was a chunk of anchor that had blown clear across town: a fat harpoon. From the *Mont Blanc*, said the creatures who lived there, the powder keg ship whose collision with the *Imo* had sparked the whole nightmare. The papers called it an accident; in the Grounds, folks just shook their heads. It'd taken a team of horses and nine men to dredge the shank from the hole it'd gouged in the earth; then they'd just left it lying there, like a petrified limb in a clump of Japanese rhubarb. That's what Artie Babineau said, the fellow next door who soon befriended Harry. Hard to believe, that shaft travelling so, but there it was, proof, an iron mote rusting away. Harder to pass by it without feeling as if it had somehow singled them out, yet missed. Even when the knotweed blazed up around it, walking by, Lucy had to fix on a nearby shack, a little place shaped like an inkbottle, with chickens pecking the dirt outside. A fortune teller lived there, Artie said.

In the woods just up the hill was an abandoned house with a barn. The Big House, it was called. Whoever'd lived there had owned all the Grounds before divvying them up. The cabin was around the point, at the end of a trail choked with blackberries and wild pear. Harry chopped them all down to open the view — the Arm with its boathouses along the other side, and the cove below plugged with an island. On it stood a building shaped like a shoebox surrounded by a jagged wall. The glasshouse, as it was known: a quaint name for a jail there since Napoleon, housing prisoners of war. Trotsky was locked up over there, supposedly. The Bolshevik, and Krauts? Got them, too. "The enemy, right in their midst," Artie said. "Food for the shark they had circling the place; a little salt 'n' pepper with that Kraut, boy?" Artie was so full of it, it wasn't funny.

Still, it was hard not to listen for strange tongues, especially when fog amplified every sound crossing the little channel. But those prisoners could've been dead over there or lying around in a typhoid stupor, as the newspaper suggested, mentioning pestilence. Besides foghorns, the only things Lucy heard were loons and, when she rocked

Jewel at night, noise from next door. The baby would whimper, the pucker of his chin enough to curl her heart, as scratchy fiddle drifted in on the coolness, tunes she recognized but couldn't name. Sometimes singing — Harry's? — would ring out, along with the sound of glass breaking.

Through work Harry seemed to recover, riveting plates to damaged relief boats and destroyers. Petering out, the ads in the paper — *lost, missing* — gave way to news from Europe. *Huns Hurled into Flanders Furnace. Double Layer of German Dead Carpet Hillsides.* Like tea berries? His paper hiding blisters in the tabletop, Harry would grimace then beam with satisfaction. This was the last place on earth the riffraff would invade. "Wouldn't have to, with the neighbours, not to mention those birds rotting over there in jail," she'd say, flipping the page to a shrinking patch of ads. Then he'd ask what was wrong, his voice brusque, saying, "Look, there's no sense — you have to, we both ... you've got a *baby* now." As if Jewel had always been the only one.

MOVING SLOWLY UP THE gravel lane away from that squealing guitar, she feels for the paper tucked up her sleeve. It's as if Harry's in the clouds now, watching. She can almost hear him speaking — to Robert, when he gets better? Across the cove, the marina bristles with glinting masts, the club where Robert hopes to work.

A shark?

The thought of Robert babysitting people's yachts makes her want to laugh; all his talk about "going back to the land" and "establishment weasels, beggars." Picking up, the breeze shirrs the Arm, whipping rope against spar, a steady, urgent clanging that reminds her of birds clamouring to be fed. Dwarfed by the clubhouse, the old prison looks rusty, its cells used for storing gear and paint, so Robert says. She wouldn't know; most of her life spent here, she's never set foot on the island. No reason to, not owning a boat. A spaceship would be preferable as far as she's concerned, the Apollo, for instance, that put those men on the moon. The thought of Mr. Armstrong in his helmet warms her: if he and Buzz Aldrin could feel the moon underfoot, is it crazy to hope Harry will recover?

Beyond the forest of spars, boarded-up cabins dot the point. A wonder they're still there; in most people's opinion they should be bulldozed — even Harry wouldn't object. "Move on," she can almost hear him, though he always was a fine one to talk.

At the end of the lane she slows even more. Sweet Dinah, her knees. By the road, below the embankment, a couple of men swig beer in a dinghy. A little farther out, a wooden box swings on the current, a floating shack that makes the ones on the point look like those fancy joints on the *Beverly Hillbillies*. Voices carry; shouting. One of them she recognizes: oh Mother, if it's not Benny the traveller, mouthing off as if he's just outside her house again. Harry would've sent him packing all right, faster than any rocket. Then a bad thought hits her: what if, well, supposing, this is how Robert ends up? Benny certainly has a different lifestyle.

Cars whiz past as she steps onto the sidewalk, and Benny appears on his makeshift deck. It looks as if he's got car seats for furniture, and company — the woman Robert was talking about? Don't look, don't *look*, she tells herself and that presence, whoever or whatever it is, beaming down. Picking up her pace, she still catches a glimpse: billowing black, a dress. Benny's lady friend is in mourning? And she's well-to-do? Could it be that Robert's friends smoke that wacky tobacco people mention on TV? If so, she ought to be more worried, not less. But there's no time to fret: if Benny sees her, the next worse thing is he'll come rowing over.

Even with her head high and her chest lifted she feels him watching, and suddenly it's as if the whole world knows something she doesn't. "Harry?" she hears herself utter, walking faster. What if the hospital's called, and she's missed something? Next time she'll let Jewel drive her, she promises herself; isn't it just easier for everybody when you do what they want?

Once she's safely past and almost home, she remembers Robert's little verse, if you can call something that doesn't rhyme properly verse. The writing on the page jumps out in proper daylight.

RAMBLING, FOR GRAMPA.

Go to school everyday don't got no pay
Don't got no love cuz it come from above
Yeah, yeah
It's outta sight, don't get uptight
Like the sun in the morning and the rain at night
Dig it man you gotta fight
Dig it dig it dig it dig it

Hmm. Well. Perhaps there was hope somewhere; perhaps she'd interest him in gardening? As somebody'd said, maybe it had even been a poet, every cloud had a silver lining.

IF HARRY'D HAD HIS accordion back then, maybe he wouldn't have liked his liquor so. Maybe it would've kept his hands busy. But, blown to smithereens, the 'cordine had fared no better than anything else, save the little cup. Dreadful but, compared to the rest of their losses, laughable. It might've been fine, if all he'd done at Artie's was play hearts or rummy. But it was hard not to boil over when he crept in at dawn, spent Sundays snoring off Saturdays.

One October night, the moon a silver dollar, his singing had echoed in, almost a howl coming through the cabin window: *Goodnight Irene, goodnight Irene, I'll see you in my ...* Just like at the party where they'd first met, when she was barely seventeen and Harry but a year older. The accordion almost sliding from his knee. "Doll-face," he'd called her: "There's a face that'd stop a clock." And clocks *had* stopped that morning a few years later when all had been lost and time itself melted then froze like a watch crystal, eelgrass hands trapped under ice.

Bundling Jewel into his crib, she'd slipped across the stony yard next door. There were dancers in the windows, someone torturing a violin, people raising glasses. A lady staggered outside, her silhouette blurred by the party's swirl behind her. A child's crying pierced the music. "Well," the woman had slurred, "if it isn't herself." Clutching a doll, a little girl rubbed her nose on the woman's skirt. The woman snatched the doll and pitched it down the steps. "Lookin' for your husbant, I suppose. What, it's his bedtime?"

Lucy'd handed the doll to the child. Stumbling outside, Harry had reached for the woman's waist, then started. "Lucy! You're still up." Then he'd backpedalled, mumbling something about tea. The woman, Lil, smirked even as Harry'd tried coaxing Lucy to stay, as if she could leave Jewel. She hadn't bothered answering, the wind through the pines wheeling her home.

Next morning he was shaky and hardly contrite, refusing to get up. "You'll die sleeping," she couldn't resist, and he said he'd get up when he felt like it: sometimes a fellow just needed to forget, and what was wrong with that? Jewel had howled from his crib. Then he'd said that her trouble was, she wouldn't forget. "You can't just quit, can't spend your whole life —" Waiting, she knew he meant. Hoping. "A person has to get —" *On with things*: her voice could've cracked the blurry mirror, Jewel's scream reflecting back. "That's it." Harry'd flapped the quilt and *Goodnight Irene, goodnight* eddied back, and the thought of his hand on Lil's waist. Easy for him, she'd said, plucking Jewel up.

THE SCENT OF YEAST and molasses fills the house. She's halfway to the kitchen when the phone rings, and she steels herself. It's the league selling raffle tickets. *Tickets?* "Mrs. Caines?" The voice could be long distance, though the church is just down their little street and across the busy road. The caller's sobriety is irksome; here it comes, Lucy thinks. One request always loaded with another for more — and her urge to give always reined in by some need or another to conserve.

"Can we count on you to bake, too?"

"Pickles," she casts about for a substitute, not quite an excuse. "I have lots of those."

"Oh. Well, okay," the woman says, asking, too, if she can pray for someone's niece.

Harry's condition is a tangle that her chumminess teases out. "Actually, I have a request of my own — ah, for my husband." That's all she can get out before the tightness in her chest returns, and her need once more for the hollow quiet of the kitchen. The voice is too careful, asking if he's all right. "No. But we're hopeful." That fake brightness of hers again, as if everyone is a troubled teen needing help.

"Now what about that famous bread? Can I talk you into giving a loaf?"

A weight like a fun fair beanbag seems to fall from the sky. She can't wait to get the woman off the phone. "We'll see."

Under its tea towel, the puckered dough resembles an old timer's maw — and I'm one to talk, she thinks, flouring the counter. Heavy and limp, even in the oven it won't rise back up. Folding and tucking their ends, she flings the loaves into the pans anyway, then, sticky-handed, phones the hospital. Nothing new, says the person she speaks with, and rhymes off visiting hours.

A little while later Jewel phones; when can she be ready? He sounds distant, edgy; if she didn't know better, she'd say put upon. "He probably won't know we're there," he says.

"But he'll feel it, dear. Perhaps."

THAT FIRST SAD AUTUMN, leaves had sifted over the Grounds in a perpetual fog. She spent a lot of time walking, without much purpose or direction. A relief just to escape the cabin with its smell of diapers and mould, wood damp enough to grow toadstools. Steering from the shore, she walked miles in circles over trails crisscrossing up hill and down, around boulders and through pine woods. Bundled against her, Jewel would smile up with his eyes, their colour enough to make her look away. Without warning, Mama's voice flooded back:

Oh, Lucy Locket, look at the pretty baby! Don't worry, dear. The sun'll turn her pink, pink as can be. Sometimes, back in St. Luke's basement, or on the street with Harry, the same voice had reminded her of things she needed. *Soap, darling; sugar, thread.* Once, she'd glimpsed the back of someone identical to Mama disappearing into a store; another time, a coat just like hers. Helena was harder to summon: her tiny drawl, her tinier vocabulary: a few split words. Day by day, what she preserved of it weakened: a thread spinning into nothing but crying, an echo that grew fainter and fainter.

One Sunday she found herself outside St. Columba's, newly built, it appeared, by the gleam of paint. Families trooped in, mostly women and children. Jewel weighed on her, his eyelids drooping. It was the singing that drew her, solemn but inviting, restful. *Holy holy holy, Lord God Almighty.* The inside of the church smelled of fresh wood and varnish; the pew felt sticky-smooth beneath her. Timbers arced overhead: it was like being inside an overturned boat. Then the Latin started: Mama would've turned in her grave! But Lucy heard another voice — Dad's? — admiring the woodwork. *Lucy Locket lost her pocket, Kitty Fisher found it*, it seemed to chant. As the priest switched to English, sermonizing in a flannel voice, "For now we see through a glass darkly, but then face to face ...," her eyes grazed the statues. Graven images. The Virgin's alabaster cheeks; Christ's honey-coloured beard. Jewel dozed in her lap, and the tinkling bells and murmuring voices trickled through her, as ticklish and soothing as having her hair brushed. A hundred velvet strokes, the ghost of Mama's hand.

A tiny smile creased Jewel's sleeping face — did babies dream? A little voice rose: *Mumma.* Her nipples tingled: sparks lit her spine. The priest lifted the silver cup as if it were a weighty furnishing. *Deo, Deus, Dei.* The whispers in her head: tiny feet on linoleum.

Behind the church, the cove sparkled like crushed glass. Leaves fell silently as ash as she found the path. Bricks, a chamber pot and some bedsprings lay in the bushes, objects as random yet settled as the shaft of *Mont Blanc's* anchor. Jewel stretched and let out a squawk.

Rounding a hill she'd come upon the knotweed patch, and that cottage shaped like a toque. Smoke curled from the pipe poking from the roof, carrying the smell of bacon. Ida Trott was outside chopping wood, mannish in her trousers and turned-down boots, hens pecking around her. Swinging her axe, she hobbled over. Grinning, barely a tooth in her head, she stuck out her hand and peered into Lucy's face as if they were acquainted.

"My, my, that's some cute," she'd said, asking if it was a boy or a girl, saying he reminded her of her own when *he* was small. Stroking Lucy's palm, she'd probed it with a stubby finger. When Lucy tried to pull her hand away, Ida gripped it, studying the lines, good and deep, and she'd explained, "This here's your heart, this is your heeead, and this one's your life." As Lucy's gaze slid to the axe, Ida had nodded appreciatively, saying the right hand was fate, but the left — everything else — that was up to you. "Choices," Ida rolled the word around in her mouth.

Jewel had screamed and before Lucy could shrink away, Ida gave him her finger. Next best thing to a tit, the old woman said, and, oh, couldn't folks see she had a way with kids? And with a promise to read Lucy's tea leaves — for a fee of course — licking her thumb and running it over her blade, she also offered to babysit.

Harry was up and dressed and had tea on by the time she got home. Jewel settled in to nurse, his hand roaming her breast, then going limp. What had been on Ida's finger? "All that fresh air knock him out?" Harry didn't ask where she'd got to, peeling back the little rugs knit by strangers, stroking her nape as she laid Jewel down. As he pulled her to the bed, the idea of that drunken Lil evaporated in a huff of laughter. Moving his hand under her skirt, he slid his tongue between her buttons. The bumps at the top of his spine like the crown of a puppy's head. Closing her eyes, she'd given in, kissing his scarred brow.

JEWEL WAITS AT THE door while she gets her sweater. "Becky's coming, too," he reminds her. "Wouldn't want the old man to think —" What?

That his best girl's abandoned him? she wants to say, looking for her purse.

Staying put in front, Rebecca smiles, looking a little behooved, a vase of blowsy carnations on her lap. The miniature kind are much prettier; still, it's the thought that counts. The vase tips, spilling water as they back up. "Oh, frig! You bugger."

"Beck." Jewel's voice cracks down. Meanwhile, Lucy feels like a little kid alone in the back seat, or, perhaps, the way Robert does going anywhere with his parents. But it keeps her occupied, studying the back of Rebecca's elaborate hairdo. It's as if she's forgotten to comb it, that shade almost like Orange Crush, and the whole thing the texture of cotton candy.

"How're you making out, Ma?" Rebecca half turns, flicking water from her fingers, those clawed nails painted a pearly white. Today her lipstick matches, a ghoulish accent to that buffed complexion. Her dress is a tropical turquoise, perhaps to go with her shoes? Morning fresh, is the phrase that springs to mind, if she had to describe Rebecca right now: a phrase from a commercial for some thing or other. Her look doesn't match the time of day. Maybe it's best not to answer. Distracted, Lucy forces an absent smile. "Oh, Ma." Rebecca wags her head, staring at Jewel, but his eyes are fixed on the intersection ahead.

In the hospital Rebecca makes a fuss refilling the vase, which only adds to the clutter at the bedside. Inexplicably, beside the tissues and tubes of salve there's a glass with a straw and a tiny container of juice. For Harry sleeps on, all the wires and tubing in place — though the nurse is cheery, alarmingly so, and doesn't seem to mind that they're breaking visitor rules. "Soon as he wakes, we'll get him drinking," she says, and Rebecca laughs almost gleefully, hearing how it's important to keep *them* in fluids. Already Harry's been sent to the realm of *them*.

"But, he's holding his own," Lucy ventures, trying to squeeze some hope into her voice. The nurse's smile seems slippery, transparent, saying the regular doctor will be in on Monday, if they'd like to speak to him then. To Lucy's dismay, Rebecca begins to sniffle. Tugging at tissues, she knocks something over, which Jewel retrieves. The last thing anyone wants is a scene, of any kind. As sedately as possible, Lucy leans close, trying to keep despair at bay. "Harry?" she says, too loudly. "Harry, dear, can you hear me?"

The nurse moves the carnations. How much better they'd look as boutonnieres, that fierce red: boutonnieres for a field of grooms or boys escorting girls to a prom; or on a Remembrance Day wreath — or even in a floral arrangement for a wake, like the one for Artie Babineau, years ago. But thinking of it fills her with a sudden panic: Good God, what if the flowers are all Harry sees when he wakes? If he wakes, and there's no one to stroke his brow and explain.

"Excuse me," she says, as the nurse adjusts the intravenous, squeezes the yellow bag stowed indiscreetly at the side of the bed. "The other day, yesterday (had it only been yesterday?) he seemed ... able to hear. The doctor thought —"

"Time'll tell, darlin'." The nurse can't be much older than Robert; how can she be from the same generation? Talk about the gap they're always bemoaning on TV. "Just have to be patient." Darlin'. Lucy braces for it, but without another word the nurse slips out.

In the distance a train whistle blows, or perhaps she's just imagining it, above the machines' beeping and the respirator's wheeze. That in-out-in-out sighing that makes her think, with a fresh stab of regret, of Harry's accordion. "Wouldn't a tune perk him up," pops out of her — it's either that, or give in — and Jewel and Rebecca stare, sending her that puzzled, half-suspicious look they share, more like siblings sometimes than husband and wife, more two peas in a pod than either lets on.

"Well, yeah," says Jewel, "if we knew anyone that played, Ma."

But Rebecca stops sniffling; something lights her eyes, and she even winks. "Why didn't you bring it up earlier?" As if Lucy is somehow to blame here. "*Not* a problem," Rebecca insists. Now she's done it: Rebecca will have Robert bring in his guitar. Come to think of it, though, she hasn't heard him play in a while, so maybe he'd bring in a poem. As if either could bring someone back, like the Pied Piper pulling children and rodents from the sea. The drowned. Her mind flits over the surface of it, and suddenly she imagines Harry singing — the way he did when Robert was tiny, staying over while his parents went out. *Someone's in the kitchen with Di-nah, someone's in the kitchen I know-o-o-o.* That small voice of his chiming in — glory, he was cute; what happened? — *Dinah wontcha blow, Dinah wontcha blooooow, Dinah wontcha blow your ho-o-orn!*

She smoothes the sheet over Harry's chest, the flannelette cool and stiff. But sure enough, yes, there's warmth under it, the warmth of a heart beating, however feebly. Jewel's eyes dart uncomfortably. "What're you smiling at, Ma?" he wants to know, as if she's grinning at a funeral. But it's not that at all, and once again the tightness fills her. It's the tightness of salt-dried skin, only on the inside; the after-feel of a wave that's tossed and sucked her outwards before flipping her back ashore.

"Oh my soul," she murmurs, grasping for something, humour a buoy. Saying that if he had his fiddle, they could bring it in and give him a shock. "Fit to raise the dead," Rebecca adds enthusiastically, then bows her head. If Lucy didn't know better, she'd swear she was praying; suddenly Rebecca's so still she might as well have left the room.

"Oh, my. Remember, darling?" Once more it's as if Lucy's head is above water; even better, she's sitting on warm sand. "The two of you in the cellar, playing guess the tune? When you first came back —"

"Yeah." Jewel glances away. Before they were meerreet? Rebecca pronounces it, the way she pronounces her maiden name.

The squeak of soles makes everyone straighten up. Jewel feels for the cigarettes in his shirt pocket, where the stitching has begun to unravel. It's that nurse again, blinking; maybe there's mascara in her eye. Their time's up, she tells them; *he* needs his rest. So Harry is singular once more, if unnamed, yanked back from the faceless, ominous *them*. This in itself she takes as a good sign. *Frout*, she can imagine Robert saying. Still, the least the nurse could do, being one of *them* herself, would be to call him *buddy*, that all-purpose, one-size-fits-all endearment.

Five

AS SOON AS SHE gets home she turns on the oven, though she'd be just as wise to throw out the dough and start over from scratch. But ... waste not, want not. So she shoves in the loaves, trying not to think of Harry being put into the ambulance. Lo and behold, the bread comes out like bricks, something Rebecca would bake. She could palm it off on the church raffle and sale; that's a possibility. But ... do unto others, she tells herself. Leaving the batch to cool she trudges dutifully upstairs: sticking to a schedule helps, even if there's no one around to notice.

Still, it's awfully early for bed, and as she lies there the world funnels through the window, every possible sound unspooling from the darkness. The chugging of a train breaks the breezy flow: the Ocean Limited or a freight train? Too late to be the dayliner. *Dinah wontcha blow, Dinah wontcha ...* And it returns to her, that time *way* back, before Robert was so much as a twinkle in anyone's eye, technically, even, before Jewel was born, just months shy now of fifty-two years ago to be exact, when the fellow in the Relief office had said there were trains, relief trains, echoing what she'd already read in the paper. *Someone's in the kitchen with Di-nah.* Indeed, indeed, she thinks, turning her face to the pillow. *Strummin' on the old banjo.*

HARRY'D SUNG THAT OLD standby on their wedding day, in the kitchen before the service and afterwards at the party. He'd stashed liquor in a washtub behind Dad's work shed — heaven knows where it'd come from, Prohibition in full tilt. Mama'd played the piano, Harry's friends from the refinery the guitar and violin. The party soldiered on four doors down, Harry's pals wheeling the piano along the gutter then hoisting it onto the veranda. That's what they heard, anyway, later on.

She and Harry'd had other things to do, things put on hold since that morning.

Mama'd been out borrowing extra linen, Dad and her sister, Ethel, off somewhere, who knows. Bad luck for a couple to see each other before the wedding, but there he'd been, three hours from the altar, packing bottles like fish into that tub, then covering the whole works over with nightshade nourished by the neighbour's horse. "Can you see it from the house?" was his excuse to come in; he'd covered his eyes: "Can't see a thing, honest to Pete." Next he was covering her in kisses, everything all askew. Kissing and tussling, halfway under the kitchen table when they heard a noise out front. Kissing and tussling like it was the end of the world, and just as he'd sneaked out the back, Mama appeared, but in all the flap no one noticed Lucy's hair still in rags but most of them falling out. Bathing, primping, she'd entertained a dreadful thought: what if he changed his mind?

But he'd turned up in good time and later, while everyone danced and caroused, she and Harry curled together between their wedding-gift sheets, a mist of happiness sifting over the drafty, half-empty flat. *Fee-fi-fiddly-i-o, fee-fi-fiddly-i-o-o-o-o!* and into the morning they made love to the sound of cars being shunted and coupled over at the glass-roofed station. *Can't you hear the whistle blowing? Rise up so early in the ...*

THOUGH SHE LONGS FOR it, longs for it almost more than anything in the world, sleep eludes her. Thoughts shuttle and bump, the darkness hemming her in. Lord knows the time; the Little Ben has stopped, its useless hands glowing green. She imagines Harry in his bed again, the soundless drip-drip-drip of fluids. He might as well be on the other side of Pluto right now, as the past, that plague of memory, becomes a cord that winds itself around her. At a quarter to two she gives up, finally, puts on her slippers and goes downstairs. But the ghosts are there in the kitchen, too, the ghosts of smells: half a century of suppers, Harry's beer, and underneath it all, a kind of primer, the odours of old lead paint and linoleum, the scent of newly foundered nails, for pity's sake. She's forgotten to wrap up the bread; no chance now of foisting it on the league. Not even the badgering deserve that, thanks be to no one for cheap or cost-free charity: *O Caritas*.

Peckish, she saws off a slice just for the heck of it. It's not so bad, with butter; passable, perhaps, dipped in milky tea. It almost revives her. And, oh glory, there's the mail lying unopened on a chair for two days now: a coupon for Chinese food ("garden compost," Harry would say) and the water bill, whose pollution charges make her think of the cabin's spider-infested outhouse. The "arachnoshack," Harry used to call it, until under Artie Babineau's influence it got dubbed the shitter, his expression of course.

Besides the bill, there's a letter addressed to her in wavy, unfamiliar handwriting, which gives her a little shock, one quickly replaced by a flush, the same prickly heat as when she used to get those old flashes. But suddenly it's as if it's ten in the morning, the briskness of feeling fully awake like having the crow's feet around her eyes pulled smooth. The mail is from the new priest, a form letter soliciting prayer requests.

Sawing up the rest of the bread, she ventures outside to toss chunks of it from the stoop. Good Lord, if she happens to be awake and watching, Mrs. Chaddock next door will swear she's off her rocker, this time of night. But the crows will appreciate it, Lucy tells herself, the pieces of crust a murky reflection of the stars, making a trail over the black grass.

BY HOOK OR BY crook, somehow the post had made its way accident-ally to Ida Trott, who must've found it amongst her own before, out of the blue, having the decency to deliver it. The envelope was already opened but Lucy wasted no time fretting over that, never mind the diapers boiling on the stove, Jewel scaling her shins. Plunking the baby in his crib, she'd torn across the yard, for she and Harry had no telephone, and luckily Artie did. Harry was there, of course.

It was hard to hear with Lil and Artie bickering and that crowded, messy room spinning, the eyes in the buck's head on the wall staring her down. The lady's voice was blandly suspicious; the name she gave was Mrs. Margaret Edgehill.

"You have a ... child?" Lucy could barely breathe: it was like being flung and landing upside down under that buck, then jerked upright. "A girl?" The woman hesitated. But yes — yes, she'd seen their notice.

The squabbling suddenly stopped. Harry breathed in her other ear as Mrs. Edgehill gave directions. Were they only sixty miles away? The woman's voice could've come from another country, Lucy's heart was banging so. Harry grabbed the phone. "Well, sure; first thing," he said, looking shell-shocked as he hung up. "This calls for a drink," Artie'd yammered, saying it'd been all over the paper, some kid found under an ash pan. A boy, he thought, eyeing Lil. "Speaking of kids," Harry'd choked, "where's —?"

"That little hellcat?" Artie'd snorted. "At Lil's mother's. Look, I says, didn't I Lil? It's me or her. You know how I feel about kids."

THEY COULDN'T BOTH GO, but Harry got the day off to mind Jewel. She demonstrated how to funnel hot milk into a bottle, test the temperature by flicking some on her wrist. The times she'd taken the train she could count on one hand — for Sunday school picnics — and she scalded herself, rushing. As she was grabbing her purse and second-hand hat, Harry, holding Jewel like a stuffed turkey, told her not to get her hopes too high.

Through the rain she ran all the way to the siding near the post office. The Ocean Limited was running a little late. But once she'd climbed aboard, each clack and grind swelled the hope inside her. Someone had left a newspaper and she read it front to back, then counted lakes and cows as they rolled deeper inland. When the train finally made Truro, she got out Mrs. Edgehill's letter and started walking; street names floated up as if in a dream. Outside a big grey house she stopped: 158 Willow. Her lungs pinched as she climbed the steps. The details in the letter had been sketchy; she'd absorbed little more over the phone, and as she pressed the bell her hope fluttered. If the child inside were hers, wouldn't she have known? Wouldn't she be certain, emboldened somehow by the leaded glow through the panes? *For now we see through a glass ... but then ...* Oh, yes, she told herself, anything is possible.

A tall, silvery woman appeared; Lucy'd expected someone thicker, dowdier. Margaret Edgehill rang a little bell and a girl Lucy's age took her coat. Showing Lucy inside, Mrs. Edgehill repeated what she'd put in the letter, about her husband dying at the Front and how she'd seen the advertisement one day when the help was cleaning windows using old papers. Then she rang for the child.

Waiting, Lucy thought her heart would explode. The blood washed from her face when the maid reappeared with a little girl. Both of the child's eyes were covered with patches — she was maybe three or four years old. Mrs. Edgehill tugged on a string sewn to the little one's sleeve, pink to match her dress and the bow in her russet hair. Sitting the girl on her knee, Mrs. Edgehill murmured into her ear. Biting her cheek, Lucy had tasted blood.

The maid returned with tea and milk and crumbly fudge, which Mrs. Edgehill fed to the child as Lucy felt the parlour sway like the coach car. Horrible to stare, but she made herself study each delicate feature, the little mouth and chin with its jagged blue scar, the tip of the small, straight nose. A numbness spread inside her, a numbness like that induced by ether. *What colour were her eyes — do you know?* she imagined a monster inquiring. "Can she hear all right?" she asked stupidly, wishing she'd brought a candy apple. When she touched the child's hand, the girl shrank against her guardian's shoulder.

As if watching through gauze, Lucy imagined the silky feel of her cheek.

"How ... old?"

"We're not sure," Mrs. Edgehill had smiled wearily, prying small fingers from hers. Saying the nurses had thought maybe three, three-and-a-half. Her voice trailed off, the look in her eyes beseeching: "The tea, goodness, it's cold ... and you've come *so* far." The child had scratched a mole on her wrist, a mark the shape of a bean. Staring at the carpet, Lucy could not wait to leave. "Another pot," her hostess had instructed the maid, over Lucy's objections. "We can't interest you in a sweet?" But by then Mrs. Edgehill had sounded uninterested. Sliding from her lap, the child felt for the candy dish, then tottered over with it, her foot hooking something. Lucy'd reached out too late, as Margaret Edgehill caught her. "The train isn't for another couple of hours, you know." Patting the child's wrist, Lucy had risen, thanking her anyway.

At the station she waited on the platform, grateful for the drizzle keeping the other travellers inside. The wet had seeped clean to her skin, in a grimly satisfying way rounding out the numbness, giving flesh to her despair. It was dark and pouring by the time she disembarked, and Harry wasn't there to meet her — just as well, sparing her his knowing look: *Best not hope too much; when life throws surprises, usually they ain't so good.* Ida's chickens scattered as she slouched past, the old lady herself inside, waving. At home, a perfect stranger bounced Jewel on her knee. "Mum-mum-mum," he brayed, when he saw her. The woman's face seemed kind of familiar; she said her name was Erma, Lily's ma, and that Mister had an errand.

Lucy kissed the top of Jewel's head and counted the hairs, hugging him till he cried. When Harry finally appeared it was plain he'd been drinking, as if he'd known from the start her trip would be a wild goose chase, all of it too much to hope for. His breath sweetened with rum, he'd rubbed her back, but still it had been as if the mildewed walls would fold in and crush her.

THE MEMORY, WHEN SHE lets it, still streaks the dark: the rain falling straight down as she stumbled outside trampling circles in the goldenrod. As if she'd partially lost her sight, too, tears sharp as darts; and somewhere in the fog — fog as persistent as all that splintering grief — had been Mama's voice singing her favourite hymn: *I bind unto myself to-day the strong name of the Triniteeee.* In the window's glow, Harry'd held the baby, Jewel wailing and reaching out; and the singing had tilted, then risen — a toddler's, words barely formed: *Wundun bwidge iss fawin down.*

Helena. The name had broken from her, a cry that glanced off dripping branches, lifting through the woods. It was as though she'd crossed to another place, where the dead brushed past, then laid themselves down flat and faceless as cards. The only sound the patter of rain; and yet, for a slick, hazy moment it had been her little girl in Harry's arms. A glimmer of blue through grey, Helena smiling, her sapphire eyes, her rosebud mouth touching glass — till Jewel waved his chubby fist.

DAWN BRINGS A RACKET of starlings and it hits her, the queer certainty that Harry's fading. He must be. At this moment, alone in the silent ward. The nurses on coffee break sharing recipes or the latest on the soaps — the stories, the ladies from the league call them, Rebecca too. Oh, the stories. Hungry for afternoon amusement, Harry — the picture of health, sort of, just last week — switching the TV on and off, disgusted. Griping how all they were was women whining and crying and stealing everybody else's lover boy.

Theft, she thinks, as a gnawing starts inside. Almost but not quite dislodging dread, it's hunger, another, louder emptiness descending as if from on high. She's had nothing much besides bread and tea for a couple of days now. But how can she eat when Harry's lying there, hovering, drifting towards what? How can she think of food?

Dialing almost frantically, she feels a rushing in her ears. "Is he ...?" She can't bring herself to say it over the phone, especially not at this pale hour. The nurse's good-natured twang reminds her of Rebecca's, without the put-upon pout, or even Robert's; she sounds girlish enough to be in high school, but with her head screwed on straight. For a second, a giddiness seizes Lucy and she'd like to ask — to forestall the bad news? — how the nurse feels about "the land" and the moon, and, oh, for pity's sake, about young women taking off their shirts and rolling in mud at that concert just weeks ago in some field down the States. 'Magine," Harry'd said, seeing it on the news. "Can't get my head around that, can you?" Harry trying in his silliness to be "hip," which makes her think of bones and steel pins. Or being "in," as they also say on TV, which makes her want to ask, in *what*?

"We'd phone if there was a change," the girl says evenly. "Best you can do is steal some sleep." Oh, the kindness of strangers! Stealing: Lucy's mind flits around the notion, as if someone's picked Harry up and stuck him in their pocket. The very thought a reminder of the times she'd have given, no, thrown him away.

SO WHAT, DOLLY, IF he drowned his sorrows: didn't he have a right to? That's how he'd put it, pushing the baby into her empty hands, throwing up his own. The mornings especially weighed her down that lonely, desperate autumn, mornings and the baby's crying, and Harry's wincing. The scar below his collarbone a jagged tattoo as he lay there, young still, but more like an old man, one who could've easily given up. Telling her to get a diaper on Jewel before he whizzed, he'd say, "There's a christening I don't need." And she'd oblige, a girl playing house, yet old herself, old enough some days to lie down and die, even as she did what she had to, folding, tucking, wiggling in pins. "Practice makes perfect, Lucy," Harry'd tease, watching. Like kids they bickered, kids mimicking adults, except it was serious. The train ride and Truro a puff of smoke as grey as the rest of it. "You getting up today, or what?" Lucy stifling "your highness," then letting slip a question, how Lily was last night. "Like a buttercup," he had the gall to answer, in the same breath asking for tea and calling her the frigging Inquisition.

Oh yes, his was the high life, all right. One day he didn't get up at all, but had an excuse. A fellow had escaped from the prison — a Hun on the lam! Artie'd heard it straight from a guard: "Scalp you like a red Indian, them Huns," he said. "Any sense, though, and the bastard would've shipped off to the fatherland." But Harry'd figured the "bastard" could be hiding right out back in the woods, and stuck around all day keeping things locked up. But by evening, heading next door for cards, he left everything wide open. "Da-da-da-da," Jewel babbled as she rocked him, the moon glimmering through the window. Watching it rise across the cove, over the wooded hill almost but not quite ringed by water, she thought of the shark, then imagined someone drifting in a dory. Ending up where? Stranded off a shoal in the harbour or washing ashore in Europe, the window seemed to answer, to be counted among the dead soldiers.

"Lucy Locket lost her pocket, Kitty Fisher found it," she crooned into the blackness, never mind what might be lurking: who cared? There was only the sky after all, an upside down bowl, and the three of them, the small, noisy triangle of their hearts beating their separate rhythms: hers, Jewel's and Harry's. The sun would rise, the days unfold, and yet ... How could tomorrow come, how would she stand it, without some sign? Something as small and inconsequential as a falling star, a shard of glass or a doll's arm washing up: or was this asking too much? Something, it no longer mattered what, to let her know that, despite everything, somewhere inside the great black bowl Helena floated, alive. Something Harry would miss, no doubt, off dealing cards: God forgive his stubborn soul.

When he went to work next day, it was all she could do to get dressed. If there'd been someone to talk to — but who, Lil? If stubbornness was Harry's right, pride was hers. And on the heels of pride came what? Shame. How easily these got muddled in the fog of despair. She longed to be able to separate it all into strands, like pulling apart a length of rope or a palm leaf, the kind they gave out at church before Easter.

Fresh air helped the concentration, as did the lapping of waves, so perhaps it was their fault they drew her. The baby bundled against the autumn chill, she'd scaled the rocks. The tide was low, just turning. Something had swung on the current — a crate? — but as the wind pulled it, she saw that it was curved in the shape of a torso, a woman's, swollen. A guitar coming unglued, with a man painted on it, a man under a palm tree strumming another guitar, like the one someone had played on their wedding day.

The October sun spangled the Arm — diamonds? — but the fog inside her had spread till all she felt was its cold vapour, the numbness that was a cousin now, a "cousint," as Harry would say, or a Siamese twin. Laying Jewel in a nest of boulders, she listened for reason: Mama's. Not a hymn, but instructions. *Lucy, girl. Go home, make a stew. Wash the floor.* Instead, a voice not Mama's, not hers, but the fog's, had hissed: *Ladybird, ladybird, fly away home, your house is on fire, your children alone ...*

Sparkling at first, the water dulled as it swirled and bit at her ankles. Yellow as the heel of a bottle, it seemed to sharpen the stones; good thing she had shoes, thanks to small miracles. Reaching through swaying weed, she scooped up a rock, amazed, a little, by the cold, her dripping sleeve. It fit in her pocket, just. But what about Harry, and Jewel? The water didn't answer. Somewhere behind her, far behind her, Jewel's cries were a gull's. The cold sawed into her thighs, but so what? The weight of her coat and of the fog itself was shroud-like. A foretaste, as the wind tugged *so* gently, and the waves rose. The spirits of the dead — the living? — taking her hand ...

Mum-mum-mum, Jewel's wails were almost hers now, about to greet Mama. The rock an anchor, so there'd be no doubt. Soon, in the drop-off, would be her little girl, sweet baby girl, rising through greeny black to meet her: their reunion a swift, sparkling shower ...

The clack of marbles grinding together. Stones. *Fraulein!* Splashing. Ice. A hand gripping her elbow, not Mama's at all but, suddenly, a man's. *Miss!* Jewel's screaming yanked her back, as had the man's arms dragging her, and his smell of sweat and fear.

Her heels left a slug's trail on the rocks. His wet coattails, their ragged hem, and the edges of his sleeves where grubby hands began and ended. All she saw, really, were his hands, and the side of his stubbled jaw as he ducked into the bushes, disappearing, an olive flash through the twigs and the blood-red huckleberries. Marooning her ashore with Jewel's shrieking as she clutched him, millstone *and* lifesaver anchoring her to land.

HARRY, COMING IN FROM work as usual and going straight to Artie's, never suspected a thing. And that Sunday she'd returned to St. Columba's, where Father Marcus, the short, balding priest, preached that despair was a sin against one's hope in Christ. A blaze of sun lit the window, a bejewelled scene of Jesus himself blessing loaves and fishes. The red of his cloak bleeding over her skirt, the glow from his hands warming hers. Shamed by the sky-blueness of his eyes, she drank in the safety of Mass, Latin soothing as cocoa. Her gaze roaming, she carefully avoided the figure above the altar: those greying limbs, that sagging head. *Lift up your hearts. We lift them to the Lord*: the priest's voice was as perfumed as Mama's. Tears tickled both Lucy's cheeks while people blessed themselves as if swatting flies. The breaking of bread, the breaking of hearts. *That we may evermore dwell in him, and he in us.* Mama's scorn for Catholics hardly mattered now, as she fixed on Mary's statue, Mary mother of sorrows, that smile like melting ice cream, and let the incense lull her. Afterwards, she ducked past the priest's hand, his murmured *Bless you.*

In the lane cutting back to the Grounds, some little boys had squatted by a puddle, fighting over some taffy. They'd gawked as she passed, then returned to their game. *Rock paper scissors!* Their shrillness following her. The lane narrowed to a track lined by tiny bungalows nothing like the houses lost in Richmond; vines crept over verandas piled with junk. Then more woods, the mossy path bordered by rattling-dry ferns, opening into an orchard with stooped trees; the air had smelled of rotting apples. Ahead lay the barn and the Big House, the back end falling in: she'd somehow walked in a loop, ending up almost where she'd started. Harry would wonder where the heck she'd got to, his day eaten up with babysitting. Peering up at the roof's sagging ridgepole, she thought of Dad's carpentry, Mama's sewing, that lost world where things had been square: joists and stitches.

The veranda had rotted; a rope dangled from a post — a clothes-line? Doves cooed, conjuring the music Harry could make blowing into a bottle. Along the path straggled the ruins of a garden: wild rose poking from the grass, day lilies, aster. Just the thing, lilies, to spruce up a dog-patch yard: who'd notice if she helped herself? Hoisting herself up, she peered over a rotting sill: the room inside soot-black, a pool of glass glinting from the floor. The stone founda-tion loomed through a hole. *What kept you?* she imagined Harry's sigh. *Them catlicks tie you up, or wha'?*

No sense crying. Crying won't bring anyone back, she'd almost heard a voice coaching, as she inspected the lilies. A caw from the orchard, and glancing up she caught movement. A man huddled under the branches, his greenish coat sweeping the grass as he scrabbled for something — windfall — like a deer; stuffing his pockets. When he looked up, her heart had raced. But before she could turn and run, he'd sunk behind the trees, covering his face.

THERE'S POLITENESS, AND THERE'S necessity. Refusing to wait, as soon as it's light she calls. Luckily Jewel picks up the phone; she never knows how Rebecca will be, especially before she's had coffee. Her fix, she calls it, which reminds Lucy of Harry tinkering at his work-bench. Maybe Jewel's the same, as hooked to coffee as he is to cigarettes! He asks what time it is, sounding like he's still in bed. Or maybe Rebecca's been putting him through his paces, ahem, her paces; she never lets up, that one, always at him to fix this or that. Yes, she's a big one for fixes.

"Were you sleeping, son?" Now she feels guilty; patience, after all, *is* a virtue.

He's gruff more than groggy, explaining that Bucky was out all night with the car. "At least the little bugger's asleep now. But he could get into trouble unconscious, swear to Christ," he adds. Watch your tongue, she wants to say, biting hers. No need to curse. His voice deepens: "Anything new?" *Expect the worst and you won't be disappointed*: that attitude of his father's is some gift, especially now. "You've pulled another all-nighter, have you?" he asks flatly, his tone indulgent but not quite kind. Does he need to hear her premonition? Better to say than stifle it, though, even if it is crossing over into doom and gloom: "I have this awful feeling, dear."

More resigned than alarmed, twenty minutes later he arrives with two cups of takeout coffee in a tray for ice-cream cones. Better they were ice creams — she doesn't even like coffee, though the heat through the Styrofoam is a comfort. Wherever did he find it, so early? "Thank Christ for the Cove." Mr. Jimmy's store, he means, up the road and across from the marina. Then he has to tell her who was there. "Your pal — Benny? — and his lady friend." Stocking up, he explains, buying anything that comes in a can. As if she needs to know, he describes them getting into the rowboat. "The size of her!" he says, and she supposes he means the friend, not the dinghy, going on about how she looks unwashed. "Living like that, a woman. Though from what I've heard, she comes from somewhere. Money." You hear that all the time, he snorts, people living off cat food, their mattresses stuffed with money. Nobody she knows of; Jewel's great for talking through his hat. Shooting the shit, as Harry'd been known to say quite rudely after a beer or two. But who feels like arguing? Jewel's just being chatty, unusually so, the sound of his voice as soothing as tea.

"Each to their own," he shrugs. "Live and let live." Never mind their nerves; his grin reminds her of when he was five, maybe six. "For all we know, our friend Benny's the same." Loaded, he means, and not liquored up, ranting then about the type who get rich by sitting on it, and he laughs as if nothing is wrong. A laugh that reminds her of thumbtacks being shaken around in a jar, the thought of which makes her cringe. It's as though he's telling himself a joke, one he can't let go of. "Yup, poor old Jimmy was scared those birds would capsize and we'd have to haul them out."

She has to stop and think, who? Ah, Benny, the knife-sharpener, and his lady friend. The one that Robert ... It hits her how she should've asked him more, what he really thought of people living in a floating shack. Not gossip exactly: friendly research. Now Jewel's looking at her, his eyes full of concern, and without warning the gnawing starts in her stomach again. Will they think she's off her rocker if she calls again? But he's already picked up the receiver, dialing in that violent way of his. "Nothing new?" he finally murmurs, cupping the mouthpiece. Hanging up, he looks almost embarrassed, but of what? "Oh, Ma," he swallows. Her boy — this greying man, that wrinkled golf shirt stretched over his belly. His breath rank as he busses her cheek, saying he's going home to shower. "Becky could take you shopping," he offers, "how about that?" The last thing she wants, not a thing she needs. But his sigh echoes everything to be fretted or fussed over, not just the respirator's wheeze, but the teasing of a comb through Rebecca's perm, Robert's lip over school. "Suit yourself," he says, jingling his keys, and she thinks again of Benny the traveller, wondering aloud, "My Dinah, how on Earth does he manage on that boat?" It's a question, and to think of two people on board! A miracle it floats, and that the spirit of good taste hasn't cut its moorings.

"*House*boat, Ma." That laugh again, just like when he was younger, rubbing his chest as she observes a little slyly that there can't be plumbing. But the thought sparks guilt; she could've hired the fellow for something: to do the fence, if Robert won't. Then Jewel says there should be laws against squatters: what's the difference, if they live on the land or sea? "Though you can't legislate taste — or craziness," he concedes, and a coolness fills her, a longing. Not much anyone can do to stop people from doing what they want. *Doing their own thing*, as they say on TV, and she thinks again of Robert, living off the land or going back to it or whatever. It's not that hard to imagine him rocking off to the horizon in an ark like Noah's, only the size of an outhouse and with no critters. Maybe that's his problem, the root to what Jewel calls his don't-give-a-crapness, the fact that the kid never had a pet, growing up. No responsibilities. Though he got the moon in every other respect, being an only child — like his dad in some ways. Then she thinks of Benny; at least he has company, and no wonder a woman like that would charm him, considering the one he'd popped out of.

Jewel eyes her oddly, sighing again, "Just say the word, when you wanna go back to see the old man," as if Harry's orchestrated all this bother. It occurs to her then, why hold off? Find out now what Harry was going to, before everything changed. Clearing her throat, she asks after Robert's plans. "Plans?" He pulls a face, as if it's her fault — it's somebody's! — that the boy is like a whirligig. As he crumples his cup, she grabs his hand, his fingers huge and clumsy in hers. "For chrissake, Ma. One worry at a time. Wait'll Dad's ..." But he doesn't sound very hopeful. Squeezing his thumb, she tugs even as he pulls away, reminding him that it's wrong to give up on any-body, that despair's — "A sin against God." He rolls his eyes, saying Becky'll think she's lost her marbles, talking that way. Heaven forbid.

IDA TROTT WAS THROWING bread to her hens and a flock of black-birds, a rippling, pecking wave of feathers, as Lucy'd stumbled up. The wind rattled the knotweed, shaking its dead flowers. "Good God, missy — ya seen a ghost, or wha'?" A couple of hairs sprang from Ida's chin. Her eyes were the colour of tinned beans, warming. "Come and sit," she'd said. "The young fella, is it? Teething?" Lucy shook her head. But Ida'd steered her inside. Her house sloped and angled everywhere, as if on a dime it could be folded and moved. Not the clutter though: dishes and pots on the rusty stove; mountains of papers, rags; and in the middle, a couch spread with blankets, a bouquet of drying weeds hung over it. Take a load off, she'd muttered, filling the kettle from a bucket, saying Lucy looked pale, and that there'd been flu over at the jail — Nature cleaning its oven. Her mouth full of stumps, her breath foul.

When the kettle boiled, Ida spooned tea into a cup, splashing in water then sliding it over. Her eyes like augers as she patted Lucy's hand, saying, There there, the worst was behind her. That leathery touch opening a floodgate as she said to drink up, but not be greedy and leave a bit. Telling her to swirl the cup three times and make a wish, then overturn and spin it on the cracked saucer. For a long time Ida'd said nothing, peering inside, then a smile creased her face. Near the rim lay her future, she said — well, that afternoon, or the next morning — and at the bottom, Lucy's past clear as mud. Flecks like bits of seaweed at high tide. Not so lucky, but full of promise, at least at the top.

"I see a ball," she said, "and a baby." Birds, too — good news — and an anchor, which meant a decent night's sleep. Then she spied a suitcase, no, a sack, meaning somebody'd flown the coop. "Lock your doors!" she joked, spotting an eye, too: "Beware, missy!" Except, there was an envelope: more good news, and a dish and a duck and a circle. But the tea's bitterness lingered. A child, tossing a ball? "The young fella," Ida said. A duck? Money coming, she foretold. And a dish? Trouble at home. Then something had crossed Ida's wizened face as she hedged, saying the ball could be an apple, a girl munching it. "Cute little thing, pretty as a pitcher."

Ida's prediction about trouble proved correct. Harry lit into her the second Lucy stepped in, barely waiting till she'd cuddled Jewel, accusing her of running off, priests and nuns waylaying her. The place was upside down, laundry everywhere. Lifting her hat, he said, Well, at least she still had her hair; those nuns shaved theirs off, didn't they? She'd yelled at him to stop, but he'd snatched up her apron and flung it, his nightshirt hiking up to show his parts so vulnerable-looking that she thanked God women's were like central heating. Oblivious, he'd asked for his dinner. There were apples by the sink. "Fill your face," she'd flung back, and he'd slammed outside, but not before the damage was done. Forget it, he'd hollered, saying Lily would feed him.

Six

OH, GLORY, THIS TIME it's Rebecca who answers, telling her to hang on a sec, as a windy sound blows over the line. "My nails, just did 'em. Still there?" In spite of everything, a peevishness pushes her sigh. "What's wrong? Pop's not ... You haven't heard —?" All she wants is to hear Jewel. But Rebecca doesn't know where he's taken off to. "Around the cove, visiting, maybe? Seeing one of Pop's old buds?"

Of all the times to go off tooling around! And they wonder why Robert has no sense. "It's fine — really." Sorry for interrupting, she almost adds; why this feeling all the time of needing to plead? This met with Rebecca's dodgy silence. She'll see Jewel at the hospital, she says, telling Rebecca to have a lovely day.

Time's wasting, after all; if she waits around, it could be supper-hour by the time she makes it to town. There's a bus in fifteen minutes; it stops in front of the church once an hour, less often on Sundays. What day *is* it? Racing to get ready, she pulls on the gauzy dress, fixing the collar under her dark blue cardigan. On a whim she adds Harry's diamond earrings, and a slash of lipstick for good cheer. Her glasses have weakened — the glasses, not her eyes — and she has to squint applying it, the way Robert did as a tyke colouring, struggling to stay inside the lines. Back then she would've been just as happy watching him scribble on paper bags, but oh no, his mother had insisted on colouring books full of wide-eyed children and animals. The pages smelling of the drugstore with its dusty cold cream and emery boards. Never enough just to let Robert doodle; Rebecca would make sure he didn't go over the lines; how unlike her, too. But somebody'd said it was good training: for what, though, Lucy was never quite sure. Anyway, it hadn't worked, seeing how the boy loves being out of bounds.

Outside St. Columba's she sees women ferrying things from the parking lot into the basement. Oh, Lord, she's completely forgotten the raffle and sale; hadn't they said Monday? But before anyone notices her, the Fifteen arrives, whisking her off, saved — for now. Clutching her purse on her lap, she's sitting back for the ride when a little boy points to her knees, their bluish stain showing through her nylons. "Ooh," he says, crying when his mother yanks his arm.

At the very next stop a young fellow gets on. She recognizes the greenish jacket before recognizing him. What a treat! More so because unexpected, a Taverners drop from heaven, sweet but hard, because he doesn't see her at first, not till she slides a Tender Tootsie into the aisle, and he looks up, his teeth sunk into his bottom lip, starting to sneer. "Fffuuuhh — *Gran!*" Robert looks surprised, not altogether pleasantly. She pats his knee when, reluctantly, he slides in beside her. "Nice scenery," he smirks as they rumble past a couple slouching along the shoulder, the wiry, reptilian Benny and the woman, who's a foot taller and wider by a mile. "Gross!" Robert nudges her. "Grouse," it sounds like, and at first she thinks he's spotted a bird, a wood grouse? They used to be plentiful in the Grounds, once. Then he says it again, "Some grouse, that one. Nothin' like a chick with a beard, eh?" She pokes him back; all this bird talk. But then she thinks of poor old Ida Trott and her chin hair. "It's pretty beead," he draws out the *a* the way his dad does, asking if she can guess what he's seen. "Her skinny-dipping. Right in the cove. Now *there's* some-thin' grouse." He cranes back, they both do, as the pair shrinks from sight, poking along. But then she can't resist, even if it is catty.

"I thought you'd admire that," she casts around for the word: lifestyle. It's fun to tease and Robert's so easily ruffled, at least with his folks. But not her, he'd never hold a joke against her, or rebel, as they say nowadays about anyone young enough not to be grey. Which causes a pang, when she thinks how Harry once had hair so black it shone blue. "Ain't there stuff chicks can do about that?" The beard thing, he means, eyeing her chin, and she wants to laugh, never mind Harry, and the Ferris wheel that's become her stomach. "*Isn't*, dear." Suddenly she's his Grandmother Frog again, he's her Robbie, and they're riding the bus to the midway, the sticky tangle of rides that would come to town each June. But then she's curious. "What do you mean, anyway?"

It blows his mind, he says. In this day and age? That a girl would let herself have facial hair. "Like guys aren't gonna notice. Even an old pit like Benny." A *pit*? "Grease pit," he says, as if she's stupid, then relenting, "Okay, so he's more of a geezer, you're right." She'd like to give his wrist a slap, as she would've years ago babysitting. A little reminder of who was who: respect for the pecking order, as Harry would say. But enough of that, especially in public, she reminds herself; he's going on eighteen, treat him like the young man he is. How long, though, since they had a real conversation, about something besides that blessed fence and his father's rules? Straightening her purse on her lap, she says, "So. Will it be Mars next, you think?" He stares as if she's completely senile. The moon, she explains, asking where he supposes they'll land next.

He's blushing, even his forehead through that stringy hair, teasing, "Jeez, Gran, you scared me," saying he'd give fifty trips in space to have gotten to some show instead. Some big thing down the States, on somebody's farm. "The Dead were playing, and friggin' Hendrix," he says, and might as well be speaking Swahili till she remembers the news: mud, and thousands of kids on drugs doing unspeakable things, and noise, godawful screeching noise. All in the name of —? "Peace, Gran." Abruptly he's getting up, flashing a crooked grin that fades to uncertainty. "Give Grampa a hug, all right?" But before she can shake his hand or squeeze it, or, God forbid, give him a kiss, he's swinging like a large monkey up to the doors, and as the bus jerks to a stop he's gone, as if she's only dreamed him.

By the time she arrives at the hospital, her dress looks mussed in the elevator's chrome, her lipstick faded. She feels raw, suddenly, and more than a little uneasy for coming ahead alone, without waiting for anybody. Her reflection only makes her edgier; there's no time to find the Ladies' and primp. Her knees and back ache from the bus, her stomach lagging a floor behind as the elevator rockets upwards.

Harry's door is closed; he's being bathed, says the nurse, a young gal. "You want him all nice and sweet-smelling, don't you?" Beaming, she has bouncy red hair, a gap between her teeth. "Ta-da," she announces, pushing back the curtains as if Harry is a prize, or a gift. Setting her purse down, Lucy takes pains not to disturb his wiring. "Dear?" Her voice is a froggy whisper, his cheek papery. It's like kissing a dead leaf, and his skin is so grey, as grey as the corners of the room — a dinginess rife with germs? Gently massaging his hand, she's startled by its warmth.

"He didn't have such a great night," the nurse says evenly, her tone neither cheerless nor encouraging. Tidying up, she dumps greyish bits of gauze into a kidney-shaped dish, saying the doctor will be in later, and is going to want to talk with her. The room goes stuffy then, the machine attached to Harry bleeping out its endless, ominous signal. It's as if Lucy's on the ceiling looking down at herself, a blue dot on the avocado chair. Patting her arm, the spit-holed little nurse murmurs about a chaplain. "Okay, love, you know where the buzzer is," she finally says, tiptoeing out with her basin.

Somehow Lucy wrestles open the window; a crack is as far as it'll go, enough to admit the noise of cars and ships in the harbour, that drone of horns and engines. If God had a sound, she wonders, would this be it? Glancing off nearby buildings, the sun slants in, and across the bluer-than-blue sky a jet paints a path like paint from a roller. It does no good at all to cry; what would crying accomplish? Closing her eyes, she times her breathing with the respirator's, that forced rise and fall, in and out; a balloon being blown up and leaking, till each of her breaths is oxygen gulped inside an airtight vault.

There's a whoosh of white, a fresh hand touching her arm. It's Doctor Sheridan, the resident, he reminds her, saying he's glad she's here; there are things they have to discuss, decisions they'll have to make. In surprisingly short order, Jewel and Rebecca arrive; they've even got Robert — who knows where and how they've found him so quickly. No one says anything about too many visitors.

They gather silently around Harry's bed; in her mind at least they all hold hands — she and Jewel, Rebecca and Robert. As if it's a wake, or a seance, as Rebecca blurts out, blinking at the ceiling. And yet, from somewhere, part of her can almost hear Harry yelling at them to cut the gag, and come off it. "Good heavens," she hears herself, her own voice farther away. Tears blurring the room. "If he comes to, he'll think he's dying. Look at us," she tries to joke, "he'll swear he's a goner."

Rebecca rubs her shoulder so hard it hurts. Robert taps his foot as if to some frantic rhythm, Jewel looking stricken. Then, out of a daze, she realizes that he's set up a tape deck of all things, a boxy contraption with reels rooted out from who knows where. He stabs at the buttons, and squirrelly squeaks and chatters burst forth, followed by shouting and music. Fiddle and accordion, a kitchen party someone's recorded, with so much background racket she can't make out the tunes.

"Edgar Boutilier had the stuff kicking around his place," Rebecca explains, as if it's important. "A good blast of 'cordine," she whispers with determination, "if that doesn't get his blood pumping ..." Her eyes jump and she swipes at them, making a soup of her blue mascara.

"Shut up, Ma." Robert's attempt at being funny, or respectful, or whatever it is, falls flat, his Adam's apple squirming in his throat.

"Don't talk to your ma like that," his dad snarls, and Rebecca swats the air around her head as if shooing black flies, just as a nurse appears. She checks Harry's pulse, takes his temperature, then tries to straighten the plastic snake poked into his mouth. It's tied into place with gauze, as if he might try to pull it out. The nurse's eyebrows remind Lucy of tiny, hovering wisps of cloud as she glances around at them all with a busy sort of sympathy, then rustles off.

Spending no time on niceties besides how-do-you-do, the doctor tells them quietly that brain damage is to be expected. "It all depends ... how ... well ... without the ventilator ..." His voice too reminds her of clouds.

"You mean he could stop breathing," Jewel blurts, making a sound like wind scrubbing branches. The same wind tugging at Lucy, laying everything bare.

"His feeding too; it's all being done intravenously," the doctor explains, his hesitation filling the room; if his voice had a colour, she thinks, it would be the shade of watery juice. Hunched there as if nursing a cramp, Robert taps his foot faster, if that's possible, bouncing his knee. "If he does survive," says the doctor, "you're looking at a nursing home."

How can he say this? The insult, his presumption! "Doctor —" she hears herself plead, her haughtiness a shock. Saying she'll feed him at home, of course. Breathe for him, too, for pity's sake, if it comes to that. Her mind races, and suddenly her chest could burst, her heart pounds so. A world without Harry, one where even the bad wind forgets to blow. Looking tall and uncomfortable, a skeleton maybe, or just molecules of air or water inside that crisp white coat, Doctor Sheridan gazes at his well-groomed hands. He smiles around grimly, nodding, and then, exactly like a white Mr. Freeze or a Popsicle melting, evaporates from the room, quietly, invisibly, slipping out.

"Ma," Jewel murmurs aimlessly, sitting there, his jaw set. As her mind casts about for something, anything to hook itself to, she wonders when he last shaved. The lump in her throat could be a marble or Plasticine, yet they're all looking at her as if she has the power to fix things. "Rebecca, dear," she hears herself. "Please stop crying." Reaching across her, she strains to pat Robert's knee, the first in a tower of necessities, it seems, in putting back together what the doctor has wiped out. *Humpty Dumpty sat on a wall,* she thinks wildly. The boy's skin shows through his frayed jeans; its warmth jars her. A thudding in her ears, she takes the five dollar bill out of her purse, tells him to get himself something. A burger. That amount would buy five; it doesn't matter, though naturally Rebecca picks up on it.

"What do you say, Bucky? Remember, Gran's fence." But the gift of gab fails even her, and Lucy lets it go, Robert's awful nickname. Like the money, she gives it over to the room's silence.

Facing the window, she waves them all off, needing solitude: can't they allow her that, a tiny opening to breathe? Slowly they file out, but not till each has murmured something to Harry, their muted goodbyes like ones on TV. Only when the room's empty is it safe to turn. *Goodbye, my darling. Au rev-war.*

She finds Jewel and Rebecca pacing in the dim little lounge several doors down the hall. Mutely Jewel takes her by the arm. Outside, they wedge her between them in the front seat, as if she is a child, or might try to do something silly like jumping out.

"Where's Robert?" she asks before they drive off. Rebecca rolls her eyes, beautifully liquid in the dim interior; movie star eyes with all that makeup, never mind how it's run.

"Oh, God," she sighs, saying he couldn't wait, and something about a girl that's been hanging around him.

"Jesus Murphy," Jewel swears, as if it's medicine. "Only a kid could think of *that* at a time like this."

Leaning forward to elbow him, Rebecca bumps her instead. "Life goes on," she hears herself warble.

"That's Buck's reaction, anyways," Jewel says, but his sigh means *baloney*, or as Harry himself would thunder, *Whatta loada buffalo crap.*

MAYBE IDA'S TEA LEAF-READING had bolstered her; more likely it was nerves fed by despair. Off she stormed anyway; she'd give Harry what-for, him chasing sin like a dog after steak. Then again, hadn't the priest called despair a sin and of the worst kind, a failure of faith? So why go to the neighbours? If despair was a sin she had bags of it, if sin was what Harry wanted. *Store up for yourself not the treasures of earth, but of heaven.* Either way, despair — self-pity? — made her greedy for something, Jewel squirming in her arms as she banged on the door. Eventually Lil had appeared, sloe-eyed, dazed, and dressed in a velvet robe. Lucy didn't beat around the bush: if Harry was there, send him out! Scowling, Lil shushed her, saying they were busy dealing, for chrissake. As if they hadn't had their fill of poker the night before.

Surprising herself, Lucy'd pushed her way in. The house was a disaster; nobody'd thought to clear out the bottles. Dangling from the antlers of the buck's head on the wall was Harry's cap, lipstick fresh as blood on the poor critter's mouth. Passing a flask, Harry and his friend stopped talking, Artie leering up. As evenly as could be, she'd said dinner was on and he'd best come home. But the liquor had already started to work: Lily had invited him, and it'd be rude to scoot, and in front of everybody he'd boomed, "Haven't I done my duty, while you gallivanted off to —" Mass, Lil tittered. But then his voice had warmed — slightly, though how could she trust it? "Can't you see, dolly? We're conducting business." Then Lil had sniffed at the air, saying she smelled something burning, maybe next door, and if Lucy wasn't so jeezly busy she'd have invited her, too. She'd even batted her eyelids, and not a hint of anything cooking on her filthy stove.

Jewel had started squalling. "Suit yourself then," she'd jeered at Harry, hoping no one saw her tremble. Later, if she could've locked him out, she would've. "You're such a killjoy," he accused, shouting as Jewel napped. Bad enough that she couldn't let go, he said, but she expected him to go down with her! "You're dead a long time, girly," he yelled, saying he aimed to enjoy things while he was able. "Frig knows what'd blow in tomorrow" — he wasn't wasting it on his knees, whatever the frig she'd have him doing! His liquored talk worse than a case of the back-door trots, on and on: "*You* wanna mope around, chasing wild geese with your nose up your backside, well, go right ahead —" He flopped down so hard the chair under him gave out, and he blamed her for that too. Then she'd shot back, "'Magine, someone so *hopeless* having that effect on you. Lord knows what Lil gets you up to!" Pounding the mat, he'd said to leave Lil out of it, hollering that there wasn't a thing about Lil she needed to know. So, the gloves off, she'd demanded to know about his winnings, or were they losses? But he'd just sneered, "Wouldn't you love to know."

AFTER THAT, THE LONELINESS just deepened, a mossy well to be climbed out of. Harry wasn't much of a ladder. But, like a rope being dangled, didn't despair offer the nugget of hope that came with having little more than a pinch of coon shit to lose, as Artie said?

While Harry shaved for work, she'd pictured that strange man — the prisoner — foraging under the trees. If Harry could squander hard-earned money, it wasn't a stretch to offer thanks, charity. Hunger was hunger; Kraut or not, hadn't he plucked her that day from temptation, the ether of forgetting? *Give us this day our daily bread.* Throwing kippers and canned milk into a bag, she pocketed a spoon. It would do as a trowel for digging up lilies, and though not a fork or slingshot, would be better than nothing if the fellow came near.

With Jewel's weight pressed against her, she hurried past Ida's, skirting the anchor. The orchard was dotted with starlings, crows screaming from the woods. Intending to leave the bag in a tree, safe from rats, instead she'd circled to the barn.

Jewel pummeled her with his heels, when there was a scurrying — squirrels? — and a pair of eyes flashed above a rusted rain barrel, watching. Dropping the bag, she'd fled, but not before spotting a boot, filthy toes where the leather gaped. Jewel's bellow like the whine of a torpedo trailing them through the woods.

DAYS LATER SHE'D UNCOVERED Harry's old boots, the ones he'd had on when the soldiers dug him from the rubble. Lord knows why he'd saved them; the kindness of strangers had outfitted the homeless, and not just with south end hand-me-downs. She poked a tin of kippers into each boot, then stuck both on fence-posts. They were gone the next day when she took more milk and an old shirt of Harry's, hanging it from a picket.

For people left with nothing, there seemed no end to the stuff piling up in the cabin. Stuff Harry wangled or had palmed off on him by his new friends — in lieu of cash, for all she knew, those evenings next door. Drink turned him into a pack rat. "Easy come, easy go," he'd say, "but you can't take it with you." Why would he want to? Sometimes it was hard being civil. But a week's charity reduced the pile.

"You meant business!" he'd slurred, trying to be funny. And then, "Good on you, since we'll want to start fresh." Fresh? He'd been thinking, he said. *Thinking?* Come spring; of breaking ground. *You're talking through your hat*: it took every ounce of strength not to say it. But to his credit, he never asked where all his stuff went, and that week the war ended, out of the blue a halt. The eleventh hour, day and month. If it was that easy, why not sooner?

There were cheers from the prison. Harry drank himself sick. Disgusted, she'd threatened to leave if he went off the deep end like that again; so fast, she said, even Artie's head would spin. "As if I'd care," he moaned, as if ducking bullets. She'd gone right on pumping water — water, in a place where drink was more plentiful, though the whole country was supposed to be dry. In the Grounds it rained liquor. *And where exactly would you go, dolly?*

While he was at work, juggling Jewel, she took his good blue shirt off its hanger and up by the Big House tried tying it to the fence. Not easy, with the wind ripping fit to tear off shingles. With a ripple of guilt she'd imagined Harry rooting around, wanting to know where she'd put it, but she'd let the gusts push her towards the barn anyway. Brazenly she'd knocked.

PULLING OUT OF THE hospital lot, Jewel slams on the brakes for a pedestrian who's already made it to the curb. It's hardly enough to cause whiplash, but Rebecca grips Lucy's arm protectively, those nails digging in. "What're you *doing*, hon?" she goads him. At a time like this! Squeezed there between them, Lucy thinks distractedly of deals, bargains. Daring herself, daring someone: God? If she can just have Harry back, even if only half the way he was, a slab of himself ...

As Rebecca adjusts her skirt, fluffs her hair, a memory stirs itself: she and Ethel when they were little, playing *Queenie Queenie, who's got the ball?* And that other game, Knock-off Ginger. All the way down the street, rapping on neighbours' doors, then hiding around corners and behind bushes. *Dare you, double dare you, sissy.*

BRACED FOR HIS SHUFFLING, she'd waited. The barn would be drafty as a basket inside, she knew, but there'd been barely time to think about it as the door tipped forward. Those eyes had met hers, spools of light that emphasized the fellow's gauntness. Her breath snagged. He was young, younger than she'd thought: like her.

The door had swung wider. Neither moved. His mouth a grim line, in the shifty light his eyes were the colour of the Arm on a winter day: that brutally innocent blue.

Shell shock? But the idea had crumbled like a sand-dollar in a pocket. Gazing steadily, she handed over the blue shirt as if he'd been waiting to have it ironed. The coolness of his eyes turned her limbs to taffy as he held it up. Smelling faintly metallic — of rainwater? — his breath had clouded the air.

Danke. An accent, a word like the washtub being dragged and emptied outside.

How long since he'd bathed? His face looked scrubbed, if pale, his hair in frozen spikes. *The Huns, godless barbarian hordes. Fields mulched with corpses.* Pictures spun through her, and the images of Helena's pram, the ghost of her daughter's warmth under her palm, and of Ethel bracing her feet against the oven while Mama bobbed her hair. The very last time she'd seen them ...

She'd been a map, the man studying her. His face glistened with sweat; from some fiery place the idea rose of spitting and raking her fingernails over it. But hatred curled up, shrivelling into pity. Barely aware of herself or of Jewel on her hip, she'd lifted a wrist to his cheek. Its heat a jolt, his eyes liquid as he'd clutched the shirt like a child clutching a toy. Harry could turn the place upside down searching, but the expression in those eyes would wipe away any guilt.

Before she could move away he'd touched her hand, the warmth of those fingers a shock. Jewel straining against her, she steadied herself; and yet something inside had teetered and slipped — almost like when she'd seen Harry for the first time, Harry at that kitchen party, juggling his accordion and a quart of beer.

AS JEWEL EASES INTO traffic, stopping then jerking ahead, she feels herself merge too, with Rebecca's Tabu-scented warmth, and Jewel's, except he smells of tobacco. She fancies herself the squishy filling in a sandwich. Except the thought of food turns her stomach, so instead, and for now, she's an uprooted plant in a weedy garden, held up by others' bracts and blooms ... Whether tuna or daisy, isn't she the soft, nurturing thing between them? Something Lucy never planned on, and even after years, she can never quite figure Rebecca out.

"Come on, Ma," she keeps nagging. "You're not going home till we've at least fed you." Is it pride, a daughter-in-law's refusal to give up? Even jammed in like this, so close, she takes it upon herself to fix Lucy's collar; the nerve, those nails like talons. Her breath is sour, too — sour as the hospital's smell. Or maybe it's hunger, since neither of them has likely eaten much either.

THE MAN'S FINGERS HAD curled around hers. Under Jewel's squirming weight her heart beat faster. Suddenly she'd felt exhausted — each day since that snowy birth a stone, the months a rocky, shifting beach. Longing only for softness, she'd wanted to sleep — there, on her feet, so much weight buoyed by the man's desperate grip, a lifeline. Moving closer, he'd opened his mouth as if to speak.

Shell shock. It was easier to abide than the truth.

Jewel had flailed his little fist, and the man stepped back to let her inside. In the dimness pigeons flapped; the smell of droppings was like shoe polish. His eyes on her ankles, the hem of her skirt. There was a scar on his jaw, visible through stubble the colour of cattails. Against one wall had been a nest of spruce boughs. That scent of Christmas trees. She'd imagined lying down, the fossil print of needles on her cheek.

Thoughts had brushed like wings. A married woman. One thing to be charitable, another to be utterly, unforgivably stunned!

He'd hung the shirt on a nail above Harry's boots, beside Harry's ripped trousers. Her handiwork a kind of shrine, as if Harry himself had been spirited off. Then, faster than the fellow could lift his hand stifling a cough, she'd beat it out of there.

What in God's acre had got into her?

The next morning snow sugared the ground. Harry'd woken her up, fumbling at her nightie. His breath was thick, her mind murky with dreams: there was a cistern, a pail without a rope. Harry interrupted just as she was trying to dip it, and even as he'd worked the flannelette over her hips she'd heard a mackerel splashing: the sign that the water was drinkable. It was a long way to the dresser and her Dutch cap, longer still to the kitchen chair where she'd hoist up one foot and try to get the thing inside. *What're you doing? Cooking a turkey?* His breathing, that groping silence as she'd stumbled back to bed, Jewel chirping by now and shaking the crib.

At this rate, she'd never have another kid, Harry'd groused, then told her not to wait up; there was a do that night at Babineau's.

That afternoon she packed half an apple cake, would've taken tea if she'd had something to put it in. Bundling Jewel up like a mummy, by the time she set out the sun was low. The barn door was open, and as she approached, the man leaned out, almost smiling. His eyes went to the parcel, his expression shifting like clouds. Reaching down, he touched Jewel's head, and Jewel grimaced; then he held his finger to the baby's lips.

HUNGER. IN A SHIMMER of memory as green as leaves, Lucy thinks of herself feeding people, offering pie after meat and potatoes, the carrot after the stick. Somewhere in the watery past she'd pushed cake at a lot of them, too, usually apologizing, *It's not much*, or, *Gee, it seemed fine out of the oven*. Even when tough and doughy was more than some deserved. Well, that'd be one good thing about passing away, she thinks: no more cakes, or chewing either. But then she remembers Harry, and Rebecca's warm weight leaning into her. Oh, mercy, please, not an invitation for supper! At the best of times, Rebecca's meat loaves and jellied salads make Benny the traveller's menu appealing: tinned beans and spaghetti, if what Jewel says is true. Though maybe now he's got that woman aboard, his diet will improve. *The meals've never been better*, had always been Harry's way, at least, of saying *I love you*.

Rebecca babbles about something you can make from a box. In a jiffy, she adds. Pizza, with spices and everything, including something that tastes like licorice. "That's a kind of pie, isn't it. From a mix?" Lucy tries to sound interested without being too encouraging.

Jewel quickly proposes that they go out; "We'll grab something, how's that?" He means well, her boy; the way he's jumped in makes her want to pat his cheek. Yet it drags on her spirits, what's left of them. Why can't he and Rebecca see that the last thing on her mind is food, and that she'd rather just hole up on her own? But the evening stretches before her like a levelled street.

THE MAN HAD BLINKED at her offering wrapped in paper, shaking his head. Maybe he was dumb, it had occurred to her, dumb as dirt. Jewel had gnawed at his mittened fist, jabbering *Mum-mum-mum, da-da-da*. For an instant the man had opened his mouth as if to speak, opened it wide enough that she'd spied a gold filling. His eyes never wavered, their gratitude burning through her. When he'd touched her arm, it was gentle but sure, as if they knew one another. Under his coat was the blue of Harry's shirt; the hollow at the base of the man's throat made her look away. But into the gloom she'd stepped, through a plank of sunlight; her eyes adjusting as he peeled away waxed paper. Wordlessly he broke off some cake and fed it to Jewel, who smacked and sucked at it. Please don't let him choke, she'd thought, as the man held out a piece to her. Where had his hands been? What did it matter? Slipping over to the layer of boughs, he'd crouched, smoothing a place. Making a cradle of his arms, rocking it, he patted the clothes bunched there, and like a bird-dog she followed, setting Jewel down. Sticky crumbs ringing his little mouth, he'd tried to eat spruce needles. The cold stung her nostrils as she settled herself there, and he offered more cake. She'd felt the warmth of his arm as his sleeve brushed hers. When she shook her head, he ate it himself.

His mouth tasted of cinnamon when he kissed her, his beard grazing her cheek. Jerking backwards, she'd felt her face burn. Jewel crawled onto the dirt floor, his face shiny with bits of needle. Springing away, she'd scooped him up, the baby flailing.

"Is there anything special you'd like?" she'd muttered into the baby's hat.

His cough rattling in his chest, the man had mimed a cup, his eyes bright as he'd pretended to drink. *My name is Lucy*: enunciating it, she'd looked away. If he responded, it was drowned out by the wind rushing through chinks in the walls, and the pigeons' cooing. From the glassless window she'd watched the sun balance on top of the Big House. And she'd raised an invisible teacup, like Harry saluting the neighbours from their porch, her voice plying the stillness: "Next time, maybe."

That Sunday the priest's words were darts. *Covet not thy neighbour's wife. Love thy neighbour as thyself.* As if that weren't enough, after Mass Father Marcus pulled out a catechism. "To get you started," he'd said, "the little fella too, once he's ready." When it was Harry most in need of commandment, waltzing off and leaving her to suffer the insult of that sleeven of a woman next door showing off her wares. Lucy'd slid the catechism under a cushion, for his benefit if he'd have sat long enough to warm his scrawny arse.

"You *could* come too, *if* you wanted," he'd offered once, as enticingly as if asking her to come for a dip — in the swamp by the old barn, where someone or other was supposed to have drowned. And then, hadn't Lil appeared at their door, all dolled up — all right, so she was striking. Those almond-shaped eyes green as a cat's peering in; that loopy russet hair, never mind the dress half-undone, which up close resembled upholstery goods, or that flirty drawl: "There you are! Harry, you're keeping us waiting." Lucy had tugged on his sleeve. But his smile wasn't for her. *What's wrong with a guy having a bit of fun?*

He was very late that night, her loneliness like the tide washing the rocks, shifting and dislodging things. With the baby asleep, confronting him meant tiptoeing around the worst of it: Hadn't he said this was temporary; they'd move when they could, in the spring?

Yanking off his socks, he'd slurred, "Break ground, maybe."

Despite her hurt, despite her anger, she'd been seized by a new terror: what if they moved, and word came, not like the message from Mrs. Edgehill, but legitimate, an answer to their prayers, and they missed it? Reading her mind — even on a bellyful of rum he could do that sometimes — he'd thumped the pillow. "For the love of Christ," he'd griped, "give it up." Helena was gone, he said, and the sooner she accepted it, the better — for them all.

Then Jewel had started wailing, and he'd asked, "Can't you do something about that?" saying she could barely handle the one kid, and wouldn't have a hope with two. "What would you know about hope?" she'd said right back, burying her face in the baby's curls. And he'd pointed to Jewel on her lap: "There it is right there, missy. Girly name and all — just like Lil says: a boy loaded down with a handle like that!"

Seven

TIMES LIKE THAT SHE could've laced his stew with bluing, or served him nightshade berries right off the vine: *What do you mean, dear, a funny smell? Nothing wrong with those teeny tomatoes!* Later on, when he acted up she could've chopped up one of her houseplants for a salad — a houseplant like the one in the restaurant she finds herself in now, squeezed next to Rebecca in a gold vinyl-upholstered booth. It's a dumb cane, the spindly yellow thing showcased in the plate-glass window. *Dieffenbachia*, she pushes the word slowly through her mind, not to be confused with that spluttering politician, Diefenbaker, whom Harry still admires. Swallowed, one small bite will strike you dumb if not deaf, so the books say; a mouthful and you'll lose more than your voice forever, she seems to recall, shame creeping over her like a prickly rash. Truth be told, she might've munched on such a salad, too.

Besides that dumb cane barely clinging to life, the Armcrest has a scruffy philodendron climbing the wall around the big, smudged window. Come to think of it, philodendrons are even more troublesome, quite possibly deadly. One that size would've silenced that whole rowdy bunch in the Grounds, back in the day. She could nibble on some herself, though, for thinking it — although, as Rebecca prattles on about this and that, which heels to wear with what, and what goes best with orange and lime, maybe dumb cane salad wouldn't be a bad thing. But then, if Rebecca went mute, God forbid, the silence would be deadly.

They're the only diners in the place, tomato soup and crackers the only things on the menu with any appeal. Swinging through a door with a grimy porthole for a window, the waitress tugs a pencil from her hairnet, and Jewel and Rebecca order coffee, liver and onions, fries. The very thought of liver, of its chalky, metallic taste, makes her queasy. "Too bad Robert's not here," she volunteers all the same, as brightly as possible, as if it's up to her to spark some sense of occasion. It's not every day, after all, that she dines out.

"Gawd — the last time he came out to eat?" Jewel shakes his head and she waits for him to explain, but he doesn't. Rebecca lights a cigarette, twisting her mouth to exhale away from Lucy, thank you very much. She stubs it out in her saucer when the food arrives with a speed that's as suspect as the plants. There's something even more suspect in the soup, a short, dark, brittle hair, or perhaps it's a bit of wire.

"Oh dear," she says quietly, speculating. A piece of Brillo pad?

"Send it back," says Jewel, but suddenly she's starving, too weary to fuss, picking out the offending object with her spoon — yes, yes, it is steel wool — then slowly, mechanically making her way to the bottom of the bowl. Never mind that it has no taste; its blandness fills her, and she fancies herself Mike Mulligan with his steam shovel in that picture book Robert was obsessed with at five. Bent over their plates, Jewel and Rebecca chew quietly through their dinners, and she focuses on the sweet, greasy smell of the onions. The only sound is the squeak of cutlery against their plates, until from the kitchen a radio crackles to life, rattling out some tinny music, the waitress singing along. Pushing her plate away, half the food untouched, Rebecca asks for more coffee as Jewel wipes up every last bit of gravy with his roll, and finally, groaning, they sit back, arms folded.

She never could abide liver. Once their plates are removed, the atmosphere feels a bit more pleasant; even the gold decor takes on a certain coziness in the twilight coming through the big blank window. Suddenly appreciative, she could sit here for a good while; the Armcrest is limbo, a hopeful sort of purgatory, it occurs vaguely, all that gold vinyl a slippery, cheerful netherworld between the empty blue of home and the hospital's dismal green. The squeak of the seat underneath her, the salt and pepper shakers squared against the ashtray, the salt with its grains of rice like fingernail parings; even the plants — all of it fortifies *ordinary*, the kind of ordinary Harry loves, that she'd give anything to have back. An ordinary that, temporarily at least, holds the doctor's words at bay. Yes, she could sit, and sit. Until, her mouth no sooner empty, Rebecca starts in again.

"What else can we getcha? Come on, Ma. That wasn't enough to feed a bird! You gotta eat more than that. You'll get sick if you don't!" As if one person's nagging isn't bad enough, Jewel sits there nodding, and she pictures herself like a hydrant full of orangey soup. Hollow-eyed, he lights a cigarette for Rebecca, and one for himself. The pair of them inhaling expectantly, as if prepared to sit forever till she consents to Jell-O or soggy pie. Monkey see, monkey do, she feels like saying, gazing back. But to please them, she opens the crackers that come with the soup.

"You might try cutting down, yourself," she lets slip, not meaning to sound snarky, though they both scowl, and it's funny, how alike they can be when they least intend it. Don't try to figure them out, she scolds herself, just love them. "So. Tell me," she changes tack, hoping *this* is acceptable, because she's genuinely curious, "about Robert's little friend." *Friend?* "The little girl he's —"

"Oh." Rebecca snorts, then holds her breath, grinning at the ceiling. The rest comes out in a smoky choke, then laughter. "In lust with, you mean."

Jewel laughs too, but in his eyes she sees Harry hooked up to those wires and tubes, and the doctor's expression, and the thought of his cool, medicinal manner creeps in like a weed. It twines itself round the thought just rooted, whatever it is Rebecca's just said, even as Jewel starts explaining, "Well, the latest is ... now he's talking about living in a teepee, or some stunned thing. Can you imagine?

Je-sus Christ." It doesn't matter what he's saying, really, for his words alone are a balm. Even the cussing, under the circumstances, because surely the Lord God himself, if he's listening, given their troubles, would forgive it too.

BEFORE THE BABY'S NAP time she'd done her hair, and as brazenly as you please, before she could talk herself out of it, had thrown together root beer, a mug, biscuits and Harry's favourite cheese. Jewel was sound asleep by the time she tiptoed into the barn, where dust had sparkled in the frosty striped light, and wings beating from the rafters stirred bits of straw. Swallows? Hanging there was that row of clothes, all but the blue shirt, and Harry's plaid one balled into a pillow on the boughs, beside a little stash of paper.

She'd heard herself breathe, then a patter from the loft, scuffling. Rungs creaked; there'd been a whisk of greenish wool as the man descended, his look marbled with a fear that quickly melted. Touching his mouth, he pressed that finger to Jewel's cheek, a butterfly kiss, then drew it along her jaw, his fingertip cool. Bending closer, he'd traced her lip with his tongue.

The rest of her had turned to kelp. *Mustn't wake ... mustn't ... Rock a bye baby*: the lullaby swung and lifted through her as the man took Jewel and gently laid him on the branches. A baby in a manger, he didn't stir. *When the wind blows the cradle will fall and down will come ba —*

His kisses were grass tickling her neck. No protest as his hands had slid under her coat, a chill like raw silk brushing her skin. They'd lingered on her nipples tough from nursing, and his teeth had grazed hers, that metallic taste ... his hands cupping her. He'd pressed his face to her coat, parting it, tugging her blouse free; run his tongue along the valley of her ribs.

Overhead, feathers rustled, and on his spruce bed the sleeping baby made sucking noises as the man worked at her underthings. Turning liquid, her heart blubbered. He'd slid her stocking down, his mouth tasting like bark — the way she imagined sap tasting: bitter, with the hope of sweetness. Her hat had snagged on something. Her heel was in his palm, the air cooling her sole; her leg like a cup handle. Gently, silent as a fog bank moving up the Arm, he'd pushed inside. That strange, sharp jolt of delight, a peculiar heat. The shudder of life as dust danced in her head, before the dimness had sifted back, and shrouded her. The two of them, perfect strangers, stumbling apart.

Her foot had hit cold earth. His eyes had been calm and blue as the water above a shipwreck. "Tell me your name," her voice so proper, properly desperate. Expressionless, silent, he'd held her, his arms like fallen branches.

NIBBLING A SALTINE, SHE puts the rest of it back. "Robert's going camping, then." As bland as the cracker, her remark dangles, neither Jewel nor Rebecca rising for it. "He'll want to be going soon, then," she prompts, "won't he?"

"I don't think the weather matters, somehow." Exhaling, Rebecca rubs her eyelid, then painstakingly wipes the greenish smudge of shadow from her finger onto a serviette. She can be so fastidious — about some things.

"Next he'll be joining buddy on his houseboat — taking a cruise." Jewel grunts, patting his stomach. If it's supposed to be a joke, no one laughs.

"No room," Rebecca says after a while, leaning forward to poke him.

"Serves you right, I guess," she tries to add her two cents' worth, "raising him right next to the cove." What price, humour? It's all she has by way of applying brakes, of forestalling things, sticking a finger in a dyke and enjoying the dryness while it lasts. But the joke falls flat, and Rebecca sniffs, and before any of them can think how to salvage it, the waitress sidles up with their bill. Tearing it off, she anchors it with three stale-looking candies: humbugs. She seems in a rush, though it can't be late, and they're still the only customers.

But Jewel stretches back as if just getting comfy. He always was that way, obtuse; wear your blue socks, she'd say, and he'd want brown ones. They can see themselves in the plate glass now, their reflections against the deepening dark. "Last time it was chicken bones, wasn't it, hon?" he says as if they have all night, and she realizes, just as obtusely, that in a way perhaps they do. "Better than a kick in the arse, I guess," he sighs when Rebecca doesn't answer. Whatever that's supposed to mean. They could murmur and shrug like this forever, avoiding what needs to be discussed. The thing that presses in on her urgently now, a murky, soundless wave, all its smothering force merely put off by liver and onions. The restaurant feels cheap now and worn, the wood-grain and vinyl smudged and sticky and cracked in places. Rising as quickly as possible, Lucy snatches up the bill — she's the mother, after all, only right that she treats them, and it wasn't a bad thing, coming here — but opening her purse she finds only change.

"Here, Ma. Don't worry about it."

Such a funny thing to say in the wake of everything; she could as easily laugh as cry waiting with Rebecca as he pays then trudges back to slide some coins under his saucer. The waitress waits before she wipes the table, pocketing her tip along with the humbugs. Soon, too soon, Lucy thinks, there'll be just the dark house and the chilly spacious bed, its lopsided sag in Harry's place. Almost better to stay and help the waitress wipe and tidy; how foolish is that?

Outside, in the crisp darkness, the smell of onions fills the car's interior, and Jewel fumbles with a toothpick, holding it like a little spear, the heel of his other hand braced against the wheel. "So, Ma," he finally puts the question so carefully avoided till now: "What're we gonna do?"

The breath she draws is as slow and deliberate and deliberately vacant as his or Rebecca's when they're dragging on tobacco. "Do, dear?" And he responds just as impatiently as she does to their stinky habit, as if the whole world knows better. "For Pete's sake, Ma. About Dad?" As if they can *do* anything, as if it's up to them, doctors included. "The respirator, the drip — ?" he prods, as though she's stupid. His voice a tired whisper as if he's small again, rubbing his fists in his eyes, resisting bedtime. A strange, sweltering feeling weaves through her, a wooziness so off-putting she wishes she could put her head down; if she's patient, it'll probably pass. "Well, my darling," she sighs, the heat twitching and jumping above her left eye. "You know what they say: It's up to the good Lord, I suppose."

AFTERWARDS, SHE AND THE man had huddled together, God have mercy on her weak, slovenly soul! Instead of running, fleeing, after grabbing at life — admitting her own craven, singing need; not only that, but letting it push inside her — what had she done but eaten biscuits? He'd opened the root beer on a nail; glug glug glug, it went down his gullet. Then he'd picked and eaten the crumbs off his coat.

As Jewel woke and started fussing, the man had mimicked her shush, making a sound like the sea inside a shell. But by then she was glad of the barn's dinginess, pleasure having fanned itself into shame, a hot, thick feeling moving up her throat and filling her ears. The baby wiggled upright, chewing his mitt and whimpering. The man's eyes had filled with a cool, bitter longing, and before Jewel could work up to a proper howl, she'd bundled and slipped away with him, lingering just long enough to straighten his little hat. Turning once, she'd forced a grin — one she hoped was brave, or at least dogged — and she'd wondered, would a woman like Lil have been that brazen? In the dimness the man's eyes were opals; his face was drawn. As she ducked into the light, he raised the mug she'd brought, and might've begun to speak.

The rocks and trees jumped into sharp relief — even the pine needles on the path — as if freshly minted, unseen before. Harry was home early, pacing, wondering what a man had to do to get fed. Then he'd grabbed his coat, shouting that he wasn't hungry anyway. Heating water, she'd filled the washtub and climbed in, Jewel gumming the edge and grabbing the cup for rinsing, christening her and the floor.

After that day, she'd returned to the barn once more, stopping first at Ida Trott's, dropping the baby into her arms. She'd seen her going to church, Ida said, blinking as he struggled. Ignoring his shrieks, Lucy blew kisses, all the way uphill past the rusty anchor, Ida's look twisting through her. Whatever it was inside her like an engine, cranked.

The clothes were gone, the only sign he'd been there a sprinkling of spruce needles. The air smelled of dust and flies. Pulling off her gloves, she'd clapped her hands together, watching her breath. As if she'd dreamed the man — and their behaviour, as Father Marcus might call it, his homily yawning through her: *True life is avoiding sin.* All its pulses and beats, sin like garden seed, endless varieties waiting to sprout: she'd been the ground in spring, the man a rake and hoe. As the emptiness spread around her, she'd thought of Harry's good eye: how he turned the bad one to the pillow when he moved on top of — the last time, when?

The man's gaze, his mouth on hers ... what the body remembered, the soul forgot? As she groped the walls for his ghost, slivers pushed into her palms till they resembled a gardener's tearing up roses, tracked with thorns. Stumbling downhill, she ignored Ida's offer of tea. The bottle she'd left was almost empty, syrupy milk rolling in the bottom like an eye. Sit, Ida'd coaxed, bundling Jewel into her arms — glad to, clearly. Clutching him, Lucy'd pushed money at her, and Ida'd pushed it back, those eyes squinting through her lens-less spectacles. Then she reached for Lucy's hand, asking if there was something she'd like to know. Stroking her palm, those scratchy fingers pushing the slivers deeper; saying she didn't want nothing for it, if that was a worry. "Ah, let's see," she said, "Babies: them two tiny creases in the side of your hand?" She told Lucy she had a heart line like a skipping rope, and a good strong lifeline, asking if she'd been chopping wood, then out of the blue: "That fella of yours an' Artie are chummy, I hear?" Lucy'd pulled away, Ida swatting at something, saying she'd never tell anybody nothing bad, *but* if she wanted to know about that fella ...

That night when Harry asked what she'd done to her hands, she answered with a shrug, the dishwater a salve.

WHEN THEY DROP HER off, there's a whisk of coolness and crunching gravel, then just the tail lights like cigarette ends as the car pulls away. Woven into the twilight and the curtain lace is Lucy's silent, sketchy prayer. *God willing. On earth as it is in heaven*, a tiny voice seems to mimic from the empty rooms and hallway, a voice from the past chased by a country tune. Some blonde bombshell's twang: "Heaven's Just a Sin Away," that song Harry's been dying to learn to play. But as she takes off her sweater, the voices and music explode, the emptiness of the house closing swiftly around her. She thinks not just of Harry, but suddenly, jarringly, of Helena. And in the thickness of memory, caught off guard as she is, once more the sky rains soot and the boiling, greasy sleet of splintered steel.

WHEN HER MONTHLY WAS five days late, she went to confession, set to barter. The empty pews hummed a silence deeper than any secret inside her, candlelight guttering as her innards crawled; she ought to have studied the catechism, its recipe for making a *good confession* (was there a bad one?). But the click of rosary beads had pressed her forward into the casket-like cubicle. The small, screened square had filled with light and Father Marcus's shadow. *How long since your last confession?* There'd been the smell of shaving soap, the priest's weary coaxing: "Through Penance, my child, all sins are forgiven."

All sins? Venial? *Mortal?* It was as if the man, the prisoner, were breathing beside her, his fingers on her skin. "God forgives the contrite," Father Marcus prompted, asking if she'd been impure, entertained unclean thoughts?

"I lied," she'd fibbed. "To my husband, Father." How many times? he wanted to know. *Times?*

A rustle then — had someone been listening? "Once," she said. "I lied to him *once*." Never mind the falsehood; she'd longed to beg an excuse, the excuse of life dug from despair. Also, she'd have liked to ask about someone's drinking and repeated "lying." But the priest's forgiveness was without zeal, her penance five Hail Marys, and the advice to honour her husband with heart *and* mind.

The Virgin's statue had smiled down as Lucy worried the prayer, its words tumbling inside her, and that familiar numbness returned as if she'd been knocked on the head. *Mater dolorosa*, Mother Mary full of grief. A voice like Ethel's seemed to chant: *Mother May I? Queenie Queenie ...* But compared to the Virgin's sorrows, what were hers? Smooth as oil, the mildness of that sculpted expression slid through her; and at bedtime that night she'd started to bleed.

IN THE KITCHEN, THE red of an oven mitt jumps from the table, out of its usual spot and as jarring as tail lights blinking down the street. What other things, she wonders, has she dropped — misplaced? — in the darkness of these past couple of days? Restless, needing the sound of a voice, a real one, she turns the knob on Harry's little radio there on the counter, dust — or flour? — caked into its grill. The radio clicks on, its tiny red light like a bunny's eye, but all that comes out is static, as though it can't quite work without Harry around, either. Still, though, the little light's a comfort, red as a Christmas ornament. Which makes her think of Jewel, and Harry too, back when Harry was still pretty green, and so was she, too green to know it! But like the remnant of a good dream, the image that floats up is airy as sheets billowing on a line: Jewel in his father's arms, his tiny hand closing around something from the tree, something pretty and bright as a cardinal.

PRACTICE MAKES PERFECT, HARRY had sniped, salvaging wood from Babineau's toppled outhouse. The plan was he'd figure out how to build a shed first, before going all out and buying land. A voice like her father's had filled her: *You wouldn't know a plumb line if it snuck up and bit your arse*. But Harry stood firm, the rum talking no doubt, as if riveting plates to hulls was the same as building a house. Then Lil had rattled the screen, her lacquered face looming; she was wearing what appeared to be a dressing gown. He'd forgotten the seat.

Later, outside in the frosty gloom, his voice was gleeful: "I'm not building another shitter, dolly." The air had smelled of snow, and a foghorn's moan was as needling as flying metal. Taking her back to that hillside, straight back to the feel of greasy, spiked grass, the sound shook then dangled her, suspended. As though, if she'd held her breath, listened carefully enough, it might've disclosed something. But then the baby gurgled, and tickling his chin, she'd chanted: *There was a crooked woman in a crooked little house ...* As if Lil had been a two-bit traveller at the door selling rags.

Quickly the shack took shape, an eyesore rising out of the grey woods: Harry's little haven, while hers became the gleaming womb of St. Columba's in the hush of Advent. Who knows what he got up to out there, but on Christmas Eve, surprisingly sober, Harry brought in a pinwheel he'd whittled then painted red, and a scrawny spruce for a tree, which she decorated with bows made from an old red shirt. The pinwheel looked like a bird sitting in the branches. *O Tannenbaum.* She'd wished with all her heart there'd been two.

"I'll huff and I'll puff and I'll blow your house down!" Holding Jewel she'd tried to make the pinwheel spin, but it wouldn't, not till Harry greased it with butter. And then he'd said, "Sometimes I dream, you know." Of what, she'd wanted to know, thinking, oh Lord, Lil Marryatt? But then he'd rambled, "Like what happened to us never happened at all," and he swore to God that sometimes he could hear *her* laughing, and those games Lucy would play with her: London Bridge, Sally Saucer. His good eye, clear and blue, had gazed out at the island, the prison under the soggy snow, and lacing his tea with cheer from next door, he said how he'd always had this idea how she'd look grown up: "a princess, maybe. Beautiful, like — like someone, anyways."

THAT WINTER, ICE BRIDGED the channel, clotting the Arm till it looked like a floating mackerel sky. Once she saw men playing hockey in their boots, which only socked in her loneliness. There was always Ida; she could've visited her, but something held her back; and slowly, eventually, the days lengthened and the ice melted, stranding seals on the rocks. One March evening Harry came home early. He was like a little kid; there was land for sale up behind the Big House. Room for a garden and everything, Artie'd said, the owner a buddy of his gone off to the States.

Her skin prickled as if she'd rolled in sand. Then he'd started in, wanting to know what he'd done, calling her the Queen of Sheba, saying if she'd wanted an estate she should've picked another fella. But at dawn he dragged her out of bed to see it.

The land was across from where she'd spied those little boys playing in a puddle, fighting over candy. A skewed rectangle hemmed by picket fences, the plot was mostly rock dotted with spruce, the houses on either side small but almost tidy. Curtains twitched: someone watching? "So, dolly?" he'd said.

Building a shed was one thing, a house quite another. And she couldn't help thinking, too, of Artie and Lil, and Ida, of course, through the woods and down the hill, eyes in the back of her head. "What about something in town," she'd answered, where he could take a tram to work? But Artie'd told him he could get it for a song.

"Can't go wrong buying land," he said, making eyes at Jewel. As if it were a done deal, the cabin with its mould and the crib crammed by the bed a piece of rotting history. Swaying her with the promise of space for flowers. Rounding up the last of their relief money, he never did tell her the price, and she didn't ask, though there was no doubt his poker playing helped. Soon as the ground thawed, he promised; by the fall they'd be in it.

Artie and some cousins of his helped dig the hole for the basement. Harry's muscles bulged from moving rock, and suddenly Lil Marryatt seemed to have fallen off the planet. He'd crawl home after dark, happy despite complaining that it was work for jailbirds; lowering himself next to her he'd soon be asleep. Listening to his snore, in the shadows thrown by the prison lights, some nights she felt high and dry as something washed up, lying there wanting him.

But at least the long, bright evenings allowed her to watch the progress. Clamouring to walk, Jewel would push her away when she tried lifting him. "Never seen such a kid," said one of the cousins. "Mine would rather hang off his ma's tit."

"Can't blame the blighter for that," Artie grunted as he drove the pick, his shirt riding up to show his crack. Harry gave her a look, mopping sweat with a rag the same colour as that shirt he'd never missed. "Never seen so much goddamn rock in all my life," Artie ranted. "Me, I'd leave a crawlspace." So it was her fault they had to dig to frigging China! Laughing, Harry gave him a shove and called him a lazy bastard who didn't like work.

That night Harry'd made love to her like a skinny machine, all muscle and bone. Afterwards they whispered in the dark, as she mulled over a picture in her mind as simple as a child's drawing: a house with two walls and a roof and a pigtail of smoke curling from the chimney. It was too much to imagine rooms and being inside looking out, until Harry'd prodded, asking what she wanted. Then the list had gone on: a letter slot, an upstairs with a landing, closets. "Mid-October," he promised, "November at the latest, Christmas for sure."

All summer he worked long past dusk, framing. The day they put up most of the roof she almost cried watching him drive nails up there in the muggy heat. With brawn he'd gained grace, scaling the catwalk over the stairs like a one-eyed tom. Wary of his vision, never mind his balancing act, she'd close her eyes, hold her breath. But he was an acrobat swinging a hammer, nails between his teeth; it could've been her dad in his carpenter's apron, the thought setting off the whirling, dusty sting of loss.

"Frigging cock of the walk up there," Artie would sneer, swigging beer. If the place came together square, he'd eat grass; they all would. Harry'd yell down at him to shake a leg, saying he and his cousins weren't much use half cut. Gophers, he called them behind their backs, and she wondered why they let him boss them. "They owe me," was all he would say. God forbid he was paying them by the hour! "Who's up there hammering," he'd turn on her, "me or you?" Still, bringing water to quench his thirst, she'd be stopped by the sight of him bent over a sawhorse, his shirt off, his chest slick with sweat, that scar like a streak from a leaky pen. As she and Jewel made shaky towers out of scraps, all she wanted was to have Harry lay down his tools. She missed him, was the truth of it, and who'd blame her after so many nights watching the stars by her lonesome?

TRY AS SHE MIGHT, she can't seem to tune the radio to anything solid; voices and songs drift in and out, the static like someone feverishly crumpling paper. At first, putting up with it is better than going to bed. She can't face the upstairs, not yet, the quiet worse up there, gathering the way heat does at the top of the house, lingering and close even from the landing. Like heat, better to brave it gradually, and the front room's a sojourn from the kitchen anyway, a resting spot like a rock in a river. But Harry's absence soon weaves through the soothing darkness bathing her. There's the photo, faded and curling inside its frame, taken when the house was built. The darkness obscures their faces, hers and Harry's, but who needs to see to remember? The image of that day is fixed in her imagination: she's chewing her lip, trying not to look too proud; Harry's curls are plastered in a little wave atop his broad forehead, and he's looking down. The picture cuts off his hands and most of his body, but she has no trouble filling them in; his fingers wrapped around the beer bottle, the baby clinging to the knees of his trousers, which is why his braces look taut.

Harry. As she holds the photo close to her face, its coolness touches her lip: the coolness of skin, almost. It's easy to imagine him peering back, his gaze a little off-centre, almost but not quite avoiding hers. An idea bubbles up: if she were younger, if the hospital would permit it, she'd pack a suitcase and camp out there. Not only that, and the idea grows practically into a plan, something they'd pull off on TV: she'd lock the door and untie that useless strip of gauze around his jaw, yes, she would, and she'd breathe. Straight into his mouth, like those St. John Ambulance people with their stretchers and first aid. Oxygen pure as the Holy Ghost himself, straight into Harry's lungs until, rejuvenated — reborn? — he'd open his eyes and look at her, maybe just a little startled. Even better, he'd speak, her poor crippled Rip Van Winkle: *Lucy? Where the hell are we? Where've I been?*

But that wouldn't be the half of it. *Shhh*, she'd whisper. *Get dressed.* Because, like Lazarus, he'd be up and walking around in his johnny shirt. But on second thought, maybe they wouldn't worry about clothes, and he'd just stroll right out of that room and down the hall in his bare feet, his skinny white legs and bum showing. And to complete this pearly scene, Jewel would be waiting outside, chewing bubblegum in the getaway car — Harry's favourite jalopy, that 1940s Dodge, or had it been from the '30s? — and he'd have Rebecca and Robert with him, and the engine running. They'd slide in back, Harry in the middle, she and the boy hemming him in so there'd be no more fears of losing him.

THE NIGHT THE ROOF got done, as the light waned she'd put Jewel to bed, then gone outside to cool off. The August sun was a rosy ball sinking over the water, the clouds pink mountains reflected on the Arm. Just as she'd settled back, a fireplug of a figure bundled in rags had come hobbling over the mud. Part of her had wanted to slink inside, but she'd stayed put. Stopping on the shore right below the cabin, layer by layer, Ida had peeled her clothes off. Not much Lucy could do by then but watch, feeling more than a little dismayed, guilty. The sad flash of drawers, skin, as the crone draped her glad rags over the rocks. If Harry'd been there, he'd have choked, laughing. Struck there against the blackening water, Ida'd gazed up once, her hair wild in the blazing prison lights — but if she noticed Lucy, neither let on. Toeing the water, she'd flinched, then ploughed in. A heavy splash broke the lapping waves as she vanished then bobbed up, that tugboat body of hers slowly straining ashore; and Lucy'd thought of a pilot whale she'd seen as a child, walking the piers with

Dad. Hanging from a gaff, the creature had been gutted, its blubber curling outwards.

A hazy moon dusted everything white as she slipped inside, careful not to get Ida's attention, or to wake Jewel as she bolted the door and crawled to bed. The old woman's footprints would've washed away by the time Harry shuffled in just shy of dawn, smelling of beer and a sweaty kind of triumph. "Wake up, girl!" he was hollering. "She's done, dolly! Wha'd I tell you?" Done like dinner, she'd murmured back, dazed, as if dreaming everything.

Eight

WHEN SHE FINALLY DRAGS herself upstairs, sleep soon rescues her; was it something in that tomato soup? Drifting off she thinks of housework, Brillo pads and a vague image of Harry scouring something with steel wool; the thought shimmying like a bubble, of Harry at his work bench ... But her sleep is alive with sounds: hammering, scrubbing, voices, all echoing as if from a basement. *Lucy Locket lost her pocket, Kitty Fisher found it. Nothing in it, nothing in it, but the binding round it.* It's her father talking; Harry is nowhere, and she's five again, rolling marbles down Roome Street — doughboys and sea-green pretties — then trundling off to work with Dad. Inspecting studs and shingles, his shadow scales planks, passing through walls and windows. The jawbreaker she's sucking on tastes of his pocket ... It's a dream she's dreamed before, one that used to haunt her when the house was being built.

THAT TASTE, LICORICE, HAD filled her mouth one morning when she'd woken to find Jewel aiming a ball at her head and Harry whipping off the quilt. Artie had a line on some free lumber, and Harry needed a hand moving it. "Why can't he help you?" she'd moaned, sleep pulling her back ... and once again she'd been on Roome Street, a tiny, slippery version of herself, twirling around this time on the piano stool, her braids flying, and Mama yelling, "Stop!" But not before it'd tipped over, its fussy claw-like feet clutching marbles, useless. *Ashes ashes, we all fall* —! Her laughter the same as water splashing tin as she picked herself up and struck middle C. But then, in the dream, Mama'd slapped her, slapped her hard, and Lucy's face wasn't hers anymore, but Helena's.

"Lumber's not cheap, you know," Harry'd rasped, shaking her. "Artie's doing me a favour." The light blazing in had made her shiver, a feeling as though something — a rat? — had touched her with its tail. Then Harry'd tried to butter her up with compliments from Artie, of all people, saying how lucky he was having someone so strong to lug that kid around everywhere, and not hard to look at, either.

His flattery went nowhere. Scrounging was scrounging, like picking bones, she said. But still she'd found herself outside the Big House, half the Babineau clan already there scavenging, trampling the lilies. As she went to scoop Jewel up, he'd beelined to the barn; Harry caught up to him first, but not before Jewel had darted inside.

THE BLUE OF THE streetlight wakes her briefly, leaking in through the blind — slats of light, and its chilly silence. Like inside the barn that day, despite the sun baking down, warm, warm as blankets ...

The barn where people went to spoon, or watch the underboat races, as Artie said. Harry's eyes had a funny look as Jewel wriggled and kicked, caught in his arms. He'd just set him down when the boy started for the ladder. "Coming?" he'd yelled down to her, almost banging Jewel's head as he hoisted him through the hatch. She'd balked, mumbling about trespassing. A patter overhead as Jewel scooted from the hole, then Harry'd beckoned, "You gotta see this, dolly!" Teasing, "Joolly-Jool — don't tell me your ma's a candy-arse."

Maybe it was how Alice had felt passing through the rabbit hole. The loft was sweltering, the air soupy as she emerged. Sunlight striped the rafters. Bouncing on Harry's shoulders, Jewel had gripped his ears, squealing. "He'll get heat stroke!" she'd protested, feeling faint. But Harry was busily inspecting a wall: petals of pine cone nailed in place to form names, dates. A tingling had started in her neck. Squirming, Jewel had let out a yell as Harry ran his finger over a rusty nail. "Wouldja look at the work," he'd marvelled, wincing as Jewel yanked on his sideburn. There were dozens of names: couples. Boutiliers, Babineaus, Babineaus and the odd Marryatt, dates going back years and years. Like the *Book of Genesis* without the begats, Harry'd smirked. A throb in her ears, she'd read till the names themselves pulsed. Then a pair had caught her eye: Franz Heinemann & Luzia, 1918.

The heat and the birds' cooing made it hard to breathe. As everything swirled, she'd reached for Harry. *Forgive us our trespasses.* But already he'd made for the hatch with Jewel, and was helping her down, taking her hand. His face smooth and ruddy, impassive, when surely hers had been a notebook, everything written there. But at the bottom he'd kissed her cheek, anxious to get a move on before the wood was too picked over.

At the Big House, Artie and his cousin Ralphie were just climbing out of the cellar, the door propped open with a rock. "Beat me to 'er, you sons of bitches," Harry'd yelled, wasting no time lowering himself down. A throaty laugh then, and Lil had appeared, blowsy as ever, that chestnut hair a burning bush. Pressed up against the shingles, she'd groaned as Artie licked at her, like she was an all-day sucker. *Mutton dressed as lamb*, sang out a voice, an inner one, alarmingly like Mama's.

"We don't got all day," Ralphie'd yelled, and something about the floor caving in.

Lil had moaned, and Lucy's ears burned but she wouldn't look. Finally Harry'd poked his head out, holding a couple of rusty nails and a hook. A waste of time. Then he'd gone pale, Lil snickering and batting her eyelashes: "Well *hullo*, Harry." He'd coughed, eyeing the ground then swooping Jewel up and seizing Lucy's arm. Out of earshot, she couldn't help saying it was a funny way to act in front of her husband. Then, reddening, he'd looked at her as if she were stupid, saying he doubted Lil was the marrying kind. *Doted*, was how he said it, adding — with a tinge of bitterness? — how she wouldn't tie the knot with anyone unless she was desperate.

DESPERATE IS HOW SHE feels once the light's too bright to ignore any longer. If dread had a colour, it'd be the same as the grey behind the blind; its dullness bores through her innards. Lying there just makes it worse, and reluctantly she gets up, making the bed with a fussy care before going downstairs. No amount of sleep and not even the sweetest dreams could prepare her for what's ahead. In their own way, perhaps each of them feels just as desperate, Jewel and Rebecca, maybe even Robert, even if they haven't come out and said so; desperate for something to shake Harry awake, to bring him back to life.

She's not the only early riser. Even Robert's up, Jewel says when she phones. "Up and at 'er, and about to load the hi-fi into the car." The what? "Worth a try," he says vaguely, offering some rambling explanation, some idea Rebecca's cooked up. "Who cares?" he gets a bit defensive when she asks, a bit cagily, if the hospital will allow it.

"Can you do something for me?" he cuts her off, rudely she thinks. This is no time for rudeness; besides, when has she not? Done things, that is. It's like asking if she'll cook. There's a sigh, well, more of a wheeze, the sound of him exhaling. "Ma, can you dig out a few albums?" Albums? At first she thinks he means snapshots, which is silly, since Harry's never gone in much for sentimental stuff. If he's got anything left upstairs, in his head, all the pictures he could ever want are stored there, safe and sound, the way hers are. Then Jewel explains: Harry's records, the Islanders and whatnot, saying it would please Rebecca. They've talked Bucky into coming, too, he says, hoping they can get him to spin the disks.

So Robert's in on this, too. The thought cheers her as she rounds up Harry's favourites, just about everything put out by Don Messer and his crew, and Marg Osburne and Charlie Chamberlain. Dusting off the sleeves, she slides them carefully into a big brown grocery bag, then puts on lipstick, forcing a smile at that face staring back from the mirror. Before long, they come for her. Robert bounds up the steps to get the records; he's all for his mother's idea — till he opens the bag between them on the back seat, and sees the selection.

"It must be so dull, lying there," she murmurs, almost but not quite as an apology. In the hospital, she means, thinking of poor Harry as still and useless as a punky log.

Letting the car idle, Jewel sighs, "Oh boy," and she can tell what he's going to say: "It's not like he knows, Ma." But then, brightening: "Good on you for coming, Buck. You know it'll make your grampa happy."

Robert's scowl hurts, though she should be used to it; they all should be. It's an act, this behaviour, sure it is, put on just to irk people. Still, it's like fighting a current, seeing through it. But for some reason nobody's moving, though they've got to get the show on the road, as they say. It's as if something refuses to budge, the atmosphere in the car as heavy as the dripping leaves overhead. "I said I'd come. But you said I'd pick the music," Robert's voice is sour, surly; he could've been weaned on a dill. What did he expect, rock 'n' roll? She thinks of the word he made up once, no doubt influenced by his mother's expression, an especially rude one about poo on a stick: *That's a shitsicle, Gran.* Just as she thinks it, before anyone can stop him, doesn't the little cuss open the door and jump out?

"Wise-arse!" Jewel hollers, then, stepping on it, pulls away without him. As if things aren't bad enough. Twisting around, she sees Robert slouch off in the opposite direction. Glory! She watches till the crick in her neck forces her to look forwards, Rebecca staring straight ahead and blowing her nose. They drive the entire route without a word.

In the parking lot, there's a fuss as Jewel unloads the record player. "You sure about this, Becky?" he says, wondering what the nurses will say.

"Not like it's hurting anybody," Rebecca sniffs indignantly. Complaining that the least Robert — "the little turkey" — could've done was stuck around to help, Jewel smuggles everything past the nursing station. Whispering, he and Rebecca set things up on the floor by Harry's bed. Except for the respirator, the room's as quiet as a chapel, and Harry's face like a statue's. Lucy has the odd feeling that she's invisible. But maybe Rebecca's idea isn't so crazy, though it wouldn't do to disturb anyone. They're already bending the rules.

"Softly, now, dear," she says, "not too loud." Jewel resembles a large child, a balding teen, kneeling by the record player, holding the needle.

"Who do you think I am, Ma? Bucky?" A gurgle comes from Harry; the rattle of spit in the respirator. They've replaced the old gauze with a fresh strip, and his lips glisten, swabbed with Vaseline. "You think this is a good idea?" Jewel tries to joke, embarrassed.

"We won't know, hon, till we've tried," Rebecca snorts. You'd think they were doing something illegal. But when he finally gets the record going, fiddle leaps out, a jaunty reel echoing from the room's bareness. So much green, and so ugly: battleship green and avocado bleached to a faded mint. If dying has a colour, this would be it. She's never been a fan of this shade, or of this music either. Yet, she can almost picture herself and Harry bookending the sofa, tunes from the *Messer* show shaking the window panes, and him feverishly bowing along.

A nurse peeks in, baffled, then smiling, wiggles her fingers in a wave, and leaves.

It's good for the spirit, Lucy has to admit, softly tapping her knee in spite of herself — the Islanders never were her cup of tea. Then the music switches to a mournful solo, that baggy-eyed Mr. Chamberlain accompanying himself on 'cordine: "Oh Danny Boy." Even with her jaw clenched and the annoying tweedly-dee of the violin starting up, she thinks she'll dissolve, those piddly hospital tissues inadequate. But there's a scratchy sound, silence, and then, thank heavens, a jig, hick music like something Granny and Elly May would dance to on the *Hillbillies*, back before the bubbling crude. *In the name of the Father, and of the Son*, she feels herself murmur inside, her own pulse breaking up the deedly-deedly-deedly-dee.

Jewel, meanwhile, slouches there poring over the newspaper he's brought along. Pretending to read; she can tell by the pucker of his chin. "Remember, dear?" She nudges him, smiling suddenly through the blur, and the years are like bandages peeled back one by one, the pictures in her mind's eye almost transparent, gauzy squares of light. It feels like just a blink ago, she says, the two of them hiding out downstairs, his dad making him guess the tune.

"Yeah, and thanks a lot — you'd never rescue me," he swallows, without looking up. "Thank Christ for the 'cordine. I was never so glad as when he quit that damn fiddle."

"Your dad and his music," she murmurs, saying how she'd have rather stuck needles in her ears than venture to that cellar when they got going.

"Music?" Jewel shakes his head. As if she didn't know. "Just an excuse to get polluted!"

There's a noise almost like the radio's static, a rattling sound coming through the tube in Harry's mouth that makes her think of a vacuum hose and a nail being sucked up. Next comes a twitch under the blanket, and they all stare at the shape outlined there. A tiny, almost microscopic flutter — an involuntary movement, the nurses might say, the ones who keep insisting that having a tube like that down his throat doesn't hurt. A sign of life, or have they just imagined it? The needle bumps round and round as Jewel struggles to his knees to lift it from the record.

"Goin' to the barn dance, are we?" a voice butts in, a fellow in white who barely looks old enough to shave, but calls himself an intern. Right behind him, a nurse bustles in and pulls the curtains around the bed, the billowing wall shutting everyone out. Once more it's as if Harry isn't hers at all, but some poor beached creature whose carcass is to be further picked and poked.

Jewel clears his throat — "Sorry for the noise" — sheepishly sliding the record into its case.

"Noise?" All you can see are their shoes, the nurse's white ones with soles like thick fat, and the intern's scuffed Wallabees. There's a pause, and a popping sound: the cap coming off a thermometer? "Oh, the music. I'm sure he can hear it — somewhere in there," the young man mumbles.

Then the nurse trills, "Knock, knock, hey, Mr. Caines?" as if to say, Anybody home? "No harm in a little hootenanny. As long as you keep the door closed." After what feels like an hour, they both emerge, the intern fidgeting with his stethoscope.

Nobody mentions Harry's breathing, or his feeding tube, or anything about a decision or choices to be made, and Lucy doesn't ask. So *this* is how it is, she thinks, Harry in this bed in this room, like a scene inside a little plastic globe: if you don't give it a shake or turn it upside down, the snow won't fall. Or the poop hit the fan, as the look on Rebecca's face says, that tongue of hers as foul when bitten as it is wagging; they've all been around her long enough to know exactly what she's thinking. Cheerily, the nurse tugs back the curtains; cheerily, Lucy decides, because there's no point, really, in imagining otherwise. In this spirit she hopes for some small, encouraging murmur, but instead it's back to business. Visiting's over, the nurse says, adding, "If you wanted to leave the record player, I don't see why not ..."

But Jewel's already unplugged it, and glancing up once more like an oversized boy fiddling with a new toy, jokes uncomfortably: "Not a chance. My kid'll think he died and went to hell without it." Saying the *H* word like that to a stranger is something Rebecca would do, but that's not what gets Lucy. It's the fact that Robert's hissy-fit is water under the bridge, as if it never happened. Harry would have something to say about that, she's pretty sure. But she'd ask, why not? Maybe that's how parents should be with kids. Slow to anger and quick to forgive, love like quicksand — most of the time, proper thing.

ALL SHE'D WANTED WAS a house with a weather-tight roof and room to move without bumping into things. Harry gave her the moon: a big kitchen with wainscotting *and* a dining room, an upstairs with a landing, a basement, a carved mantelpiece and lintels, hardwood floors, plate rails and linoleum in the latest leaf-pattern — everything but an indoor loo. She'd ordered a decoration for the parlour from *The Family Herald*, a picture of a blue-eyed, blond Jesus crowned with thorns. As she hung it, Harry told her to mind the mantel; the varnish was still sticky. But she'd touched it anyway, distracted by the blueness of Christ's eyes, the colour of forgiveness, she'd thought, something you couldn't put into words, like the sun lighting a mackerel sky. The crimson of his robe matched the sofa Harry purchased from Eaton's.

She'd balked at the expense, but they couldn't furnish the place with junk, he'd said. In the corner where the plate rail dovetailed, she'd placed the little pink cup, that relic from their life before; and when the last coat of shellac was dry they threw a party. His idea, inviting half the Grounds and the shipyards, never mind her fear of a houseful of ghosts; the party rivalled the wedding one, with Artie bringing most of his relatives and their old neighbours, Edgar Boutilier the fiddler, and his wife, Birdie, and a few she'd never laid eyes on. Harry acted like he'd known everyone forever, slapping backs and handing out drinks. The gals he passed off on her: a ragtag bunch in cheap dresses and laddered stockings, who ogled everything when she gave them a tour. Her heart had swelled — *Lord, forgive me the sin of pride* — as they ran their fingers over the balustrade, and flicked lights on and off, cooing at Jewel asleep upstairs. *Ain't he some sweet?* She'd saved the front room for last, but Birdie and the others filed right past to the kitchen, even when she tried herding them through the dining room with its gleaming birch floor and rose-patterned paper. It was no use; around the kitchen table they gathered, the red one saved from the cabin — like bluebottles to manure, as Harry said; maybe they were just hungry. Ralphie Babineau had a guitar, and Boutilier dangled his fiddle while Artie knelt, sawing away with the bow between his teeth. She had to holler, offering tea; only Lil's mother, Erma, nodded.

The counter had bristled with bottles, liquor dragged in by the case. Popping a cap on his teeth, Ralphie had spit it into the pristine new sink; beer had washed the leafy floor. Then he'd dared Harry to play. "You know I'm no fiddler," Harry said, and Artie got testy: "No one says no to *my* cousint. Play us a goddamn tune!"

She'd squeezed through to cut the cake, which was lopsided — that oven had taken getting used to — then Lil's mother and a girl in a velvet skirt had traipsed after her into the front room with their plates. The girl chewed with her mouth open, then disappeared, leaving her plate on the sofa. Erma's eyes kept flitting to Christ's picture, and Lucy'd asked politely after her little granddaughter, the answer drowned out by "Turkey in the Straw" and scuffling feet — Oh Dinah, the new linoleum!

In the kitchen, things had got rowdy. "*You* play the goddamn thing, Boots," Harry'd yelled, "you brought it!" Laughter rose as somebody strummed and strummed the same chord. Then Boutilier had struck up a strathspey that pulled at her heart in spite of itself, a tune gloomy enough to make you jump in front of a train. *Enough of that slow stuff, Boots! Give us a jig!* Erma had left, and "some glass got broke," as Harry put it, and as Lucy was sweeping up, Lil had arrived with her little girl. Better late than never, somebody'd yelled. The child's eyes had followed Lucy's every move. A cute little thing, what, three years old? Never mind the hem falling out of her dress, her bird-nest hair.

Harry'd chugged beer. "Gimme an accordion and I'll play you one, buddy!"

"You can't play nothing," Ralphie'd jeered, and Harry'd jeered back, "Watch me, you friggin' squirrel!" Then Lil's girl stuck her finger in the cake and licked it, talk about a wild animal: no daughter of *hers* would've done such a thing. As Lucy wiped up another puddle, the kitchen went so quiet she could hear people swallow. Artie leaned against the range, undressing Lil with his watery eyes: "Let's hear you, then, bud: 'Sleepy Maggy!'" And Lil had heckled, "I hates that; give us 'She Put Her Knee on the Old Man.'"

Harry'd protested, but Boutilier had handed over his fiddle; then Lil laid a hand on Harry's wrist as he hesitated, waving the bow. His gaze had jumped to Lucy clutching the dishrag as Lil tumbled into a chair. His foot on one of its rungs, his head cocked, he'd thrust the bow like a knife, dragging out a reedy shriek. His face splitting in a laugh as Lil cursed and covered her ears. The little girl had grabbed a fistful of frosting then, and Ralphie'd cut himself, everyone hooting at the blood. But then Harry's gaze had sobered: "This one here's for dolly, all right?" And as he walked his hand over the strings, bobbling the bow, all she'd thought of was his lost accordion shooting skyward like that ship's anchor. Its bellows turned to dust and ivories a shrapnel of bone and teeth.

Upstairs in his room with its sloping ceiling, Jewel had started crying. Lil had slid onto Artie's lap, her moon face broad and empty; when the little girl whined that she was thirsty, her mother said, "Drink your spit." And Boutilier was telling Harry he'd cut him a deal on the fiddle, figuring he'd pick it up quick. The banister still felt tacky as Lucy hurried upstairs, slipping on the tongue-and-groove Harry'd taken such pains laying. Her temple throbbed. Jewel was standing up, moonlight pooled around the crib as he reached out. The ache spread behind her eyes as he'd bounced up and down, wailing fit to raise Methuselah, as Mama would've said.

Downstairs the music quit, and quarrelling rose up. Sliding to the floor, a splash of moonlight her only blanket, she'd curled like a fiddlehead. Jewel shrieking, rattling the bars like a monkey while she counted; wasn't that what she was supposed to do?

Sucking his fists, hiccupping, Jewel had eventually sunk to his knees, then onto his belly. From below, there'd been the squeak of the door on its new brass hinges; curled there, her cheek to the cold, polished birch, she'd felt the house empty. When all was quiet, she'd crept to the window and seen Lil and Artie kissing in the road, the little girl bashing something under a rock before the trio zigzagged into the woods.

Downstairs, lights blazing, Harry'd slumped, snoring into what was left of the cake. Someone's cigarette had blistered the lino, greasy footprints sullying its pattern; glass glittered in the sink. The front room at least was untouched, not a smudge or ring anywhere. She gave Harry a little push, but he'd snored on as she worked away at the burn, and from somewhere a long way off, the doorbell whirred stiffly.

The sight of Ida's wizened face through the pane was a shock, her rheumy eyes absorbing everything. "Don't tell me I missed it," she cracked, "or maybe you forgot me? Well, well, missy. I remembered, if you didn't." Harry's snore burbled behind them. The bundle Ida pushed into Lucy's hands smelled of hen: "A novelty, my darling, to brighten your digs." And she said how Lucy'd come up in the world, and how she never could see why anyone would run with that crowd by the jail. "Them Babineaus," she'd sucked her spit; "that Marryatt one." Blowing her nose on her sleeve, she wheedled about something being Harry's business, saying if there was anything a-tall Lucy'd like to know, she could tell her a thing or two —

Lucy'd thanked her hastily, shutting the door, Ida's brittle laugh coming through the letter slot. *Wouldn't tell you nothin' bad, dear. Nuttin' you wouldn't want to hear.* Then she'd gone and sat in the front room with the bundle on her lap, the hall light casting its gleam on the picture above the pretty mantel. *In my Father's house are many mansions.* Who else hadn't she invited? Father Marcus; now that would've made for entertainment. The business of the prisoner in the barn a downed tree across her conscience, for months now blocking her way to church.

Harry stumbled up to bed, by some fluke remembering to shut off the oil, so the fire was dead. As she scrabbled for matches, the wrapping on Ida's parcel gaped, the gift inside made of cloth a twilight shade. It was a tea cozy crudely stitched together — sweet of Ida all the same. *Like it, missy? Something you can use?* that croak seemed to rise from it. Then something opened up inside Lucy, a feeling like falling through ice. It was forget-me-not, the blue of Harry's shirt.

She'd thought of Ida watching her trek up past the Big House — water under the bridge? — the wind nipping as she slipped outside, across the yard. The burning barrel was heaped with scraps for kindling; striking a match she'd watched the flames eat through the lumpy cloth and burrow down. The sky had jumped with stars, the upstairs windows black as rinks on a snowy pond; and letting the fire consume itself, she'd made the night's last trip to the outhouse. Comforting herself: Be like Harry; worry about what you see, not what you cook up but the here and now right in front of your schnozz, as he'd say. *Put that in your pipe and smoke it, eh?*

But curiosity gnawed like hunger, and steeling herself, she'd later gone knocking. Ida, old wag that she was, delighted to see her. "I knew you'd come," she said, "sooner or later." She'd joggled Jewel on her knee while Ida boiled water. No beating around the bush, she'd drunk the tea, spun the cup, then asked what Ida knew about Lil Marryatt. Ida'd picked at something on her head. "I see a fan," she'd said, waving a stubby hand, "flirtation. A bunch of grapes on a big, long table: prosperity." Then, her gaze narrowing, she told Lucy not to be scared, but there was an eye. Jewel squirmed to the floor. "Caution, missy." Ida's voice dead calm as she spat into a bucket, saying not to fuss, because there was a harp.

"A violin?" Lucy had piped up, which seemed to irk her. "Love, harmony, missy," she'd snorted. "And a horse's head! *There*. A lover, dearie," she said, "galloping off." Blushing, Lucy had pointed at a tiny fleck: and what was that? "A mouse," she'd grinned, "thievery." And despite a feverish feeling, Lucy had pressed: one more thing, did she see a child, a girl —? "Ah, Lily's, you mean," Ida sneered dismissively. "No girl-child, missy. But there's a chair: a guest. And an ostrich; see the neck? Gossip, scandal ... and somebody goin' on a trip." Then, scowling, she'd pointed to what she said were a knife — "Are ya blind, girl?" — and a cat, saying they were the friendship Lucy'd flung in her face. Rising stiffly, she'd hawked into the cup and said if Lucy didn't mind, she had her birds to feed.

THAT NIGHT SHE TRIES watching some TV; there's a nature show that's usually quite nice, featuring exotic animals that Harry likes comparing with folks they know. *Ah, look dolly, isn't that baboon that*

Chaddock woman? Look at her, to a T, bet she's even got a blue arse like that under her stretchies! Or, *Dolly, quick, isn't that critter just like your friend, buddy with the wagon? Like a friggin' road-runner, looka that!* But she finds it hard to concentrate, and has to change channels when a gazelle gets stalked by a lion. The other station just has baseball, which is like watching cement set. But at least it makes her sleepy enough to go upstairs, and in bed she thinks of all the other creatures Harry's linked with people. Rebecca a baby orangutan these days, with that orangey hair, and quite a while ago now, poor old Father Marcus a pigmy-type boar, and Edgar Boutilier a platypus. Lord knows what she was, or had been — a kangaroo or an anteater, or maybe a bitch; at times she could've been a stingray. Then she thinks of Lil, and how on the *Hillbillies* anything with a face and fur is a varmint.

BUT IN HER DREAMS, it's all machines. Instead of animals stalking each other, there's a train: rails sticky with soot, an engine pulling from a platform as stealthily as glass being tweezed from a wound. Even the snow is smoking; everything reduced to black and white. Inside the cars are passengers, quite human. Nobody speaks as they cradle bloody stumps, weep black tears from sightless eyes. It's just like at the Front, a nurse in a uniform white as rabbit fur murmurs as a baby whimpers and a little girl cries over and over and over, *Mumma, Mumma* ... There's one man who can see, his eyes like a husky's, blue and brown. But his face has the dazed, vacant look of a soldier's. *Did you see her go up?* he keeps asking, and finally someone answers just to shut him up, a moon-faced fellow as grey as stone: *Had the sense to run, bud; you don't know what's on these fooking ships.*

As the train gathers speed, she herself is a bird growing wings, a crow hovering over. Through the falling snow she can see things floating in the Basin: doors, rooftops, pieces of ship. Half a hull lies under the thickening blanket, a carcass. Then her feathers fall away, wafting gently through white — pepper and salt — and once more she's back onboard, invisible but jerking to the cars' rhythm. In the caboose a marble rolls in a galvanized pail. *Where're we going?* a chorus of animal voices whispers. The herd has its own language, which she understands. *Frigged if I know. Hospitals are full up, bud. Sit tight* — The conductor is a wolf with no eyes. They're heading up to the Valley, he tells everybody; there's room there. She hears herself caw about the weather; *that's right*, someone agrees, *it's too goddamn early for this.* Put up or shut up, the wolf orders, saying they'll be the last ones out today, if it keeps up. Their bloody stares are lost on him. But a whistle blows: a signal from heaven?

The Ocean Limited, they've made it! the wolf cheers. *We will too!* And then its head spins, threaded like the seat of a piano stool, and when it stops they see it's got eyes after all, brown-bean ones, and a different face, the face of an old woman: Ida.

When Lucy wakes, the air in the room tastes black.

Nine

SHE'S JUST MADE TOAST when the hospital calls, the voice on the phone cool and transparent, a man's. It takes a moment to put name and voice together: Doctor Sheridan. He asks how she's doing, which makes saliva pool in her throat. Preparing her for the worst, she thinks, and then he explains how they want to try weaning Harry.

"Excuse me?"

From the respirator, the doctor says, too patiently. They want to try it little by little, he repeats, to see how Harry does on his own. "*If* he can breathe on his own," he adds quickly, and she imagines his white-coated presence behind a desk or even, absurdly, filling a phone booth with vapour like the stuff these long-haired so-called musicians have at concerts. Dry ice, Robert calls it, and wouldn't that describe Doctor Sheridan's tone?

"If he stops breathing," that chilly, distant voice winds through her, a voice like a gas, like ether perhaps? "We'll resuscitate, don't worry." Resuscitate sounds like something you'd do to a car. But the thought is slightly cheering, somehow; didn't Harry say once in the middle of *Ben Casey* that we were all just like old Fords anyway, the heart like a carburetor, whatever a carburetor was? "But I need your permission," the voice seems to echo; maybe it's the phone that's bad, bad like the radio.

"Permission?"

"To try weaning ..." he clears his throat, and she thinks not so much of Harry as a baby being offered a sugar-tit, but of him being mad and saying she was weaned on a pickle. Weaned on piss, he'd even said once in the heat of the moment. But then she thinks of Jewel taking his first steps and refusing the breast; her relief back then chased instantly by a slippery feeling of loss. "Mrs. Caines?" The doctor sounds wary.

Let Jewel do it, let him say yes, she thinks wildly. But the doctor knows best, or should, she tells herself, not convinced. Suddenly she's on a Ferris wheel again, the very feeling as when she'd accompany Robert, swinging her legs at the top and dreading the downward rush, but desperate to have it over with, too. Forcing all her worry, her fear, into a dizzy grace, slowly she says, "If it's for the best, if it's something you have to do?" As if the question will let her rest at the bottom, her stomach in her mouth, but still in one piece — even knowing the wheel will jerk upwards again, having a mind of its own.

"We'd like you to be present, then," the doctor says — no escaping — "you and your son."

SHE'S COME TO SEE the plastic snake as almost friendly, as good as a snake can be with Harry's poor lips closed around it. But the gauze holding it in place is frayed and bloody; the corners of his mouth are raw. Except for that, the rawness, she realizes that she's gotten used to this, the way one gets used to anything if one has to. Harry lying there like a landscape, constant yet still, there but not there, hills hidden by mist. She can't even think about what's locked inside him, the dips and bends of memories.

Jewel's face is stony as he grips her hand; she feels like the child as they watch, and in a dizzy way the scene becomes framed, wavy, as if there should've been a test pattern first, that Indian in a headdress that Harry's been known to stare at. She tries to imagine that they've been plunked into an episode of *Ben Casey*, only Doctor Sheridan isn't nearly as handsome. The whole picture tilts as the nurse snips through the gauze strips knotted too tightly to untie.

There's a dreadful gurgle and Lucy stops breathing as the tube slides out, slowly, slowly; could it be like a magician extracting a dove? Please, please, she wills Harry to breathe, but then comes a choking sound, like water coughing through a hose. Another nurse, the gap-toothed one, holds Harry's wrist as the doctor murmurs something, and Lucy sees that they've already unrolled fresh gauze.

And then Harry's chest flattens, his body a brook under snow; or is this an illusion too, a cruel sleight of hand? For it looks to be the moment, the fine, sharp sliver of time that, for as long as she can remember she's dreaded seeing, the passing of someone — someone else — the line dividing life from death finer and maybe fainter than the horizon between grey sky and sea. Hadn't she thought it would be like watching a blade drop from heaven, silence stretching forever on the other side?

Someone else: Harry. But she's already somersaulted ahead of herself, so intent on seeing the line that it's as if he's a specimen, a dummy for their experiments, and none of it real or serious or permanent, just a game someone's decided to play, a lark. A trick to jog him from his sleep, a slap to shock him back to life. Except that Jewel's eyes are the eyes of a little boy marooned on the rocks, hollering. His grip on her hand is so tight it hurts, and suddenly he gasps *No!* It's like having her knee tapped with a mallet, or receiving a karate chop from behind, as Robert had once demonstrated, long past his cute phase. The doctor's mouth forms the hard line she's been looking for as he shakes his head. *Not yet*, says his look, and the little nurse nods and the snake is quickly replaced. *Not yet.* And before her very eyes, hers and Jewel's, once again Harry breathes, pulled back to the safe side; of this much she's certain.

In the wake of it, she barely feels Jewel leading her to the lounge with its flowered curtains and ripped magazines; it's as if she's had her oxygen cut off, then been lassoed from the dead. "Take me home," is all she can say, relief spilling and tumbling over, leaving her all but paralyzed.

RINGING OR NOT, THE phone becomes an instrument of torture; every time she passes it she thinks of a book in Robert's room, which he'd pulled out once from under a heap of clothes. It was full of devilishly ingenious gadgets to maim, even kill people after ripping secrets out of them. "Have a look, Gran," Robert had gleefully flipped the pages to something named an Iron Maiden.

Rebecca's laxness, no doubt, allowing such trash in the house. Not that it's easy shutting out the world, and she thinks perhaps it wouldn't be so bad living aboard the Apollo, or Benny's awful little houseboat: at least there'd be no phone. Don't answer it then, is Jewel's advice, as if she'll heed it; not answering is something Robert might do. What'll it be next? *Have a cigarette, Ma, a few drinks?* For Pete's sake, next they'll be saying she ought to try that illegal tobacco!

So when it rings of course she picks it up, and as usual now (does this mean it's permanent?) her heart's in her throat. But this morning, rushing around getting ready to visit Harry, once more she's thrown off guard. "We missed you at the raffle, Mrs. —" The voice is sharp and vaguely familiar, though not familiar enough. "We thought you were gonna come and donate." Her pulse in her ear, she has to stop and think, what on earth? Except in her head it's Harry gasping, *What the bejeezus?* "Mrs. Caines? Lucy?"

Like a bird landing, recognition. But then she beats the air for an excuse; the last thing she wants is to talk, explaining that the bus is in half an hour. There's a pause, rather deadly, as she explains where she's off to.

"Oh, gosh," the woman exclaims, a notorious talker. "Are you sick? My mom — Mrs. Slauenwhite? — well she just went in for tests and, oh my —"

"It's not me, dear," she struggles to interrupt and explain; glory, it takes so much energy, energy better conserved. Mrs. Slauenwhite's daughter takes a short breath, then there's a long, forced "Ohhhhh." For Harry's never set foot in St. Columba's, never has and never would; all these years he's staunchly refused to. A matter of pride, she's always supposed, blind stubborn pride that's left her feeling at times like a bike with no back wheel. At least that's how she figures people see her, since everyone knows she's got a husband; they know she's got a son. Word jumps around here like flames from dry branch to dry branch, so it could be that Harry's fall is old hat, last week's news. His fall, she's already labelled it; it's simpler that way.

"Look, I'm that sorry, Lucy," the caller chimes in, so morosely that it's infuriating.

Now she has to backpedal; why, oh why, has there always been this need to protect Harry from someone or some thing or another, including himself? "Oh. Don't be sorry — yet," she pussyfoots. "He's not out of the woods, *but* ..."

Mrs. Slauenwhite's daughter sniffs solicitously. "We'll keep you in our prayers, luv."

Luv? She's a far cry from her poor old mother, thinks Lucy, but then, maybe not. Misery loves company, the daughter's voice tempts — already passing judgment?

But Lucy won't rise to it. "I'll remember that," she murmurs politely. "We both will."

She just makes it to the bus. Hurtling towards her, it reminds her of Robert and their trips to the fair, his grading present every June till his twelfth birthday; the memory itself mostly pink and sticky, riding home with him, his mouth full of cotton candy. The driver barely allows time to pay; she falls into the nearest seat. There's hardly anyone aboard besides a clutch of people at the back. Rude to gawk, so she fixes on the fare box, the driver's creased pant leg. But there's a smell, quite distracting, of sweat and, oh for goodness sake, pee. Its unpleasantness transports her to the hospital room, the plastic bag suspended under Harry's bed. For a dismal moment she frets that the odour might be from her — impossible to avoid the odd little leak, rushing the way she has been. But the smell wafts from the seats behind; the driver even glances back, wrinkling his nose. Well, that's it; who can resist peering around? At least she smiles. There's a teenager, he could almost be Robert in his ragged jeans, and someone in a suit. And near the back, Benny the traveller, that odd duck, slouches in a seat, pressing his face to the window. Just opposite, staring out the window is someone who could be Benny's lady friend. They don't look like much of a couple, seated an aisle apart, but then she thinks of herself and Harry. The driver gazes up at his mirror for what seems like a dangerous length of time.

"Take a pitcher," Benny's snarl drifts up, "it might last longer, bud." Before her eyes dart away, his meet them, small and beady as a turtle's in a face that leathery.

"Calm yourself, Ben," his lady friend warns; *cam*, she says, the way Harry does, and once more it's as if Lucy's been lifted then plunked prematurely in the hospital room; the reason she doesn't mind the bus is because it takes a while to get there. But then she realizes the "calm yourself" has to do with her.

"Nice day, ain't it, even when you're all stuck up!" Benny starts in, his voice uncommonly shrill. Then he begins to rant, starting off with the Yanks putting an effing man on the moon and bombing effing Vietnam, then launching into the weather, how it's gonna be "some jesus winter, 'cause the squirrels are some busy." His language would strip paint. But you've got to be prepared, he says. "Ain't that right, Driver? Huh, Missus? Out ridin' around, la-de-da," he jeers, repeating how you've got to be ready "for every event-u-al-i-ty, or *else*," then switching topics again, as if everyone there needs to know about some nice little sloop in the cove that some knucklehead got for a song and "don't give a shit about," and how he's got his eye on 'er. "Oh yeah," he rambles, sounding preachy. "Always gotta be pre-pared. But you know no man's a fuckin' island, even when he gotta live like one —"

"Okay, philosopher. Tone it down," the driver finally shouts. Pinning her eyes on the big wiper in the middle of the windshield, Lucy can hear the woman make shushing sounds.

But Benny won't be silenced. "Gotta earn a living somehow," his voice rises even higher. "Got my tools, oh yeah. Keeps a fellow goin' but you gotta eat, like death and taxes, winter's coming, thank you very much, we got that right, and —"

"Shh, Ben." The woman's voice is soft but firm, almost bossy, motherly in a funny way. Well, better late than never, thinks Lucy; the poor critter couldn't have had much mothering as a kid, and got nothing at all in the way of fathering, by some accounts.

"Shut up, man," shouts the teenager, who's kept surprisingly quiet till now. In his place surely Robert would have the sense not to yell like that, because it's the wrong thing to do.

"You buncha fuckin' hypocrites," Benny hollers back, and she supposes he means everybody. "Lookat you. Easy street, eh?"

Barely tapping the brakes, the driver swivels around again, telling him to watch his language. Lucy focuses on the handle of her purse, where some of the stitching has come away, and thinks deliberately of Harry. Goodness, why can't people just sit quietly?

Not soon enough, the bus sidles up to its main stop by a department store. "Come on, Ben," the woman coaxes, taking his arm as the doors lurch open, and Lucy steals a look at her. Where do they come from? she thinks. Not all that old, the woman might've been pretty once — well, in another life. And smaller, perhaps, she decides, the woman's bulk shifting under her puffy dress. Maybe her size helps keep Benny in line, though he doesn't get off without seizing the last word: "You bastards have a fuckin' nice day, a'right?" That word hovers in the air like a bee even after the bus pulls away. The bad smell is gone, though, but not Lucy's queasiness, a feeling now of being somehow remiss; instead of making her feel less stuck on Harry, all this ruckus has just rubbed it in.

A new raft of people squeeze aboard, so that she has to make room. Normally, she'd find entertainment in studying them; researching, one might call it. Normally, she might even play Harry's game: picturing some climbing trees or grooming each other like apes on that nature show. Though the rest of the route meanders, she doesn't even bother with the knitting stowed in her purse. Socks begun ages ago, thick ones for wearing around the house, since Harry has always hated slippers.

When she finally gets off outside the hospital, dread almost stops her. Not only that, the September sun has buttered everything with such warmth it almost feels sinful to go inside. *We all gotta do stuff we don't want to,* she imagines someone — Harry? — lecturing Robert; a lot of good it would do, too, but never mind. Up up up, she travels, the elevator and corridors a steely harshness of chrome and fluorescent light. All around her, voices blur and footsteps shuffle and click along as if marking out some diehard rhythm.

Cluttered with thank you cards and a fruit basket, the nurses' station reminds her of an abandoned ship, nobody at the helm. But in the greyish distance a crowd's gathered outside Harry's room, and her heart beats faster. A blur of white — uniforms, caps, shoes — they're like snow people, or angels maybe. She thrashes around for whatever it was Robert said that day when Harry first landed here, about somebody else's grandpa. Angels: that's exactly what Harry might think if he woke and saw them hovering like this. But then he'd ask where they'd put the trumpets! Dear God.

As the thought settles, her stomach does a loop-the-loop and the hand gripping her purse goes weak; it's as if the elevator has risen too rapidly but she's still inside and the doors haven't opened, and she could just as easily push a new button. You could just leave, something inside her advises — a voice rather like Robert's, no, Jiminy Cricket's. Some tiny critter's, anyway; maybe Greta Grub's, the worm on that *Maggie Muggins* show that Robert used to adore. But it's too late. Before she can turn away, someone waves and lopes toward her, more quickly than the little voice can repeat itself. Down the hall the elevator dings, the light above it flashing *up.* It's the young nurse again, the little one with the spit-hole, as Harry would call it; maybe she reads minds, because she's smiling. Harry and his way with words.

"What timing," she beams, saying they've been calling and calling. "Hubby's awake — opened his eyes this morning." Her voice bubbles over; it's as if they've won the Irish Sweepstakes. The corridor goes fuzzy, all that green bleaching to yellow, and it's as if Lucy herself is melting, the feeling washing from head to toe; a wetness like in the moments climbing out of a steamy bath — or after giving birth. Oh glory, an instant, tiny dribble — a joyful drop. As if wading through an ankle-deep yellow stream she finds herself at Harry's bedside.

"Harry? Sweetie?" She's never called him that before, ever; would've choked on it before, the way one would a stale humbug. And suddenly she *is* choking, swallowing tears and saliva, everything inside her tightening, then lifting and pushing open like a bud. "Lord God Almighty!"

The poor, poor fellow, he's a sight, like Rip Van Winkle all right, lying there so withered. She could stick a knitting needle down her throat for every bad thought she's ever had; she could eat a whole dumb cane. As she strokes his yellowish wrist, an eyelid flutters, half-opened, reminding her of a camera shutter that's stuck. He looks like a mushroom, that pale, after ruminating so long in the darkness, a darkness of the sort she can only guess at. Quickened by dreams? By death, more like it.

"Harry? Answer, dear, if you can hear me." It's the same as begging God for a favour, the way she used to when she was little, believing in her heart that all one had to do was ask. But lo and behold, the dullness of Harry's eye responds, a glimmer. Then one of his hands moves, a tiny, spidery movement — the hand not paralyzed — and touches hers. *Harry.* His touch is faint and chilly as a draught, and its lightness sends a phantom tingle through her, as remote as if her arm's been severed.

It's more of a shock seeing him now than it was while he slept or journeyed, whatever and wherever — the damage in plainer view and worse than she'd let herself imagine. Somehow, it strikes her sharply, underneath all her pickling and praying and feverish dread, a little of that girlish fancy had fanned itself back to life, unawares: *of course* Harry would be all right — in the fullness of all right, and not diminished. In her darkest doubts, she'd clung to that. For she'd always figured he'd been at his lowest lying there on that church cot, years ago, most everything about his life blown away like dandelion seeds in a single puff. But, tough as a weed, he'd come back. *Of course.*

And by some fluke, by some odd, unforeseen favour, here he was again, at least in part.

Don't look a gift horse in the mouth, she imagines the puppet mouthing on *Ed Sullivan* — Charlie somebody — the ventriloquist nodding along. And Harry himself teasing, *Smarten up, unless you want a slap upside the head!* Tucking that cool, limp hand beneath the flannelette, she'd give away both her arms, legs too, to hear him say that — but who'd want them? Tears prickle as something clamps down inside her. "I'm here, my darling, and I won't be leaving," she fights for some humour, plucking it from the clouds in her head, "— not till someone gives me the boot, that is." She makes herself laugh and it feels like a sun shower, tears, and using those muscles for better economy; but maybe it's true, it *is* less work to smile than frown. And how long since she's called him *my darling*? Maybe he's wondering the same thing, as the side of his mouth sags and there's a bubble of spit.

"Jewel's on his way," she says, speaking from a place above her collarbone, a place that perhaps uses fewer muscles, too. But then a new worry arises. It is as if Harry's just returned from a very long trip; who knows what, if anything, he's brought back? Speaking slowly — he may as well be foreign — she explains, "Jewel, darling — our boy."

And then, more than she could've bargained for, a miracle happens. "Looschee," she hears him say, or believes she does.

Ten

LITTLE JEWEL HAD GROWN like a weed in rainy weather, faster than either she or Harry could've predicted, and he soon outgrew his baths in the sink. But adding plumbing upstairs meant losing the spare room and running pipes up the kitchen walls. *Awful costly*, Harry'd balked at first; no accounting for this sudden belt-tightening — and over a loo? "Suppose you'll want a big fancy tub too," he griped. "God knows how we'd get it upstairs." Odd, after his fixation on other luxuries, the lilies carved into the mantelpiece, for instance. A lot of good they were when you had to dash out in a blizzard to pee.

"Give me till spring," he'd finally agreed, just to be left alone screeching out notes on his new violin. Never mind that his favourite time to practise was Jewel's bedtime. "Can't you do that downstairs?" she'd say. But he was determined to master "Turkey in the Straw" if it killed him, and he said it sounded better in the front room.

Jewel, meanwhile, was into everything, the fireplace included, his sooty hands everywhere. "Do that again, and you'll catch it!" she'd threaten, leaving it to Harry to explain, "Listen to your ma, or she'll tan your hide." Then, in his next breath it'd be, "Dolly, guess the melody" — a few mysterious bars as Jewel beelined back to the grate. "Twinkle, twinkle little star?" she'd volunteer, her answers never right. *You got wool in your ears, Luce, or what?* He'd flee to the cellar in disgust, but at least he was home. *Tan your hide. Put your head in a sling*: these were the threats that came to mind when he wasn't, or when Lil's name arose, and it often did. *Better the devil in front of your face than the one at your backside,* a voice like Dad's would whisper; and so she tolerated, and at times even sort of appreciated the fiddle.

One spring day she'd measured the spare room for fixtures, while, droning like a hornet, Jewel drove his little truck up and down the walls, and she'd thought of Mrs. Edgehill in Truro, and that child. It was like a train chugging through her, even as a greening sweetness drifted through the window, the scent of apple blossoms almost a tune of optimism. And quickly she'd thought of the claw-footed tub they'd have, the Swiss dot curtains she'd sew.

Later, on the way to the post office she and Jewel met Lil coming from town. "Hear you're getting a john," she'd sneered, the peacock feather in her hat quivering.

So the news had travelled, now that Lil was a fixture at Artie's, or so Harry'd happened to mention: like a table, she'd thought, or a broom. But he'd actually made fun of Lil's cooking: "Artie oughta take out insurance, eating them dinners."

Jewel had held up a pine cone, Lil acting like he wasn't there. "My, my, herself on a throne," she'd sniped, "proper thing for a princess." Walking on, Lucy'd tingled all over, incensed, then she'd felt deflated. Why bother? Holding out hope for anything was like awaiting word from Mama. As if she and Helena, Dad, Ethel and all the others had ventured, temporarily, to the same gauzy place — but then, she'd told herself, maybe it wasn't so far away, that place? Buoyed by the wind's fragrance, her spirits lifted faintly by the time she and Jewel stopped for the mail. But when the clerk handed over some bills, just as quickly her mood plummeted. She'd thought achingly of Helena, her hope ebbing — as if Helena were on a tiny raft and she herself on a shrinking shore. The memory of her daughter's face and her small shape almost fuzzy now, mysterious and ghostly as a scent.

Jewel gummed a key he'd found on the floor, and as she plucked it from him, the clerk produced something else: "This wouldn't be for *you*?" It was addressed to *Luzia, General Delivery, Armview Post Office.* "Some people, eh," the clerk had snorted. "Like throwing a bottle into the sea!" The mail was postmarked Delmenhorst, Germany. The clerk raised his brow — *Krauts!* — whistling "Pack Up Your Troubles" as Jewel yanked on her stocking. It was as if the whole post office were Harry's good eye.

Outside, the stink of low tide had driven away the flowery smell as she opened the envelope, her hands shaking. Penned in a heavy scrawl, the note was months old, dated *13 März 1920. Liebe Luzia,* it read. *Danke für seine Freundlichkeit, mit viele Dankbarkeit, Franz Heinemann.* The return address a *strasse.* A bill fluttered out; Jewel tried to grab it. It was an odd size and had more strange words in a language stubbornly familiar yet written in code. *Reichsbanknote, 1000 Marks. Eintausend.* Her pulse raced, and a coolness rippled up her thigh as a garter let go: holy good Dinah, saints above — the sum! Sweeping Jewel up, she'd reread the letter, her head spinning. Surely her eyes played tricks: *one thousand?*

The prisoner's breath, the memory of it, seemed to lift from the paper and settle on her skin till she felt clammy. Any thoughts of Lil and her fancy feather turned grey as a molting pigeon. *Freundlichkeit.* What did it mean, that he felt obliged to repay her? For her charity — in exchange for his giving her her life back, the small, cool treasure of self-preservation she'd curled her fist around, despite the guilt. As she fingered the banknote, her heart thumped in her ears.

At home she tucked the envelope into Father Marcus's catechism and slid it under the sofa. The letter would have to be disposed of — but, a thousand marks! Manna — enough for fifteen loos! But then a dreadful notion had crept in, one that sucked the air from her. She was no better than a Lily Marryatt, a proper sleveen: he was paying her! Filthy lucre. Lead us not into temptation, she imagined the priest leading a prayer, never mind that she hadn't been to Mass in a dog's age. But then she'd quickly shoved the thought away. One thousand marks: that would more than cover the improvements upstairs, with some left over. But how ever would she explain — that she'd won it?

Harry arrived home early with Artie in tow. They'd both been drinking, Harry too lit, perhaps, to notice the look on her face. "Where'd you put my fiddle?" was all he said. Giving Harry a shove, Artie asked if he could count on him, and he'd winked at her: "If not, bud, I'll take that as a sign you're agin me." Then the two of them had disappeared to the basement, Artie cursing a blue streak to the squawk of "Roll Out the Barrel."

That Saturday, out of the blue, two fellows in a truck dropped off a pedestal sink, tub and toilet. Harry's doing, though he still quibbled. "What if we end up with another brat? Where'll we put him, in the outhouse? That'd make a fine nursery." Or music hall, she'd felt like sniping.

Didn't he know what it summoned up, the mention of a baby? That newborn tenderness, the thought of it like a whirlpool, the ghost of a small, fading smile spinning through her, pulling her down. Coyly, she'd remarked that she didn't know he wanted another. "I don't," he'd snapped back, then resumed playing, "Lord Lovat's Lament" veering like a car off the rails.

Next she'd heard him on the phone: I'm cutting back, bud. Saying it was her doing; she didn't like him playing poker, not every night, anyhow. As if it were her, and not the fiddling that interfered with his gaming. Never mind the front room crowded with porcelain, a storeroom for bathroom fixtures all of a sudden. She'd just got Jewel into the sink when Artie appeared, the yeastiness of his breath reminding her of lilacs. "I been thinking," he told Harry, raising a beer, "maybe we could figger something out." Dwink! Jewel had lisped, pointing, and before she could stop him, Artie'd held the bottle to his mouth: Long as he don't chug it, eh? And then he'd turned business-like: "Okay, Harry. Show me what I can do you for. Cash, up front? Scratch my back, I'll scratch yours. Right, missus?" he'd boomed, asking if she was sure about losing that bedroom, before the pair of them thumped upstairs to take a gander. "I mean, what if," he said, "you find that little one youse've been missing?"

SHE TRIED MAKING A game of it — *Humpty-Dumpty sat on the wall, Humpty-Dumpty had a great fall* — teaching Jewel the motions to the words as the plaster caved and crumbled overhead, the handiwork of a team of men thundering around up there. She just had to trust that they knew what they were doing, making way for the pipes. The room looked like it'd been shelled, the pounding enough to drive a saint crazy, that and that infernal fiddling. It took five fellows to wrestle the tub upstairs. "Watch she don't go adrift!" one kept yelling. Meanwhile, Harry paced and sweated over what it would cost, while she kept mum — which ratcheted up her guilt, and made the prospect of springing her windfall on him all the more delicious, but scary. What the heck would she say? *By the way, look what I found under a rock?*

As she washed dishes beneath the groaning joists, men piling around her cracking beers, she'd spotted a chance, well, half a chance, and brushing off Harry's *What's there to eat?* slipped to the front room. The toilet was in the way, but she managed to squeeze around it. The envelope was where she'd left it, undisturbed. Waiting till she heard Harry go out back for more beer, she'd scooted upstairs. Tucking the brownish bill into her purse, she'd given Heinemann's note a final skim, its meaning still no clearer. The men's banter filtered up through holes in the floor; a riddle, laughter. *Whaddya call a lure? A hooker, get it? Ah, our lady Lily!* Artie's rasp: *You jealous little bastards!* then his laugh. *Forget Lil, you fellas — it's the gubbermint keeping me in business.* The gubbermint?

Skirting the holes, she'd stepped round the tub marooned there like a giant shell; below the window gaped the opening they'd punched for the hot and cold. Kneeling, she folded the note into a hard little square, and dropped it in. But a worry buzzed, and she went and got Harry's bow.

Below, laughter turned to groans about finishing up; in the next room Jewel woke from his nap. Poking the bow down into the cavity, she'd probed around, its hairs snagging a stud, but that was all. Harry hadn't bothered with insulation, not a scrap of newspaper or seaweed to get in the way. Then a creak came from the stairs, and her hand jerked. Slipping, the bow clattered down, disappearing. Glory, how stupid, careless! Harry would have an utter conniption, missing it; worse, what if he found it? Not only it, but ... *Gimme a hand with the sink, fella*, she'd heard. *Mind that pedestal, it cost me a fortune.* She'd reached down as far as her arm would go, but nothing.

Picturing the bow sitting on the sill plate in a hill of sawdust, Heinemann's letter for company, she imagined Edgar Boutilier hectoring, *Pizzicata*, Harry! Then boots had scuffed the landing. "That'll learn you, putting a woman in charge," Artie moaned as the others barrelled in with the sink on its little white pillar. The sight had made her think of Lot's wife, and salt. Then Artie'd winked, his saggy eyes all over her. "Bad luck, fellas, keepin' a lady waiting. Harry, you paying us by the hour, or wha'?"

A strange giddiness bubbling inside, she'd been unable to resist, "Lil keeps you hopping, I guess," aiming it at Artie.

She only meant it as a joke, but after the men left, Harry demanded to know what she had against her, anyways, and she'd pretended not to know who he meant. "You know damn well," he'd muttered fiercely.

SHE WAS DAMNED GLAD of Jewel snuggled against her, a shield, when she slid the banknote through the wicket. "What's this?" The teller had seemed flustered, going off to get advice. When he came back, he pushed a couple of five dollar bills and a few ones towards her. Baffled, she'd felt her face go red and then pale, her breath warming Jewel's curls. "There must be some mistake," she'd said. The teller pursed his lips. "Don't you read the paper? Hun money, honey." He flushed at his little rhyme. "Peanuts, ma'am, but with nutting inside."

Lacking the heart to start supper, she dawdled over the dusting, the whole house in need of it. Harry banged pot lids, baffled: "Nothing cookin'?" She was polishing the mantel when he opened his violin case. There was a silence, then he started scrabbling around, looking everywhere. "Where the hell —?" he said, accusing Jewel of getting at it. Turning things upside down, searching high and low, he'd ranted about respect, wondering how any decent woman could let a kid — "No one touches Artie's stuff!" he bellowed, and she could only grit her teeth for so long.

"All right," she'd said, standing up to him, "so what kind of woman tells her little one, 'Drink your spit?'"

He swung the violin before laying it back in its case, the thing forlorn as a calf-less cow. Laughing bitterly, he told her to get over it, that Lil was a good head, a good sport.

"I'm sure she is," she'd faced him squarely, "but what I'd *like* to know —"

Okay, okay, he'd waved his hands. "So she helps — with Artie's business, all right?" and he'd explained how she drew customers, players he meant, and kept them in line. Then, like a little kid, he asked if there was pie from the night before, saying he was near perished. And she'd snarled back, why not ask Lil for pie, or some cake? Or was Lil too caught up in business to bake?

She'd thought of their housewarming party, the daughter's fingers in the frosting. "That poor child," she sniffed.

He practically jumped down her throat: "Becky, you mean? Give it a rest, for chrissake." Latching the case, he stalked into the hall, yelling, "Wouldn't you like to know," when she asked where he was going. His voice the same as when he made a mistake: measure twice, cut once.

Wheedling about the bathroom, she heard herself say she'd whip up supper, something nice. But he'd shoved on his cap, and she'd lost her temper — "For Pete's sake, what would *Lil* cook up?" —

sounding hoity-toity, but hurt, too, and instantly regretting it. Because this thing with Lil was a trifling, wasn't it? A fling of the imagination?

But then he'd thrown it back at her: "If you've got something to say, say it," blaming her for having too much time on her hands and listening to priests. Which was ridiculous, since she hadn't been to St. Columba's in what, a year?

But Harry hadn't stopped there, ranting about Ida: "That bloody old rag-bag," he railed, accusing Ida of filling her head with this rot about Lil and him. "Garbage," he dragged it out. And she'd goaded, "What *about* you an' Lil?" until he'd hollered, "Don't tempt me, dolly," and somewhere in the house Jewel started screeching, as she dared him to raise his voice like that again. Yet, he'd grabbed the last word, asking, "Know what's good about Lil?" Since Lucy seemed to know so much, he said, calling Lil a *friend*. One who knew when to keep her trap shut, "and when friggin' not to!" Then he'd slammed out.

Sometime in the night, though, he came home; she'd woken to the sound of pounding. In the morning, there was the throne itself freshly installed — *Her Majesty's Waterworks, June 20th, 1920* scrawled on the plaster above it — but positioned so close to the tub one had to sit sidesaddle. She found Harry downstairs trying to make coffee; other than that, it was as if the fight had never happened. But then the noise of splashing erupted upstairs — how had Jewel escaped from his crib? Harry on her heels as she dashed upstairs; and then he'd proudly demonstrated. *You push the handle, like so.*

Jewel blinked and laughed with delight, and the phone rang — never mind that it was just after dawn and likely some crank on the party line — and Harry ran down to answer it. "Lemme see what I can do," she heard him say, and that he'd be seeing Babineau later, and they'd settle things after that. The plumber, he'd explained, coming back up and lathering his face for a shave. Jewel swishing his hands in the bowl, flushing and flushing again. *Tanyerhide mum-mum tanyerhide.*

FEELING GUILTY FOR HER absence, she re-entered St. Columba's through the sin-box, as Harry called it, though he'd never darkened the church doorway let alone a confessional. The spirit was willing, she'd wanted to plead, but the rest of her got waylaid. Father Marcus had barely blinked, prescribing two Hail Marys, no meat on Fridays, and keeping the Sabbath. It was only wise to obey, for Jewel's sake, since St. Columba's was also the nearest school.

Harry took delight in frying bacon on Fridays. "Oops," he'd say, telling Jewel to get it off her plate; they didn't want her going to hell. Hard to say which was worse, his teasing or his fiddling; he'd already gone through another bow after replacing the first.

"Hellinahambasket, right Daddy?" Jewel would crow right back, old enough, before they knew it, to start grade one.

As usual Harry had something to say, never mind that he waited till she'd seen Sister Jerome, the principal, about signing the boy up. "Bloody Catlicks," he'd started in, asking what they taught there, exorcism? They could practise on you, she'd wanted to say, focusing instead on her knitting. Then Jewel had started, refusing to go for his bath, his dad fiddling "Shave and a Haircut" as she dragged him upstairs.

Digging his heels in, Jewel said he didn't want to go to bed — or to school. Who could blame him? Harry nattered, saddled with a name like that. "The kid'll be teased six ways to Sunday — watch," he said.

The gall, to raise it after nearly five years!

"Sounds like 'drool' with a lilt," he'd added.

A little voice had piped up from the stairs, "I *like* my name," saying it was jiggly as green jelly. "Green like an emerald, right Ma?" He sounded so pleased, even when his dad hollered to get upstairs.

She'd found it funny enough to ask, "What colour's 'Ma,' then?" And his father's name? No colour, and brown like dirt, apparently. She'd stifled laughter, threatening, "Upstairs, before I put your head in a sling!"

Harry wasn't amused, though. "Think he was a pansy, talking like that," he said, accusing her of raising him like a girl. Behind the grate, blue flames hissed as singing travelled downstairs: *Run, run, fast as you can, can't catch me I'm the gingerbread man.* And she'd thought of Helena, the name like white smoke wafting upwards, and where she'd got it: the tale from the Greeks she'd heard in school of the woman whose love for somebody launched a war; if any war started here, it'd be Lil Marryatt behind it! Surprisingly, Harry'd gone along with 'Helena;' 'Helen' was too plain, he'd said, holding the infant girl up to the sunlight — holding her as if she were a piece of china, used as he was to things of metal, or wood. Mama had loved the name, because it made a person slow down to say each syllable.

Dropping stitches, she'd had to rip out a row. "Enough, *finis,*" she'd cut Harry short, borrowing the word from Sister Jerome.

"A forn language now, is it?" he'd sputtered. Putting his bow safely out of reach, he'd grabbed his coat, muttering that there was a big game that night, so she needn't bother waiting up.

She'd found Jewel awake upstairs studying an ostrich in his little illustrated dictionary. "Snow works as good as sand, I bet, if you're like him," he said soberly. "Except, if he's a bird, how come he can't fly?" The spat with Harry ringing in her ears, she'd tried coaxing him to say his prayers, like pulling teeth. He wanted to know if Jesus had to go to school — "that guy in the pitcher" — and where he lived. *Now I lay-mee down ta sleep,* he finally mimicked. *If I shoul' die be-four-eye wake ... I pray the lord myso' to take.* Even parroted back, the words had weight.

One afternoon she'd caught him lying on the road — like the gingerbread man baking, he'd protested, as she swatted, *tanned,* his behind. Then there'd been the winter morning, not long enough ago, he'd wandered off while she was cleaning. She'd been washing walls, had just wiped down the plate rail, the pink baby cup nearly slipping from her hands as he straggled in, half-frozen, his little duffel coat dripping. "I seen ... *saw,*" his voice had wobbled, "the abdominal snowman!" Then it dawned: he'd taken himself all the way to the swamp by the barn, and had gone through the ice. Queasy, mute, she'd hugged him till the wetness seeped to her skin, and he'd pulled one of Harry's new cufflinks from his leaden mitt: "Look. Ma — a table for a little pinhead guy!"

After his prayers, she'd just got to sleep when he screamed that there was a sea hag in the window. "I can smell her!" he shrieked, trembling in the doorway, pointing to the landing. The furniture polish, forgotten in the midst of a chore. Then he whined, "I don't *wanna* go to school." More sobs, as his sturdy arms hooked round her neck. The sea hag had eyes, he said, like the eyes of a dead reindeer. Just a dream, she'd murmured over and over; and after a while he'd tugged at her hand and smooched it, asking if he was a flower, like Daddy said. "Oh, my darling," her voice had slid out, saying that flowers grew in gardens, and what would Daddy know about that?

The first day of school, he was as balky as ever, refusing breakfast, and Harry, swatting fruit flies with the paper, barely speaking, didn't help. There was always the Protestant school, she said, though it was a bit late to change plans, and his father would have to drive him. By now they had the Model T, the tin lizard, Jewel called it. But all Harry said was, "Well, if *you*'d learn to drive ..." But then who'd have gotten the meals? Too nervous to eat, she'd taken Jewel's hand, walking him over, despite his complaints. *I'm not a baby!* Never mind that he clung to her in the dusty schoolyard, watching the other kids swarm around. The air full of chamomile, a clutch of mothers comforting the smaller ones.

A girl with braids, a year or two older than Jewel, was chasing a ball; her smile sent a jolt through Lucy as the child tossed it to a dog lolling there. Someone waved, a woman Lucy knew vaguely from Mass, and pushed her boy, named Samson, at Jewel. Samson stuck his tongue out, just before Sister Jerome appeared, a bell dangling from her sleeve, not a hint of a smile on her stony face. Mannish shoes poked from her habit sweeping the scuffed step. One sharp jingle, and as the children formed lines Jewel latched on to Lucy's waist. Prying him loose, she stood there bereft as the lines chugged forward, disappearing inside.

Out by the road, leaning against the statue of Christ was Lil of all people, having a cigarette while her little girl kicked stones. Having shot up, the child had grown pretty in a feral way, bony but cute in her droopy jumper. "Why do I have to?" she was whining to her mother. "*You* never went."

Lil smirked as Lucy passed: "Kids, eh?" But all Lucy could think of was Jewel's frightened look.

Further up the road she'd passed the tinker — the traveller, as some called this fellow who'd turned up and seemed to live in the woods. No more than a teenager, he was leaning against a cart with what looked like a whetstone. *Pots, pans, knives. Fix and sharpen. Reasonable.* He'd followed her right down their street, finally stopping at Mrs. Chaddock's; she could tell by the barking. At home, she'd busied herself with housework so as not to fret over Jewel. The front room had become a dust trap, Harry forever bringing home knick-knacks, when he was in a good mood. A china cat and a crystal scent bottle were too nice to hide upstairs, so they'd joined the pink cup whose china would always remind her of bones — the relics of saints Father Marcus went on about, as if to lure parishioners on some grisly pilgrimage.

Before lunch, she'd hurried back to meet Jewel. A yellow breeze teased the branches, the cove and the glasshouse with its iron walls looming through the trees. Jewel was slow coming out; sniffling, he wiped his nose on her skirt, saying he wasn't going back. In front of everybody she'd held him in her arms, though he was big for his age, telling him to be a brave soldier; everyone had things they didn't want to do. The traveller was still next door when they passed, Jewel's eyes lighting up at the sight of his wagon.

The house smelled too clean as he pulled out a limp sprig of chamomile and gave it to her. When she asked why he hadn't given it to Sister, his teacher, he sulked, "I don't got a sister."

"Sister Rosa?" she'd prompted. When she asked what they'd done all morning, he said that "Father Circus" had visited, and that his nose resembled Mr. Babineau's.

"Becka'd even said it did."

Becka?

Then he'd asked, "Whose father is he, anyways?" mentioning how they'd heard about wisdom and fruit and *a* words, like *axe-cement*, like the time he'd gone through the ice. Then, with grim delight, he asked if she could guess what Becka did — "You know, Missus's girl?" — and said she'd peed herself, in her seat. She was retarded, he said; he'd seen how she acted at Mr. B's. The Marryatt girl. So much for Harry minding Jewel at home while she was at Mass!

Jewel balanced a marble on the tip of his tongue, and kicked the table. All the way back to school he whined and dragged his feet, till she bit her cheek so hard she tasted blood. When the bell rang, he tried to hide behind her. School had only been in an hour when they phoned, asking her to come right away. As she raced over, there was a noise like the Lizzie backfiring. The traveller was lounging in the schoolyard. Something red slicked the steps. Stepping over it, she'd gone inside, following the corridor to the office. A nun quite a bit younger than Sister Jerome answered her knock. Jewel was standing in a corner, a red-haired boy in another. Introducing herself, his teacher scribbled a note and slid it under a vase of wild asters. Slightly askew, the desk practically filled the dismal little room. "We don't tolerate such behaviour," Sister Rosa said sternly, in a voice that didn't match her heart-shaped face. Then she asked Lucas, the red-head, to explain.

An Embrie, Lucy could tell, related to the Boutiliers. He had wet splotches on his shirt. "I seen everything," he said: Jewel in the "warshroom" playing with the soap. "Squirtin' it all over, cross my heart and hope to die." The nun murmuring what a mess it made, soap everywhere for the custodian to clean up. Lucy asked to see the principal, but Sister Jerome was indisposed, said Sister Rosa, clearing her throat, and saying there'd been an accident. Lucas launched in, "Seen that too. Dog went right for her, didn't he Jool?" Sister Rosa sniffed: "I'm sure you'll agree, punishment was in order." Lucas couldn't stop himself, saying that as soon as Sister Jerome lifted the strap to Jewel, "whomp! Lucky striked!" nearly ripping her fingers off.

Jewel's chin twitched; it was a struggle not to pull him to her. Lucas marvelled, "Her *own* dog, Sister J'rome's!" saying how they'd watched her feed him at recess, out of her hand. "We seen the blood, too," he said, and Sister Rosa blinked; on the floor was a spattering of red dots.

Murmuring that it wasn't his fault, Jewel wanted to know where Lucky was now. Explaining that the custodian had taken care of it, the nun's voice had warmed slightly: "the poor thing." But when Jewel asked brightly if Lucky was in heaven, she barked that dogs didn't have souls, only people did. And since the day was almost over anyway, he should go home and think about the state of his.

In the schoolyard, Ida Trott was lounging around with the traveller, spitting the seeds from an orange. She yelled, "You there, Missy! Fine then, be stuck up!" as Lucy kept walking, and hollered how Lucy should keep an eye on her son — "Boy like that; you don't want no harm coming to him" — and how she'd seen an owl in Lucy's cup, though she'd said nothing at the time, and a cat too, before Lucy'd crossed her. "Not good, missy!" she cackled, till the traveller finally shouted, "For the love of Christ, Ma, *shut your gob.*"

SHE DIDN'T KNOW HOW she'd broach Jewel's trouble with Harry, imagining his rant: Goddamn mickey school, that'll be the last time they try laying a finger on my kid! But after work he just stopped long enough to change his clothes, in a rush to see a mandolin Boots — Edgar Boutilier — was selling. He must've noticed that something was wrong, "Your lip should be in a sling, girl," but groused that there was no pleasing her. Pointing out their latest acquisitions, a table for the phone, a picture of a ship he'd wangled someplace, he said, "What do you want from me?" *You*, she'd wanted to blurt out,

I want you to stay put and listen. Instead, she murmured cryptically how she wished Jewel didn't have to grow up. "Cripes, not *now*," he'd grimaced, asking how she figured he paid for all this stuff. "It doesn't grow on trees, you know."

At bedtime, Jewel said that Lucas Embrie was a liar, that he'd never touched that stinking old soap, and that Lucky'd saved his hide. "Shoulda seen Sister's hand," he said. "Like the time Mr. Boutilier's dog killed a rabbit!" But he sounded frightened, saying they were still going to strap him, so for sure he couldn't go back. Sister had it in for him, especially after Lucky "striked."

"Struck," she said as calmly as possible, and, looking thoughtful, he'd mentioned that Lucky Strikes were Mr. Babineau's favourite smokes. Then, pleading for a puppy, he asked if she believed in witches. "Don't be silly," she'd said, and, wanting to know the differ- ence between a witch and a nun, he'd asked about the chicken lady, Old Backdoor Trotts. "She's a witch," he said, "don't you believe in her?" She'd buttoned her lip then, smiling till his thoughts turned in a different direction, his voice tiny: "Lucky wasn't lucky at all, was he?" And he asked what would happen if you swallowed a marble, the two of them eyeing each other at the sound of the Lizzie pulling in. Part of her had wanted to skitter free, like a pile of ashes. *Ladybird, Ladybird, fly away home, your house is on fire, your children alone ...*

By the time she stumbled downstairs Harry was lying on the couch, almost corpse-like, in a suit she hadn't seen before. The stink of liquor oozed up. One lapel was stained, and his shirt open, his tie — a tie? — askew. Strangest of all was a bruise on his neck, a yellowish one with teeth marks. Tiptoeing upstairs, she'd found his fiddle and brought it down, dragging a shriek next to his ear fit to raise the dead, before shaking him. Not a bit of good it did, her efforts as useless as tits on a bull, as that damned Babineau and his kind would've said.

Eleven

"IF THIS DOESN'T CALL for a party, I dunno what does!" Rebecca shrieks into the phone, nearly taking Lucy's ear off. She's not ready for this; heaven knows when Rebecca gets something in her head there's no stopping her. But Lucy tries anyhow, reminding her that it's a hospital, and she doesn't think ... "*Welcome back. Get well soon,*" Rebecca charges on, "What would he like on the cake?"

Cake? "But he's only just opened his eyes," she says; it's rest he needs, and what matters is that he can see their faces. Lordie, it's like tiptoeing around an avalanche, being diplomatic, telling Rebecca she *knows* she means well, but ...

Since when has she ever listened? "Stay right there," Rebecca answers back. "Don't move, we're on our way." The line clicks dead; that's right, she can't help thinking, go get Jewel all churned up. A party! Now watch, after getting everything in an uproar, who's the one who usually disappears? Still, she feels a bit mean hanging up, remembering it's a hospital phone, harbouring who knows what germs? Too late for her own benefit, she remembers the fresh tissue up her sleeve and gives the mouthpiece a wipe. For it's as if angels are smiling down, the corridor aglow with benevolence. *Harry, Harry, Harry*, she cheers inwardly, like a fan at one of those matches that, God willing, he'll soon be watching once again on the beloved boob tube.

Despite Rebecca's enthusiasm, it's a dog's age before they come trooping in, the whole family, even Robert. Rebecca leaves an imprint of her lips on Harry's pasty brow, then bustles off. They can hear her in the hallway asking for directions. Jewel touches his father's shoulder as if it belongs to someone else, then folds his hands, gravely gazing down while Robert nods at his grandpa in that way young fellas do, acting like men. An eighteen year old imitating some old goat: the thought deepens her smile. Dampening another tissue, she wipes the lipstick off Harry's forehead. His eye follows her hand the way a dog would follow a cut-up wiener.

Soon, sitting around the bed, thanks to Rebecca they're all drinking tea — even Harry — from Styrofoam cups that taste of plastic. Lucy holds Harry's as he sucks his tea through a straw, sputtering like a tap when the pipes are frozen. His eyes squeeze shut with exhaustion as she mops his chin. The shifting light — birds passing the window? — brings back that dark time when she'd spooned soup into him. But Rebecca would have no inkling of that.

"There you go, Pop! Bet that tastes some good, what, after that godawful sugar water?" she cheers, and his eye opens, a wary slit. Then, quaking, his hand pushes the cup away, a confused yet obstinate look replacing suspicion. The nurses have left Q-Tips dipped in Vaseline; wiping his chin again, Lucy swabs his lip still caked with blood from those dreadful gauze stays.

"Now don't you go to sleep on us," Rebecca coos down at him, then slips into the teensy bathroom. "Surprise!" she hollers, emerging with a cake still in its Sobeys box, hastily picking off the price tag. It's white, with hard-looking blue roses and little silver balls like BBs; mercifully, though, it's been left blank. All they had, she says, on such short notice. A nurse peeks in, an unfamiliar one, and asks whose birthday it is; her busy cheer makes Lucy feel inadequate. Wiping away tears, Rebecca beams at Harry, eyeing Robert as if he should explain. At his glower she sighs, "Well, now that you mention it, guess you *could* say ..." It's a resurrection cake, Lucy hears herself murmur as a floor polisher rumbles by, and maybe they've misheard, the nurse blinking when Robert cracks a grin, and grinning too but looking baffled, Rebecca calls out giddily, "Congratulations, Pop! Today's the first day of the rest of your life."

"Oh, Jesus." Robert coughs, slumping on a footstool, a giant with his legs thrust out. "Hey, Grampa," he says, taking a big swallow of tea then crushing his cup. Only Jewel has kept quiet. Using the bed for a table, Rebecca cuts the cake with a tongue depressor, handing out slices on tissues. Luckily she's rustled up a spoon from somewhere, and Lucy loads it with icing for Harry to lick. But he lets out a hiccup, and then a moan.

"See?" Rebecca jumps in. "You're liking that, aren't you, Pop? Aren't you, Harry?" If only she could keep the dismay out of her voice; it's as though she's wobbling on the edge of something; and why does she have to shout?

"Honey," Jewel finally speaks, "the stroke didn't hurt his hearing."

"You dig that, Ma?" Robert lights into his mother, licking his fingers. "I know it's heavy." He's teasing her? Ignoring him, Rebecca slouches back, picking at her cake.

Lucy can't help it — better late than never — and reminds him, "Manners, darling." Someone has to, if his parents won't.

Rebecca sucks icing from her teeth, blinking, annoyed? "Wait a sec," she sniffs, "I almost forgot. Jewel, hit it, would you?" What now? Jewel flushes, mumbling about toning things down, and how she needs to think of his dad's nerves. The way he says it makes Lucy feel bad for not going along with Rebecca a bit more; she's only trying to help, after all, and it's not her fault, maybe, that nothing registers till it's a national event! "Fiddle-faddle," she clucks dismissively, which fills Lucy with a little wave of relief, as if she's been let off the hook. As Rebecca squats to put on the record, her skirt rides up and there's a ripping sound — nylon? — and a flash of bare thigh. She's well-intentioned, if not always appreciated.

"Watch it, Ma!" Robert shoves his mother out of the way and carefully lowers the needle; the record wobbles like a flat tire. But a reel jumps out, and closing his eyes as if trying to dream himself somewhere, anywhere else, the boy moves his head slowly, fingering what must be the frets of a pretend guitar. Well, he always did have a good imagination. But then a curiosity, maybe even nosiness, hits her; what's going on behind those lids? Blouse-less hippie girls dancing, their long wet hair swinging in the rain? In his smirk she can almost see naked skin slicked with mud. Oh, glory. Not that there are girls like that in *this* part of the world, none she can think of, anyhow; they're only that way in the States, or maybe in Vancouver.

Barring speculation, Harry's pale hand lifts suddenly from the blanket and falls, lifts and falls again. Rebecca slaps her knee, picking up on it. "See? 'Got my dancing boots on, got my Sunday best,'" she parrots the singers on *Don Messer*, nudging him. "Hey, Harry?" Her eyes full of something that makes Lucy look away. *You frigging doom-and-gloomers*, that smile seems to gloat. As if he's her own.

THOUGH HARRY'S IMPROVEMENT MIGHT seem small potatoes, to her it's a blooming miracle, and the first chance she gets, Lucy hauls herself off to Mass. There's hardly anyone there, mostly just ladies from the league, and it's not easy dodging their looks. It's not as though Harry's home free, exactly. Call her superstitious, but it's early to bubble over with relief: it might be bad luck.

The new priest acts like a master of ceremonies, and doesn't seem to mind the lack of an audience for his sermon. It's too bad there aren't more listening, she thinks, though he has an irksome habit of adding *k*'s to his *ing*'s, and of rocking back and forth on his toes, saying what it is to seek the "kingkdom" of heaven. Ah, but the visions of rightness this conjures: Harry happily dozing in front of the TV, his beer virtually untouched. And Robert, yes Robert, shaking someone's hand and collecting a diploma. His mom marching past the perfume counter, telling herself she's sweet enough already, and thinking twice about flashing that infernal Chargex card, poor Jewel footing the bills. Lucy's mind drifts, then hooks itself around the words "mustard seed."

"Sproutingk and takingk root right under our noses," the blush-ingly young man enthuses; his excitement almost vibrates. "The smallest seed on the planet. Growingk and spreadingk its branches, all the birds of the air nestingk there, and the snakes of the field," his eyes needle her, and once more she's imagining Harry, only this time he's watching *Untamed World* or whatever that show is, and grinning as if he's got all of humankind pegged. *Donkey, ape, dingo. Goddamn chihuahua!* Lil Marryatt had died too soon to get a name, the thought wafts down like dust from the rafters, enough to make her sneeze. A rabbit, maybe? A skunk? No, Lil's scent had drawn men, not repelled them. Maybe she'd have been better tagged in the plant kingdom: some sort of prickly shrub, with Lord knows who or what nibbling on its buds. Or a Venus flytrap, that would've been Lil — though equating her likes with a green, growing thing was distasteful. *Stop.*

Tuning herself once more to those *ingk*'s, she forces herself to think piously of twigs turning woody, leaves unfurling in fast motion the way they do on TV. Lord only knows what a mustard plant looks like; easier just to picture an apple tree. Blossoms. But next she imagines someone lying under one. A child, maybe; a little girl in a pink dress? Staring up through the branches, her limbs outstretched like the points of a star. A little girl with a dirty face; no, worse, a man's face. Alone and lost as that prisoner, oh dear God, how many years ago? That poor Mr. Heinemann scrounging around for wormy fruit. Glory, how the brain meanders! The *ingk*'s lasso and corral her thoughts, but only for a moment. Except, *except*, she decides, resolute: the sky overhead would be clear, wouldn't it? The sky above the tree. A cloudless, transparent blue, the blue of forget-me-nots. As if it's part of a dream, she imagines Harry's shirt, its faint smell of sweat, even after she'd washed and pressed and given it away ... *Stop it.*

"Imagine, brothers and sisters!" the priest intones, looking barely old enough to shave. "While *you* and *I* are eatingk and sleepingk ..." And he blesses himself, and mercifully, it's time for Communion, which she sits out, eyes shut in a pose of prayer. Like the ostrich, its head conveniently buried: if she can't see the league ladies, they can't see her, so she won't have to explain, or brook their murmured encouragement. Their encouragement just now, she realizes, would be like getting dunked in a claw-footed tub of ice cubes. If the road to hell is paved with good intentions, the one to limbo must be steamrolled with the need to smile and nod as other people's troubles get offered up as examples meant to succour or boo-ee the spirits, as Rebecca would say.

At the end, Father Langille nails her just as she thinks she'll slip past, asking how things are. A ridiculous thought creeps in as he blushes, clearing his throat. As if he hasn't had the last word! But she shouldn't be so critical; it's not every young fella chooses the life; imagine Robert in that robe and collar. Still, her mind whips round to Harry; he's never been more with her — *What critter, what critter is Father Langille, do you think?* Harry's voice plays inside her head. An otter, maybe, with those wet black eyes?

"Better," she says, smiling foolishly, blushing too. Making for the steps, but not before Mrs. Slauenwhite's daughter corners her, describing when her boy's girlfriend's father had *his* stroke. "Thing's are good," Lucy heads her off, adding that they could always be worse.

"Well that's something, anyway," Father Langille pitches in, seemingly relieved.

Gone, though, is that excitement over the kingdom, whatever and wherever the kingdom may be — an estate walled by wind, she supposes, with a castle built of the same, or a mansion like the Clampetts', only made of water that resisted running away. The idea makes something inside her swell, not worry or grief so much as guilt. Despite his downy cheek, that keenness, maybe Father knows a thing or two. Maybe the mustard-seed kingdom was a place where things came out in the wash while you were busy flossing your teeth or emptying the teapot, or shaving.

"So, you're surviving," says Mrs. Slauenwhite's daughter approvingly.

"Doing fine." Surely her brightness will throw them off; the last thing she wants is sympathy, the snoopy, doting kind trotted out on the afternoon stories Rebecca watches. "Surviving," she trills, nodding, what a person would say after getting slapped with a cold, or the flu.

BIG DO TONIGHT AT *Babineau's*, Harry'd winced the morning after he turned up in that snazzy suit. Rolling over, his breath had been like Keith's brewery as he kissed her cheek. She'd stared at the ceiling as he groped under her nightie, and said she'd sooner eat dirt than go. As his fingers quit their crawling, she'd come right out with it: "Where were you, Harry?"

His mouth had twitched, just a little, as he repeated the same old same old, that business of seeing Boutilier about an instrument. When she pointed at the suit jacket on the floor, he'd asked if she liked it, then gave her the usual, *Look, I can explain.*

And still not bothering to ask about Jewel's day at school, he'd stroked her nipple: "So, this party — you wanta come, or not?" But wasn't seeing for herself better than sticking her head in the sand, or turning a blind eye? So she'd agreed to go, though he looked disappointed and said she'd have to leave the little blighter at home. As if she'd have brought him along.

Just before eight o'clock, Mrs. Chaddock had come to babysit, armed with her crocheting. The dark woods smelled mouldy as she'd hurried to keep up with Harry. Light from Artie's cabin spilled across their old place, which looked even smaller, overgrown with creeper. Artie'd claimed it for guests, Harry said, strolling into the party. A gale of music and laughter. Glass in hand, Lil strode right over. Painted up, she was wearing a dress that looked all wrong. *Houdini*, she'd called him. She'd seemed heavier, somehow, but still beautiful, dewy-eyed yet blowsy as a peony past its best. Her smile soured as Lucy hooked her arm through his; still she'd held out her drink and stroked his lapel, insisting, "Have a nip," and that it didn't take much to get feeling good. Then she'd laughed, and the fellow swinging a bottle behind her laughed too.

The place looked pretty much unchanged from the few times Lucy'd ventured inside. Some crepe paper dangled from the buck's antlers. In a haze of smoke the Boutiliers slouched round a table, Edgar and Birdie, and a girl Lucy recognized from their house-warming. Raising a glass, Artie'd hollered something about Harry bringing his wife. His eyes roving over Lil's dress. Then Boutilier had waved his fiddle, slapping Harry's back: *Got something over the house you might be innerested in, bud*. Dodging the reach of fellows playing cards, Lil swished past to boil water. Stockings drying behind the stove made Lucy think of cut-off legs and feet.

A strange pair of hands had grabbed Lucy's waist. Grinning, the fellow'd kicked away the mat in the middle of the room, dancers stepping back as he'd lifted a hatch and shimmied down into darkness. "More where that come from," he'd hooted, hoisting up bottles. Then Lil reached inside her dress and passed him something. "Who's mindin' the young fella?" she'd asked sullenly, plunking down Lucy's tea. Under the makeup her cheeks had looked doughy.

Lucy'd murmured something about Lil being lucky having her mother to babysit. Lil just rolled her eyes, hiking her skirt and spinning into that fellow's arms as Boutilier started playing. Then he and Lil disappeared, and a light had come on in the old shack next door as a fight broke out over cards. *Show me your hand or I'll fix your fookin' face!* Harry'd had that look that meant he was getting quietly soused, not so much as glancing up when she buttoned her coat and fled.

The wind was raw and heavy with salt that night, and a peaty scent that'd made her think of smoke — of fire travelling the roots underground She couldn't get home fast enough, though Mrs. Chaddock insisted she should've stayed out longer as Lucy tucked money into her fist. Upstairs, Jewel had every light on, studying a book on knots, something Harry'd picked up. She'd taken the book and laid it down, cracking the spine; next, for pity's sake, his father would be bringing home a boat! Kissing Jewel's forehead, she'd drawn up the blanket. "You smell like Daddy," he'd said.

AS SCHOOL WENT ON, his nightmares worsened. *Kid might's well be glued to the tit, and you encourage it!* Harry would stay out till he figured the boy would be asleep, though he sometimes miscalculated. He'd crank up the wireless to drown out Jewel's hollering. *So much for a fellow's listening pleasure.* One more row, she'd tell her knitting. Socks for St. Columba's tea and sale, the raffle prize a trip for two to Sainte-Anne-de-Beaupré up in Quebec: a once-in-a-lifetime visit to the shrine, the new basilica being built there. When the screaming continued, she crept upstairs. Jewel wanted to know what they'd done with Lucky's head, and thought maybe Sister Jerome had it on her wall, like Mr. Babineau's reindeer. "Buck," Lucy corrected, and he'd asked what Daddy and his buddies meant when they said, "Pass the buck, frig that, gimme the doe." *Oh, for the love of Dinah!*

Downstairs on the sofa, Harry leaned his head back as if fielding secret messages. You could've heard that radio outside. Picking up her needles, she busied herself counting stitches. "Socks," he badgered, "You trying to outfit an army?" and the smell from the kitchen range, with its hint of kerosene, roused her memory. "What's wrong now?" he wanted to know. Jewel being gone all day left more time to think, she told him. "That'll never do, dolly," he said, "thinking." As an ad for soap bubbled over the airwaves, suddenly there was peace upstairs. "No wonder I'm so frigging exhausted," Harry griped.

So many irons in the fire, she'd agree sarcastically when he came out with such comments; it was hard to sound neutral. *Business*, he'd say. *Look around you, Lucy.* As if she was stupid. For it was true: he'd done a splendid job furnishing the place, filling it to the rafters. Curio cabinets lined with ornaments, a fancy sideboard and drop-leaf table for the Tiffany lamp, the real McCoy. A friend of Artie's had brought it back from the States, given Harry a good price on it, so he said. Still, it would've been nice if he'd consulted her now and then, instead of bringing home surprises. And how could she tell him that the nicest things in the world didn't ease the panic she felt sometimes, the past hollowed out like a gourd? Or the longing that plagued her despite Jewel's best behaviour? Persistent as dampness, it was emptiness that pushed her to St. Columba's, where distraction, at least, was a gentle tickle, the *Holy holy holy, Blessed triniteee* wafting in and out of nothing. A relief, never mind how fleeting, when it came to roost however briefly. And didn't that fancy Tiffany lamp-shade remind her of stained glass windows?

But he'd surprise her some nights, following her upstairs. Outside Jewel's room he'd draw her close, smelling of pomade, as they peered in. "Joool Jekyl," he said once, kissing her temple almost shyly, then explaining, "I meant it, you know — about thinking. Don't put much store in it, myself." Then he'd murmured that what a person saw was *it*. "You could blame your almighty God for everything," he said, his voice trailing off. About as useful, that, as blaming Ida Trott for their loss. When she told him about her dreams, he said, "Lordie, visions? You'd best stick to knitting," even when she tried explaining that sometimes she saw Helena, in her mind, as if ... Shrugging down his suspenders, his shirt open, he'd held her hand to his scar. Clasping her fingers, pressing them lower, he asked, "Remember me, your husband?"

Even as Lil burned in her head like a light in their old cabin, he knelt, laying his cheek on her knee. His hair slicked back as he stroked her thigh, he joked, "Convert me, dolly." And she'd thought of the thirteen dollars hidden in her drawer, too mean, too shameful, to spend. Forgetting and giving up: weren't they the same thing? Then Jewel had peeked in on them, singing *A tisket, a tasket, a green and yellow basket*, and wondering if they could guess who'd got the strap for talking and nearly making Sister blow a gasket. "Becky Marryatt!" he said, asking, to Harry's alarm, if he was still gonna get it.

"A licking? Dolly? They're going to *hit* my boy?"

Behind the bedroom door he'd railed against the holy catlick church and her, too. *Spare the rod and spoil the child — is that it? A bird in the hand worth two in the bush?* A dead one worth two singing, whatever that meant. Depending on whose hand, she hedged, and what bush. Then, lying there in the creaky dark, she'd leaked the truth, saying that everywhere she went, she saw Helena; in every little face — something. He told her not to be so crazy, his dead eye gleaming in a stitch of moonlight, and his breath in her ear. "What you need to do," he said, "is keep your eyes on Jewel."

He was gone when she woke in the night. But at breakfast he gave her a music box. Mahogany, with a ballerina that pirouetted to "A Bird in a Gilded Cage." Jewel opened and shut it, balking over his egg. "Like it, dolly?" Harry asked a little anxiously.

It was lovely, but where would they put it? And where had it come from? "Artie's," he'd explained vaguely, saying that someone had given it to Lil.

"Note to head," his voice changed quickly as he jotted a list: rosin, furniture polish, candy — "Jawbreakers or licorice babies, Jool-my-boy?" — saying he'd see them that night.

In the schoolyard the traveller was snoozing under his wagon. Clutching his throat, coughing, Jewel asked if he was dead, then pleaded to go home. Redheaded Lucas was bouncing a yellow ball of blubber that an uncle, a whaler, had brought back for him. "My uncle could pound the tar outta your dad any day," she heard him jeer.

At home she stuck the music box under a bag of onions in the mudroom. But at suppertime Harry arrived with another surprise. Someone owed him, he said, humming as he replaced her picture above the mantel, stepping back to admire the new one, a painting of a waterfall as she imagined a waterfall in England might be, mossy and gentle. Folding the maroon socks she'd just finished, she told him about the raffle and how you could win a trip. "*Queebec?*" he said, as if she'd lost her marbles. Bouncing in, Jewel asked his dad how hard you had to hit someone before they saw tar. "Jesus Murphy," Harry blurted, "what kind of question —?" Scrunching up his face, Jewel said, "Listen, Daddy. A fart!"

BY THAT EASTER SHE'D knit through five pounds of wool: ten pairs of socks, grey, blue, red, maroon, plus brown ones Harry had his eye on. Two days to Good Friday she delivered them. Inside the church, the league ladies were dusting the purple-draped statues. The building creaked in the wind, sleet pinging the blackened windows. "Bought your tickets yet?" they grilled her. "You wouldn't want to miss out." The prize trip was booked for the Feast of St. Anne, patron saint of grandmothers — "*and* housewives!" they added in a flurry, the sign of the cross like a nervous tic. A shrine to the mother of the Blessed Virgin, Saint-Anne-de-Beaupré had a relic: a bone from her venerable wrist. Gathering up their buckets and rags, the ladies then left her alone — alone as Jonah inside the whale, the walls and ceiling a ribcage, the wind mimicking waves while, next door, Jewel practised printing: *The quick brown fox jumps over the lazy dog.*

Fixed on the drooping figure over the altar, she'd imagined the Son — not a baby lying on straw, but a carpenter young and wiry as Harry, except with flowing, girlish hair. In her mind's eye, though, the Son's face had loomed close, eyes blue and unwavering, wide with knowledge but haunted, too, and in the rocking wind, she'd imagined his breath on her cheek, so sweet that her breath caught, and a tingling started in her arms. Then the wind wailed and she'd thought of a baby in a cradle, a mother cooing — and in the flickering light the sweetness dissolved.

"Hinky dinky parlee-voo!" Harry teased when she asked for ticket money, reminding her that Quebec was practically a "forn" land, and that she'd never been past Truro. As if he had. He wouldn't even come to the sale, where the socks went in a jiffy, ten cents a pair. Most of the neighbourhood turned up, except Lil, though her daughter milled about with her grandmother. Erma's housedress kindled in Lucy thoughts of humble St. Anne — and the bolder one of herself climbing the shrine's Holy Stairs, a replica, according to Father Marcus, of the ones Christ the Son climbed meeting his earthly judge, Pilate. The draw got delayed when someone mislaid the ticket stubs, and she got roped into drying teacups until the fellow appeared, waving a bucket and asking for volunteers. Sucking a lollypop, Lil's daughter elbowed forward. Blindfolding her, the man spun her around. *A trip for two! All aboard!* "Who's gonna see the sacred bone, scale the *Scala Santa*?" he'd shilled, calling Lil's girl *sweetpea* and telling her to pick just one.

She reached in, snatching something, but when the man went to take it, she wouldn't let go. He'd tried to pry it from her, asking, "How many humps does a camel have, dearie?" She just grinned, the sucker poking out her cheek. He'd asked if her mom was there, or her dad. Someone snickered, and he made a grab for the stub. Lucy could hear it rip as Erma scuttled forward, telling the girl to smarten up before she whapped her. Another little girl bobbed forward, a hush falling as the man held out the bucket.

"And the winner," he shouted, "the winner of this once-in-a-lifetime, all-expenses-paid trip to the greatest shrine in all of North America —" He looked around, and Lucy's throat tightened; such a prize would only mean trouble. "The winner is ..." A curse, really: Harry would never let himself get dragged along, and she could hardly leave him and Jewel to themselves for a week. "Mrs. Lu —" a whoop, and a woman covered her face "— cinda Slauenwhite!" Then somebody yelled from the back; half a stub lay underfoot, Lil's daughter off playing tag. Retrieving it, the man unfolded his piece, scratched his ear — "Ahem, a trip for *two*" — and thanking everyone for their patience, called out the other winner: "Mrs. Lucy Caines." *God in heaven*, she heard herself say, pumping his hand, as if she'd died and gone there.

THE SOUND OF A truck braking on the hill wakes her. Lordie, it's light out. She's overslept — not that Rebecca will mind; to Rebecca ten means eleven. Marryatt time.

She's been dreaming again, this time of her sister, and the thought of Ethel keeps her still, listening, grasping ... It's like clutching at smoke, and now Ethel's only a voice, the echo of a voice. And the shadowy impression of a little bone, perhaps, a magic one in a fairy story, a talking one. A finger bone? In the dream they've been playing marbles, crouching at the top of the hill on Roome Street. *A tisket, a tasket,* someplace inside Lucy the little bone still sings, *I lost my yellow basket!* and keeping her eyes tightly shut, in her mind Lucy's chasing a doughboy. And Ethel's no longer a bone, talking or otherwise, but herself. Except, when she holds out her hand — *Give it back!* — she's tiny and blue-eyed. Not Ethel at all, but Helena ...

The phone is ringing; not yet out of the woods, not yet free, she steels herself, padding down to get it. It's Rebecca, of course, offering to take her shopping, insisting that if there's one thing she'd *love* to do, it's just that. No wonder she and Harry get on so well, two sides of the same coin when it comes to buying things, never mind any differences in taste. It's the hunt that matters. "Make a list, okay?" she coaxes, meaning items Harry could use. "We want Pop to be comfortable, right?" As if that railed, metal bed could be a La-Z-boy, and the monitor he's hooked up to a top-model colour TV.

"Oh, I think the nurses see to that," Lucy says, as Rebecca rhymes things off: a bed jacket, jammies. Boxers, vests? A new razor, for sure, and deodorant. "Rebecca, dear," she has to cut her off. "It's not like he has to go out." The gal means well, yes, but it's always as though she's got to have a leg up. Next she's going on about his sponge baths, as if the water for them comes from the harbour! "I have everything he needs right here," Lucy interrupts, but as usual Rebecca has to have the last word: "Well," she sniffs, "a man can never have too many changes of underwear. Trust me." Oh Dinah, *her* undies must be in a twist. She thinks the world of him, that's all; *she just wants what's best,* Jewel is always defending her. *Yes, my darling,* Lucy's felt like saying more than once, *and the road through the Grounds is paved with taffy.* "Don't worry about making tea or nothing," Rebecca tells her before hanging up, saying she'll be right over.

It's all Lucy can do to make herself presentable. The honk outside puts her even more on edge, and without any discussion, Rebecca heads towards the nearest department store, the radio blaring about Vietnam and Ho Chi Minh. "I never know if that's a place or a person," she babbles, zipping past the post office and the Ocean Limited's whistle stop, "I can't keep it straight, can you?" It makes Rebecca's bossiness almost forgivable, since most news about the war confuses Lucy too. She murmurs that she could've saved her all this bother and walked, but Rebecca ignores this, scouting out a parking spot. Preying on one is more like it, as she whips ahead of someone else, never mind that there are lots of spaces farther away. Rebecca behaves like a hunter at the end of the season, though she does try to hold the revolving door. It clips Lucy's elbow, sending a pain up her arm as Rebecca herds her inside.

It's been ages since she shopped for anything but groceries; when was the last time, before or after the men returned from the moon? The store gleams too brightly, a world inside a giant bulb, all clean sharp lines and shine, shine, shine. Maybe that's how Earth looks now to the astronauts. Anyway, it makes her uncomfortable. "We only need a couple of things, dear," she whispers loudly, tapping Rebecca's hand, still tanned from the summer, even leathery. A mistake agreeing to this shopping spree. All she wants is to be outside, under the Indian summer sky — better yet, in the garden. The asters'll soon be done, it occurs to her with a bit of a shock; for weeks now she's thought of nothing but Harry.

Rebecca sees her impatience. "Now, you don't want to scrimp," she teases. If only that goodness of hers weren't so officious. "Maybe we'll see about a bathrobe, then," Lucy gives in; the sooner she complies, the sooner she'll be out of here. Taking her arm — since when was she a cripple? — Rebecca leads her to men's wear, where a saleslady in an orange pantsuit is helping someone choose socks.

Oh glory, it's Father Langille of all people, and he blushes when he sees her, reddening even more and nodding as he notices Rebecca. "Ladies," he says in a scratchy voice; whatever happened to *sisters*? Gazing too intently, he clears his throat — "And how's your husband?" — as if, alive again, Harry must be lurking.

"Harry's doing good," Rebecca answers the way she'd parked. "We're getting him a new wardrobe." As if they need to explain. Elbowing Lucy. "Right, Ma? He's gonna need it, isn't he." Father's smile is benign, but curious. He starts to ask vaguely about their plans, when a voice over the intercom says anyone missing a child should come to the toys section. "Thanks be to God, then," the priest murmurs. "Your prayers've been answered." Rebecca gives him a look, saying, "Well — I don't know about *that*."

"It's still early yet," Lucy puts in quickly; sometimes it's as though Rebecca were flesh and blood, the way she needs to protect her. Baffling, frankly, how short the gal can be on common sense, not to mention manners. Not that it's her fault, perhaps.

"Ah, not out of the woods, yet. Well. We won't forget him," says Father Langille, adding that prayer chain meets this evening, and she's on the list. His neck strains against his collar, and she tries to imagine him without it. But Rebecca's tugging on her elbow, the one that still hurts.

"Errands, Ma," she urges; in case Lucy forgot, she's got to be back to wake Bucky up. The priest stammers an apology, asking if Rebecca's her daughter.

"Daughter?" It's as if a feather's stuck in her throat. "Oh, Father, no. Forgive me," she blurts, introducing her son's wife.

"Nice to meet you," Rebecca bares her teeth, and he mumbles something about circumstances and visiting. Lucy coughs, fishing for a tissue. Father's tidy features glow, and his collar looks too white, rigid, against the silk ties and boxers.

"Perhaps you'll join us tonight," he says hopefully, "for a proper vigil."

"Thanks," Rebecca yawns, saying she doesn't think so.

Glancing at the socks he's chosen, argyles in yellow and red, Lucy can't help smiling. "Lovely shades," she remarks, "fallish," and he blushes again, or maybe he's naturally ruddy, his colour exaggerated by the artificial light.

"Thanks, yes. Gosh, you're right." Then he pats her arm — how she hates it, being consoled — telling her to keep her hopes up, that God is faithful to those faithful to him. "Ask, and it shall be given," he says in a pinched way, nodding once more before moving to the cash.

"What drug's he on?" Rebecca rasps, though he's barely out of earshot, steering Lucy towards bathrobes. "Oooh. Look," she fingers velour, "Wouldn't Pop love lounging in that! You'd never get him off the couch." Maybe it's funny to her, but Lucy pictures Harry in his johnny shirt, the nurses sliding a pad under his rump, as Rebecca admits it's pricey, but insists, "Lookit, let me — let *us*. Jewel wants his dad to have the best." She grabs the boxers Lucy's chosen, and, snatching some pajamas off the rack, marches up to pay. Mercy, does this mean they can leave? The pantsuit lady asks if they've found everything they need, and Rebecca hesitates, as if staring through the sights of a rifle, grabbing some men's cologne from the little display. Golly — now she's got Jewel wearing perfume? "Chargex," she says, corralling her buys as though they might end up in the wrong bag. Never mind they're the only ones standing there.

"Rebecca, you mustn't," Lucy says feebly, but she just pushes her hand away, saying it's not like they do this all the time.

Something tickles her throat; it must be the air, dust from the clothing? She might as well be with someone from the league, suffering their kindness, saying Harry has no use for —

Now she's done it: Rebecca's lip curls, falling into a pout, not the angry kind she saves for Jewel, but hurt. There's a treacherous pause. "You're saying he mightn't come home?"

Lucy glances around nervously for Father Langille, but he's vanished. Pleading, "Rebecca, *dear*." Scolding herself: how hard is it, just going along? It shouldn't be that much to ask, a bit of motherly humouring. Lord knows in Rebecca's life it's been in short supply.

"You have to think positive, Ma," Rebecca says, and she agrees, smiling to prove it. But who knows if Rebecca catches this. She is now in a sudden rush to whisk her outside, their mission accomplished, just as Lucy spies a rack of sale items, some darn good buys. This time she lets Rebecca go first, waiting till the revolving door's stopped before stepping in; otherwise it's like an egg beater. Outside, Rebecca taps her foot impatiently, her high heel clicking against the cement. People stare dully, waiting for the bus; one fellow has bell-bottoms like Robert's, except his belt's up around his waist. Bumped against the concrete wall is a shopping cart piled with odds and ends, rusty metal and what looks like copper pipe, and a couple slouched there, guarding it. Oh, Lordie. Benny's lecturing the woman, that's how it sounds, though the woman seems to be listening raptly. Glancing up at Rebecca, she smiles vaguely and waves her stubby hand.

"Oh Jesus," Rebecca mutters, but smiles, waving back, saying on the way to the car that she's heard she does houses. "Probably can't trust her as far as you can throw her," she tosses out, launching into a raft of gossip. How, over at Jimmy's one day, she'd heard the woman bragging that she kept house once for "some big professor up the Valley" and how her people had money, too. "Go figger, eh?" Rebecca shrugs, "There but for the grease of God, goes I?" and she says how *that* would put the fear of God into Bucky, someone like her rifling through his room, scrubbing. "The state of it," she snorts. Smoothing the bag between them, Lucy thinks of how Robert had fished his poem from the mess. Far as she sees, kids just do what they're used to, and his room's not the only pigsty over there. Rebecca's got all the time in the world to clean: why doesn't she?

Sometimes it's as if Rebecca's got ESP, and expects the rest of the world to have it too — the damnedest thing. Pulling up the street she looks right at Lucy, saying, "Jeez, poor thing." A queer thing to say, after how they complain about him. But it makes Lucy smile inside, telling Rebecca it'll all come out in the wash; give him time and Robert'll be fine. But Rebecca frowns, almost dinging the fence.

"That poor crazy lady, I mean, living with that nutcase. Or maybe Benny's got something we don't know about?" And she winks, that dirty grin like Rowan's on *Laugh-In*, that show Harry's always trying to get her to watch.

Twelve

IN THE HOSPITAL, THOUGH, Rebecca's humour comes in handy, asking Harry if he likes his new maroon robe. "Don't that colour just get the old blood pumping!" she nudges him. "*Doesn't* it, Jewel?" It takes the two of them to hold him up while Lucy tucks it around his shoulders. But there's something in his expression, or his lack of expression: gratitude. Lifting from the bed, his good hand motions *sit*. "Sheesh, he's like the Pope now," Rebecca ogles, "all he needs is the ring."

"Becky. Please." Jewel reaches for some juice on the bedside stand, peeling back its foil lid. "Jesus Murphy, it's dry in here," he sighs, and Rebecca picks up on it, teasing, "Any excuse for a drink, eh Harry?"

Stop, Lucy wants to say. Enough. Taking the juice, she leans in to position the straw; Harry's lips quiver as they close around it, his look like Jewel's as an infant nursing. "God," Rebecca says, "he must be croaking for a smoke."

In spite of himself, Jewel smiles, then grimaces at his shoes, patting his shirt for cigarettes. "God, Harry," Rebecca persists, "here you've quit cold turkey."

That index finger lifts and points feebly to the record player pushed to a corner on its bandage cart: a nurse's bright idea. Moving his head, he jars the straw. Cooing like Rebecca — "oopsy-daisy" — it's as if Lucy's twenty again, a new mother wiping his chin. Now his whole hand moves, pointing towards a glass of melted ice cubes. "All gone, Harry. Empty." Leaning back sharply, Jewel sends it toppling. It splashes the sheet, but doesn't break.

"Now see what you did?" Rebecca snipes. "Clumsy."

Muttering that it was an accident, Jewel says, "Can't you give it up?"

What's with these little flare-ups; surely they could save them for home? "How're Robert's plans coming?" Lucy pipes up, for the sake of peace. "Too bad he doesn't have a friend —" To travel with, she means.

Jewel gives her a look. "Friend? *She's* the one's got him worked up in the first place, all about going west." To live in a beehive or a teepee, he says, to hear them go on. "Stay in school, I keep telling him. Just get through the year." The most Jewel's opened his mouth since Harry's fall, he goes on, "That one says jump, Buck says how high," ranting how the kid may as well live on the moon, the wrong side. He's not exactly thinking with his *head* these days, Rebecca pitches in. All Lucy can think to add is that maybe the moon's not so bad. "Right," Jewel glances at Rebecca's shoes, "if you're dressed for it."

She feels like a referee on wrestling. Asking him to play something, a Quiet Time number, she suggests, something nice and slow: Marg Osburne? "That'll put you to sleep again, won't it Pop," Rebecca shouts and Harry blinks. But there's the hint, ever so faint, of a smile. "Give him a jig," she orders.

As Jewel gets up to put the record on, the good side of Harry's mouth opens and out comes a sound. Wiping his chin again, timidly, Lucy leans so close his lips brush her ear. "What, sweetie?" A grimace. Trembling. His drawled word could mean anything: *courting*?

"'Cordine!" Rebecca exclaims, as if she's special.

"He wants his accordion," Jewel repeats as if needing to translate, and the needle makes a noise like a boot punching through frozen snow. "One Don Noble coming up."

ONE SPRING MORNING WALKING Jewel to school, between his night-mares and Harry's shenanigans, she'd been so tired she could barely walk straight. She'd woken to find the bed empty, and Harry on the landing like a little kid waiting for Santa. Along the road the maples were a reddish haze; a storm had showered buds everywhere, and cars churned up pinkish mud. Instead of turning in at St. Columba's, throngs of kids were running towards the cove. Jewel raced to catch up; she'd started running too.

The tide was out and a crowd was gathered, people spilling over the rocks. On the shore below their old place the Mounties were hauling crates from the water: lobster traps? Jewel kept pointing out a boat tied up in the shadow of Deadman's, the hill crouched opposite. Babineau's boat, he was telling everyone, as people whooped, laughing at the haul. *Jayzus, look what the cat drug in! Finders, keepers*, someone jeered, as a policeman fired his gun straight in the air. She'd felt queasy as Father Marcus approached. "Let the wicked fall into their own nets," he'd wagged his chin, saying the Lord knew who was responsible, if the coppers didn't; "even as God knit them in their mothers' wombs." Ducking back up to the road, she'd wondered who else, verily, had eyes in the back of their head?

It wasn't long before the Mounties paid Harry a visit, interrupting his attempts at "My Lovely Black Maiden." Drop the fiddle, they said, it was criminal business.

The words *alibi* and *wife* had volleyed back to the kitchen, where she was making divinity fudge. She'd almost burned the pot when the constable peeked in, lying that Harry'd been home constantly, practising. Father Marcus's words knocking inside: *the wicked, falling*. They knew where to find him, Harry'd chimed in at the end of their questioning; anything a-tall they needed.

An hour later Artie'd shown up, making fun of her knitting before Harry rushed him downstairs. Their voices murmured up through the pipes, incoherent but sober. When they emerged Harry seemed sweaty. Lil was back at her mother's and Artie wasn't doing so hot, he explained, and if anyone asked, he'd been staying with them. "That's right, missus," Artie'd puffed, "eating your loverly cooking and helping junior with arithmetic." Then telling Harry that sometimes he envied that crazy tinker living under his wagon; would live in a can if he could, the bugger. The cops didn't muck with fellas like that, he said, why bother? "Wouldn't go that far," Harry snorted.

The same week a truck pulled up, men making a delivery. A mistake, she thought, but they wrestled the Victrola inside anyway. Three hundred bucks new, one of them said, "Don't look a gift horse, my darlin'." Artie wanted her to have it, Harry explained. Opening the cabinet, taking out records thick as plates, showing her how to turn the handle, place the needle just so. *Wicked, nets.* Father Marcus's words had echoed, but as the song leapt out — a man mimicking a little child: *la-la-la-la, I fall down and go boom* — despite everything she laughed and let Harry waltz her around till the singer's voice got woozy. "Sounds liquored," Harry'd joked, cranking it up again, not too tight, in case the spring snapped — even as she protested how it was too big a gift to accept. "Not like you haven't earned it," he said, asking blithely when she was going away, then flipping through the stack: "You're the Cream in My Coffee," "Ain't We Got Fun."

Two days to the Feast of St. Anne, he and Jewel saw her to the train, Harry saying not to worry about a thing, nudging a box of Turkish delight at her. The porter wrestling her suitcase from the boy. She'd waited so long for this; now the moment had come, she'd wished she'd just dreamt it. Pouting and clamouring to come too, Jewel refused to kiss her. She'd waved till the pair of them were smaller than fleas. "Do them good to muddle through," clucked Mrs. Slauenwhite, the other prizewinner, taking the aisle seat. "Motion sickness, you know." Unwrapping a sandwich, she'd tucked the wax paper into her purse, then launched into descriptions of her children and grandchildren, and all her other pilgrimages. That bone, the relic, she'd said, crossing herself, was "a testicle" — a *what?* Lucy'd wanted to squeal — "to immortality. Proof, dear, that the sanctified would be raised up." Like bread dough, Lucy'd thought, Jewel's pout branded in her head as the train rounded the Basin, as if the parts of her life that mattered had been left at the siding.

Mrs. Slauenwhite prattled on, asking how old Lucy's little fella was, and if her husband was Catholic. It was hard to enjoy the scenery, last seen through sleety rain, dressed up now in summer blues and greens, like the same body under nicer clothes. *The resurrection of the dead, and the life everlasting*, Father Marcus's words had come out of nowhere. As woods slid by and her companion preached that a change was as good as a rest, she'd opened Harry's candy. "Tastes like more," Mrs. Slauenwhite said, helping herself. The sweetness was cloying, and nearby, a man smoked cigars. Light skittered through Lucy's eyelids as she tried to doze, and Mrs. Slauenwhite rambled on anyway about what a pity it was, Lucy's husband's lack of religion and their "mixed" home. "Too bad you haven't a girl," she'd added, saying girls were nicer in one's old age. It was all Lucy could do to ask how long the trip might be, feeling a little ill. A church flew by and a cemetery, and Mrs. Slauenwhite crossed herself twice, suggesting they'd have lunch past Truro, though complaining that what her daughter'd packed wasn't fit for a bird.

Lucy had tasted bile, the porter's eyes doubtful when she told him she was sick. "A medical emergency," she called it, as he trundled off to find her bag. An apology was all she could offer Mrs. Slauenwhite, gazing past her puzzled face as the train came to a standstill. *Shubenacadie*, said the sign over the platform. The air had smelled of manure, and though the return train wasn't due for hours, she'd felt instantly better, despite the sleepy houses, blinds drawn against the sun. The weight in her stomach lifted, and crickets sang in an octave that matched the wires' hum.

It was twilight by the time she climbed the front steps, having spent prize money on a cab from the siding. The radio was blaring, Jewel in the front room with his feet on the sofa, and Lil's daughter beside him. They were eating taffy apples, spitting the seeds.

"Quit it now, Becky, or so he'p me, you'll land back at Gran's!" a voice shrieked from the kitchen.

Blessed Mother, who was in there digging through the ice box, *her* ice box, but Lil?

Lil's eyes had widened like a cat's, her hands skimming her thighs as Artie wandered in, a beer in hand. "My — wasn't that a short jaunt," Lil sneered and seemed to soften as Artie laid his hand on her neck, mumbling about Lucy being a vision.

Then Harry'd yelped from the mudroom, "For chrissake, you turd, get the electrical tape!"

His face twitched when he saw her, his tongue tripping over itself, some cockeyed explanation about Lil and Artie and the kids helping out. He had a wrench in his hands. Lil made some quip, what did a saint have that he didn't? "You got a bone or two, dontcha, Mister?" Artie'd laughed first, rubbing Lil's neck till she winced.

Setting down her suitcase, Lucy fled to the dining room, her face tight as she grabbed the first record lying there, before noticing the Victrola was gone. Miserably, she'd followed their voices outside where it lay gutted, its thick black spring looped over the grass like a bowel.

"That's what happens when you wind 'er too tight," Harry muttered, trying to splice the ends together. *Goddamn kids.*

"Not Becky, though," Lil swooped her eyes. "Becky wouldn't —" Artie poked her and told her to can it, and Harry'd yelled at them both to give him a hand; maybe they could shove the whole works back inside? But Artie'd blown up, asking how many favours Harry thought he owed him, telling him to fix it himself. He and Lil had to peel the child off the sofa, judging by her screams.

Lucy'd just knelt there, and let Harry stagger around with the spring, trying to replace it. "Might's well pitch the whole goddamn thing," he ranted, till she demanded to know what *she'd* been doing there. "The little one? Some handful, isn't she?" he'd demanded right back, and then he'd jeered, his eyes hot: "So. Father Who's-it pull the plug on things, or what? Or did he just give you a broom?"

The Victrola ended up in the cellar. *Easy come, easy go.* Harry couldn't understand why she hadn't stuck things out. "You're too damn sentimental," he said, bowing along with the radio as she tried to explain how the train and the view and Mrs. Slauenwhite had reminded her of things too painful to stomach. "Those records were too fast to play to anyhow," he said, turning up the volume, fiddling harder. Almost more than her lost opportunity, she missed those squealing clarinets and silly lyrics, the frantic glee pressed into the grooves. At least the radio threw up a wall between them, just high enough, bricked in with voices and music. Filling in where talk failed, for he'd started keeping queer hours again.

Next door Mrs. Chaddock's bulldog had died, so there was no warning the night Harry was off supposedly playing cards. She mightn't have answered had she heard the wagon. It was hard to tell the traveller's age as he stood there shivering, asking if she had anything that needed fixing. Harry'd been threatening to dump the darn Victrola into the Arm. When she asked the traveller if he could fix a spring, his eyes shifted. Smirking, he'd come right in; she'd let him go first down the stairs. "Beyond fixing?" she asked, as he eyed Harry's tools hanging everywhere. She was stupid to let him in; Harry would've had a conniption. Nervously she'd slipped upstairs, and a little while later he appeared, his eyes following her to the pantry where she kept the money jar.

Afterwards Jewel had hollered down from his room, asking who was there. Nobody, she'd said. Then, down below, she'd put on a record, turned the crank. Just a little resistance, then out had come a yodel gaining in pitch and tempo with each turn, and a thud every so often announcing where the spring had been spliced. When Harry came home she told him to move the thing upstairs where it belonged.

For Christmas he gave her "Blue Rhapsody," which she played till the thud melted into the rhythm. Once again, for a while at least, it was as if his friends had fallen off the Earth. "Lil says bend over and that dummy Artie says 'how far?' Who needs it?" he'd chortle. But what was that look in his eyes? That New Year's Day, she'd put on her new record and Harry'd got out his fiddle, its shrieks poking holes in the melody, pulling all its lovely threads. She'd held her tongue, though, till he started to massacre "On the Sunny Side of the Street." Then she'd lifted the needle.

There'd been snow and they'd been cooped up, and she suggested they go for a spin. Like it was *spin* weather, he objected at first, glowering as they piled into the Lizzie, Jewel perched on some blankets in back. Snow twirled down, everything padded white as if with quilt bat. On a whim she asked to go to the old neighbour-hood. Gears grinded, and they skidded. Eyeing Jewel in the mirror, Harry'd rubbed her knee. "That hill will be a bugger in this!" his voice had chirred like the chains on the tires: "You *would* pick a dirty day." Dirty, *unclean*, a preachy voice had piped up inside her, a shriller version of Father Marcus. Mind in the gutter. For the first time in weeks she thought of Lil.

Above the shipyards Harry'd pulled in alongside a snowbank, and from the frosty cocoon of the car, they'd marvelled at the rows of new houses built of blocks like grey sugar cubes. A woman and her children had come along, one of them missing a leg. Rubbing a hole in the frost, Jewel pointed, and Lucy'd grabbed his finger, studying the ferns on the windshield as he kicked her seat. It had spilled out of her: "Sometimes, Harry, if I wait long enough, pray hard enough, I think ... everything'll just melt, and there she'll be." Their little girl, she'd meant, like something left out all winter, then revealed, come spring. Afraid she'd cry, she'd stopped talking and he'd patted her knee, digging for his hankie as Jewel complained about being "froze." The snow swirled in blasts. Even when he'd started the car and the jingling chains helped lug them forward, the sadness wouldn't budge. As Jewel whined that he could've been home playing Meccano, she curled her hand over Harry's. Words caught in her throat: They'd never told him about her, had they, dear?

Jewel blew frosty rings in the air. "Who?" And she'd imagined that mother and her family inside their sugar-cube house, that boy setting aside his crutches like Tiny Tim. "Your sister," she said, "you had a sister once, you know." She spoke as if reminding him about a test, and to do his best. Harry'd lit a cigarette, waving the match, mumbling that he wasn't their only one. Only one what, saved by a dog? Who could spell "Musquodoboit" backwards? "I want to go home," he'd whined as the chains whirred, making the same noise as the sewing machine she'd also found under the tree.

She'd pulled at Harry's hankie, spelling out Helena's name, repeating that she'd be eleven-and-a-half now, eleven-and-a-half years old, and he'd said he wasn't retarded, asking, "Hell-in-a — what, handbasket?" And then: "Well. Where did she go?" The Lizzie'd lurched as Harry geared down, Lucy murmuring that she hadn't *gone* anywhere, they'd lost her.

As they skimmed along, the smell from the brewery filled the car. *Pee-ewe!*

Harry tried to be funny, as if Jewel weren't there. Saying how a little ale would do about now, and that he should've joined the navy; talk about a ready supply. "A bit of fun," he'd sniffed, his voice hardening; they could use *that*. "You used to like fun, Lucy, didn't you," he said. "Wonder we didn't end up with ten kids. Throw my pants on the bed, next you're pregnant!"

"The kind of fun Lil liked?" she asked, as if Jewel weren't there, adding that she never knew he was so family-minded, and if he *wanted* more children ...

"Look," he'd spat, "it's no skin off my nose." Her anger was stoked by the cold, never mind Jewel listening.

"So," she'd demanded, "how much fun *is* she?"

And he'd sneered, why buy the cow when he had milk at home? But it didn't stop there; the argument turned to religion. "Do unto others, and all of that!" he ranted. The way he saw it, she had two religions, the catlick stuff and her own blessed church of the divine Dutch cap! Or whatever she called it. *If* she'd take the opportunity to use it. That priest of hers knew the half of it, he said, she'd be excommunicated! "His holi*ness* would chop off your —"

What came next sliced closer to the bone: he accused her of upsetting the boy. "'Not the only one!'" he mimicked. "Like the sun don't set except on him, then, *boom!*" And he blamed her for never unpacking her troubles, as if some saint would come and kiss things better. "Well it won't bring her back," he'd said flatly. "Nothing you can do or say. For the love of Christ, would you just *let it go*."

THE HILL BEHIND BOUTILIERS' was perfect for coasting, no shortage of snow back then. Jewel wasn't old enough to go on his own, so she'd shadowed him as he raced ahead with his sled, its red runners freshly filed. Jewel acting as if she were a bad smell; she should've been home starting supper. Yellow ice hugged the shoreline as kids flew downhill on pieces of cardboard that snapped in the wind, then trudged lemming-style back to the top. Not a thing she could do to stop Lucas Embrie and Mrs. Slauenwhite's grandson, Samson, grabbing the sled and taking off. Those runners flashed as Jewel pushed Lucas and dove onto his belly, all three boys wrestling. *Give it here, you little frigger!* She shook her fist, but no one noticed. As Lucas hurled a snowball, something moved in the woods; *the chicken lady*, he hollered, and Ida Trott limped from the trees, leaning on a bladeless hockey stick. Samson and Lucas piled onto the sled, shrieking as they shot downhill, zoomed past the rocks. There was a shout; she couldn't hear what over the gulls' yowling. But suddenly everyone was streaming towards the shore. Coasting on his stomach, Jewel got up and ran too.

Ida hobbled out onto the ice, which made a kissing sound. *Sweet Mother.* Lucy'd stumbled closer, Jewel melting into the crowd. The ice dipped and shifted; farther out, beyond a crevasse, a hole had loomed. "For pity's sake," she'd breathed, as Ida knelt then started to crawl. Her stick a spar, she'd rolled like a patchwork seal towards something orange. The top of Lucas's toque as he bobbed, then heaved himself up. Flattened there, Ida thrust out the stick. Children let out a sound like waves curling. Everyone's eyes on Lucas as he wriggled, kicking, wallowing ashore. *Samson!* the shout had echoed as he vomited on the snow, Jewel crouching over him, wanting his sled.

"Run to Boutiliers'," she'd heard herself shriek, cradling Lucas before his red-headed sister pushed in. Birdie came running in her slippers, her bosom joggling over her apron, then ran back screaming, "Git the boat!" Lucy racing to catch up, gasping that it was the Slauenwhite boy — and Ida. *Not Mrs. Trott* — not *Ida!* Staggering out in his suspenders, half loaded, Edgar Boutilier had clawed at the snowy hump in the yard, the dory he used trapping lobster. His dog baying from its rope. "Get Babineau," he hollered, saying the bastard must be good for something.

Running, she couldn't feel her toes. Artie'd taken forever coming to the door in his undershirt, Lil and some man in there playing cards. "I'm Sitting on Top of the World" blaring. "A child," Lucy kept gasping. "Ida, too." Fanning her cards, Lil had stared; she'd smelled peppery — was it lavender? "Not my girl?" she'd cried, panic in that velvet drawl. Telling Artie to move his arse, her almond eyes lit with fear. What in God's acre had made Harry file those runners so sharp?

Lucy helped drag the dory down to the ice. Children huddled, adults now too. Men kicking the snow. The boat was useless, little kids climbing in and pretending to row. Jewel had breathed in her ear that they'd come up, Samson and Mrs. Trott: "They can swim, you know." She'd pictured the sled gliding like a fish with red fins as Father Marcus arrived, announced by his collar in the bruised, dusky light; the woman with him, crying: the one who'd organized the raffle. People hugged her, then Mrs. Slauenwhite herself had appeared. Jewel's stomach growled, and Lucy tightened her arm around him, not looking as Artie shambled up, Boutilier, too. Shivering, he lit a cigarette, holding the match for Artie who roughed Jewel's sleeve, and told him to get his dad. *The more men, the quicker the search. Give the poor mother something to bury, at least.*

Above the sound of weeping, Father Marcus prayed. A look rippling over Jewel's face. "What about the chicken lady?" he'd wanted to know, and Artie'd grimaced, "That crazy old twat, she's down there too?" He'd whistled through his teeth, and said they'd better find her son; where the hell was he, that lunatic, Benny? Then Boutilier nudged Jewel, saying, "While you're at it, tell your old man I got a mouth organ he might like."

POOR OLD IDA UNRAVELLED like a sweater, bits and pieces of wool washing up here and there — though at first all that appeared was a mitten, on the spit near Artie's dock. But all that winter and into the spring it was hard not to think of the boy and her under the ice, the glitter of eyes like plankton. The currents broke things up, Harry said, but anything the tide didn't take, that spit would hook.

"So where *is* Samson?" Jewel had wanted to know.

Lucy couldn't help seeing *his* fingers curled around the sled's rope. "Safe now," she told him, "out of harm's reach." But where did you go, he nagged, once you were dead?

Harry, too, never knew when to stop. "Lobsters have a big feed," he'd told him, saying they especially liked faces.

Evil to speak that way of the dead, and for a whole week Jewel had woken up screaming. "It's just a dream," she'd soothed, over and over, but one night he started singing: *I have a little sister, peep peep peep, she wades the water deep deep deep. Climbs the mountain high high high. Poor little twat only got one eye!*

As for Ida, her hens pecked the snow and then each other till the ground was nothing but feathers, and as it thawed, girls invented a skipping rhyme that Jewel brought home.

Chicken lady, chicken lady
Whatcha gonna do?
Chicken lady, chicken lady
Looks like stew
One two three four
Count the chickens at her door
Five six seven eight
Bones by her inkbottle laid out straight

Chicken lady, chicken lady,
Make me some tea
Hush up hush up
Wash 'er out to sea

A small wonder no one set it to music.

WAITING BY THE NURSING station, a woman blinks when she sees them coming, Jewel lugging Harry's accordion. "That's some fancy suitcase," she remarks, as a nurse slips out from behind the desk, admiring the Don Noble's finish. Lucy's dusted and polished it to a sheen before letting them bring it.

"It's Pop's," Rebecca's voice ripples down the corridor. "Occupational therapy!" The nurse makes a face; they should be used to her by now. The hospital's become like home after all, a sterile, regimented home, with its film of cleanliness covering all the dirt and heartache settled in its corners. Just like in keeping house, though nobody says so, the fight for order is a losing battle. One still has to try; surely even Robert sees that.

"Come on, Bucky — smile!" Rebecca goads him. To quiet her, Lucy says that it's good enough he's come.

"Right," Jewel mutters, saying they had to bribe him with the car, as if she needs to know. Then he yammers at the boy about checking the oil.

"You'll try a tune for your grampa, won't you," she says softly as they creep into the room. Robert looks embarrassed, muttering *just because he plays guitar*. Rebecca propels him towards the bed, never mind that he's a foot taller than her and everyone else. Once a mother, always a mother, Lucy thinks; the same goes for a child, she tells herself, from a safe, almost watery distance.

"Should've heard him serenading Shirley," Rebecca moons.

He corrects her: "Sheryl, Ma."

Whatever, says Rebecca, rolling her eyes: his girlfriend.

"The latest attraction," Jewel smirks.

Greeting Harry, she hears herself call him *sweetie* again, peeling off her gloves. The weather's turned; it's definitely fall, and all of a sudden, too, giving a hard blue edge to everything. Carefully she smoothes Harry's brow and his eyes open, his good one mildly curious. She tells him it's Sunday; "Look, we're all here!"

That's right, Rebecca says: "Party central."

Harry's eye flashes, alarmed. Why the mass visitation? she imagines him thinking. What's the bloody occasion?

"Don't worry, Dad. It's not a wake." Every now and then, it's true, Jewel surprises her with his sense of humour. As she elbows him, a sound gurgles from Harry — a laugh? That eye of his lights up as Robert opens the glittery, lacquered case. Robert's hair, clean-looking today, reminds her of Shirley Temple's. Shaking it out of his eyes, he handles the instrument as if it's a dead animal. *What now?* his scowl says.

"'Yankee Doodle'? Give it a try, Buck," his mother jumps in. "That's pretty easy, isn't it?" He gives her a pained look, just like his dad at that age, but obliges, squeezing out a few wheezy notes. Harry's hand comes up, his finger trembling, motioning *down*.

"How's school, anyway, darling?" Lucy pipes up quickly. He's gone back, as far as she knows, for the time being. But a look yawns between Rebecca and Jewel.

"Peachy, Gran. Groovy," he drags out the word, his eyes darting. Lord knows what it's supposed to mean, that stunned expression; it makes her think of records. Maybe that's what he has in mind, putting one on instead of playing. His curls jiggle as he closes up the Don Noble; freshly washed, his hair's a pretty reddish gold. Just a bit more red and it would remind her of goldfish. "School's a blast," he sighs unexpectedly. "Like I just can't wait to get outta there," saying all he wants to do is travel. With Sheryl, she guesses.

"He wants to be on his own," Jewel mimics, as if the boy's already gone, not just from home, but to another city, saying what a deal he has, the run of the basement, the car whenever he pleases.

"The basement," Rebecca moans, fluffing her hair. "Elinor had a hell of a time down there."

"*Heck* of a time, Becky." Jewel looks at her and then at Lucy. Has she missed something? Either it's got lost in Rebecca's chatter, or she's getting old timer's disease.

"Who the devil is Elinor?" she has to ask.

Rebecca smiles, amused. "Benny's woman? Like I told you, Ma, she cleans? So she had a *heck* of time with Bucky's room. Lucky he wasn't —"

"Wouldn't trust that one as far as I could ..." Jewel perks right up. Nothing these two enjoy more than gossip! "Stole from her last employers, that's what I heard over at the store," he says, repeating what Mr. Jimmy told him, how the people had to let her go; wondering why no one pressed charges. "People get away with murder these days," and he gawks at Robert.

"Oh, just leave it," Rebecca blurts out, exasperated; who can blame her? Jewel can be a piece of work sometimes, looking for the worst. "Leave it," she says again, louder, batting her eyelids, "which is what I finally said, Ma, when she started on Bucky's carpet. Banana peels stuck to it, would you believe? And glue," and she demonstrates, pretending to pick some petrified gum off her chair. "'Seen a lot worse,' Elinor said. That family she worked for?" she eyeballs Jewel. "Pigs, I guess."

"Takes all kinds," he lobs right back. "You'd know, wouldn't you hon."

That curmudgeonly streak of his — it almost reminds Lucy of Harry's old crony, Edgar Boutilier, whom she'd rather forget. Was it something she did, raising him? When he and Rebecca go on like this, she'd like to knock their heads together the way Moe does with Larry and Curly on *The Three Stooges*. Still, she has to wonder about Rebecca, hiring that woman. Even if she were lily-white, good as all get-out, there's the real issue, bringing a stranger in to see one's dirt. If she had someone in to clean, glory, she'd have to kill herself making the place presentable first; otherwise, it'd be the same as hanging out her dirty Hannas. Not that she'd hire that woman, or anyone who lived that way, certainly not to keep house.

"Cleanliness *is* next to godliness" — it just jumps out of her, and now they're all looking, as if she does have old timer's disease. Really, it's the thought of germs and filth popping to the surface — what else was Robert hiding in his rat's nest, besides poems? — a monster mess taking over. A person could devote her life to wrestling dirt, and dirt would always win. So why not backburner cleanliness? Take a vacation from it. God himself probably wouldn't've minded a break from godliness at times.

Jewel grimaces at Rebecca, and she grimaces back; still Lucy can see that underneath it all they're in cahoots, taking everything that pops out of her mouth as if she means it exactly. The flat-earthers! If they'd been around in Columbus's day, they might well have told him, *Don't bother sailing.* But since he did, to take advantage of the salt out there, more than a few grains in the ocean! Just as she thinks it, something else pops out, but this time it's meant to tease them. "You'd think God has no sense of humour, you two," she chides, "the way you behave."

Only it's Robert who latches onto this, looking doubtful. "Yeah, Gran. A real funny guy. Where's the spot on *Laugh-In?*" At that, Harry's eye lights up; it's not her imagination.

Giggling, Rebecca says, "Well, speaking of the Bible," — had they been? — "Elinor's got this great book, *How to Clean Everything.* No shhi-sugar," she grins like a pumpkin, craning over, suddenly pushing Robert's curls back. "Ohmigod, what's on your neck?" His hand flies up to cover whatever it is, and he reddens, mumbling about mosquitoes. "This time of year?" His mom rolls her eyes, letting them rest on the ceiling fixture that resembles a lone headlight. "Well, maybe it's true," she says, apparently to herself. "It is pretty comical, a friend of Benny's being a cleaning lady. If you look at that boat."

"One big frigging cosmic joke," Robert says sagely, tugging up the collar of his ugly old army jacket, as if only just feeling the chill.

God in heaven, perhaps he's written a poem about it, this kid who'd go out in a blizzard without boots. Funny all right, till she pictures him hitchhiking through the Rockies in sock feet.

Eyeing him, Jewel mumbles something about Benny and tides and poo — "The ocean takes it away, I guess" — then, watching Rebecca, asks if Bucky's girlfriend's related to Dracula.

But Rebecca's not listening, her mind like a Timex under water, way offshore. "What'll they do in winter, you suppose," she says, "her and Benny in that floatin' outhouse?"

Calling them a pair of connivers, Jewel says not to worry, they'll take care of themselves, "Like on this thing on TV, right? How after the rest of us are gone, the bugs'll take over."

The likening of Benny and his friend to insects seems to perk Harry up even more. Not that Jewel or Rebecca notice when he rubs his head up and down against the pillow, nodding. Picking a bit of lint out of his hair, reminding herself of an ape, Lucy strokes his wrist. With any luck he'll see his show again, slot back in, comparing folks to critters. Enough speculating, though; a girl in a hairnet rolls in a cart full of trays. Dinner. Lifting a lid, Lucy picks up the spoon. The food's a mystery — greyish peas and fish mashed together? — the sight enough to drive people away. An excuse anyway, Robert shaking Harry's limp hand. When Jewel does the same, she tugs his sleeve, reminding him to take the accordion. Rebecca blows kisses, Harry's good eye following everybody out, like a fly on a lead, then fixing dully on his plate.

"Open sesame," she coaxes, and in the stuffy, sterile quiet — the smell of that dinner filling the room — he does what she says. And isn't he like a baby booby, some rare type of gannet? "Good dear, good," she pats his shoulder, saying keep it up and he'll soon be home.

Thirteen

THOUGH SHE'D DONE EVERYTHING possible to drill in the value of school, Jewel never took to it. Once, Sister Jerome made him write a hundred times: *I will not allow distractions to disrupt my pursuit of knowledge.* He'd swear at his homework; a girl would never have acted that way! More interested in dawdling, reading the paper one night he'd pointed at something. The prison was going to be used for storing ordnance. *In the event of tampering,* he'd read out, *a detonation of benzene would be catastrophic.* Her voice quavered, telling him to buckle down, get back to work. She wasn't surprised, only alarmed, when Sister phoned one day to say he'd disappeared before a test, had possibly escaped out the window and down a tree.

Through the cool June woods she'd searched, spying them below Boutiliers' hill, which was ablaze with dandelions. On the rocks, not one kid but two, flat on their bellies. Bare feet, and the backs of knees. A fishing pole propped between them, Jewel jigged the line and the girl squirmed, her laughter teasing, *You think babies come from* where? As Jewel scrambled up, weighing the rod, Lucy threatened him with a licking and no radio for a year. But he crouched, pulling, the pole bent back almost overhead; and as he pulled, something surfaced, streaming upwards. Fringed with eelgrass, wool a greeny blue, it was a scarf — *Samson's,* Lil's girl shrieked. Lucy slipped as Jewel unhooked it. Something moved under the yellowy water, a huge bug trapped in amber? Trailing seaweed, its eye sockets were empty.

Get Birdie, she'd heard herself holler, the pole riding a little wave. Before she could've stopped them, both children had seen. Flotsam, like a marble rolled down a hill, lost; the very worst, another child.

She waited till after the burial to deal with Jewel, who blamed their playing hooky on the girl. It was all her idea, he said, stealing the pole from Boutilier's shed. After that, she could barely stand to let him go swimming, hanging around to watch him cannonball off the rocks with the other kids. Something sickening about all that blue, and the thought of someone sinking in the drop-off, buried in water green as a cat's eye. But it didn't bother him. At home he kicked his wet trunks under the bed; once, when she went to retrieve them, a bottle rolled out, peat-coloured and foul with periwinkles stuck to it: one hundred-proof rum. A present for Dad — he was going to throw it back at first, he said — yelping, "It's payment to Mr. Boots, for losing his rod!" as she poured it down the toilet. Payment, my eye.

His dad was no help when it came to liquor, or any other parts of his education. What *was* Harry thinking that fall night before a math exam, when he asked Jewel to come along? Fishing, he said, in Artie's boat; not many more chances, almost November and dark as your arse by six. What would they possibly catch at night? she'd wanted to know, marching to the front room, expecting Harry to follow. But he'd stayed in the kitchen, telling Jewel she'd gone off, praying. Or holding a seance. "A what?" Jewel boomed, his voice having deepened that summer. His father wheezing with laughter, saying it was when people tried dragging dead spirits back. Then Jewel had asked what Sister meant by x equalling y; Harry answering that Artie would put his nuts in a sling if they kept him waiting.

She'd tried to stop them; she didn't like him dragging Jewel along. Harry nearly jumped down her throat, saying if it made her feel better, Artie and Lil *were* properly married; she had the rock to prove it. As if she gave a tinker's damn. They were going for a goddamn boat ride, Harry'd sighed, saying Lil got all out of joint if Artie saw too much of the boys, which was why he kept the boat way the hell over where he did. "Women, Jewel, they're all alike," he'd teased, saying Lil had better things to do than tag along.

A draught blew in as they left. Throwing coal on the fire, she'd imagined the flames were blue poppies, trying not to think of that woman rubbing against strangers like a cat. Then she'd stepped outside, the night moonless but starry: the sky a hat pricked with holes. Somewhere in the harbour a horn blew, and the wind rose. She should've been sleepy, having spent the day scouring. But the dark felt restless, alive, and going back for her coat, she'd wandered out to the gate, where Mrs. Chaddock stopped and her terrier sniffed Lucy's leg.

Back inside, she put on "A Good Man Is Hard to Find," the singer hiccupping through each thud till the record stopped. Then the radio played a drama about the Wild West. But when it ended, there was still no sign of them, and without knowing why, she'd dug out the rosary she'd squirrelled away. One *Hail Mary*, two *Hail Marys*: she'd worried the beads; even Jewel had started teasing that she prayed so much, wasn't it crying wolf?

She was on her way upstairs when they finally appeared. Harry's face had looked blanched, beads of sweat above his lip. He kept rubbing his cheeks. Jewel's eyes jumped, and as she went to hug him, there was a sourness — vomit? Harry shoved past to the kitchen; as she tightened her arms around Jewel, she heard him on the phone. Jewel slumped against her, such a big boy at twelve, already dwarfing her. It was Mr. Babineau, he'd whispered, Harry's voice drifting in: "No chance, sir. No, sir — I don't know what he was thinking. Enemies, sir?"

A thickness inside her, she'd crept upstairs, saying above the thud of her heart that she was off to bed. Jewel at her heels, staying by the door; she'd heard him rifling through the closet. When she got up, his Meccano was all over the floor. And noticing blood on his boots, she'd gone numb.

Harry let out a strangled sound at her touch, and in a dull voice blathered that they couldn't see a goddamn thing; there was a shot and Babs took it. "Babs," he called him, "like a bird picked off a wire."

They were right there, he kept saying, swallowing as if gagging; they'd seen the whole thing, and he'd told the Mounties everything he could, still they wanted more. Artie can't die, her mind had thrashed: who'd keep Lil? But Harry's bloodshot eye stared back, his whisper steely as he said they were in the boat, just offshore, hauling traps. She'd waited for him to start laughing, the whole thing a misplaced April Fool's joke. But he grabbed her arm and shook her, saying it'd been just them in the boat, him and the boy and Artie.

The constables looked too big for the kitchen, wanting a statement from Jewel too. Into the night she held vigil in the front room while he and Harry answered their questions. Worrying each bead of the rosary, she let Jewel's murmurs weave through scratchy prayers in her head. *He was lying there and stuff started coming out and Dad tried helping him but but but ...* Her shock turned to rage. Harry was responsible: he'd transplanted her flower into a bed of weeds, Artie and his crowd — while she'd stood by, failing to cut them down or root him out. *Be with me*, a voice inside had begged, as the policemen cuffed Harry and took him out. Then she'd run Jewel a bath; impossible to look at him without seeing something sweet and dark and awful leaking away. While he soaked, never mind the hour, she'd pillaged cupboard and closet, pitching things.

Dawn reddened the treetops by the time she'd piled Harry's gains outside, the profits of his poker winnings. Knick-knacks, trinkets, silverware, and even clothes still bearing tags. The clouds were the colour of watered-down blood — *the blood of Christ shed for sinners*, Father Marcus might've said, sinners like Harry. The clank of cutlery brought back that of handcuffs, and Harry's shamed, furtive look that of another prisoner, Mr. Heinemann, and, oh God, the perfume of spruce: her own sin.

Swollen-eyed, Jewel fished pieces of Meccano from the pile as she made a sign: *Free. Help yourself.* Then she'd ranted, blinking as if the ceiling might open: she wouldn't live with his scamming, not now, not any more. Though all this time, she'd never asked, and now he was up to his eyeballs in it. *Work bonuses*, my *eye*. She was through with his father, she told Jewel, did he hear? Through! All the while *Be with me, be with me* stinging her throat, and tears reddening the pimples on his cheeks, while she blazed inside like Christ's heart in the image relegated to the cellar by Harry. Tossing his picture, she cleaned mildew off hers and re-hung it. Raving that if Jewel took after his father, it would cut her in two, and she'd break his head, so help her Dinah! A girl would *never* pull this on her mother; thank the good Lord Harry's hadn't lived to see this! She'd never seen the likes! It took till nighttime to calm down. By then neighbours and strangers alike had cleared off the veranda, barely leaving a thing for the poor box. It went without saying, she later supposed, that Jewel wished he'd never seen the likes either, but by then she felt she'd lost him too.

HARRY COULD'VE BEEN CHARGED with trafficking, but wasn't. It was a murder after all; his part in the bootlegging was small potatoes. He was released in time for Artie's wake; "Aren't you glad to see me?" he wanted to know. In a daze, she'd watched Mrs. Chaddock raking leaves, and he'd said, "Fine then, if you're not gonna talk." Then he'd turned to Jewel, saying the funeral parlour wouldn't touch Artie, poor bugger; imagine.

"No bootleggers, alive or dead," she'd blurted out, just repeating what she'd heard at Mass. Then Harry'd looked around, distraught, as if the place had been robbed, asking what she'd done with his lamp, his tie-clip ... "See my finger, see my thumb? See my fist, you better run!" she'd sauced back, saying he'd better not expect her to go paying respects. She'd relented though, baking squares for the wake, never mind the thought of darkening Lil's door was worse than the butterflies she got before going to confession. Harry'd looked stunned but grateful.

When Lil staggered out to greet them, the air behind her was already blue with smoke. "Artie loved a party," she slurred, collapsing into the mob ringing the casket. It rested on sawhorses, Artie the centrepiece in a green suit with a red boutonniere, his head propped on a lacy pillow. His eyes glued shut, his cheeks powdered, and comb lines in his oiled hair, he seemed as solid in death as a hunk of granite. He didn't look like he was sleeping, Jewel had whispered accusingly. He hardly looked like a person, in fact, but more like a big grey doll — though dolls were usually trim and smiling, and he'd appeared to be clenching his teeth. Lil had raised her glass, her eyes wild and distracted, drool on her chin. "Jesus Murphy," she toasted Jewel drunkenly, "some tall isn't he? Almost a man, eh."

Lucy'd set the squares on the table, nudging aside bottles. Standing as near the door as possible while Harry helped himself, she studied the muddy roses hooked into the mat as a squabble drifted from the bedroom: kids fighting. "Eat, drink and be merry, all of youse," Lil crowed, tears glittering. "How 'bout a drink there, youngfella?" Jabbing at her eyes, she tottered to the ice box, handing Jewel a mug. Her mouth looked broken; then she'd leaned down and kissed Artie's cheek. His voice cracking, Jewel had asked after her daughter, who was with her gran again, apparently, and had been for a while. "Artie wasn't big on kids," Lil juddered, leaning into the scrawny man beside her, who set down his glass and patted her head.

"Clear out of there, you little buggers," somebody'd yelled, "so Missus can lay down," and as she staggered off to bed, they'd all gaped at the body soon to lie underground. Bedrock.

Ashes to ashes, Lucy imagined the priest intoning. *Lay up for yourselves not treasures on earth, where moth and rust consume, and thieves break in and steal, but the treasures of heaven.* Towering over the other kids, Jewel had looked ill.

Outside, Harry took her elbow, saying, "Don't let it go to your head, dolly, but those squares were your best batch yet." He winked at Jewel, but even in the dark his face looked sunken. Speaking into the wind, her heart a-flutter, she asked if they'd figured out who'd done it. Tripping on something, Jewel swore, and Harry sighed. Then something had snagged inside her: *Forgive us our trespasses, as we forgive those* ... It could've been Harry lying back there in that box. It was cold and it was late, and Jewel had school next day, but she stopped, leaning against a tree, and in spite of everything slid her arm round Harry, as Jewel griped about his missing penknife. Harry'd tugged her closer: "You know what they say, my son: spare the rod, spoil the child," and then, to her: "Dolly, you didn't just *give* the stuff away?"

THE DAY THE GOOD news comes, it takes them all by surprise. The hospital's done as much as it can for Harry; he'll soon be all hers. Rebecca makes dinner to celebrate, saying it's Lucy's last supper "as a swingin' single!" All the talk these days about "swinging" and "swingers" makes her think of gates and hinges needing grease — and the fence, which everyone else seems to have forgotten. Too cold now for painting.

Dinner's more than just an occasion to mark the end of this fall of falls. Rebecca's house has never looked tidier. To Lucy's surprise, there's another guest at the table, Robert's little friend. She doesn't look a bit happy to be here, Rebecca preening over her.

"Garlic bread, Shirley?"

Sheryl, Robert corrects. The main course is lasagna, which Rebecca's apparently made herself, her eyes glued to the girl carving a noodle into tinier and tinier pieces. "It's not that bad," Robert whispers, elbowing her. They could pass for brother and sister; the same glumness, and that untidiness that seems typical these days.

"So you're the traveller, Sheryl," Lucy ventures, just trying to be friendly, asking when she expects to be leaving. The girl gives Robert a blank look, and he shrugs, eyeing Lucy through his bangs, if that's what you'd call that mat. "Robert tells me ..." she tries again.

"*Who?*" Sheryl digs her little finger into his belly, swooping her eyes from his face to his lap. "*Bucky*, you mean?"

Lordie, she's fresh, Lucy thinks, refusing to look where she's looking. A girlfriend! It seems no time since he was four years old, watching *Maggie Muggins* while his mom was at work. That first old black-and-white TV a godsend — to Harry, certainly, who treated it the way most folks treated their Sunday best, especially when it came to others watching it. *Wibbit*, Robert would croak with glee when that freckle-faced Maggie came on, and Lucy'd race to get supper on. The sofa croaking, too, under his bouncing feet as he aimed the fireplace poker at Maggie's puppet friends, shooting them. They had such unlovable names: Big Bite Beaver and Greta Grub, and worst of all, Grandmother Frog. *I wanna stay with my Gwan Fwog*, he'd whine, clinging, when his mother came to pick him up. Once for a whole week he wouldn't eat his snack because her warty hands had made it. *Enough*, Harry'd hollered, stomping in from work, not too pleased to find his TV blaring goofy animal voices.

Rebecca's grin sends all this packing. She's being so chummy, as if Sheryl's her best friend. "Bucky's grampa's coming home tomorrow, did he tell you, darlin'?" Saying Sheryl's lasagna must be cold, and does she want it heated up? *Darlin'?* Lucy would no more have called Jewel's girlfriends *darlin'* than flown to the moon.

"What?" Sheryl says dully, her bottom lip hanging, a touchiness to her raccoon eyes. She's pretty enough, in a skittish, scrawny way; why does she wear all that war paint, Harry would call it, especially around her eyes? Lucy's forgotten her glasses, but even without them it looks garish, and doesn't fit, somehow, with Robert's back-to-nature talk of teepees, or is it wigwams? Heaven forbid, if Harry was here he'd get Sheryl to come closer, asking who had a knife so he could scrape off all that goop. "What's wrong with your grampa?" the girl finally asks Robert, pushing back her hair. It makes Lucy think of a pair of curtains, the way it's tucked behind her ears.

Robert just blinks, shoving his plate away, the lasagna licked clean, telling her she doesn't have to eat hers "or nothin'," if she's not hungry. Rebecca sniffs, eyeing Lucy's plate, saying she's eating like a bird. Now that would be something, wouldn't it? A bird would fly right out of here. That must be what Robert has in mind, when he pokes his guest — "Let's blow this joint, okay?" — and the two of them slouch off without being excused. Sheryl does take her plate with her; that's something, anyway. Maybe she'll set a good example? Girls can have a civilizing effect; some girls. But the prospect seems lost on Rebecca, whose attempts at gourmet have fallen flat.

Sighing morosely, she glowers at Jewel shovelling in seconds all the same, as if it's *his* last supper. Her voice grates when she asks Lucy about her plans. Plans? The bugger is, as Harry would say, she hasn't a clue. Now that it's almost here, Harry's release looms like the launch pad at Cape Canaveral. She's hardly able to think beyond pushing his wheelchair to the elevator and pressing *Down*. She's picked up a card for the nurses, though, and signed it: *In appreciation of your kind* (scratch) *loving* (scratch) *care*. I'll leave it on the desk, she thinks. "People do that," she murmurs aloud, and a noisy silence wells up, as if she's having another old timer's moment.

Across the table Jewel says, "What?"

But she's thinking of a bird again; the sleeves of her blue sweater are wings taking her off on a little *tore* somewhere: Peggy's Cove? Rebecca's too hung up on her food failure to notice, lamenting how everything was made from scratch. Never mind the tinny taste, thinks Lucy; if she were alone she'd spit into her serviette, or maybe even like Harry, into the sink.

"A holiday," she hears herself chirp to change the subject, as someone mentions dessert, Whip 'n' Chill. Rebecca brightens a bit, one reddish eyebrow arched, saying, yeah, yeah, after living apart for two months, it *would* be a holiday having Harry around again, wouldn't it. A regular honeymoon, Lucy wants to say, smiling back. So like Rebecca to put a brave, silly face on things. If there were more weight to it, she'd give her credit.

At least Jewel seems to know better, saying if it's too much looking after his father, they'll arrange something. Like putting someone out to pasture, she thinks, as simple as going on a date. The taste in her mouth turns acid; is it really only two months she's been on her own? "Your dad would never stand being in a home," she tells him the way she might've, once, to clean up his room.

"No digs like your own, I guess," Rebecca jumps in, looking around proudly. There are vacuum lines in the orange carpet, and one can actually see through the windows, the leafless view stretching across to the yacht club, the old decrepit prison.

"Amen to that," she nods, wiping her mouth delicately, never mind that the serviette is an old one, probably re-used. Hoping Rebecca will be just as delicate and take her plate. But then music blasts up suddenly, vibrations coming through the rungs of the chair. The drums remind her of Harry's carpentry. Jewel stares up at the ceiling, expecting it to snow dirt, but mysteriously the cobwebs have vanished, and abruptly the drumming stops, replaced by slow, plodding piano. It's not half bad, she thinks with a shock, it's almost musical; maybe Robert's growing up?

"Hey Jew," it sounds like when Rebecca sings along, eyeing Jewel with a faint smile. "The first song Elinor heard," she says, "when she came to town."

Here we go, thinks Lucy: more juiceless gossip. You'd think Rebecca was in love with the woman, the way she goes on: how Elinor took the train down, just last year, her first time out of the Valley. "Well, except when she was a kid," Rebecca interrupts herself, "if you can believe it," explaining how Elinor'd heard the song on the radio the last time she saw her brother, on and on, or whoever it was that drove her to the station. "Coltsfoot by the side of the road and 'Hey Jude' on the radio," Rebecca puts on a drawl, saying that's what the cleaning lady told her, picking up that album off the floor.

"When she was running away from the funny farm," Jewel snorts, more interested in the progress of the Whip 'n' Chill. No need to be nasty, Lucy wants to jab him, remembering how she'd threatened to put his head in a sling for being mean. But the thought of a song being named *Jude* warms her, especially for Robert's sake: the patron saint of hopeless cases, not that he would know. When the song ends, silence hums from the basement.

"Now what do you suppose those kids are up to?" she wonders aloud, not that she means anything by it.

But Rebecca grimaces, draining her cola, cola with something added. "Gawd, you don't want to know. The little slut," she adds, as if Lucy's not there, then leaning in so close that even without her glasses Lucy can see a crumb of mascara on her eyeball. "Swear on everything holy," she blinks, saying it scares the tar out of her, how easily Bucky's led. "The vagrancies of love," she sighs, blinking harder.

"Come on now, Becky," Jewel teases, making some remark about "self-defecating" humour. Stacking their plates, he goes and listens by the basement stairs — like a coon hound, his dad would say. He could stand to lose a few pounds, especially off his middle, she notices, thinking of his heart. It would do him good.

Then Rebecca gets up and listens too, muttering, "If that little tart gets up the stump, so help me Jewel, he'll never drive again."

As she tramps downstairs, Jewel says, "You didn't hear that, did you, Ma." Seconds later she reappears, her face blank. They're not in his room, she says, who knows where they went. She doesn't seem to notice Lucy clearing space for the dishes.

"You check the garage?" Jewel looks disgusted. "There's always the car."

"They'd think of that, wouldn't they." But Rebecca jingles some keys triumphantly, saying she beat them to it. "It's locked up tighter than a virgin's ... Sorry," she says, looking at Lucy. Why does she say things that demand apologies?

"You'll have to excuse Becky," Jewel jumps in, saying all it takes is one drink any more. And when hasn't she excused her? For years she has, so have they all. Washing a glass, Jewel sets it on the shelf, Rebecca's lapse and Robert and his girlfriend's as important as the leftover lasagna. They seem to have forgotten the dessert supposedly setting in the fridge, Rebecca suddenly digging through a drawer. Pushing aside a *Joy of Cooking* — *Cooking* crossed out and *Sex* penned in in childish printing — eventually she finds what she's looking for, a dog-eared tome: *How to Clean Everything*. Perhaps she really is turning over a new leaf?

Flipping pages, she points out remedies for every conceivable stain. "Remember my turquoise dress?" she enthuses. "Bacon fat on the sleeve?" But then she says it's not the book, but Elinor herself who's the whiz.

"Right," Jewel smirks sourly, peeling off a Rolaid, and as Rebecca elbows him, something slides from the pages. A clipping so yellow the print is blurred. "Lord Jesus, not a recipe," he kids. "Can you imagine that one cooking? 'Sewer-fed lobster.' Poor old Benny!"

Calling Jewel "Mr. Knee-jerk," Rebecca says that woman can do anything she puts her mind to.

"I guess she'd have to, wouldn't she, living that way." What else is there to say? With *him*, Lucy means, and *not married*, though she's careful to keep that under her tongue.

"Benjamin Trott, Esquire," Jewel pipes up; according to Bucky, that's what they call him at the yacht club.

"He's not a member?" Lucy asks; it's a joke, for pity's sake, but neither he nor Rebecca laugh. Maybe it's true that senility's a second childhood? Perish the thought.

"No, Ma," Rebecca says absently, perusing the clipping. Reminding her that Bucky works at the club after school, "minding things." Napping in the cells, in other words, Jewel says.

But Rebecca lets that one by, preoccupied. "The poor creature," she murmurs, admitting that the last time Elinor came to clean, she'd let her use the bathtub. It can't be a picnic, she sniffs, living without conveniences. Jewel just mumbles how Benny and his lady friend could star in a "creature feature," whatever that is. Lucy's still digesting the thought of a stranger in their tub. Rebecca gives him a shove, squinting at the clipping's dingy photo. "Jesus — that's her?" she says, and peering close, Lucy can just make out a girl in a pale dress sitting on an old man's knee, a cranky-looking woman and a young man posing behind them.

"'The Van Buskirk family,'" Rebecca reads out painfully; how did she make it through high school? "'On their farm near Kentville. John Van Buskirk Sr. died this week, leaving ...' Verrry interesting," she interrupts herself, mimicking that German soldier on *Laugh-In*. "Frigging apple *barons*, 'Van Buskirk and Son Orchards *Limited*,'" she says, lifting her eyebrows, marvelling that Elinor wasn't just talking through her hat.

"So ring my chimes," Jewel says flatly, more of that "hip" lingo, as if he and Rebecca are speaking in code. Just then, Robert and his girlfriend slither in from outdoors, and without a word troop downstairs, a smell trailing them. It reminds Lucy of something burned in a ditch, of spring, and people burning lawns. Odd, with winter so close.

Giving Jewel the eye, Rebecca follows them, the basement door clicking quietly behind her. Jewel fidgets, asking if she'd like tea, then opening the fridge and closing it quickly, but not before she's glimpsed dessert, a bowlful of something soupy, a grasshopper green. Another small disaster, one that fills her with a childish disappointment. She wishes Jewel would dish some out anyway; there's nothing urging her home, back to the bunker, as Harry would say. But while the tea steeps Jewel disappears, and perching on a tipsy stool she opens the cleaning book. Without her glasses, the recipes, if that's what you call them, are in print so small they're not much good, but there's the clipping, the headline large enough. *Died suddenly at home. Found in barn* ... and the date, smudged and barely readable: November, 1929? *Trouble in the apple industry*; her eyes co-operate just enough. Something about the market crash, words that summon a building collapsing — God above, she imagines the glass-roofed North Street station in the Explosion, shards raining down, only on vegetables and fruit.

"What's so in'eresting?" Jewel startles her. He seems worked up, slapping at his pockets — is he that hooked on those cigarettes? But then he checks his wallet.

Squinting, she scrutinizes the photo, that stern-looking family. There's something almost bovine about the couple, especially the mother. No hint of what illness might've taken the father. The girl — she looks thirteen or fourteen — has a sullenness about her, that teenaged chippiness quite obvious even without her glasses. A handful, likely; no wonder the mother looks weaned on a ... "Pickle," she sighs, as Jewel slides a cup towards her, giving her a stare and asking what on earth they're doing downstairs, reading tea leaves?

"Pardon?" she says. Then she bites her tongue; it doesn't take a genius to imagine a showdown, and a few minutes later the girl comes skulking upstairs, leaving without so much as goodbye or thanks for supper. Rebecca appears, looking flustered, and Jewel lets out a sigh that sounds as if he's been holding it in for months.

"I knew it," he tells her, like a judge on the stories pounding his gavel, "the twenty bucks on my dresser? Poof, *gone.*"

Fourteen

JUST AFTER LUNCH, THE ambulance surrenders Harry. Jewel's taken the day off work, helping to get things ready. Rebecca's tied a yellow balloon to the tree outside, a poor colour choice given the memory of that bag under the hospital bed. Still, it reminds Lucy of the day they brought Robert home from the hospital when he was just a mite, never mind how unceremoniously Harry is deposited upstairs. But the room is cheery, the Don Noble and the TV positioned so he can see both from the bed. The nurses have given tips and instructions to turn him every couple of hours, and feed him slowly so he won't choke. Jewel's old room, her sewing room, has been crammed with waterproof pads and aids: a bedpan, wheelchair, walker, crutches. Could it be that Jewel's gone overboard?

"Let's be optimistic," he says quietly as they stand back, watching the medics place Harry between the sheets. She should be happy, but this moment she's been hoping for stirs up panic as raw as the feeling that'd crawled through her years ago in that church basement, as she coaxed Jewel to take the nipple. Now what? Now that he was here, how would she manage? But like a gift, now that it's given, how can she even think about sending it back? Ashamed, she busily plumps pillows, kisses his chilly forehead, welcoming him home. Maybe Jewel feels it too, the weight of what's ahead? Not Rebecca, though, flitting around arranging things. Whatever's got into her lately has taken hold as firmly as the Yanks claiming the moon! As Lucy imagines the astronauts planting their flag, Harry's eye flashes a look of apology, as if it hasn't yet taken in the others, only her. *You've got the shitty end of the stick, dolly*, it seems to say. Then his lips fumble: a moan, a bit of drool — gobbledygook — and finally a syllable: "Lucsch?"

Rebecca sets down some Vaseline, looking a little shocked, maybe even dismayed. None of this seemed quite so alien, so difficult, in the hospital. Jewel rushes to smooth things over, asking Harry what more he could ask, having the best nurses in town. "Old man," he calls him, eyeing Lucy; if his father weren't so frail, she could imagine Jewel punching his shoulder. It makes her blush when Harry rubs his head up and down enthusiastically. Gratefully. *That's my dolly*, she imagines him saying, if he could talk. *Like a dog with a bone.* At least he's still in there somewhere, isn't he?

Rebecca vanishes; they hear her down in the kitchen rustling something up. Oh, Lord. She comes back with food on a plate, sticky buns that are store-bought, thank God, but of a texture that wads and would block an airway in a second, the voices of a dozen nurses seem to holler. Just as Harry sucks and smacks at his, Lucy, terrified, reaches into his mouth and pulls it out, and he almost looks like he'll cry. *Stealing candy from a baby*, says Rebecca's stare. She and Jewel have the tact, at least, to leave before Lucy has to manage supper.

As she follows the mimeographed instructions — a life sentence of soup and soft foods? — the kitchen's drafty silence is a comfort: the way the Earth must've felt to Mr. Armstrong and Mr. Aldrin stepping back on it. Carrying Harry's meal up on a tray, she tries to look at the plate as, well, a relief map, like Robert made once for geography, with a lot of mounded brown and green, of papier mâché. At the sight of it, half of Harry's lip curls, an effort at a smile. *Nothin' like real food, dolly. A fella oughta take out insurance, eating that hospital crud*, she imagines him joking. Spooning small bites of hill and dirt into his opened mouth, she fancies herself a mother booby, and him a chick that's tumbled from the nest but managed to fly back up. Yes, there's something miraculous and only good about hope come home to roost, rewarded, and for a fleeting moment she feels relief sweet as mashed carrots.

Later, though, bathing him is a different story, the basin balanced on her side of the jiggling mattress. It's like bathing an overgrown, helpless infant as she draws the cloth over his neck where food has dribbled, and between his fingers, then tenderly pats him dry. If there's one thing she's learned, it's not to think beyond the chore in front of her. Positioning the bedpan, she makes sure the TV is good and loud, though, the way she'd turn up *Maggie Muggins* if Robert got whiny. Emptying it, to keep from gagging, she thinks of Robert as a baby, and then Jewel — and, unwittingly, of the baby before him. How had she managed, when she hadn't been much more than a girl herself, still too young to appreciate that babies grew up? How did any mother manage, let alone the mothers of babies who didn't, or couldn't? But then *Untamed World* comes on, a gift from the airwaves. She fixes Harry's pillows, making him comfy as a wildebeest charges across the Serengeti. "Who's that, dear?" she nudges him, her voice almost bubbling over with cheer. But when she glances over, he's asleep.

That night he's a deadweight beside her, that right arm of his a withered branch that would just as well fall or get snapped off by wind. She doesn't sleep a wink watching the clock, those instructions ticking through her, when or when not to turn him. "Upsy-daisy," she grunts, rolling him onto his other side. It's like moving a boulder, the effort eating her strength. But, with whatever strength's left over, she presses her palm to his cheek in place of a kiss, and closes her eyes. Wanting to nestle against him, but afraid to. For he smells wrong, of starch and antiseptic and pee laced with chemicals. Like a vehicle, not new but passed off as reconditioned — strike her dead for thinking such a thing! But watching a real car's lights trace the ceiling, she listens to him breathe, the sound more laboured than any snore, and letting her toes touch his, feels herself melt at last into the mattress and what Rebecca would call an "airy-fairy" normal. The stuff of the stories. *Goodnight, my darling. Sweet dreams.*

How can it be, having Harry present and yet *not*, not the old Harry, anyway? The lights on, as Jewel would say, but nobody home. She should be used to it, his *there* and *not-thereness*; Lord knows she's had practice. Not that practice helps, when it's as if she's been stowed in one drawer, and Harry in another, which wasn't so bad, as long as one knew the other was safe. *A tisket, a tasket*, the clock's ticking, monotonous as a child's chant, finally draws her under. *A green and yellow basket.* A basket full of weeds, the thought presses down; and she imagines coltsfoot in a ditch and Harry's snore as the idling of a truck.

HER HEART HAD JACKHAMMERED, seeing Jewel off. Her boy, her baby, so tall and skinny, the uniform buckled at his waist: he'd been just three days past his twenty-second birthday. The scratch of wool against her cheek, the smell of damp khaki — *kayaki*, Rebecca would've called it, had she been around back then. Anyway, it was like kissing a giraffe goodbye. *Our soldier*: pride had pricked at her, she and Harry waving in the December drizzle, bereft. They could've at least had a band, sending the boys off. No "Auld Lang Syne" or "Roll Out the Barrel": the stuff of the first war, and of newsreels. But a spectacle would've killed her.

Maybe it was the cold, but Jewel's face had looked beaky as he marched up the gangplank. They watched till all they could see was his peaked cap. Brass, pipes, a bit of ceremony would have been in order, but even Jewel himself had tried to keep the sailing a secret. "God Save the King," Harry'd hummed quietly, muttering God save them all from that fruitcake in Europe with the moustache and bad haircut. What was it about those Jerries? he'd wanted to know, "And God, where's *he* at?" Don't blame him, she'd said. They'd dabbed at their eyes; tears just made it harder. As the ship's whistle blew, Harry's fingers had tightened around hers, her boxy little purse bumping him. She'd made herself think about canning, preserving. Their last few moments: the warmth of Jewel's cheek, the smell of tobacco and boot grease. *So long, Ma! Auf Wiedersehen*. Harry's *See ya* the same as sending him off after Sunday dinner.

She'd watched him disappear in a blizzard of faces. Breathing in the stink of bilge, she'd stared at the pier as Harry gulped, What a beautiful boat, the *Empress of Britain*. Straightening her pillbox hat for her, humming "We'll Meet Again" as the ship slipped from her moorings. The engines' shudder the shudder of Lucy's heart, which Harry'd warned Jewel not to break, like telling the Jerries to go decorate tannenbaums. The army was better than the navy or the air force, he tried to cheer her, as the *Empress* slid out into the foggy dark, a line of foam breaking from her. The shapes of more ships moving by, spirits rumbling in the night, a convoy. *In the name of the Father, and of the Son, and of the Holy Ghost*, she'd crossed herself. The more the merrier, Harry'd joked. As though all those young fellas were off on a trip, just to see the world.

As they tooled up from the docks in the new-ish Plymouth, they saw sailors reeling everywhere, never mind it was the middle of the night. Crossing town, Harry zipped past their street and St. Columba's, the prison and Dunphy's, the dancehall somebody'd thrown up near Deadman's. If they raced, they'd see the ships going out; never mind that he could barely see to drive, with the fog and not a light anywhere with the blackout. Slow down, she'd said. Any slower and a dog could piss on the tires, he'd answered, admitting, though, that without Jewel around it'd be "some jeezly quiet." Compared to the sickness in her heart, maybe. Except for the two weeks Jewel had come home after quitting work and enlisting, they'd forged a routine, she and Harry, based on quiet. And it wasn't as if Jewel had hung around; he'd whooped it up, God knows where or what habits he'd formed at Black's Shipping, and rooming downtown. *I'm working*, his excuse every time they'd asked him to supper. Sure, Harry'd said, a single guy and wartime in a town that was a hooker's heaven — as if Artie Babineau were a ventriloquist six feet under. But war prospered sin, Father Marcus declared every week: look around.

Harry downshifting for the next cove, the harbour'd opened before them, and they'd cut down a lane hugging the cliff. Not so much as a candle flickering from a window as the "arse end" of the convoy slid past the submarine net, making good time, Harry observed. The drizzle silver-plated everything as a corvette cleared the gate boats anchored there manning the net. In daylight they reminded her of Christmas ornaments, one green and one red, or two sitting ducks. "You can take the kid outta Hellifax, but you can't take the Hellifax outta him," Harry joked, to comfort her. "Don't even think about it," he'd said, meaning the U-boats lurking at the harbour mouth with their torpedoes. But as the last ship disappeared she'd prayed aloud, not caring what he thought. *God have mercy*, she'd told the void that was like water rising, displacing them both. *On my boy, and everyone else's.* Impossible not to imagine fire, and the frigid black sea filling lungs and sinking them all to the bottom.

Good things come to those that wait, the priest never quit saying, and business boomed at the shipyards, Harry working overtime repairing damage done by the Jerries. She had the house to tend, he reminded her, as if her war effort were reclaiming the space Jewel had so briefly filled. "You get in a knot every time the kid comes and goes," he said, and he was right. But time stalled around them like a ship in reverse, forget that having Jewel underfoot those couple of weeks had been awkward. *Who needs the Jerries when they've got you, Ma?* Once, he'd come home near dawn, and she'd woken to the sound of the sofa squeaking like a jiggled pram. That's when she'd found out about Mona: nothing serious, just a lark, he'd said.

"Seeing anyone?" she'd grilled him, before he'd moved back home, and he'd said there was Mr. Black, the boss, and his secretary who weighed two hundred pounds wet, not counting her moustache. Then Harry'd nosed in, saying all girls were after was a meal ticket. She'd nearly dropped the teapot when Mona came to meet them. No bigger than a minute, she had starry eyes and a blue sweater so tight her ribs showed. But she'd helped with the dishes, and there was something sweet about her sharp face. Jewel had made them all squeeze together while he snapped a picture. *Cheddah*, Mona said instead of *cheese*. She worked at the tobacconist's next door to Black's, and knew who smoked what. Jewel had taken Mona dancing at the new place by Deadman's, but later, Lucy'd woken to hear him retching. So much for a steadying influence.

But as the weeks dragged after his departure, she thought fondly of Mona, and once, from a tram, spotted a look-alike. The street was choked with sailors and girls, and, beelining to Eaton's, Lucy'd lost sight of her. Blackout curtains were on special, a necessity, but a dismal green.

She was about to leave when a brassy voice called out, "Looking for something, Missus?" A far cry from Mona, the gal seemed familiar. Fingering cheap fabric, Lucy couldn't help staring; it had been an age — ten years? — since she'd seen her. She'd grown by a foot, but had the same catty grin, though her hair was slate-coloured, and wasn't Lil's daughter a strawberry blonde? "Just looking," she'd said, smiling faintly, and couldn't help checking for a ring.

But the girl persisted — she had things to learn about serving customers — saying, "You're Jewel's mom, right?" and asking where he was. As if the bags under Lucy's eyes weren't telling enough.

Loose lips sink ships, she'd thought, and asked if people were actually buying these curtains, even as the image of the *Empress* leaving the jetty crowded in.

"Fugly as sin, aren't they?" the girl joked, "some friggin' ugly."

A minor thing if Jerry buzzed overhead, she'd answered quickly, buying six pairs.

The curtains spoiled the look of the front room, but it was best to be on the safe side — of what, though, she'd wondered; what could be worse than waiting? Every week she wrote, packing shoe-boxes with Hershey bars and cookies. Jewel wrote back, describing buddies he'd made, how the food stank and the showers, when they got them, were freezing. Reading around the crossed-out bits, she'd composed a fuzzy picture for herself of young fellas touring around, carousing as they would at home. Sometimes Jewel gave details, like the Jerry car they commandeered, rigging a tank to its engine to heat water. Travelogues with the place names inked out, his letters. Once he mentioned a tank burning, but then it was on to the next village.

In spring he mentioned apple blossoms, the letter arriving while she cleaned house, a salt breeze swinging in and out of the opened windows. In the note that came months later he discussed chocolate; she was weeding the garden when the postman stopped. *Love*, Jewel signed it, the rest saying precious little.

Months, and a year, and another year crawled by. A letter here, a letter there. Leaves to London. Pubs. Then Paris. Shifting details, from food to slit trenches and hundred pounders. "It's only lingo," Harry'd tried to soothe her. Words like *Brits* and *Yanks* were crossed out, the censor's hand sometimes unsteady. *Dont worry*, Jewel wrote, his punctuation gone to the dogs. Reading of the war in the paper, the endless bombings and sinkings, she'd dreamed of his baby face, features blending into those of the child she'd lost. Like a portrait captive inside a locket. *Dont worry.*

She prayed the rosary first thing each morning, last thing each night — and Wednesdays at noon, stretched out in the cellar. Weekly air raid drill, the signal and its routine old hat after a while. Still, she had to stop what she was doing — peeling an egg, rinsing a pot — to go and flatten herself to the concrete. Lying there that first Wednesday, Jewel's absence an open wound, she'd focused on Harry's tools, then remembered Mr. Heinemann's note deep in the wall. She'd almost wanted to die, suddenly: the casualty of a Luftwaffe bomb. It could happen, people said, though at night they just drew the curtains as usual and went to bed. But a ship was sunk off Sambro; this could've been England, Harry said, as if the walls of the world were crumbling. Waiting for the siren's whine to stop, she'd imagine soldiers with swastikas on their sleeves climbing in the windows.

When Harry didn't have the radio blaring, she played the Victrola, jumping at each bump. Nervous Nellie, he called her. If Jewel came back in one piece, she'd have Harry buy a new one, but in the meantime they'd wait. *Don't tempt fate*, Father Marcus said. What good, a new anything, without Jewel there with them? She'd thought along the lines of the priest's advice, as in giving up chocolate for Lent, or awaiting the Second Coming: keep busy, but not too busy. The records' bumps kept her on her toes. But one steamy night the spring had broken for good, and then time really dragged, with just the radio and nothing anyone would want to hear. The shipyards working round the clock, Harry was on call constantly, even with girls replacing men gone off to fight. Mrs. Chaddock had a niece with her welder's papers; but then Mrs. Chaddock also had stories about U-boat crews wading ashore for beer and a night out. Maybe Mona had traded her cashier job for something mannish? Jewel's latest letter said she'd married the receiver at Black's. No accounting. And suddenly no chance, either, of buying a new Victrola, not for love or money, even if she'd wanted one, every spring and screw funnelled into war. Jewel's letters had grown glum, full of crossed-out lines, Harry often at work when she opened them.

"Don't wait up," he'd said, one muggy evening, heading off to Dunphy's.

How could she stand to be alone? The Arm was flat as a cookie sheet as she rounded the cove, Jewel's latest note in the pocket of her good dress, one with blue roses and a twirling skirt — pretty, though it didn't do much for her waist. By the time she found the trail through the woods, she'd felt quite wilted. Queer place for a dance-hall, even Harry said, stuck out on that swampy spit. Through the trees had loomed the ruins of Babineau's dock, and across the channel the empty jail, munitions moved to a depot on the Basin. The trail cut to a rocky path, the glide of a clarinet drifting closer. *Dunphy's Social Club*, said the sign tacked to a tree; *Dunnuttin's*, somebody'd dribbled in red paint. Lounging outside, a group passed a bottle, someone giggling at Lucy's dress.

Inside, the clarinet had given way to tinny piano. A lady with yellow hair took Lucy's money, stamped her hand. Oh, God, she'd thought, hoping no one from St. Columba's appeared. At one end of the dance floor was a stage and at the other a counter, girls hogging chairs along the walls, while onstage a man bashed at the keys. It must've taken some doing, getting a piano there. The air oozed liquor, which had made her wonder about complaints in the paper about nowhere to drink. The Mounties would've had a field day, stumbling on this place; she felt dirty just walking in.

As the pianist banged his way through "Jeepers Creepers," sure enough, she'd spied Harry clapping along. He was sitting with someone; Lucy could just see her hair and doughy shoulders, and they were passing something between them. He'd leaned close enough to kiss the woman's cheek. Then a gal shimmied past with a sailor: Lil's daughter in a dress with straps that cut into her flesh, and with her, two others in bright red lipstick. A flotilla of skin and flimsy cotton, they'd swept Harry up and he'd laughed, tucking the bottle under his arm. Then Lil, none other than herself, had turned unsteadily, winking. "Oh shit," he'd murmured, spying her — sloshing liquor as she approached. "At least you're not drinking by your lonesome," Lucy'd said, feeling stung, and wanting him to feel that way too. But he'd caught at her arm, offering her a sip and blathering that he was helping Lil out. "Sure you were," she'd said, her voice icy, the mugginess a slap as he followed her outside, shoving the mickey into his pocket. *It's nothing, dolly — I can explain*, he kept saying, as the darkening woods closed in. *Explain away*. She'd fled up the path, stumbling over roots as the trail steepened, Harry breathing behind her. They found themselves on the top of Deadman's, the Arm shushing below. Dampness rose up through the bushes, carrying the funk of dead leaves and the spongy earth underfoot. To weasel out of the spot he was in, Harry brought up Artie's stories, about the dead buried there in unmarked graves. "Yankees, Frogs, slaves; maybe even the odd Kraut," he said, his laugh a little desperate, "prisoners of war, hundreds of 'em. Undesirables." Like the Marryatts? she'd asked.

Moonlight groped through the pines as he tipped back the bottle. A prickly feeling had climbed her neck, then embraced her, a chilly hug, and watching her, he'd said how the place gave him the creeps. It wasn't as though he quelled her jealousy, her perfectly reasonable disgust, but suddenly the chill had made Lil a fly in the ointment. All she'd wanted was the safety of the veranda, to sit watching moths bump the light. For something Father Marcus said had come back, about thin places, places like this, burial grounds and near water, where the spirits of the dead hovered, lingering. Never mind whose bones moldered underfoot. Then Harry'd grinned, losing his baleful look. A twig snapped; she'd heard it too. Rustling, giggling, then breathing; and through the bushes a flash of cotton. A sailor, probably, and bare arms in the moonlight: Lil's girl?

AS THE WAR DRAGGED on, the foghorns droned nothingness — and for months the weather stayed poor. Sometimes it seemed she herself was smoke threading over water, or a mournful wail crossing grey ocean. Whenever the phone rang she steeled herself. Once it was Father Marcus asking if she could help with the Christmas campaign. Christmas an insult, *campaign* viciously loaded. No idea where Jewel might be, she'd forwarded his parcels to a post box in Britain. The return address "An East Coast Port," though anyone with half a brain knew: Hellifax. It was the holy season, Father reminded her, and there was a widow in need in the Grounds.

"You might take comfort helping the needy," he'd said, reminding her that God remembered those who remembered others. That, according to St. Francis, the reward was not to be loved, as to love. Herr Heinemann had crept to mind; apple cake, and bits of Harry's clothing. An eye for an eye, or tit for tat? If only it were so: just desserts for selfless acts. But being middle-aged, forty-two, she wasn't stupid; she knew by now that things didn't work that way, rewards a matter of grace, not a ledger.

The priest asked her to deliver something, a shoebox; the league had made up dozens for servicemen, to which she'd contributed. Toothpaste, candy, homemade socks; too bad knitting left time to think. Clearing his throat, Father wondered if there'd been any word. "Not a peep," she'd said quietly, and he'd told her that God was steadfast in mercy, and she mustn't lose faith. But then one of his sermons reared itself, about loving thy neighbour, which really meant loving thy enemy. "Remember this poor, lost soul," he'd coaxed, adding that all were brothers and sisters in Christ. His direc-tions confirmed her suspicions; never mind that the poor widow had a daughter. Old Mrs. Slauenwhite's hands shook as she handed over a box and some food. Palsy had locked in her frown, more or less permanent after she'd lost her grandson. "Ah, Missus! Better you than me," she said.

Wet snow blanketed the steps, and no one answered when Lucy knocked. A window was broken, an overcoat stuffed against it. A bottle rolled as she let herself in; she could see her breath. "Lily?" Her call was met by a groan from the room where kids had fought at Artie's wake, Lil's sunken eyes peering up from above the filthy quilt. "Look what the cat's drug in. What the Jesus do *you* want?" she'd slurred bitterly, asking if Lucy's hubby had sent her, or what? The stink was awful: sickness and rot. As Lucy set the parcels down, Lil grabbed at her, her fingers half-frozen. How much easier to have pried them away, and run. "Nobody home," she could've lied; but the priest's voice intervened: *You win hearts by feeding stomachs. Win-ning hearts for Christ is* the *reward.*

Picking at some turkey, Lil had retched, vomit decorating the quilt. Mocking her for being "a good sport" and calling Harry "one lucky bastard, a darlin'," saying they deserved each other, he and Lucy. She'd wiped her mouth, staring at the peeling wallpaper, and accused him of being timid. "Got the balls of a hamster," she laughed raggedly. "Wouldn't know what to do if a woman come up and bit him on the arse!" Lucy'd wanted to spit, but then Lil had said, "But *you* now, Missus, far's he's concerned, the sun sets on *yours*," and that the last thing anyone needed was charity and Lucy's type coming around. "Fish stinks after a while," she'd choked, "so *git.*" Lucy didn't stop to slide the plate into the icebox, leaving the shoebox on the floor. Feeling sick, she'd hurried through the slush, then thought of the daughter. She'd phone her at work, what anyone would do under the circumstances. No matter what, Lil was her mother. Like mother, like daughter? But when she got home, a letter was waiting, the postmark illegible, but she'd have known the writing anywhere.

Dear Ma,
    Landed o.k. in ▓▓▓▓▓ *hours crossing, sick as a dog, no sea-legs till* ▓▓. *Nice digs though. Nice view from* ▓▓, *as you can see in the snaps, looks a bit like* ▓▓▓▓. *Ha ha. Why go far when anything a guy could want is in his own* ▓▓▓▓. *Well. Got to march. So long for* ▓▓, *say hi to dad & don't worry, be seeing youse.*
    Yours truly, J xox

Shaking the empty envelope, frantically she checked inside. If he'd sent pictures, they were long gone.

THAT SPRING AN OBIT ran in the *Herald*: Lily Jean Marryatt. Forty-eight years old, daughter of the late Erma; survived by ... no visitation, by request. *Earnestly, tenderly, Jesus is calling, calling oh sinner come home.* Harry's step lightened, somehow. Not long after, she was getting breakfast when the paper thwacked the step; the boy had a habit of winging it. *Normandy Invaded!* the headline blared. The eggs going cold, Harry'd gripped her shoulder, mumbling that since they hadn't heard otherwise, things had to be all right. If not, wouldn't they know?

Time had hummed then like the wires, a buzzing dread that woke her at night and made her clammy. Once, in the wee hours she'd found Harry on the porch in his pajamas. He had an appointment at the eye doctor's next morning for a cleaning and polishing. In the moonlight his good eye had looked wet, and he'd muttered about feeling poorly, and why bother? An eye or a Victrola, what did anything matter, when your boy was absent? Neither had been able to say *missing*.

Then she'd dreamed of Jewel stopping by a river, water flowing green and opaque. Squatting on a rock, he'd splashed his face, then peeled off his uniform like a skin. A shield of lindens towered all around. Something black and white drifted by, a cow, and a uniform with red on the sleeve. He turned sharply, and it was as if she were there, too. Looking her in the eye, he opened his mouth: "Hey, Ma!" As she waved, an arm moved behind him, a helmet like a potty. Below its brim the Jerry's face bore a mark. A tattoo: three blue upside-down commas. The face was Franz Heinemann's. As the bayonet lifted, she tried to scream, tried to move her arm, but it was wooden. Somehow Jewel turned, his boot sinking in mud, and a scuffle started.

Not the water, she tried to warn him, but no sound would come out. The Jerry drove his bayonet — the movement slow as salt threading through an egg timer — but Jewel slid and spun. They were Errol Flynn and Basil Rathbone, Robin Hood and Guy of Gisbourne, sword-fighting, thrusting, parrying. Suddenly Jewel was a little boy, and the Jerry lurched. A triangle of blood blooming in his chest, and his face becoming rock, and as he gave one last thrust, lunging, his soleless boot skidded. Curling life into his fist — like the workings of a watch: first steps, words, day at school, that run-in with the Mounties, and his look on the jetty that drizzly day — Jewel blindsided the blond-stubbled jaw, sent the man reeling into the silent current.

A teenage girl with a face like hers and dandelions in her hair hid like a frog in the rushes, and let out a croak. As the enemy thrashed, Jewel thrust his bayonet. Heinemann's mouth opened, gasping, and in the dream she could see inside — the pink surprise of a tongue — and even understand. *Hilfen mich?* Useless syllables dangling over the river as it netted him. One last glimpse before his clothes pulled him under: his face was another child's, the Slauenwhite boy's. The helmet spinning away a tortoise shell. The tortoise and the hare, as the fellow bobbed a final time, the air knit with spray.

A yellow wind stirred the reeds as the river sucked, and overhead a bird tweeted. *Wir kampfen bis wir siegen?* Somehow it made sense: we fight till we win. Picking up his shirt and boots, turning his back, Jewel slipped through the lindens, and she was the bird watching over as he ran.

The next morning, as soon as she woke she wrote to him, quoting the twenty-first Psalm: *The Lord is thy shepherd, don't forget.* She omitted the part about the valley in the shadow of death, launching instead into his father's activities. *He's considering a new accordion; maybe the fiddle fever is waning?* The notion had given her a tiny jolt of pleasure. *When we met, he was quite the musician — before his fiddling, and raising Cain, ha ha!* Humming Vera Lynn, she'd crossed out that last bit, trying not to imagine him lying in a trench, or wading through gunfire. *Our Father,* she'd whispered, sealing the envelope before Harry appeared, rosining his bow.

Posting the letter was like plugging her nose and jumping off a rock. She'd imagined it riding the sea in a convoy, a candy heart in the belly of a destroyer. Crossing paths with one from him some-where in mid-Atlantic, surviving wolf packs and waves.

THEN, ONE FREEZING MARCH day, a letter had arrived for Harry, postmarked Delmenhorst. *Delmenhorst?* Resisting the urge to open it, she'd called him at work and he had her read it over the phone.

Dear Dad,
Up to my knees in blood shit & corruption. Bremen, you know: the place with musicians? Put the boots to Jerry, sleeping outside all winter. Ma's chocolate bars are great, the boys trade for smokes. You'd think you hit the jackpot here, cellars full of cash. Arse wipe's about it. They say the Jerries are whupped. Tell Ma I dream about her pie. Guess what passes for coffee? Weeds by the road. Went to some fella's house and his wife brewed some up. The Jerries are done for.
Your son always, Jewel

Father Marcus's eyes were grave but detached as he pressed the host to her tongue that Sunday. *Corpus Christi.* A tiny, perfect moon, sticky as a postage stamp. *The bread of heaven.* She'd let it melt on her palate. *Blood of Christ, shed for you.* Then Mrs. Slauenwhite had corralled her; they were starting early on the raffle, looking for donations. The prize was a quilt embroidered with the names of all the parish boys who'd enlisted, every wife and mother asked to do a square on a sugar bag, a precious item given rationing. Naturally, Lucy'd squirrelled some away. Busy hands mend busy minds.

She was pressing open a seam when the bell rang. Standing there in his cap, the man asked how she was doing. The sky had swayed as he held out the telegram. She shook her head, the iron hissing behind her. "Harry?" she'd called out feebly. But Harry was at work, of course, welding plates to a hull with a hole in it big enough to drive a truck through. *Harry?* "Sorry?" The man had kept his eyes on her apron, asking if she was Mrs. Caines.

Wounded in action, Jewel was shipped to a hospital in England, they eventually learned. *A clean place with good light,* said his note. His writing not so different-looking. *My luck ran out,* was how he put it. *All I seen were trees like torches, then a flash. Any lower, and I'd be singing soprano, any higher, and ... Sorry for the bad news. Shrapnel. I'll make it, dont worry. Others didn't, though. I love you Ma,* he signed off, *J.* Harry'd read it breathing over her shoulder, needing a drink. Impossible to tell if the sound he made was laughing or crying. Swigging, swallowing. "Jesus Christ," he'd said, muttering about what the fathers of girls didn't know.

They were both there to see the ship dock, fewer than a dozen people waiting in the spitting April rain. In a throng she mightn't have recognized him. Stooped, craggy-faced, he'd almost walked right by. She was wearing a new coat, mauve, a bit of an old ladies' colour. Harry had on a suit and tie, his neck bulging. His bad eye had developed a permanent squint, as if the lid were sick of pretending to be useful. In the five years, four months and six days since she'd kissed Jewel goodbye, her hair had gone the shade of weathered shingles. He'd looked confused when she grabbed his sleeve.

She could almost circle his waist with one arm, clinging to him. Wincing, he pulled back at first, till Harry pressed in and, swear on everything holy, kissed him. The rain a thousand pinches. He'd limped to the car, an arm around each of them, peering about nervously at every honk and rumble. Gripping his father's arm, getting into the front seat. A small torture it had been sitting behind him the short ride home, braving his sideward glances. *Holy Mary, Mother of God,* she'd prayed. Driving in silence, they'd passed sailors beating someone up in broad daylight. She'd thought of Jewel's wound, the strafing he'd survived — by grace? — as Harry asked if he could guess what she'd baked. Covering his eyes, Jewel just shrugged; and all her waiting was a knife in her side — *Stabat mater dolorosa* — even as she imagined angels singing. When she gripped his shoulder, through the dank wool he felt warm and solid: more than she could've hoped for. "A Ritz pie," Harry'd brayed — apple made of crackers. "Beat that, eh?"

Fifteen

"PILL TIME, HARRY." JUGGLING the straw and a glass of water, she takes the last blue tablet from the plastic case — a slot for each day of the week: Rebecca's idea, which couldn't've come sooner. It's like a sewing box, spaces for pins, needles, hooks, eyes. "Open up, now." It reminds her of giving a cat a pill, the moth-eaten tom that had adopted them once, briefly. Stroking Harry's forehead, she holds his chin gently, then pinches his jaws open; she's about to pop the pill down his gullet when he coughs. It flies from her fingers, a dot that goes instantly microscopic. Has he swallowed it? He rubs his head back and forth against the pillow. Even after just a couple of weeks, it's impossible to hold back the exasperation. "For heaven's sake!"

Finding her glasses, on hands and knees she scours the floor. Too late to call the drugstore, even if they do deliveries. It's for his blood pressure — or is it thyroid? Lordie, the vials lined up on the dresser, and still more in the kitchen. So hard to keep track, which makes Rebecca's brainwave appreciated.

Harry gurgles something, his hand dangling, pointing? Pain shoots through her knees as if she's crawling on spikes. Peering under the bed skirt, she thinks of Father Langille in his flashy socks, and his favourite parable. The one about the poor lady turning her house upside down searching for missing coins. *So God turns us upside down, till all the lost are found.* The new priest has a habit of slapping the pulpit, making his points.

"Luschee?" Harry starts to cry, that thick, rattling sound deep in his chest, like walking pneumonia. She'd been warned of these emotional spasms, outbursts. Two weeks, and they've been daily events, not much different from a toddler's going through the terrible twos. "Mood swings," Rebecca says, always the expert.

Searching every inch of floor and coming up empty-handed, she feels like one of those dames in the Bible: Sarah, maybe, at age one hundred or whatever giving birth. Not just ancient, but feeble. Feeble-minded. The crying makes her want to draw up her knees and weep into her hands. *Don't be a martyr, now* — how many times has she heard that? It used to come from Harry, now it's from Rebecca and Jewel. They're full of suggestions, advice, but they don't know. They have no idea. What's a martyr, anyway? As if Joan of Arc asked to be burned at the stake, and her very own namesake, St. Lucy, blinded. The saint of light, her pretty eyes gouged out by her own hand to spite an unworthy suitor. *I renounce you, vanity! Get lost!* Imagine. No, caring for someone is nothing like that. If she must think of saints, which old Father Marcus used to relentlessly, better to think of the less flamboyant and not the crazies, as Harry would put it. The ones like Jude, maybe — and Helena, it strikes her, the thought of her daughter's name a ghost creeping in and tapping her on the shoulder. Helena, the patron saint of converts and divorce; now *that* had given Father Marcus pause.

But enough foolishness; she's got to find that pill. "Where the hell is it?" she hears herself rasp, and suddenly the room swims, and there's a swarming dizziness. The thought of everything lost rushing in, despair foaming on the surface. Good God, is *she* having a stroke? *An episode*, she imagines Rebecca pronouncing, if she were here looking down at her; if *she* were so lucky. But then a voice inside intervenes, a voice like a priest's, a hybrid of the old and the new — *The Lord is patient and steadfast in mercy* — and in a queer flash she pictures a monk with hair like that bossy Stooge, in a brown robe and striped socks. She really is going loony. *Okay, so be merciful, and just take me now.* But then a tiny, hard nub rolls under her fingertip. There!

Scrambling back up, dusting it off, she pries open Harry's mouth and pushes the pill down his throat, clamping his jaw shut so this time it can't escape. He chokes and sputters, that eye of his sharp with resentment, maybe even fear. When the spasm passes, dutifully, childlike, he takes a sip of water. "Okay? All set now?" she pants wearily. Gently, guiltily, she sponges his face, swallowing back the lump in her throat. At last she can say, the way a mom would to a little kid, exhausted but mustering brightness, "All right now, dear. Lights out." But, bringing his hand up, he taps his lips with two shaky fingers. The gesture as cruel as a poke to the back of her knees. "What now?" Instantly she regrets her sharpness. Two weeks at home and barely a drop of beer or a whiff of tobacco, well, except what he can breathe in off Jewel. Oh, God, the guilt.

Tucking Harry's hand beneath the sheet, she kisses his brow; in what way *isn't* she his mother? "You know what the doctor says," she reminds him: no alcohol and no smoking. They haven't exactly been sticklers. But if anyone's broken the rules, it's Rebecca; she started offering him puffs now and then. As with a kid, once one gives in, it's hard to stop. That very afternoon, so help them all, Lucy'd lit a cigarette herself, her tongue curling at the taste, and held it to his mouth: a pacifier. "What's the good of living if you can't enjoy it?" Rebecca had a point. Though Harry coughed so hard he spat up, and after all that, refused to nap. "There's something worth staying awake for, eh, Pop?" His cigarettes, she'd meant.

Discipline, she tells herself; she needs to take charge. "TV off, now, dear," she says stiffly, bustling around the foot of the bed. The volume's already low, and there's just the flickering screen; who cares what's on? But when she goes to press the button, he shakes his head stubbornly. Since Jewel brought the set upstairs, it's become Harry's best friend; he hates being left. *You can't function, Ma, without sleep,* Jewel's voice comes back to her, the same voice that says *martyr.* For the love of Dinah, so what if the tube's left on all night, if it keeps him company?

Jewel's old room has become a magnet for every household item that lacks a proper spot, so she feels right at home in it. After that first night with Harry back, she knew she'd never get another night's sleep sharing his bed. Tugging on her nightie, she barely sees the clutter — the wheelchair piled with pads and rubber gloves for the nurse who visits him weekly, the walker, her knitting and the sewing machine gathering dust. The little bed creaks when she falls into it; who knows when the sheets were last changed. For an instant the bluish flicker in the hallway alarms her, conjuring a fire, an emergency of some kind. But then the faint trill of TV laughter drifts in, and all too soon, Harry's moans, that dreadful, choked sobbing. Yes, yes, he *is* still there inside that useless body — somewhere, more's the pity, she thinks at times.

Tumbling down into that limbo between sleep and waking, she imagines Rebecca marching in absurdly, ordering in a voice like the one that comes on when a program's disrupted, *Do not adjust your set*, then messing with the rabbit ears. She even imagines arguing with her. *But everyone needs a reason to get up*, Rebecca's imagined voice harps vaguely. *But, dear*, something inside Lucy that's louder and stronger gets the last word, harping right back, *there's a lot worse than* not *waking or getting up*.

If she lies still enough, the voices trickle away. But as they do, exhaustion replaces them, and she almost wishes her soul would leak out and evaporate into the drafty gloom. *You must die in Christ —* she imagines that hybrid monk again with a pigeon on his shoulder; a mimic of St. Francis? — *all ye who seek freedom*. Oblivion would do just fine, thank you. But next her brain's a circus mirror, Harry's reflection bending and stretching, blooming and folding as the world flashes by. At last, drifting towards a grainy peace, she thinks — dreams — of Robert. The two of them, Robert and his Grandmother Frog, off to the midway. The only one patient enough to stand at the sticky sidelines, she watches him ride the bumper cars. Cheeks sugared pink, he's ten years old, his brush-cut noggin snapping back and forth with each jerk. *Just one more ride, Gran — please, pleeease?*

When she wakes it's barely dawn and everything aches, as if she's ridden all night on a bus. Until Robert's twelfth birthday, they'd always shared a seat riding home from the fair; once he'd even kissed her. Silence hugs the dimness, the TV's hum melting into it, slightly louder than the drone of the fridge below. She can almost feel Robert's scrawny arms around her neck, smell cotton candy, hear the couch springs jouncing. The blink of years faster than forty winks of sleep.

A gurgle from the next room rouses her, a moan as soft as a nursing baby's. Before she can move a muscle, the groaning starts, low and miserable. What day is it? What month? Is it really only four and a half weeks to Christmas? Mercy, Harry, *please*, she thinks, getting up. Limping in, she takes a deep breath, forcing herself to think of air — air and lightness, butterfly wings. Butterfly breath. "Hush, now. It's all right. Lucy's here," she says, telling him to be a brave soldier, and she'll bring his pills, get him cleaned up. But in the pinkish light, she might as well be cased in cement, and it's all she can do to sit rubbing his feet. Below, there's the squeak of a bicycle, and the newspaper thuds to the porch like a dead crow. The escape of its pages enough of a treat that she pads downstairs to get it.

Hard little flurries wisp past the windows. It seems early for snow, but the paper's full of travel ads, trips to Florida and Barbados. There are bus tours, too — shopping trips to Bangor and music pilgrimages to Nashville; speaking of pilgrimages, glory, there's even one to Sainte-Anne-de-Beaupré. "The Grand Ole Opry," she reads out to Harry, feeding him his porridge. Imagine, loading the wheelchair on a coach, and pushing him around; don't give Rebecca any ideas. But if he could go anywhere, he'd once said, it would be Nashville. *What? You and all those blue-rinses? Heck — it wouldn't be safe.* She remembers saying that, not quite joking, and him asking, *For who?* and her laughing. Now she wishes they'd gone. But there'd always been something, his work and then the grandson, and when it came down to it, neither of them were the travelling type. *Hell,* he'd said, *I got Don Messer. Buddy can play circles around Earl Scruggs, any day.*

She takes her time filling the spoon and when she offers it, Harry motions for his cardboard, the insert from a pair of nylons, the alphabet printed there in big letters. She has to hold it steady. "M-I-N-N-I-E-P-E-A-R-L," he spells, his finger moving like a snail. She answers to the glint in his eye: "Can't hold a candle to Marg Osburne, can she, Harry?" Pointing to the TV, he taps his ear and tries to speak. There's porridge on his chin. "Oh, all right. But not till you're finished." The bowl is only half-empty. Pacing each spoonful, she could expire between each swallow; enough volume that he could actually hear his program would just distract and slow him down. *Important that he eats to keep up his strength*: the doctor's words. Only trouble is, what goes in has to be put there, and what goes in comes out.

After breakfast, once he's washed and dressed she cranks up the television so loud the Avon bottles on her bureau vibrate. Harry settles back, and until she rises, looks almost relaxed. She's going down to dust, she says, as if every move must be explained to ward off his panic. In two eternal weeks the whole house has grown cobwebs. Gathering up the tray, she strokes his wrist, and a faint smile twists his mouth as little children dance over the screen. A pretty gal with flipped hair claps her hands, and singing leaps out, "London Bridge is falling down, falling down," before she switches channels.

It seems she's only got started downstairs when it's lunchtime. Harry's meal is runny carrots and turkey soup boiled to a beige paste. The TV's racket fills the quiet as she spoons it into him. The local news shows a flatbed hauling a gigantic Christmas tree, an entourage of trucks moving down a freeway, lights flashing. "Boston-bound," the announcer says, before she can switch him off. "An annual gift from our city to *theirs*, in thanks for their *help* in our time of *need*. In *just* a couple of *weeks* we'll mark the fifty-*second* anniversary of the explo —" the fellow rattles off, his voice a jackrabbit hitting certain syllables. Staring straight ahead, Harry waves his hand violently, but before she reaches the set, they're onto the next "story," about a basement flooding. Dear God, as if everything's made up, life not much different from Rebecca's soaps — which have the same bleak look as news, never mind that the people look better.

The afternoon is a crawl of dishes, bedpans, laundry, with no time to knock down the spiderweb over the mantel, or read the rest of the paper in peace, with a cup of tea. For supper, more soup and an experiment: a slice of white bread. Harry sucks at it for a long time, his eyes bulging as it finally goes down. "Good, dear," she murmurs; every bit of encouragement helps, she knows. And if she forgot, Rebecca would step right up to remind her. Well, encouragement works, sort of. Reaching for his tomato juice, Harry knocks it over. Glancing off the bedside, it splatters the freshly washed spread before crashing to the floor, leaving a puddle studded with glass like the bus shelter's windows after a Saturday night. What's wrong with kids, anyway, vandalizing things? she wonders, on her knees again mopping up. A splinter jabs her finger under the nail. Wasn't the tumbler "shatterproof," another of Rebecca's bright ideas? At least the glass can be swept up; the stain's a different story. "S-O-R-R-Y," Harry spells out on his card, looking scared.

After this tiny disaster, they pass the evening watching TV; what else is new? There's a *National Geographic* special, a man with a deep voice touring shrines of Europe, which puts Harry to sleep. But she savours the man's soothing commentary as he leans over a glass coffin in France, the body inside small enough to be a schoolgirl's, a face like marble. "The incorruptible corpse of St. Bernadette," he says slowly, the picture shifting too quickly to a rushing green river.

Harry stirs, and during an ad she trots downstairs to fix his snack — tuna on the same squishy bread — then, hurrying back, settles into the show again, one eye on the tube, the other watching him eat. The man on TV pauses, and there's music: the Singing Nun, that song, "Dominique." Next, they show him strolling beside the torrent, swept along by an armada of wheelchairs. In a shallow cavern a priest raises the Host like a tiny moon, and crippled people bless themselves. Lourdes! There'd been an article in *Reader's Digest*; hadn't it been Mrs. Slauenwhite's dream to visit there? Yet, lulled by the pictures on the screen, by the pilgrims' fever *to believe*, she can't help watching for some sign of a hoax. Chicanery. But, just as the man predicts, people splashed with water rise from wheelchairs, and a young man who looks to have polio drops his crutches into the river.

Harry smacks his lips, his plate leaning at a dangerous angle. "B-A-L-O-N-E-Y," he spells out, his finger hooked above each letter. But she thinks of Sainte-Anne-de-Beaupré, and her own longing to get swept away, anywhere, up, up and away, on filmy wings. A shrine. Doesn't the word itself conjure peace, and craving — for something as simple as a pickle munched in solitude! "A certain rectitude," the phrase burbles from the box; "wreck what?" she imagines Harry spelling. But who doesn't crave something, she thinks, or pine for something that isn't?

The show continues, in the camera's glare the sun baking down. The man on TV turns invisible, speaking like the Lord or the Wizard of Oz, as a fresh tide of the sick, crippled and weary surges forth. Those who can hold up candles, the kind she keeps around in case of power outages. From a nearby basilica bells peal "Ave Maria" over and over, with the sameness, the sureness, of carols in Simpson's Christmas toy department.

Harry pushes himself up in bed, catching his plate just in time. Surprisingly quick — which fills her with a spark of resentment and more guilt. Throngs, meanwhile, grope the cavern's walls, aiming cameras. "*Petite* Bernadette," the chocolaty-voiced wizard elaborates, "eyewitness to the Virgin Mary not just once, but eighteen times!" The sickly girl had drunk from a healing spring that burst from the ground. "*Que soy era Immaculada*," he quotes the words on a statue, the image of the Holy Mother, her guileless eyes cast upward. "Greek to me," Lucy murmurs, reddening. Glory, it's like a hot flash; is it just her, or is it warm in here?

On the screen, heat shimmers, the blaze of candles; a withered rose bush sprouts from rock. In the background, the river's rushing is like that of wings. Then a boy Robert's age wobbles to his feet. "'Walk ye sinners, walk, for whosoever shall walk in my light will be saved,'" the wizard quotes gospel, as people stream to a wall lined with taps. Stooping to drink, they cup their hands so as not to waste a precious drop.

Harry moans softly; yes, *yes*, he needs turning. But not just yet. In the faces and murmurs on TV she feels hope beating down, never mind that it's second-hand, like the sunlight glancing off the river. "The asthmatic daughter of an impoverished miller," the man repeats, almost like a chorus, "venerated as a saint and a comfort to millions." A prickly heat, almost an itchiness, fans across her shoulders. Despite his saggy smirk, Harry looks intrigued. Suddenly she feels ... responsible.

"Who doesn't want a miracle, dear?" She hates how she sounds defensive. But isn't it true, not just in this house, but everywhere: in kitchens, garages, beauty parlours? Rebecca hoping for a perm that'll last, and cookies that won't break your teeth. Jewel: peace, something as simple as sleep while Robert's got the car? And Robert? For success without work or school, cash and girls without expectations; she wasn't born yesterday, it's obvious where his mind is. What would Harry want? It's too cruel to ask. A pack of Export As instead of just one; a two-four of Keith's, beer from the bottle, instead of through a straw. And what would she want? Out of the muddled blankness, the image rises, faded and brittle, of a little girl giggling, flowering into a teenager, then a woman.

On TV the man interviews a lady with a doily on her head, anointing herself with water, mumbling about arthritis. Droplets arc and glitter like rhinestones, the man watching from the wall. Its mossy stones conjure up the smell of mildew.

Tapping on the bedside table, Harry makes a rolling gesture with his hand. She pretends not to notice. The TV man returns to an echoing room: the chapel of St. Helen, he says. Honest to God, and a spark travels up her spine. His arms folded serenely, he peers out from the screen. "... As pure in death as in life, the Blessed Bernadette lay here forty-six years before achieving sainthood. Just as believers say, her body has a fragrance, which the Church likens to the scent ... of ... lilies."

"FILL YOUR BOOTS, SON." Harry would watch him eat, the first little while after Jewel's return, wondering if he had a hollow leg, or what?

"Another egg? More milk?" she'd coax — not as though she needed to, and he'd curse, saying he wasn't a little kid.

When Harry told him not to talk to her that way, he'd stomp back up to bed. He was a ticking time bomb, his father said, sleeping his life away. Sleep was good; he needed it, but the truth was, she didn't like him lying around all day, though the doctors advised rest. There was a piece of shrapnel they hadn't been able to remove; too close to the heart, they said. The first time she saw the scar, her stomach had risen. A jagged stripe, it ran from his left nipple to his navel. His father had told him to put on a shirt. She'd wanted to lay her palm against it and weep.

Once he'd recovered, Harry said maybe he'd get him on at the yards; he couldn't lounge around home forever. "Why not?" he sassed back, and his dad told him to smarten the hell up. Then he'd get red-eyed and twitchy, accusing Harry of thinking he was smarter than him. But they'd make peace over drinks, Jewel following him downstairs; and ragged notes would rise up. His tired voice, guessing, "A Long Way to Tipperary," "Harvest Home"? They used her Royal Albert for ashtrays; when she went to reclaim it, he'd be sitting on Harry's toolbox, a bottle between his feet.

"There must've been *some* good come of it," she caught Harry saying once, but the blue of Jewel's eyes had reflected nothing she'd want to know.

In early May, he shocked them both by putting on the suit he'd worn to Black's; amazingly, it still fit. He even left the house, and when he returned, reported that he'd got his job back. They'd hired a girl in his place, so there was no problem canning her. Though she'd rather hoped he'd try for something better, kneeling, Lucy gave thanks, and the next morning he caught a drive with Harry, as if he'd never left. He was at Black's a week when the paper screamed *Victory in Europe.* Harry was late getting home that day; people were going nuts celebrating, he said, smashing windows and stealing everything but the kitchen sink! He wouldn't tell her what some guy had been doing to a dummy. "In broad daylight! Pants to his ankles, arse in the air. Would I *lie*?" he'd said. He'd also seen sailors set fire to a tram, and a man lugging a dresser on his back, and Benny — "buddy with the wagon? the traveller?" — pushing a wheelbarrow full of shoes while everyone else was making off with booze. "To hawk?" he'd chortled when she looked puzzled, "Buddy's only got two feet."

She'd made stew and a real chocolate cake, setting aside Jewel's supper when he didn't turn up. Harry had just wolfed down his when Edgar Boutilier, of all people, turned up at the door with a 'cordine still bearing its Phinney's price tag. Fifty bucks, firm. Harry's excitement had turned into nerves; he'd have to think about it, he said.

Afterwards, she'd suggested a spin downtown, hoping to spot Jewel. "What," Harry said, "and get a brick through the windshield?" Jewel was a big boy and could look after himself, he sighed, especially given where he'd been. But she'd thought of his wound and that stray piece of metal, trying to sew until the news came on, and then she'd started pacing. Didn't he know he had work in the morning? she'd pointed out lamely.

In the morning, a breeze reeled in and out of his open door, shouting his absence. To have him make it home, then be lost downtown on a drunken tear, or worse! The phone just rang at Black's, then Harry called from work, saying the downtown looked like a bomb had gone off; goddamn this, and goddamn that, and asking, "Is he home yet?"

Just before supper Jewel sauntered in, his suit looking slept in. Stinking like a blind pig, as Harry said, but otherwise none the worse for wear. "Guess who I ran into?"— he was all good cheer — "Lily's daughter — remember?" Never mind that she'd been nearly sick with worry. "Get used to it, Ma," he'd pecked her cheek. But while he bathed, she slipped her rosary under his pillow, and a card she'd been saving for Harry. A picture of St. Monica, patron of alcoholics.

Thanks to God and Joseph, the patron saint of workers, Jewel kept his job. In a queer way, thanks to the riots too, the partying, for shaking him out of his shell; though people like Father Marcus called the whole thing evil. Harry was more understanding, saying everyone needed to get "shit-faced" sometimes, though there was no excuse for morons. Evil or stupid, she'd tried to argue, most people weren't *that* bad. "The ratio, good to bad?" he'd argued back, rarely using such words. More stupid than bad, she'd said with conviction, until he'd goaded, "Bad-stupid, or just plain stunned?" That was splitting hairs, she'd given up, swatting him.

Slowly things returned to normal, and as servicemen left, the city shrank. But Jewel continued drinking, keeping beer in his room. So long as he lived with them, she threatened, he'd mind the rules! But it was hopeless: he was twenty-seven years old. Meanwhile, he got promoted, and splurged on a natty new suit. She pressed it the day of the Black's party and Harry loaned him the car, the afternoon threatening rain. A garden party? Surely they'd move it indoors? Blotting out the smell of cigarettes, she'd asked if Mr. Black had a daughter, then inquired about Mona. *Christ, Ma*, he said; it was a tea party, for frig sake! What she'd have given to be a fly on the wall.

The minute he left, she went up to tidy, his room like a trench with ten men camped out. Hanging up his old suit, she'd stacked a month's worth of newspapers. Clothes spilled from drawers and butts from three of her saucers, everything reeking of smoke. Dust furred the tiny crucifix over the bed, and formed bunnies fit to smother him at night. It was too bad about Mona, who'd seemed the type that would make a good housekeeper. Not that Lucy was ready to dump him in some other woman's lap, have them look after him.

Boys love their mums, Mrs. Slauenwhite's wisdom had filtered back, as she stumped downstairs for the vacuum.

Men, she'd grimaced, moving the dresser. As a drawer slid out, something caught her eye. Photographs, a heap of them, in grainy, washed-out grey. Kneeling, she gathered the pictures in her lap. Ones he'd snapped of her with Mona — she barely recognized herself: how trim she looked, how dark her hair; Mona like a whippet, grinning. A nice shot of Harry showing off his violin — and one of a bell with a swastika on it, and fellows in uniform mugging for the camera. There was a picture of Jewel surrounded by little kids wearing wooden shoes and bonnets like the girl's on a tin of Old Dutch. Another showed something charred — a tank? a boulder? — with rags lying around. But it was a photo of a meadow that froze her fingers to its border. The meadow mulched with helmets, bodies, and Jewel standing there grinning, his foot on someone's back. Like Columbus claiming America, or Cabot Cape Breton. *The Jerries are done for now.*

She'd slid the pile back into the drawer, feeling none of the usual pain as she straightened up and resumed vacuuming. Pushing, thrusting, she'd bumped baseboards and chair legs before realizing the thing wasn't plugged in. Leaving everything as it was, she'd gone and splashed her face; was sitting on the edge of the tub when the Plymouth roared in. He'd only been gone an hour; she heard him telling Harry about some girl dressed like a *buttahcup*, mimicking her la-de-da British accent. "Hold me back, right?" he'd laughed coming upstairs, saying he was going right back out again, to Dunphy's.

Staying put, she'd held her breath and counted. *Holy Mary, mother of God.*

For three blessed weeks after that, she waffled over whether to mention the pictures or not. Just their presence made her queasy; she couldn't walk by his room without the images flooding back. One sultry afternoon, she decided to confront him when he got home from work, then smooth things over with supper. Despite the heat, she'd put on eggs and potatoes for a salad; there were shallots in the garden, poked among the marigolds. Tinned beef, Jell-O and lemonade: they could've done worse, a lot worse. She was in the kitchen when suddenly the air went still, had just finished peeling an egg when, seconds later, the whole house rocked — gunshots? A bomb? Good God. Trembling, she'd stood there, rooted, sweat tickling her temples. Another blast, louder. A pane shattered, shards tinkling into the potted gloxinia. *The Nazis*, had been her first thought, never mind the war was over. Coming unglued, she'd fled downstairs.

The cellar was cool, the cement musty against her cheek; wild fear melted her to it. There was another explosion, and another, and there she'd been, middle-aged and aproned, yet twenty years old again inside, as if her face were pressed to tarry grass.

Who knows how long she lay there before the gravel crunched outside, and footsteps pounded. Harry's boots on the steps, his yelling — "Lucy! *Lucy?*" — wondering where the hell she was, then hollering *Quick!* and trying to gather her up. But she couldn't move, her hand still grasping the ghost of a boiled egg. Though it was different this time: she hadn't flown or cartwheeled anywhere, but dropped to the bottom of the house — dead? Except, there was Harry screaming and hauling her to her feet; but then her legs wouldn't work — had they been blown off? No: just pins and needles. Looking down, she could see them. *The potatoes.* Her voice had been like a little girl's. *Forget the frigging potatoes.* Lugging her outside, he was stuffing her into the front seat when Mrs. Chaddock came running and jumped in too, her dog in her arms. They were telling people to get out. On the radio. The magazine, any second she was gonna blow ...

He'd gunned it up the hill, till, looking back at the city and the tight glint of the Basin, they saw the mushroom of smoke. Cars choked the road. There was a BOOM! and a yellow wheel of light had spun upwards, shattering into spokes; then a green one, as the cloud climbed and grew. Harry'd laid on the horn, but there was no moving. "May's well enjoy the show," someone yelled as people abandoned cars, taking to their feet. More bursts of green and yellow lit the sky. Fireworks. *Oooooooh! Ahhhhhhhh!*

Clutching her dog, Mrs. Chaddock spied a relative and took off too. "Better get moving," a fellow had said, leaning in. That was just the barge going up. If the magazine blew, she'd be a mother, he hollered, 1917 all over again. They couldn't just sit there, Harry said, as icy fingers seemed to pinch her. Jewel. They couldn't go anywhere without him.

The neighbourhood was so still that between blasts they could hear the Plymouth's purr going up the street, as if they were the only ones alive. Yet everything looked normal: Mrs. Chaddock's petunias and push mower by the fence, and on their veranda not a leaf off the clematis. "Maybe he's inside," she'd whispered, her words chased by a blow like thunder, but closer, sharper. Shellfire? But no Jewel. Empty, the house had smelled of eggs and black potatoes as they thumped downstairs.

Must've had the sense to run for it with his crowd from work, Harry'd tried to soothe her, as an explosion shook the foundation. Green lightning lit the dusty little windows, illuminating shelves of pickles and tools. Creeping back up to get a blanket, Harry spread it out. Lying side by side, they'd held hands, the floor quivering beneath them. "Nuttin' like a full basement," he'd tried to joke. It'd taken years to realize, but he'd done a good job on the house. Pity if it fell in now, she'd thought. But a mercy, if anything had happened to Jewel. Squeezing Harry's fingers, she'd tried to picture him fleeing in Mr. Black's shiny Packard.

Harry squeezed back, then his grip had eased and of all things he'd started to snore. Though sometime in the night it sounded as if the world was being attacked — each heartbeat a grenade bursting inside her, her bones pummelled by falling rock — and Harry'd slipped his arm around her as they waited to die. *Wherever Jewel is*, she'd prayed silently, *make it quick.* But suddenly the roar flattened, followed by a burst like the noon gun on Citadel Hill, or a truck blowing a tire. Then silence: if this was dying, she'd thought, it didn't feel much different from living, the cool cement as unforgiving as ever of her knees. Slowly, creeping sunlight had spread the dinginess with a soft glow, as a bird chirped and the dog yipped next door. "Jesus," Harry'd breathed, saying he guessed he'd seen everything now.

He was snoozing on the sofa when Jewel waltzed in later, looking like he'd crawled out from under a rock. Catching up on the ironing, she'd almost burned a shirt as he slouched in the doorway smiling down at himself. She'd moved towards him, not quickly enough, wiping sweat from her hands. *He was all right!* Of course, she'd told herself: he'd been playing croquet, eating potato salad — if people like the Blacks ate potato salad, maybe in an emergency. She'd been out of her mind with worry, she told him. Blushing as their eyes met, he'd smelled ... of onions? When she reached to pat his cheek, grinning, he'd motioned towards the screen. There was somebody he wanted her to meet, he said; actually, they'd met already. "My wife," he'd beamed. *Rebecca.*

If only she'd been a Black — or a Mona, that was her first thought. Then she'd figured he was kidding. Skulking there in the hallway, Lil's girl had looked in rougher shape than Jewel, her hair a rat's nest, her dress a disaster, especially wrong with the rhinestone pin she had on, a frog. Spying her ring, Lucy'd beelined for the garden, leaving Harry's shirt practically smoking. Fanning herself, it had been all she could do to keep breathing. *Dear Christ in heaven*, she'd have so gladly taken a Mona any day, even if Mona'd turned out to be lousy at housekeeping. When the shaking stopped, she'd called out for a glass of water. "She's having a baby," she heard Jewel say as he handed it to her.

"A baby," she'd heard herself repeat, water dribbling down her blouse. The sun making his face a blot. Her tongue had gone numb. *Don't expect me to babysit*, the words had buzzed out, like a pesky fly. As he reached for her, she'd reeled onto the lawn, pressing the cool glass to her cheek. *Jesus, Mary and Joseph.* "Missus?" Rebecca had called through the screen, as he disappeared inside. Then Harry's voice had travelled out, stunned, saying this called for a party!

"Where will you live?" was all she could think to say, startling everyone. *Anyone*, she thought, but not *that* woman's daughter! Rebecca looped her arm through their boy's, smiling, showing her pointy little teeth. *Gem*, she called him, as he mumbled something about a room above Phinney's, and his father spat discretely into his hankie, saying there was no reason they couldn't live here. Lord love a duck, it'd been like a scene in the stories, except, if they'd tried they couldn't have planned it worse. Then Rebecca'd piped up, her voice surprisingly gentle, promising — "Cross my heart an' hope to die, Missus" — to make them all glad, not just Jewel, but her and Harry.

Sixteen

BLAME HARRY; HE'D ALWAYS had a knack for making messes she had to clean up. The hardest part, though, was having the newlyweds underfoot. Not so much underfoot as lying around in Jewel's bed. Once they left the door open and she'd glimpsed them spooned together pretending to sleep. They'd been married by a Justice of the Peace; in spite of herself she'd thought: a white dress, a priest, a cake — wouldn't these have made it legitimate? But most of the time they made themselves scarce, disappearing to Dunphy's after supper. Sometimes they didn't stay around long enough to eat, but one evening Rebecca pitched in with the dishes, doing such a poor job Lucy had to do them again. On the stickiest night of that summer, Rebecca'd tried to make fudge. "That buzzard next door'll be phoning the firemen!" Harry'd batted at the smoke. A terrible waste of sugar.

Then the news came on: hadn't the Yanks bombed Japan. Hiroshima: the very name seemed to sear the airwaves like screaming metal, souls rushing upwards, filling the sky. She'd crossed herself as Rebecca chipped away at the burnt pot. When Jewel stalked outside, Rebecca followed, and she and Harry could hear her out there whining that she was sick of Dunphy's, and why couldn't they go downtown? "Plenty of beer here," Harry'd called out, and after a while they sauntered in, Jewel jumpy and impatient. His father got out the fiddle — "Becky? You must know this one" — reeling off a few tunes. Wiping her eyes, Rebecca'd leaned over and kissed his cheek, Lordie, shocking everybody, but she could see how he liked it. When she slumped down again, her belly looked awfully flat — but what did Lucy care? Somehow she'd been with those people in Japan, each a tiny candle snuffed out.

She'd make herself ask how Rebecca was feeling. The poor kid, after all: the first months were the worst. She'd been sick as a dog with Jewel, not so bad with ...

Helena's name and her small face would fill Lucy's head, even as she tried to imagine what this baby, Jewel's, would look like. Though Helena might as well have been specks falling from the sky, or a picture in the paper faded beyond recognition, one she'd gazed at till time wore out the details. "Maybe you ought to rest," she'd suggest, saying it couldn't be good, standing in the store. But Rebecca would say she was fine, fleeing upstairs, Jewel at her heels, and as if to prove it, not ten minutes later their noises filtering down, and Harry putting on a fake, disgusted look, his good eye gleaming. *Harry!* She'd plug her ears. After a while Jewel would appear in his undershirt, saying Rebecca was worn out, poor thing. But eventually she'd straggle downstairs, and Harry would pour beer, measuring out a shot glassful for her, Rebecca flicking the foam from it as it spilled over. You wouldn't even think about diapering a baby with nails like that.

"More where that come from," Harry would egg them both on, her and Jewel. He had a stash, of course. He'd never change: once he got wound up, there was no shutting him off: "You like a shindig, don't you, Becky? Your ma sure did." And he'd strike up that poisonous fiddle, while Rebecca twisted her ring round and round, asking if he knew something a bit more popular. As good a time as any to bring it up, Lucy seized the moment to corner Jewel — corner, not ambush — asking him to at least talk to Father Marcus about a wedding. She never did confront him about the photographs.

The ladies' league quilt had got sidelined by the Victory hoopla, but when the raffle was finally called, she'd bought ten tickets, printing *Mrs. Jewel Caines* on every blessed stub. The prize just the thing for the double bed she and Harry bought as a belated present; but it went to someone who'd lost two boys at Normandy. "Not my taste anyhow, Ma," Rebecca'd sloughed it off, thumbing through a magazine full of cooking and gardening tips, never mind that she was useless at both. Still she raved about the house they'd have someday, right on the cove, with a dock.

"When I have my *own* kitchen," she'd started in one night, Jewel downing his beer in a gulp. "Coming?" he'd blurted out; not that he called her anything but her name, no *sweetie* or *doll*, at least not in front of them. Harry'd told a Bob Hope one-liner, laughing too loudly as Rebecca lit a cigarette, staying put, and Jewel snatched the magazine. In a huff, she'd clicked upstairs, those heels of hers denting the floor, reappearing in a dress Lucy hadn't seen, its cut less than flattering. Patience, she'd told herself, imagining powder in the upstairs sink. Rebecca's purse looked new, too, seeing how she fussed swinging it over her shoulder. If they hurried, she said breezily, they'd still make the tram; she sounded so sure, even as Jewel changed his mind, preferring to stay home. As Lucy put away dishes, the girl stomped out, her footsteps gunshots. "Touchy," Harry'd cracked, unleashing a flood of gripes from Jewel. What had he been thinking, marrying her? he moaned, saying he'd thought they'd have *fun*. Fun!? His father slapped the table, Jewel blushing as red as the toadstool salt and pepper shakers Rebecca'd given her, a bread-and-butter present. Saying he'd figured he'd be like Harry's old pal Babineau, with his endless supply of ..."Whoopee?" Harry hooted, telling him that if all else failed, at least he knew Rebecca could dance.

They were listening to *Don Messer* a little later on, she and Harry, Harry bowing along to Quiet Time when the fight erupted upstairs, rattling Helena's cup on the shelf over his head. Turning up the radio, he played harder, and she'd wondered aloud whether Edgar Boutilier still had that accordion for sale. Shouts travelled downstairs, followed by a thud that shook Christ's picture over the mantel as Jewel thundered out. His heart, she'd thought, hearing him pound the step. From upstairs came sobbing, and when she went to investigate, it got louder, a naked sound through the bathroom door. A sound she'd never have expected from someone so wrapped up in clothes and makeup. It had gone right to her stomach: *what about the baby?* The door wasn't locked when she tried it, and she'd slipped in, forgetting that the girl might be indisposed. There she'd sat in her slip, a tiny spatter of blood on the floor — like Sister's, after the dog attack.

It's gone, Rebecca moaned, Lucy looking away when she heard how Jewel had accused her of making everything up, the pregnancy a lie from the get-go. But then Rebecca had grabbed her hand, training those pleading eyes on her, saying that *she* knew; she could tell, couldn't she, that she'd never lie, swear on a stack of Bibles. That it took a woman to know what it was like, having a bun in the oven, then losing it, she'd sniffled through a welter of mascara as Lucy patted her arm, which was surprisingly muscular. Blowing her nose, Rebecca said she always knew Lucy would understand how it felt, losing something, someone. Because Jewel had told her, about his sister and all.

Almighty God, it'd been like having a stranger rifle through her purse. Those greenish cat-eyes fixed on hers even as fingers picked her wallet, even the pennies, it felt like, such loss laid bare. "Ma," Rebecca kept calling her. Somehow, around the thickness in her throat, she'd told her not to fret, and that Jewel might have some explaining to do.

But downstairs, his and Harry's voices drifted in through the screen, language that would curl paint. Jewel ranting about what an arsehole she'd taken him for, him swallowing the whole load of shit! Harry's chair scraped the porch. Then Jewel's voice went monotone, asking if his dad had any idea what he'd seen over there. "Arnhem — Holland?" he spat, as if Harry was stupid. Oh my God, she'd thought: the photographs best forgotten. Wrong to eavesdrop, but before she could step away, she heard him say, "*Men*, Dad, hanging from their 'chutes. Like washing, in the trees. Hundreds, picked off, one by one by ..." Then silence, except for the *que-ching que-ching* of

Mrs. Chaddock beheading dandelions with her mower, and he'd murmured how she and his dad could not imagine.

Harry piped up that maybe he couldn't, but his ma might. "Back *then?* I was one of the lucky buggers," he told Jewel, "dead to the fuckin' world till they hauled me out," saying he could've burnt to death, but somebody — some*thing* — must've been watching out. Harry'd never talked like this, about the Explosion; all the years between them a silent pact not to. "But I smelled it," he went on, "the smoke? Sweet, almost, till your gut turned and you knew what it was. Bodies. Your mother, now, Christ only knows what she seen." Then Jewel cut in, saying his was *war*, which made it even harder for her to keep quiet. "So one and one makes two, bud," Harry sighed, "misery is misery," and they'd both glanced up, caught, spying her.

"'TOMATO JUICE,'" REBECCA READS out, licking her finger to turn the page. Harry gazes up from the bed, puzzled or miffed; why the fuss, his look says, over a little spill? As soon as she heard about it — the pill, the glass, the mess on the bedspread — she was right over, the 'bible' in hand. *How to Clean Everything:* if life were that simple! "Got a pen?" she says, saying they'd better write down the recipe, the instructions. One hundred and one things *not* to do with tomato juice; forget about bathing in it to kill the smell of skunk, Lucy's read somewhere. Now there's one thing she hasn't had to deal with.

"She didn't mean to lend it," Rebecca says impatiently, scribbling away. "Jeez, she'll think I stole it or something." Lucy must look confused, because Rebecca grimaces as if she's lost her marbles for good. "You know who I mean. Elinor? Miss Van Buskirk?" Then she asks Harry what he was trying to do, tie-dye the room, or what?

The stain isn't that bad; Harry couldn't care less. Propping the book open, Rebecca strokes the lapel of his pajamas, his favourites, blue washed to a dingy grey. She reads out the instructions, as if dictating to herself. Maybe it's her neat side communicating with the messy, the Jekyll and Hyde of her homey personality. "Sponge it first," she says in a robotic voice, "with cold water. Then work in gly-cer-ine." *Glycereeen*, she pronounces it. "If that doesn't work, try hydrogen peroxide. Or so-di-um per-bo-rate, whatever the frig that is." Touching the pen to her tongue, she finishes with a curlicue that makes Lucy think of a stringed instrument. Except she's distracted by a niggling thing that has nothing to do with the stain or its removal; she knows she should've just washed the damn spread right away. Tomato's a bugger, as Rebecca says.

Suddenly it seems important to get everything straight, even things that don't matter, especially now that her days are nothing but chores and caring. Suddenly she's confused, asking, "Miss Van *who*?"

Buskirk, Beeskirk, Bees*wax*, Rebecca jokes. "Has a kind of a ring to it, don't you think?" she hollers into Harry's ear, his hand coming up to shield it.

Lucy lunges to prevent another accident, a vial of pills rolling off the bedside table, but too late. At least the lid stays on, but Rebecca takes her sigh as a complaint, saying she needs a break. "Gwan! Take yourself shopping," she orders, "or out to lunch."

As if I'm not already, thinks Lucy. But then Rebecca turns to Harry, yelling as if he's deaf. "Where's that robe I got you, anyways? Must be here someplace," she clucks, exactly like a mother hen, telling them that if she finds the robe under the bed, so help her God, she'll ...

Like all of Rebecca's threats it fizzles out, but for once Lucy'd like to sauce back, "You'll what?" the way Robert would. No chance though, for she's bustling around — as if with a twitch of her nose the tomato stain *and* the book will vanish — and soon a rustling comes from Lucy's room. It's as if Rebecca owns the place; sooner or later she probably will, but not yet.

"A-ha!" she gloats, appearing with the Simpson's bag and the maroon bathrobe still bearing its tag, as pristine as the day they'd shopped together a few months ago. "You two are hopeless!" If it's meant as an endearment, it doesn't come off that way.

Brushing invisible dust — germs? — off its cover, Lucy places the stain book out of harm's way. If only Rebecca were like that, she thinks.

So easily shut up. But, no. Perhaps Rebecca should've been a nurse, all that boisterous good humour put to some use. Appreciated. Except that she wasn't good with bodily things, functions, and didn't like touching strangers, she'd confessed once, when Robert was small and she still worked in retail. "Touching strangers?" Harry'd snickered, and she'd gotten all indignant. "Helping them try things on," she'd insisted. If there was one thing Rebecca could be, it was insistent.

"Take a cab," she says, as if driving a nail — *if* she were the handy type. "Treat yourself. Get out of the house." Then changing tack, teasing, "Oh. *I* get it. Harry? She doesn't trust us. Your wife doesn't trust us!" Her voice is shrill, and when she laughs her lipstick thins, almost fading to a lighter coral. Harry will be just fine, she says — "Won't you, Pop? You'll be okay, won't you?" — prodding him so hard his head sags off the pillow like an egg about to fall from the nest. Listing like that, he taps his lips urgently, his gaze fixing on the drawer. Rebecca's got the package out and is lighting up before he can shpit out the first shyllable of shigarette. "Hold your horses," she chides. "Don't have a nicotine fit on me, Pop," exhaling a puff of smoke, poking the fag between his lips the way she used to jam her finger into Robert's infant mouth. No, not a nurse. Pity the patients, thinks Lucy; there would be lawsuits.

AFTER THE LOSS OF that first baby — or whatever it had been, a lie or not — Lucy had stayed after Mass offering novenas for what might've been but wasn't any more. Whether or not Rebecca had actually been pregnant became a moot point, eventually. Still, Lucy was suitably vague passing on prayer requests solicited by Father Marcus. For my son, she'd murmured: some sort of peace, and for his wife? Someday, perhaps, a child. Then Father Marcus had wanted to know if Rebecca was of the faith, quickly cancelling out his question with, "Ah, best leave the details to the One above."

The kids meanwhile — and she'd still considered them kids, never mind the goings-on in Jewel's room — finally found a place of their own above the sporting goods/music store downtown: one big room, a kitchen and bath shared with two other couples. Rebecca had soon invited her and Harry for dinner: beef masquerading as rawhide and doughnuts like pram tires, best slipped into a pocket. Before long, Jewel started coming home again for supper. "Trouble in paradise?" Harry would tease, Lucy kicking his ankle. Tired of slumming it, Rebecca wanted a house with her own kitchen; though she was a disaster in one, who could blame her? There was a place for sale down by Dunphy's, Jewel told them, saying Becky wouldn't take no.

Somehow it had fallen on Lucy to pack up the rubble in Jewel's room, things the pair had left behind. The photographs were gone, but there'd been a bill from Eaton's as long as her arm, stuffed among frayed lace and empty lipstick tubes, and in a drawer, the marriage licence folded like a receipt. *Jewel Augustine Caines* and *Rebecca Susan Marryatt* below their squiggled signatures, and two unfamiliar witnesses. *What God brings together, let no one drive apart.* It would've been lying to say that she, Lucy, hadn't thought about the weakness of city hall. Rebecca'd shoved the certificate into a pillowcase of old clothes, and hadn't even bothered sweeping up afterwards. Driving off with Jewel in a borrowed truck, she'd blown kisses, and in a cranky moment, waving back, Lucy had wondered aloud if, given the way things had turned out, Jewel had considered annulment. Harry'd stomped on her toe. "What, and lose Rebecca?"

One evening when Jewel came over, she'd offered to give Rebecca some cooking lessons; it wasn't that hard. Even when he said she preferred food raw, Lucy dug out her *Purity* cookbook and started copying down recipes, things a trained monkey could make: war cake, beans. She'd squinted — spectacles would've helped — thinking of the letters she'd written Jewel; by then it was almost as if the war hadn't happened. "One or two teaspoons of soda?" Lucy'd waffled, even as he winced at the time, saying Becky would have his arse if he didn't get home. But she'd told him to keep his shirt on, it was for her own good. Once the babies came, she'd have to cook!

As soon as the words were out, the idea of a grandchild took hold

— a real flesh-and-blood, fist-waving baby, not just the notion of one growing inside someone like a mushroom. The idea swelled as Jewel fidgeted, saying she was wasting her time, even as she argued that if one wanted results, one must follow the recipe. They'd gotten into a debate, about catechisms of all things. "There's a recipe book, didn't you used to say?" he'd teased, and she denied it, blushing as if she'd betrayed something. "In your letters," he insisted, to which she replied that Rebecca might try fishcakes. "A cat could make those," she joked, and he'd asked what she had against his wife.

"She just wants to make up to you," he said, and a flash had started, its prickly heat moving up her neck a little like brushfire. Make up for what? she'd faced him squarely, that heat making her sweat. Out of the blue, he'd raised it; his sister, "the girl you never seen grow up." *Saw*, she'd corrected, the flash making her head swim; even her eyes had tingled. Fanning herself with a recipe card, she'd said to tell Rebecca fishcakes were tasty, offering her cheek for a kiss. Instead he smiled ruefully, saying Rebecca had no time for anything not from a can.

That week the church bulletin included a recipe on behalf of the league. *Peace Pie*, it was called.

One huge dollop charity, one cup trust, one cup tenderness
One cup good humour (extra pinch won't hurt)
One tablespoon generosity
Blend with two cups unselfishness,
a dash of interest in all He does,
and one big helping of work — avoiding ruins flavour.
Mix together with sympathy, understanding.
Flavour with patience, salt with obedience.

The sentiment made her skin crawl, but she'd cut it out anyway. God knows if it ever reached Rebecca, though, or what she and Jewel did with any of the recipes — picked their teeth on the cards, possibly. All she could do was try. It didn't help, though, that she was always watching for Rebecca's looks to change, her worst fear that the girl would turn out like her mother. Sometimes, seeing Harry and Rebecca together, she'd cross herself silently, thinking what a blessing, one less burden on her mind, that Rebecca was two years older than Jewel, born before Lil was even a spark in Harry's roaming eye. Otherwise she'd have fretted even more; it could've been like something out of Sodom and Gomorrah.

Then one night she'd asked if Rebecca'd tried the war cake. They were in the backyard watering the lilies, Jewel having wolfed down enough food for two fellows on death row. "The meals have never been better," he'd said evasively, when the breeze brewed up, bending the spray. Some squealing notes ripped from the house, and Harry wobbled in the open doorway, raising his glass tipsily. "Get the gal over here, Joool, and we'll go on a toot!" he'd hollered.

There was no excuse for what happened next: had she been more pious, she'd have said Satan pushed her. But, twisting the spray towards the climbing rose, she'd let a gust push it. A few inches higher and it would've soaked Harry's belly, but as it went, he looked like he'd peed himself. He and Jewel cursed at once, Harry glaring down. If he hadn't been so loaded, no telling what he'd have done. "What the hell were you thinking?" Jewel kept saying, helping her mop up the kitchen, which got the worst of the dousing. They could hear Harry slamming around upstairs, as Jewel's cheeks reddened, like when he was small. He'd sounded incredulous, disgusted, accusing, "You're jealous. Of Becky. Aren't you." Not a question but a truth put in that grating voice, the one in which he'd asked years before about Lucky the dog's head.

Rocking back on her heels, she'd shoved a pin through her hair, the flashes coming and going in waves till she thought she'd melt. Frustration stung her face as she flailed for the words. How she was sorry, not for what she'd just done, but for Jewel himself having put up all these years with his father's carousing. Wringing the sponge, she'd felt suddenly humbled. If not for Harry, she said, she wouldn't've had him. Then he'd taken her hand as if he wanted to tell her something, touching the ring embedded in her finger, till she crouched to wipe the rest of the floor. Wiping her brow, she'd sounded like the priest talking, as if words alone would set things straight. "Peace and quiet's a gift," she'd said, "for anyone lucky or smart enough to see it. A child's a gift too; don't you forget. The only one some people ever know."

She'd been about to describe Helena, too, so he'd know something of his sister. But Harry'd stumped down in a towel, still smelling like a brewery, telling him not to talk to her. "Either it's the change of life," he scoffed, "or she's demon-possessed!"

In spite of that, she said that no matter what, a baby gave a person hope. Like a rope tossed by the drowning to the swimmer, she thought, as Jewel accused them both of acting like kids and said to forget it, just forget it, the reason he'd come over in the first place. Out he'd stalked — touchier than a woman, Harry'd marvelled — and even the car sounded mad backing out of the driveway. Then he'd turned on her, "Now see what you did?" But she was shaking, a little, not with fear or worry, but near laughter, and a feeling that she couldn't have explained if she'd wanted to, floundering for excuses. Saying she didn't know *what* had got into her earlier, and blaming the wind.

"Well don't look at *me*," he'd replied, shutting himself in their bedroom while she skulked off to Jewel's old bed, a sort of penance. Despite its sag she had no trouble falling asleep, but then she'd dreamed of a girl carrying a head. A baby's, with wispy hair and a toothless grin. In the dream a soldier in a priest's collar came up and told her not to be scared. *Seek and ye shall find*, he said. *Ye of little faith.*

Long after Harry rose for work she'd lain there trying to purge the feeling it left, till the sound of knocking pulled her out of bed. It was Rebecca returning some knitting needles she'd loaned her, and some yarn still with its label. She was dressed to the nines for work, her dress the colour of buttercups, her lips a deep red. Those green eyes slid slyly over Lucy in her nightie, but no amount of war paint could mask her complexion, a match for those peepers. "Don't tell me

I woke you?" she'd started in. That cheeriness an alarm going off. Then Rebecca'd gritted her teeth, breathing in as if there were someone behind her coaching. "Jewel *meant* to break the news," she began. "Don't just stand there. Take a good look, Ma. Guess who's expecting? No fooling. You're gonna be a grandma," she said, as if Lucy were dumb, dumb as dirt.

"When, dear?" had been all Lucy could manage, falling into a chair and gripping the arms as if Jewel were driving it, while Rebecca mewled about how over the moon Pop would be.

But then Rebecca asked what was the matter, saying that she didn't look too happy. "Sheesh, if you were my ma —"

Thank the good Lord I'm not, she'd thought, fanning herself with *The Star Weekly*, holding her tongue, fortunately, till the right words shook loose: "A grandchild? When, did you say?" Rebecca was already clacking down the walk in those ridiculous heels. Green! Her shoes hummingbird green, her hair mussed in the back and dusty-looking. "What lovely news!" Lucy'd hollered too late, then, trembling, offered up a prayer to St. Anne. *Jesus, Mary and Joseph*: a grandbaby!

Seventeen

AS GAMELY AS POSSIBLE Lucy hobbles downstairs, Rebecca's voice behind her regaling Harry with a joke, a dirty one naturally. A bit of a shock: it's begun to snow, tight little flurries circling down, but not badly enough to warrant a taxi. Bundling up reminds her of all the times she'd bundled Robert up, and Jewel before that. The frigid air burns her lungs, its sharpness a pinch: she's alive, at least. Waiting for the bus, she's a jailbird breaking free — the little man in his striped suit in Monopoly, which she and Robert played by the hour, once, waiting for his mother. Rebecca was always working back then, supervising one sales department or another, hard to keep track. "Go shopping, Ma." Rebecca's solution for everything.

It's true, though, she needs a few things, having let everything slide these past couple of months. Maybe some lipstick, though who's to see her? As the bus swings up to the storefront, a train streaks past the parking lot, and maybe it's the greyness, the gloom, but she sees herself after those train rides long ago, stepping to the platform empty-handed but with the weight of a barn on her shoulders. Well, today would be different; she'll come home loaded with parcels, just to make Rebecca feel better. Spend Harry's entire pension cheque, if need be.

The store's decked for Christmas, not a month away. "The festering season," Jewel calls it, because of Rebecca's wish lists. Never mind. Right now the warmth engulfs her, the tinselly brightness enticing even as her own plainness yells from a mirror: the wool hat and gloves, her sensible boots. A lady in a white coat beams from behind the perfumes; the scent makes Lucy's eyes twitch. A welcome, fragrant heaven, though, after the bedroom with its bedpan and pills. Just thinking about it tightens a slip-knot inside her, a feeling that mimics the pain in her back. These days her aches spread quickly: water drawn through a willow, when she thinks about it, starting from the ground, moving up. Smiling faintly, she glimpses the display — little boxes and bottles laced with silver and gold.

What day is it, again? And who buys all this stuff?

Drifting towards some clothing, she squints at the sign half hidden by a garland. She's forgotten her glasses, again. *Ladieswear*, it says, which makes her want to laugh. Some distance away, a woman fumbles through some blouses, her back to the other browsers, her purse strapped over her lumpy coat, school-bag style. It reminds Lucy of Jewel starting school. But then she notices the bread bags poking from the woman's boots. *Ben's Holsum*, she can read. Turning to the next rack, the woman glances up and Lucy looks away politely, her face getting hot. Should she say hello? It's Benny's friend, the traveller's "old lady," as Jewel has started calling her — the sayings he gets from Robert; it makes you wonder who's raising whom. As if having her do Rebecca's housework gives him licence. Shuffling up to a mirror, the woman smiles wryly, holding an orange blouse up to her bosom. It's as though she's got eyes only for herself; if she's noticed Lucy she doesn't let on. As if she should, thinks Lucy uneasily, picturing the cleaning book, herself and Rebecca riffling through it to that newspaper clipping, the photo of that family — an invasion.

Not knowing what to do, Lucy opens her purse; perhaps she should go over and slip the poor woman a donation? *Ask and it shall be given.* But she must have her pride, Miss Van Buskirk, doing what she does for a living, despite putting up with ... *There but for the grace of God.* But money might be insulting, and it's easier to escape to lingerie. *There will be poor always*, says a voice inside like Harry's, if he wore a dog collar and could utter a full sentence.

Guiltily she fingers the filmy bits of nothing on their hangers, then takes her time picking through some marked-down briefs. Everything is nylon and white, a slithery reminder of the snow. Distracted, she forgets her size, as if shopping for someone else, finally settling on medium. *You'd worry a rock to death, woman, rubbing,* Harry would say — not like she hadn't tried, rubbing beads till her fingers burned, wishing and praying for things that couldn't or wouldn't be. But maybe she could just casually buy the blouse, that gaudy orange, and have Rebecca give it as a present for tackling Robert's room. An appreciation of something, Lord knows what. Though when she looks around, Miss Van Buskirk, the cleaning lady, is nowhere to be seen, and so she moves on to Menswear. *Do they ever!* she thinks; the one thing Harry's speechlessness has spared her is his mouth. If he could curse now, their ears would curl up and die. But then she imagines Harry lying there fed up, the blue of his eye full of resentment, and fear sets in. What if he falls out of bed reaching for something while Rebecca's doing her nails? What if she forgets his pill? Helplessness engulfs her, an ache not so different from the one all those years back when she'd woken on a cot wondering what on earth had happened to him, and then to her little girl.

But it's only been an hour since she left the house; she hasn't been gone long enough for anyone to miss her. Don't be ridiculous, she tells herself as a pimply young fellow in a suit approaches. Keen to make a sale, he points out the men's pajamas, satin and silk that snag at her touch. The kind of pajamas she can imagine that smarmy Dan Rowan character wearing, if he had a life outside *Laugh-In*, a real life.

"A special gift for that special guy?" The salesman grins flirtatiously, never mind that he's young enough to be her grandson.

"A bed jacket, perhaps." She blushes — wishing she could play along?

His brow furrows; heavens, he has it down to a science. "A smoking jacket? Hm. Let's see." It has satin lapels and a little faux cravat. Forget Dan Rowan, Hugh Hefner look out! She can just imagine

Jewel's reaction. Ridiculous, but she buys it anyway. Rebecca will be so proud of her.

"Thank you, sir."

"Thank *you*, dear. Ma'am. Sorry," he says, "I get it from my mom."

Buoyed by her purchase, she rides the escalator to the second floor. There's another hour to pass till the bus home. Browsing in yard goods, she checks fabrics for their grain, cottons leaving a fishy smell on her fingers. She studies the latest in notions, pausing to flip through patterns. The books make her think of atlases, strange countries where giraffe people lounge around, bored but graceful. Some geography, she can't help thinking, the rift between these pictures and her own puckered stitches. Looking makes her hungry.

Finding the restaurant means passing through linens and home electronics, where a man and two little girls cuddle, watching a big TV, which, if not for the rabbit ears, resembles something for storing dishes. Above the rattling voices drifts music, if you can call it music, the stuff Robert likes, best compared to screeching tires, hammers and drills. There are other purchases she should make; items come to her all the time while she's changing Harry's sheets, rinsing his basin, grinding his food up — like baby crap, Robert says. But now that she's here she can't put her finger on a single thing.

A gold cord marks off the restaurant's entrance, and a sign on a chrome stand lists the special. Thankfully, the letters on it are big enough to read: soup, sandwich, Jell-O, coffee/tea. A cafeteria is more like it: almost empty, the place makes the Armcrest seem luxurious. A single customer perches on a stool at the end of the counter.

"You want may-naaze?" the waitress says when she places her order, plunking down a cup and a dish of bright green Jell-O. Juggling her tray, Lucy manoeuvres to a table by the door, hanging everything but her hat on the wobbly coat tree. It's then that she sees who's at the counter. Hunched over her soup, Miss Van Buskirk hasn't bothered removing her coat, her purse either — she's stuffed into both. The sleeves pulled up, enough to show orange cuffs underneath.

The bones in the salmon salad resemble a baby's molars, Lucy observes, averting her eyes as the woman, Benny's friend after all, upends the bowl to drink the dregs. And the flecks of black skin mixed with pink remind her of a cat's maw, as the cleaning lady dabs her mouth, the way Father Langille does after draining the chalice at Communion. If she's felt any urge to speak or offer the woman something, the feeling's passed. When she glances up from dessert, to her relief and her guilty regret, Miss Van Buskirk is gone.

"Don't borrow trouble," she hears herself murmur; good heavens, talking to herself in public, aloud! All the trouble she needs, having Harry on her plate. Trying not to think of him badgering for cigarettes, she lets a spoonful of Jell-O dissolve on her tongue, quarrying the last of it from under its squiggle of Dream Whip.

It's good to get out, Rebecca's coaxing comes back. *For God's sake, Ma, your life isn't over. Yet.* Reluctantly, yet anxiously, she slips on her coat, sliding a quarter under her saucer. *Ladybird, ladybird, fly away home. Your house is on fire, your children alone,* a *Maggie Muggins* voice from nowhere sings — off that kiddies' show Robert used to watch. But then a priestly voice inside her soothes, *He leadeth me beside the still waters,* and despite a gnawing worry, she stops for a browse through linens. What a comfort examining sheets, flowered ones that smell of manufacture — not the productivity she's used to: functions, bodily ones, Harry's. Fingering them, she imagines lying in a bed of daisies lifted off the sheets, a field of them waving; then, tasting Jell-O, God forbid, hears herself murmur aloud again: "Maybe six feet under, dolly."

"What?" It *must* be bad if someone responds. And there she is, Benny's friend, stretched out on a bed not far away, a high, narrow one designed for a princess, done up in sheets with hot pink roses. At least she's had the decency to slip part of a newspaper under her boots — the Classifieds?

"Excuse me?" Plucking at her necklace, the saleslady looks stricken. Her tone makes Lucy freeze. "What do you think you're doing?"

"Excuse *me*," Miss Van Buskirk mimics, saucing the woman. There's the rustle of plastic as she gets up, and a loud sigh. "You wouldn't talk like that if you knew who my father was." *My father*, la-de-da, the way Margaret Drysdale would say to Jed Clampett.

Pretending to price towels, Lucy slips to the next aisle, barely feeling the terry under her palm. All she can think of is the newspaper clipping, trying to recall a blur of faces: the yellowed, almost feature-less ones of that family with the dead father. But the only things that come back, however vaguely, are the teenaged girl looking rebellious, and the hoity-toity, put-upon look of the mother.

"Don't let it happen again," the salesclerk's voice carries. "Or I'll call security. Tony," she adds, as if giving a name heightens the threat. But as Lucy hurries away, she hears laughter and a mocking "Tony who? The Tiger?" flung right back. Heaven knows what Benny would do, if he were lurking. File a knife on the lady's teeth?

ON THE RIDE HOME, she spots Robert walking towards town with some kids, his arm around someone, a girl. Impossible to tell if it's Sheryl, the bus races by so fast, and they all look the same, teenagers strung across the shoulder as if gearing up for a game of Red Rover. It's stopped snowing, but even so they're hardly dressed right, their jeans sweeping the gravel. Shouldn't they be in class? Straining forward, she asks the driver for the time. It'd be nice if Robert would drop by to visit. She'd even keep her mouth shut about school. "You got the money honey," the driver quips, and wouldn't it be nice if all young men could be this cheerful? "I got the ... Hap-past two, ma'am."

"Oh my Dinah," she murmurs, thanking him. Not that she'd want him for a grandson.

SOMEONE'S IN THE KITCHEN *I know-whoa-whoa-whoooooooa. Can'tcha hear the whiffle blowin', wise up so early in the born.* Some days Robert would never be still, from the moment his mom dropped him off to when she picked him up. Rebecca'd trip over herself making Lucy feel appreciated. But when Lucy'd offered to babysit, she hadn't meant adoption. Harry would just grab his lunch pail and tell them to have fun. At the age she'd been then, fifty-seven, the last "fun" she'd wanted was chasing a three year old.

The child an octopus, that many hands, into everything: Harry's tools, her sewing machine. *My ma lets me use her scissors*, he'd say, then pester for some coffee! *A witto bit*, he'd say, then want to try out Harry's *fiddo*. All the livelong day, *How come* this and *Why* that. When Harry came home from work he'd think Hurricane Hazel had blown through. They didn't know the first thing about discipline, Jewel and Rebecca. But then the world was a different place, she and Harry would actually agree, though people were pretty much the same, and kids needed direction. His lips would still curl when he found peanut butter on his violin. *But he's so cute*, she'd rush to smooth things over.

Cute as a goddamn chimpanzee, one that picks pockets. And had a motor mouth and ears that missed nothing, plus enough toys to amuse ten kids. More than once she almost killed herself slipping on marbles, but that was nothing compared to the time she found him trying to use the rabbit ears for swords. One morning he'd pulled a homemade slingshot out of his pajama bag. She'd barely had time to wash her face, Rebecca arriving early, a buxom Judy Holliday, all made up as usual. Later, just when she thought he was winding down for a nap, slumped in a chair for a rest, she'd watched him raise the weapon, squinting like a hunter. Lulled by the TV, she didn't see him aim, his sights fixed on an imaginary bird. Helena's pink baby cup had teetered for a second, the ammunition — a marble -- pinging inside. Mercifully, it didn't break, but she'd counted to resist spanking him. Though Rebecca shrugged it off. *What was the use, anyway, of a cup with no saucer?*

Hell on wheels, Harry called him. *Hell in size three Buster Browns*. But then the boy practically strangled her with his hugs, licking her cheeks — *Doggy kisses, Gwamma!* — and singing in her ear: *I been working on the wailwoad, all the wivelong day.*

REBECCA MEETS HER ON the stairs, already in her coat, a tight-fitting belted thing so short it can't possibly be warm. "Sorry, Ma," she apologizes, saying that Robert will turn the place into party central if she's not there right after school. "Neighbours'll be callin' the cops," she jokes, quipping, "You leave anything for *me* to buy?" as if that one bag contains the store. "Got your head out of heaven long enough to indulge, I see." Heaven? Before she can show off the smoking jacket, Rebecca's out the door.

Upstairs, poor Harry gestures wildly for the bedpan. She has to move the Don Noble first, stretched as it is across the spread, covering the large pink spot that's replaced the tomato stain. It's like stuffing something into a suitcase. "There. Feel better, dear?" But it's hard not to let resentment creep in. "I don't suppose Rebecca remembered your pill." Opening the little plastic box, a reminder, in spite of everything, that Rebecca's more on the ball than she sometimes seems, Lucy does a quick count. The blue pills, his muscle relaxants, seem low. A shake of the vial on the dresser confirms it. But Harry's oblivious.

"Bucky was here," he spells out on the pantyhose card, a fresh one that Rebecca lettered.

"Robert?" she prompts. Lord, if someone doesn't call him by his name, they're liable to forget it!

Kids, Harry spells out determinedly, *Bunch*. Which reminds her of the swarm she's just seen on the road, their ratty jeans and stringy hair. "They were here to see you? All of them?" Sounding unsure is too often taken as doubting his brain. But he simply shakes his head, spelling out *Beck*. "Sent them packing, did she? Well. It was sweet of Robert to drop by." A pang of jealousy creeps in; why couldn't he come while she was here, too? Never mind, she thinks, a response that's as automatic as breathing; *atomic*, as Rebecca would've said, once upon a time.

Downstairs, she checks the shelf with Harry's other pills, a forest of vials; maybe she's imagining it, but the rest seem low as well. Not that she's great at counting, but there'd been seven blue ones, she could've sworn: one for each day of the week, and now just a few. Good Mother, it strikes her, the old slip-knot of fear tightening inside: had Rebecca accidentally doubled his dose? Rebecca and her foolish advice: *Shopping will set you free, Ma.* Yes, God forbid, while the brains dried up in their heads!

Hurrying upstairs, she studies him so closely that Harry flares his nostrils, scowling. "Are you sure you're feeling all right?" *Fine*, he spells, tapping the card. *Now.*

Then she spies the cleaning book on her dresser, forgotten in Rebecca's rush to escape? "Oh, but Rebecca means well," she remarks absently, thinking more, though, of the book's owner; and, as if Harry's not there, "and the road to you-know-what is paved with good intentions." When he wags his head, she teases, "Don't tell her I said."

The book makes her uncomfortable, as if Miss Van Buskirk herself hunkers in its pages. Ignoring it, she stumps downstairs for the newspaper, which Rebecca's left on the table. Glory, December 6th: how has it come and she's forgot? The headline blares dully, the same as last year's and the year before, and the year before that, predictable as rain, reminding everybody of what anyone who was there would rather forget. The fifty-second anniversary. There's a photo of a white-haired lady reminiscing, pointing to the lightning bolt scar above one eyebrow. The old, dreadful ache comes back, like something falling out of a drawer; but then she could kick herself. Jewel's birthday! Here's she's been out shopping and hasn't even twigged to it. No wonder Rebecca was keen to have her go; she'll really think she's senile, having let such a thing slip her mind. Too late. She can hardly leave Harry to pop out again.

As if in penance — will it ever go away, this urge to atone for every little lapse? — she skims the front page. Always the hope, however sketchy, however foolish, of discovering something she hasn't heard or read before: a raw wish that even at this age makes her ever hopeful. The paper never fails to dig up a new tale each year, things trotted out that she can barely stand to imagine or relive. As long as there are survivors, there will be stories ... though it stops her breath to think of herself that way, a survivor, like someone washing up from the ocean.

Harry will want to see the paper, of course; between supper and TV the highlight of each evening is picking his way doggedly towards the obits. *If my name's not there I know it's a good day, dolly,* he always used to say; and it's true, perusing that page has become dessert in a perverse sort of way. The news the first course, the pot roast and vegetables, he likes to take his time pointing out things for her to read aloud. But not today, especially not today, the cocktail of drugs and his weakness rendering Harry one weeping wound barely scabbed over. Who can bear to open it up? Not even bothering to check the weather page or the death notices, she tucks the paper into the garbage.

"The boy forgot to bring it," she says, its absence leaving no less a hole in the evening. Waiting for *Laugh-In*, worn out by one-sided conversation, she makes herself open the stain book. Rebecca appears to have claimed it. Notes in the margins in her hand; maybe Benny's friend has passed it on — in exchange for what? she wonders. *If you knew who my father was, you wouldn't talk like that* ... Finding her glasses, she browses to pass time; the book is not without its good bits. *Follow the jingle,* reads one entry: *Wash on Monday, iron on Tuesday, mend on Wednesday, upstairs Thursday, downstairs Friday, bake on Saturday, church on Sunday. Turn it around any way you want, but do have a plan.* Right, she thinks with satisfaction. It's not so much about dealing with messes as preventing them: words to live by. A bible for day-to-day dirt, though the league ladies might well call that blasphemy.

She puts the book aside when Harry taps the bedside clock, and on goes the TV. Chortling along through the show, his laughter reminds her of someone choking to death. Yet his eye brims with glee; and the sight brings relief, and briefly her feeling of being imprisoned lifts. As if it doesn't matter so much, looking after a man who can't really talk and won't walk again. A child who, instead of growing up, will need her more and more. Yet the thought of the room without him in it hums like a test pattern, a sound that would drive a person crazy if it persisted.

When the credits roll, she turns down the volume, his cue that it's time to take care of his needs, as she puts it, hoping he'll be asleep before the local news comes on — not that the TV is as bad as the paper for digging up dead bones. Once his teeth are brushed, his face washed, the bedpan rinsed, she kisses him. "Night night, my darling," she barely has the energy to murmur, stumbling off to bed.

In spite of herself — and the guilt it breeds over how she's let the house go, the days eaten up with tending Harry — she takes the cleaning book with her. It actually makes good reading, an encyclopedia with no thread to be followed. Like the *Book of Proverbs*, open it anywhere and something new jumps out, or, even if it's old hat, acts as a reminder. Cleanliness *is* next to godliness, she tells herself, entries catching her weary eye, then falling away, dropped stitches as she turns pages. The comfort of being told what she already knows or suspects. How to clean eye glasses, for instance: use warm water and soap. Felt: steam and a brush. Then the odd yet familiar tidbit, like preventing rust using lard and rosin (!), interspersed with the deadly: how to kill moths with *paradichlorobenzene*. Was that anything like the stuff that'd fallen from the sky that day fifty-two years ago? In her exhaustion, she half-imagines Harry rosining his bow with it.

Time to sleep, but as she pushes the book aside, the clipping slides out. The creases in it are almost furry, worn through in spots. Imagining its odd yet oddly familiar owner tucking it there for safekeeping, adjusting her glasses she can't help but peruse it with new interest, interest in the form of a queer, unsettled sympathy. Apple baron, indeed; an image creeps back of bread bags, boots on newsprint, a bed too pretty to sleep in. *My father* ... Yet here it is, laid out in all its details but the loudest one screaming to be explained or at least mentioned — never mind the wealth, the wife named Alice, the orchards, hills, dales and rolling countryside. What's missing is how "prominent Valley farmer and businessman John Van Buskirk" died. *A large house in the hamlet of Coltsfoot, population sixteen swelling to thirty-five during harvest season. A tragic loss, not just to family, but the entire Valley and the industry as a whole, not to mention the province* ... Yes, yes, she thinks: the comfort and the frustration of reading things you already know, or, if you have half a brain, can assume. But *died at home* is all that's said of what happened forty years ago, if she can trust the clipping's date, and God forbid the paper lies! A knowing voice knocks inside her head, Rebecca's or one of the league ladies', almost catty, suggesting that in the obituaries anyway *dying at home* means *by your own hand.*

Lordie. A weary body is some vehicle for a weary imagination, and wearier memories! Times in her life her mind could've driven her off the rails, and, as if it happened yesterday, the weight of stones comes back, and the Arm's icy water ringing her thighs. She braces herself as Harry moans from his bed, the flash of the TV lighting the doorway. It would be a venial sin to get up and close the door. As long as she knows he's comfortable ... and mercifully, his moaning stops, replaced by a whistling snore; as she resumes reading, some lines about the daughter, Miss Elinor Van Buskirk, catch her eye. They send her spirits downstairs where the garbage waits to be put out. *Fourteen-year-old Elinor*, the story prattles on, *adopted after being orphaned in the Halifax disaster.* Lucy can almost picture the person typing it; a man most likely — aren't all newsmen male? — though it's just as easy to imagine a gossipy lady recounting bits and pieces, a lady not so different from Rebecca, or the league women. *A miracle child, the family called her, the toddler discovered without a scratch, under an ash pan one full day after the catastrophe.* No, not a nurse, she thinks: Rebecca would've made an ace reporter. Except the typing part; she'd never manage with those nails.

Folding the clipping carefully — it wouldn't do to tear it — she slips it back where it belongs, then, listening for distress from Harry, tiptoes out and leaves the book on the landing. The house is haltingly quiet; the thought of sleeping with that book in her room makes her queasy. Like sleeping with a poltergeist, more to the point, a family of them; or worse, hanging around some place she's broken into. For that's exactly what it's felt like, thievery, lapping up details of a stranger's life. Gazing through a peephole, party to some reporter's nosiness, and not so different from stealing the souls of grass-skirted natives by snapping pictures. Or maybe she's just read too many *National Geographics*; anyway, she feels like a thief burdened with useless loot — loot that not only makes her feel guilty, but spooked.

Died at home or in the water: by her own hand, drowned. God only knows what's made that poor misguided woman, Miss Van Buskirk, the way *she* is. Tunnelling under the quilt, getting comfy, she can almost feel that oddness rising from the pages on the landing, and drifting in, a vapour. God save her from her imagination; but perhaps Harry's felt it too, who knows.

She wakes to his whimpering, a mewling sound, chilled by her dream. In it Harry's been hollering, weeping, "Help me! *Help me!*" and lying there engulfed in the darkness, the watery streetlight creeping in, her mind fills with an image aflame with pain: a doctor tweezing glass from Harry's pupil, giving up. A tiny glass ball rolling in bright, filmy red.

"Darling!" Her mouth is dry, her voice weak. When she flips on the light, there he is, sleeping, a muscle in his jaw twitching peacefully, that surviving eye roving as quietly as the moon under its lid.

WHISPERING A PRAYER, SHE makes herself take a gander before replacing the paper at the roadside. Page two has an elderly man's account, his recollection of running to school with his brothers, one landing safely when the blast hit, ending up with a hole in his stocking. The other found later, missing his head. Curiosity killed the cat: better not to look.

"Hey, Gran!" Travelling up the street, Robert's shout startles her; where was he when she was hauling out the garbage? "What's goin' on?" he beams, dangerously cheery and a little out of breath, as if her life's a circus and he's scrambling to catch up. Sweet Dinah, kids today. A girl trots up behind him, smiling weakly. It *is* Sheryl, her hair parted in the middle and pushed behind her ears, her parka unzipped so you can see her top — like one of Harry's old undershirts, or Jed's on the *Hillbillies*. She hardly speaks when Lucy says hello; shyness, or just plain rudeness? She doesn't look like a traveller, the kind who'd feed Robert those wild ideas of going west. At least not the way travellers look on TV, shows about tourists in exotic places. Not that Lucy's spent much time with any, besides old Mrs. Slauenwhite on the train that time eating sandwiches. What she'd give to win that trip now; she'd camp out in that grand basilica at Sainte-Anne-de-Beaupré, and they'd have to tear her away from that withered wrist bone! She could kick herself for chickening out back then; slap herself upside the head, as Rebecca would say.

Robert looks at her oddly, those eyes of his so like his father's. Playfully he twists Sheryl's arm till she winces, giggling. "I just wanna see Gramp for a sec," he says vaguely, and it strikes her how early it is, early for teenagers to be on the prowl, early for poor Harry, too, who's just been washed and fed and topped up with his medicines. Aren't they supposed to be in school? "Day off, Gran." He looks her in the eye, as the girl snickers, inspecting the ends of her hair so intently she could be looking for lice. And Lucy thinks how much like himself Robert sounds, Robert not so long ago riding the bus home from the fair: *You sit there, Gran. And no kisses. Someone might see.*

"But the holidays are just three weeks away." She's not letting him off that easy, not today, smiling at Sheryl. Maybe it *is* shyness; if so, the least she can do is try. "You'll still be with us then, won't you? No trips planned?" But the girl just eyes Robert expectantly, and they tramp upstairs, Sheryl following him. Her little rear end wiggling a bit in those jeans.

Harry's lying there stroking the accordion's smudged case. Glancing up, startled, he waves to the visitors, as if Lucy's invisible. "How's your music, dear?" she asks brightly, too brightly. That need to buffer him, to put herself between him and the world now, no matter how harmless. As if guests are intruders and should be frisked first; glory, she's been watching too much TV! "Look who's here," she says; Lord knows what to do with Sheryl, as wordless as Harry. Some Scripture runs through her mind: *He maketh the deaf hear and the mute speak.* Good luck with this crowd, she thinks.

Robert silently fingers the keyboard, till Harry drags it away, flexing his good hand over the ivories. *Yankee Doodle*, he spells out on his cardboard, and looking relieved, Robert plunks the instrument onto Harry's lap.

"Careful — you'll hurt him," she starts to say as the boy wiggles an arm around Harry's shoulders and somehow, ingeniously, works the bellows. In and out they wheeze, Harry glaring at first, impatient, that hand of his signalling for a smoke. Then it drops to the keys again, and slowly, painfully, presses out the tune's bass. Robert's girlfriend gazes at the pink splotch on the bedspread, twiddling her hair. Clapping, the sound of her applause echoing from the walls, Lucy stares at the window to compose herself. The girl yawns, mugging helplessly at Robert, who ignores her. Are those tears in his eyes too? "Way to go, Gramp," he nudges Harry.

"How come he don't talk?" Lucy hears the girl murmur when she flees to blow her nose; the last thing she needs is anyone, least of all Harry, seeing her discombobulated. "Sick people creep me out, Buck," Sheryl whispers hoarsely, tripping ahead of him down the stairs. But you only just got here, Lucy wants to call; if he were alone she'd waylay him with — what, cookies? It's as if he can hear her, anyway; as if the little invisible string connecting them has never been cut.

"Gran?" he yells up, a little too anxious, maybe, to please her, or to make up for Sheryl. "I'm gonna come and do the fence. I mean it." Then he says there's a book he's supposed to get for his ma. "Something about dirt?" Yes, and paint would sooner freeze now than stick. But traipsing up from the landing, she finds a bag, glad to unload the book but uneasy about trusting him with someone's treasure. The fence, he says again: "I mean it this time." She doesn't care that Sheryl's watching when she plants a kiss on his cheek, where, up close, there's the start of another tiny patch of beard. Like the hairs on poor old Ida Trott's chin, she can count them.

And she thinks of him with his slingshot, the marble inside that precious pink cup, and how, the cup spared, Jewel had almost become a casualty. Demonstrating with a cat's-eye, Robert had aimed the toy right at his dad; if Jewel hadn't ducked he'd have got it in the temple, like Goliath. A thundering, blundering giant — like Christmas barrelling down on everyone.

When the newspaper arrives, the ads are full of things like wind-up snowmen. She barely has time to skim it when there's a bang, a choking sound. God in heaven, if the man could just lie still and keep out of trouble! When she rushes to investigate, there's a drawer upside down on the floor, and Harry's clenching his one good fist in the throes of a tantrum.

That night she wakes to the same sound, his crying a cross between a hound softly baying and someone sawing wood. Harry trapped inside that useless body, the sobs of a prisoner claw at her. Instead of jumping up, she struggles for air, the voice inside her begging *Take him*, yet in the next breath ready to strangle herself for being hard. If the league ladies knew what went on inside her head. That knick-knack advice circling through her: *Give me the strength to change what I can, and accept what I can't.* There's not a thing she can do to free him.

CHRISTMAS COMES AND GOES. As soon as the turkey disappears, so, it seems, do Jewel and Rebecca, the days and nights slurred together in a dusk of feeding, bathing, *care*. The comfort of food thins to the comfort of light, the tiny stretches between late afternoon and twilight. Her quiet time: *I'm going downstairs for a bit, dear.* No Marg Osburne, though, no Charlie Chamberlain. The last thing she could abide is that brief peace cluttered with anything but the sound of the TV upstairs babysitting, the sound that carries the stillness. It's the winter light that keeps her going: the sun's hard glow on the snow and the deep orangey blue of the sky. The only time of day that

offers solace. Warmed by that fading light — *Do not disturb!* —
momentarily she's a little speck of nothing surrounded by the greasy
kitchen, the window wet with the steam of boiling turnip. Drifting
on a raft of silence, she thinks of Rebecca's cleaning lady in that
floating shack almost but not quite jammed in by ice. It's not hard
to imagine Ida Trott's crazy offspring warming himself by a fire
fed with trash, while that poor creature stirs tinned spaghetti. God
knows how they get along. But it's not her worry. Besides, God's
already had an earful fielding her pleas to heal Harry. Of what,
though? His condition is a growing list of complaints. *Okay, up
there. Pick a problem*, she adds to the chit-chat in her head, *any
problem*. But it's like banging her fists on a steel door, asking God to
change his stubborn mind. *Thy will be done on earth as it is in heaven.*

Maybe if she went to Mass ... though that would mean arranging
something for Harry. It's as if God's gone deaf: maybe he should
follow his own example and heal himself of exactly that! *Thy will be
done.* But the only things that change are the destinations in the
travel ads, places with hot sun and beaches. Which remind her of
salt, and whatever it is in each grain that keeps water from freezing,
leaving an escape route open even to the likes of a Miss Van Buskirk.
But an escape to where? She has to wonder. Not that it's her concern.
As for Mass, it's not like Harry would perish, left alone for an hour.
The truth is, the last time she went, the new priest, Father Langille,
said some things that cheesed her off. Things she'd rather not be
reminded of: how it's sinful to judge and stupid having faith without
the gumption to act.

Eighteen

ON THE FIRST WARM night in spring — spring? she marvels when it finally comes — Robert arrives with paint. She happens to look down from Harry's room, and there he is scraping the pickets. *Don't-let-yourself-grow-weary*, says its scratchy rhythm rising through the salty air, above the TV. Not till Harry dozes off does she venture out. Robert doesn't notice her at first, smiling to himself. When he sees her he waves, then asks if he can use the radio. Setting it up on the steps — what a relic, caked with dirt and old batter — he plays it so loud it's lucky Mrs. Chaddock's lost her hearing. A choir of tipsy angels and a lippy voice moaning about getting, or not getting, what you want. When she asks him to turn it down, he yells back, "You're kidding? Don't you know who that is?"

It seems he's just gotten started when he quits, leaving the fence half-done. "First thing tomorrow," he promises. Before she can ask about school — as far as she knows he's still going — he disappears into the budded twilight, his gangly shape swinging down the street. But he doesn't turn up next morning, or the next. After a couple of weeks the rain washes flakes of old paint into the gravel, and the fence gets shabbier. At least it's half-scraped instead of half-peeled, she tells herself, sitting up with Harry watching a replay of last summer's moon landing. The astronauts bounding over the pocked surface remind her of a *Nature of Things* close-up of germs exploring a patch of skin.

Later, falling into her narrow bed, the TV's pale light flaring then fading in the doorway, she feels a tingle through her chest — a sensation that moves from her heart and makes her flush. It's a crazy feeling that the kingdom of heaven mightn't be so far off — that is, if people can walk up there on the moon. Downstairs, the fridge just hums along as usual, but oddly the sound ignites a spark of joy, tiny, but more than she's felt in months.

The next evening, as she's sorting the pill bottles on Harry's bureau, something makes her turn down the volume. Shifting, Harry points at the screen. "Bippy," the word bleeps out of him, like the first time Jewel uttered *ma*. Wheeling around, she finds Harry eyeing her, a grin lifting the strong side of his mouth. She can't believe her ears, yet, doubting, stunned, has to fight an urge for precision. "*Hippie,* dear?" The tingling starts in her chest again, almost painful. "*Harry?*" "Bee-bee," it sounds like the second time, the repetition enough to make her drop a vial. Watching her, he opens his mouth and speaks again, more slowly, but clearly. "Swe-eet bip-py." The look on his face is one she'd almost forgotten. Edging towards him, she feels his hand brush her hip. "Bet your sweet bippy," she recites, such a foolish phrase, but who cares? Even so, she blushes as Harry beams, reminding her of Jewel — or Robert — tickled to death at spelling his own name.

"Say it once more, for Lucy," she can't help murmuring around the thickness in her throat. A doubting Thomasina, she imagines the league ladies snickering.

Harry closes his eyes, swallowing like a little kid dreaming of outer space. "Loocy — henrikpsen." *Henry Gibson,* it sounds like he's saying. Squeezing his wrist, she rummages wildly for his card, pressing a pencil into his hand, her eyes on his. Coaxing. He lets the pencil roll away. His next words, a question, take forever. "Whhhat time, Bippy?"

Her reply — "nine o'clock" — could be from the moon. The smallness of words and what they mean measured against the wonder of speech. Not for another hour, she hears herself say, her hand trembling wiping drool from his chin. Only then does it really hit her, the hugeness of what's just happened. A giant leap for Harry, barely a blink for mankind. It's as if she's caught his disability, struggling for words to match the occasion, kissing his mouth. "Jesus Murphy. Oh my God and all the angels in heaven!"

Jewel and Rebecca arrive bearing a mickey of rum. She lets Harry have a thimbleful, raising her cup of tea in a toast. After one drink Rebecca gets gabby, setting the Don Noble on Harry's lap and hugging him, as if expecting him to play a jig. "Gosh," she says, "Elinor oughta be here." Lucy has to scour her brain for who Rebecca's talking about. But Rebecca rattles on, oblivious, about getting the skinny on her. "Turns out she's musical, Miss Van B." Last time she came, she brought a mouth organ. A harmonica, Lucy winces inwardly; probably Benny's, used — by many, a multitude of blowers.

"Shhh," Harry slurs, waving his hand when *Laugh-In* starts, Henry Gibson's face blooming in the middle of a daisy. Rebecca keeps yakking, as if they're hanging on her every word. Prattling on, how Elinor took piano as a kid, how her parents gave her everything, to make up for ... "Everything," she says dramatically, "well, till the crash. Of '29? When the old man, you know ... Couldn't've been easy."

Harry raises his fist to shut her up — jokingly, Lucy hopes, and raises the volume. Not that Rebecca gets the hint, rambling on about what "the poor thing" went through after the father "hung" himself. "Not that she remembers. What happened *before*. I guess she looked like a tar baby getting off that train. That's what they told her, any-ways," Rebecca sticks her chin out, as if they don't believe her, muttering how "the old man felt so bad seeing all those bloody people" that he grabbed her, then and there at the station, and took the kid home to his wife. Disgusted, Harry thumps the mattress, and Lucy quits trying to make sense of what she's on about. But there's a reason Robert calls his mom a motor mouth. "The mother, *well*," she sighs, saying how the woman was quite the queen bee always having tea parties, and didn't *want* another kid, since she already had a son. "Not an acorn off the old tree," Rebecca gossips, as if they should give a hoot, "not like his father." Finally Harry draws a finger across his throat, making a noise like it's being slit. "Dear," Lucy nudges her, "it's one of his few pleasures, this show."

But Rebecca won't be silenced, saying how the girl must've been some spoilt. "Nice clothes, music lessons, the whole shebang," she says in a clipped voice. *Yap yap yap*, Lucy imagines Harry cutting in, if he could, *like a goddamn French poodle!* "Not that that's a bad thing," Rebecca blathers. "'Magine, that poor little kid on that train with all those people, some with their eyes half out. Cripes ..." Mercifully a toothpaste ad finally steals her attention, the jingle bouncing off the walls.

Tapping his glass against Harry's empty thimble, Jewel smirks, offering his dad another shot. Measuring out a spoonful of rum, he grimaces. "So how the hell do you go from *that* to being a bag lady?" His tone makes Lucy bristle, but just then Lily Tomlin — Ernestine, the telephone operator — fills the screen, licking her lips in her prissy way and dialing. Rebecca could take lessons from her, all the world a party line.

"She's *not* a bag lady, hon," Rebecca jumps in, fending off Harry's groans, when she calls the woman a "maintainer." A keeper upper.

"Geezhushchrisht!!" he finally explodes. It's not like him to be short with her, but it does the trick. Even so, Lucy can't help thinking, maybe the miracle of speech is a mixed blessing.

With the volume cranked right up, they manage to watch the credits in peace. But when Jewel pours his dad another drink — "Cheers, there, old fella" — it's as if the walls have eyes, the doctors'.

But she sleeps soundly for the first night, it seems, in nine months: long enough to have a baby. Is it only that long since Harry's fall? Dreaming, she travels back to when she did have a baby, a real one, her first. Back in their flat in Richmond. In her dreams, Lucy's body is lighter than ash floating over the quaint linoleum. Light blazes through the windows, fading to forget-me-not blue as she hovers, a hummingbird making breakfast. Poached eggs, tea. Someone knocks, but she can't touch down to answer it. *Too bad*, she whispers, pouring milk into Helena's pink cup. *Tough titties*. But she has eyes that see through the door: only the landlady coming to collect rent and ask after the baby covered in chicken pox. Shadows spill in, everything charcoal as Helena whimpers, waking from a nap and scratching at welts, a nasty one on her thumb. Her claws dissolving, she tries to wake Harry to get the money, but lacks hands to shake him, and he can't hear. *Being invisible doesn't mean I'm not here*, she tries to chirp, a clutch of feathers. Fluff from a dandelion carried on a breeze with the rust of lilies. Looking down, glimpsing herself, something of herself, black as peat, lying in a box. A bog relic. Black veils riffle as the rest of her hovers, featherless wingless *invisible*, passing over. Impossible to fly home, never mind Harry's calling, the baby's crying. Helena's wails stir dust into hornets' nests, trapping Lucy inside them.

So much for sweet dreams. The taste of mud in her mouth, she wakes, shaking. Willing it to stop, she pads as quietly as she can into Harry's room. The sight of his sleeping face is a reassurance, but cold comfort. When she crawls in next to him he barely stirs, her old side of the bed as chilly as the wrong side of the moon.

A FEW WEEKS LATER, buried below the paper's obituaries there's something about a pilgrim leaping from his wheelchair after drinking the water at Lourdes. But it's a piece in the travel section that grabs Lucy's attention, about a shrine a five-hour drive away, where someone's reportedly seen the Virgin Mary — like St. Bernadette in the famous French grotto. This woman had been given six weeks, before her cancer disappeared. Complete with a map and a photo of a church surrounded by woods, the article tells how to find it. There's even a picture of the healing spring, which looks to be a puddle with something bubbling from the bottom.

Is it greedy, she asks herself, wanting more? In spite of everything, Harry's already been granted a partial gift of the gab. Never mind her impatience and doubts. *Seek and ye shall find*, she hears, buttering bread, and it's the fridge, of course, working harder now the warmer weather's here. Still, she reddens, slathering on tuna, hearing herself say, "What?" *Ask and it shall be given*, the fridge and the newspaper spread there chime together, as she cuts the sandwich into triangles. *Right, and where there's a will there's a way*, she decides glibly, taking the plate upstairs.

"You need to get out more, Mrs. Caines," Father Langille says when she finally works up the gumption to go back there. Yes, yes, she agrees, mumbling something about summer being better.

IT'S A CONSPIRACY, LIKE something that awful President Nixon might orchestrate: they all want her out of the house. One Saturday Jewel and Rebecca come over, and it's as if there's something they're not telling her. Oh boy, she thinks, it's got to be Robert; he's failed, and that's it with him and school, and next he'll be taking off without the wherewithal to feed himself.

"Just take your mother for a bloody ice cream!" Rebecca flashes Jewel a look. "Go for a drive." Harry doesn't look too happy, but as Rebecca insists, how often do they get out together, mother and son? Okay, Lucy thinks: she and Jewel hardly get a minute alone, and there's something she needs to broach, away from the chatter. "Keep her on the go," Rebecca elbows Jewel. They do a lot of this now, talking around and above her the way they do Robert. Eager to stretch her legs and smell the lilacs, she'd rather walk, but Jewel insists on driving.

Parked outside the store, they watch Mr. Jimmy in the window flipping burgers. From the car she can see pickled eggs, too, jars lined up on the counter, specimens floating in brine. It's supposed to be a leisurely outing, but Jewel leaves the engine running. Asking what flavour she wants, he seems crankier than usual. What makes him that way? He could be an octogenarian inside a fifty-two-and-a-half year old's body. Changing her mind from vanilla to strawberry, she quips, "My treat, Jooolly," just being playful, but he refuses her two dollar bill. Maybe it's not the best time to raise what's on her mind.

Sun showers the cove as Jewel saunters inside; from the bubble of the car she watches him joking with Mr. Jimmy, who licks his fingers, wrapping the cone in a serviette. She feels a jolt of dismay as Jewel returns, handing in her lonely treat. What's more, the ice cream is white. Childish to feel disappointed, but not without reason, she thinks. Such a rare jaunt outdoors is a bit like being on the lam, as if any second she'll be pulled back home. She licks up the drips as neatly as possible, Jewel tapping along to the country-ish bleating on the radio, his foot riding the brake. It's as though he can't stand staying put, but can't think what else to do; he reminds her of Robert that way. Like son like father, she thinks, trying to eat faster, in bites. But the cold makes her teeth throb. Jewel peers anxiously into the rear-view. He smirks, shaking his head. Who comes climbing over the bank but Benny Trott, beating the bushes with an oar?

"Crazy old bugger," Jewel mutters. Mr. Jimmy, scowling through the glass, spots Benny too. Poor Benny, she can't help marvelling; a turtle yanked from its shell. Jewel must be thinking the same, snickering as the traveller gets closer. The thought of that nickname makes her smile; mention it to anyone these days and they wouldn't have a clue who she meant. A space cadet, Robert might call him, or maybe not; Benny's too old to be connected with rockets. He's by his lonesome; odd, how she's come to think of him as half of a pair. Half a deck. Dabbing her mouth, the serviette sticks to it. There's ice cream on the seat, and Jewel's so picky about his car. But right now he's fixed on watching Benny inside, Mr. Jimmy ringing something in. Their mouths opening and closing, Benny gesturing crazily. "Buddy'd talk your ear off," Jewel mutters. "Must be what happened to *her*," and she knows he's talking about Miss Van Buskirk. "Just about done there, Ma?" He's always in a race, always something on his mind, even when he's supposed to be relaxing.

It's now or never, she thinks, beginning, "I'm wondering, dear ..."
But he jumps in, on the wrong track. "How Becky's making out?" That crankiness melting to an edgy cheer. "Just fine, I'll bet; switching channels, lighting smokes ..." If he was in a hurry before, he isn't now.

She watches Benny inside counting change. "There you go," Jewel's voice is heavy with sarcasm, "Old Benny Trott the gold-digger. Missed the boat there. Too bad he didn't meet Boxy Lady when she was a kid." Not liking his laugh, she points out that there must twenty years between Benny and that gal. When she says they ought to be getting back, he looks almost disappointed. Benny's come outside, rolling a cigarette. Catching Lucy's eye, he glances away, as sneaky as the muskrats she used to see by the ditch.

"She must be a good listener," she can't help herself, meaning Benny's mate. Jewel gives her a funny look, leaning on the wheel. Misunderstanding, as usual. It's just that Becky's willing to pay her, he says. Glory, if she doesn't raise it now, she never will. So she spits out that she has a favour to ask, never mind that he'll think it's foolish.

"How about you and me, dear, taking a trip?"

He looks surprised, even amused. Benny, meanwhile, has crossed the road, and they watch the top of his sunburned head disappear below the bank. Explaining about the article, the church and the spring, and the woman with cancer, she sees the plywood punt put out into the channel, a tiny ark, its oarsman a lonely critter. But Jewel just hoots: "In Cape Breton? What the hell's up there?" She says it's not a long drive; a fine one she is, too, judging distances. But Jewel shifts uncomfortably, as if he hasn't been listening. "It's Bucky," he interrupts, saying suddenly that he's got a good idea of what the little bugger's been up to.

Baffled, she keeps quiet as he heads back around the cove to what used to be the path near St. Columba's. A dirt road now, wide enough for a car. Who knows the last time she took it, it's been so long since she set foot in the Grounds. Mentioning this, she looks away when Jewel groans, "Why would you bother?" Half the woods have been cut down and trash litters the ground. The Big House and the barn are long gone, nothing more than rubble rising from the bushes. But Ida's shack is still there; someone's painted it mauve with a rainbow over the window, and wind chimes dangle from the eaves, as though a bunch of crafty little kids have gone nuts with crayons and shells. Where the hens used to peck sits a van with flat tires and queer licence plates, from British Columbia. "Where all the little drips come from," Jewel snipes, pulling over.

A stink wafts through the window, not wood smoke but more like burning grass, the weedy reek she smelled once coming from Jewel's basement. Music drifts in too, muffled but whiny as sewing machines with the tension gone, some song about a purple haze. Good Lord. Before she can stop him, Jewel's out of the car and pounding on the door so hard it shakes. The porch sinks under his weight. He may as well be knocking on the Clampetts' door for the good it does. Slouching down the steps, he sidles up to a window and peers in, no better than a peeping tom. "Good heavens! What are you doing?" she cranks down her window, hissing, "You'll be arrested!"

"Damn heeppies," he yells back, kicking the rotted shingles before climbing back in. His blood pressure, she thinks. Rarely has she seen him this riled up, and for no good reason. "I know he's in there, the little punk," he keeps yammering, and something about having dirt for brains. "I've seen his friends. I know what they're up to."

Without warning, the door opens, the music blasting, and a girl with frizzy red hair holds up her finger in a rude way, while a burly young fellow in a jacket with a homemade peace sign on it swaggers behind her. Then, of all people, Robert staggers out, mouthing something, his eyes Ferris wheels. "Get in the car," Jewel orders, as if she's not there. "*Get in!*"

"You can't friggin' make me," Robert yells with a hate she hasn't seen before. There's a sickening thud as he hauls back and kicks something — a tire? Spotting her, he looks away, and as Jewel races the engine, he takes off running towards what's left of the woods. Cursing, the girl and the fellow with the peace sign go stumbling after him.

"They're not going to hurt him?!" She can't contain the tightness inside her, a tightness that slides to her belly. Something from TV leaps to mind, nothing to do with danger, though, or fighting, but a man mooning over himself in a doorknob while the room swayed, some show to scare kids off drugs. She and Harry had found it comical, the man's nose like a dahlia bulb, especially when they realized it was the guy who'd been married to Cher. *Cheer*, as Harry pronounced it.

Drugs? Robert? *No.*

"Let him stew in his own goddamn juice," Jewel rants, his voice thick with anger, as they head back, and he growls about kids learning their lesson. "They all have to figure things out," she murmurs lamely, patting his arm before sliding out. "He's a smart boy, he'll be all right." It's what she keeps telling herself, anyhow; repeat something often enough and sometimes it comes true. But so much for a pleasant outing.

Even from the veranda something seems different: she can almost feel it, an airiness from the house. Upstairs the TV rattles on as always, Rebecca's laughter drowning out Harry's. But in the hallway, the walls seem brighter, the smell of Mr. Clean everywhere. The cobweb suspended from the light is gone, so are the dust bunnies from the corners. *Good golly Miss Molly*, the silly phrase twists through her, and an image of pint-sized Robert mimicking her back when she had the spunk to clean despite his shenanigans. In the front room, someone's wielding a feather duster, poking at the shelf. Miss Van Buskirk, of all people. Miss Mind-Your-Beeswax, Lucy almost blurts. Tucked under her other thick arm is a mop with a pillowcase over it, a rag around her brownish hair to match. It doesn't quite fit with her swingy black dress, its orange and pink flowers — kind of pretty, though it hasn't seen soap in a while. Humming to herself, standing on tiptoe, she reaches for Helena's cup. But before Lucy can say, *Leave it*, Miss Van Buskirk cradles it in her palm, a look crossing her face. Not as if she's about to pinch it — Lordie, who would be that low? — but as if admiring something she's dusted a dozen times before. In some other house, belonging to some other employer or client or whatever she calls people who hire her. *Not* that Lucy is one of them.

"Who let you in here?" a voice not quite hers cuts the airiness, and she's aware of Jewel coming in, and silence upstairs, as if somebody's pulled a plug. The woman looks up, startled, her mouth hardening. Gives a tight little nod. Her hand trembles as she rocks up on her toes to replace the cup, rolling back on worn-down heels. Those shoes, or are they slippers that might've been fancy once: velvet with beads?

Following Lucy's stare she looks down, almost shyly. "Benny got me these," she says, as if anyone should care; as if she and Lucy have just sat down together on a bus, sharing a seat because there's nowhere else.

"I would appreciate ..." Lucy says slowly, her voice ringing in her ears, ashamed of her anger. Being prideful and house-proud are useful, but ways Mama used to say people ought not to be. Watching her, Miss Van Buskirk's eyes have that in them, pride, and some of what Lucy's just seen in Robert's. Those eyes the icy blue of the stone in that ring she once had. "I would appreciate it, please, if you wouldn't —" Lucy swallows. It's so petty, so uncharitable of her, but most troubling of all isn't this stranger's mucking with her treasures, but being in the house. Interfering — though her own hoity-toity sniff makes her blush. Where's Jewel when she needs him? To explain, to excuse her? The least he could've done was introduce them properly. But he's halfway up the stairs — on a mission, to get Rebecca in a stew about Robert? Whatever he's up to, her mind reels, refusing to figure it out. Miss Van Buskirk swats a cobweb from the curtains. There's more than an afternoon's work; she says she'll come back if Lucy wants: "Tell Becky I'll build it into the price, okay Missus?" Something about that singsong "if you want" reminds Lucy of Harry, of Jewel in a better mood.

"We'll see," is all she can manage, as Elinor — "call me Elinor," the woman insists — gathers up her rags and agents. It's as if she's been invaded; worse, having the invader — the thief? — catch her in her underwear, dirty laundry on display. The whole reason she's resisted getting someone in, never mind Rebecca's nagging. The last thing she wants, people seeing how she's managed, or not. If it got back to the league, they'd invade for sure, armed with buckets and Christ-like intentions. *The road to hell paved with ...*

Jamming her feet deeper into those slippers, Miss Van Buskirk reminds Lucy of a bristly animal, in her own little world; letting herself out, she half-whistles, half-hums something not quite under her breath. That tune Lucy's heard at Jewel's, the one with slow, plodding piano. Just as it registers, it switches to something sweet and childish, making fun?

WHEN ROBERT FINALLY COMES to finish scraping, he says he's been working at the club every possible minute, now that he and Sheryl are "definitely" going out west, as soon as he raises the cash. After that to-do in the Grounds, maybe he'd be better off out there, she thinks. She can hardly grill him about it. At least what she doesn't know won't sneak up and throttle her, and after the throttling she's given Rebecca about bringing Miss Van Buskirk in to clean, all she wants is peace. Though Jewel would say that equals being kaput. The music blaring while Robert works is some outfit called the Grateful Dead. Gratitude can take a lot of forms, she tells herself, calling him in for a Coca-Cola. Watching him guzzle it snags something inside her. He passed school, he's working, but she blurts out, "What's your problem?"

His eyes dart, his crooked smile finally settling on her. Nothing she can help him with, he says. Shaking her head, she pulls five dollars from the cupboard, from the little stash, Harry's freshly cashed pension cheque, and slips it over. A little bonus never hurt anybody, she thinks. She's upstairs when he leaves, the scraping almost done, the transistor back in its place on the counter. But when she goes to get a plate, the pile of bills looks smaller: half of them are gone.

SHE WANTS TO TELL Jewel, but can't. How to admit she's been betrayed — cheated — by their boy? And there's her trip to think of, though it's as if she's asking to be driven to Vancouver! Vancouver, with its drug dealers and hippies.

"You're not thinking straight," Jewel snorts, making excuses, even when she says it's for his dad, not her. Though maybe it is: since that day the cobwebs came down, she's begun to wonder. If Harry's ever going to improve, maybe it *will* be her doing, if only she has the gumption not to give up. "What does Dad think of this?" Jewel grills her. "Who'll mind him? Next you'll be getting his palms read." Finally he gives in, as long as it's okay with Rebecca, deciding that Bucky could help: "Let *him* worry for a change." She almost says something then, but Harry thumps for her to change the channel. "Womanish bull," *The Edge of Night*.

Too bad, in a way, her plans can't be grander. A tour of Lourdes, a glimpse of St. Bernadette's corpse, or a visit, at the very least, to Sainte-Anne-de-Beaupré, more remote it seems than ever. She has to pace herself, though, at seventy-three. Opt for the do-able, though wouldn't it be nice to go for the real McCoy, apple instead of Ritz? Especially these days, when people — some people, crackpots — spy the Virgin Mother and Child on trees and telephone poles and even, she's read somewhere, on a chicken wing.

"Make sure you come back," Rebecca jokes, a tad nervously, as if they'll be circling the globe. Lucy waits till everything's set before telling Harry. When she shows him the article from the paper, he rolls his eyes and says he won't be going anywhere except in a box. His look the same as when they lived in the cabin, and she'd go on her missions to the barn, missions of self-saving mercy.

"Like the night life, like to party," Rebecca pokes him, dumping a suitcase full of containers on the bed, shampoo and pill bottles. "This miracle water, bring me back a case, okay?" Mercy like gratitude, all right, dolled up today in a tight green skirt. Hope in the face of disappointment, that's what mercy was. Unless Lucy had gone soft in the head and touchy as those gals on the stories.

Nineteen

PILGRIMS WOULD'VE TRAVELLED MORE lightly. A dozen things to do before leaving. The garden to water, Harry's Aspirin, his stool softener. Her own preparations: the rosary in her purse, for what it's worth, and cash, the remains of Harry's pilfered cheque. A dress with polka dots that matched her handbag. An overnight bag with her nightie and several changes of panties, since a sneeze or laugh could cause a leak. And lately she'd been having trouble, too; nerves, since the day she'd found Miss Van Buskirk dusting. Nerves and headache, probably from the heat.

"For God's sake," Jewel laughs, catching her fingering the beads as they hit the highway. Even focusing on the scenery, rocks painted with slogans — *Billy was here, Make Love Not War, Jesus Saves* — can't soothe the rockiness in her belly. Excitement, or maybe her queasiness is regret. Maybe she should've asked Rebecca to come instead; the next best thing to a daughter, at least she'd understand about pads and waterworks: women's problems.

For a while, it's as if they're blasting through space — endless hills and woods, that road stretching forever. Something comforting about the middle of nowhere, being neither here nor there. Then the road narrows, plugged with motels and cafés: lunchtime. The restaurant is packed with tourists; glory, what if they're all headed the same place? "My treat, Ma," Jewel insists, as they squeeze past a boy Robert's age, and she can't help a sigh. The decor is a jumble of tartans;

imagine, belonging to a clan. But the thought's upstaged by worry: what if Harry drops a cigarette, sets the house on fire? Or falls out of bed, Rebecca glued to the stories? At least the other diners don't look like pilgrims, though nearby there's a sickly woman wearing a scarf on her head. The deadness of her eyes makes Lucy even more uneasy, but when the woman's gaze meets hers it registers nothing. Jewel orders fries and grilled cheese; when her lobster roll comes, it's mostly mayonnaise on a hotdog bun. She longs suddenly to be home with Harry sitting through cartoons. Worries crowd in — will Rebecca get him up? Will Robert help her with the wheelchair? Rubbing his stomach, perspiring, Jewel says to relax, that she's on vacation.

Back on the road he guns it past a transport truck, quipping, "I'm the king of the castle." Like Robert in kindergarten, leaping from the couch — *You're the dirty rascal, Gran!* — while Harry watched for flashes of underpants on *Don Messer*'s twirling dancers. The thought blots up some of the uneasiness; how happy those days had been, despite everything: happier than anybody'd realized. But then she wonders if Rebecca's cut up Harry's lunch enough. Belching uncomfortably, Jewel pulls in somewhere to buy gas; she feels a bit dizzy getting out, tottering off to find the phone booth.

"You're supposed to be having fun, Ma," Rebecca sounds irked, traffic drowning her out.

While Jewel pays for his Tums, she inspects the magazines. There's a homemade looking one with a church on it — *the* church where they're bound, woods springing up around it. Proof of something, she thinks vaguely, some kind of power? There's a picture of a woman showing off her arthritic fingers. *The water's of St. Margarets let Josey knit again*, reads the testimonial. Peeling off a tablet, Jewel stares at the map.

Eventually they cross onto an island, one that could be a continent. Despite the spruce, the view takes her back to that show about Lourdes — the snowcapped Pyrenees and lumpy green hills around the grotto. She can almost hear the velvet-voiced narrator touring the cramped town with its souvenirs, plastic nuns in habits the colour of a donkey Robert had as a tyke. *St. Bernadette, patron of shepherdesses, the hopelessly ill, and all who are mocked for their piety.* But these mountains are nothing like the ones on TV. There's only one road, so they must be going the right way. It's hot and her mouth feels dry; how stupid, those empty bottles in back. An ice cream barn appears, closed. They pass a road sign: *Halfway Mountain.* "Halfway to what?" Jewel blinks, almost giving them whiplash swerving into what appears to be someone's driveway. He slaps the wheel, stifling a belch.

Hitting potholes, they pass a trailer with a tarpaper porch, a field sprouting wrecked cars. Sweating, he grimaces. "Sheesh, the promised land. Where's the moonshine? Lock your door." Teasing, isn't he, surprisingly chipper. "Oh, Ma, don't take everything so serious!" Rolling up the window, she dabs her brow with a Kleenex, a fluttery feeling inside her. A narrow track, the road winds beneath some tangled maples, a spring sluicing over it. Shiny stones give way to mud. Bushes grab the doors.

"God. The *Hillbillies*, or what."

The track winds and climbs, the dirt speckled with signs of a recent sun shower. "Maybe we'll see a rainbow, dear," she murmurs hopefully.

"Christ, I hope so." Through the window, the smell of spruce pours in, the woods a tunnel of flickering sun. There's a jolt and a bump fit to break her teeth. "Jesus God," he groans, "the things I get myself roped into." You could do worse, she wants to say, picturing Rebecca sharing a smoke with Harry or trying to watch the stories while he dozed. She was addicted all right, had even phoned in sick to catch a cliffhanger.

"Jesus Jiminy, Ma. You think you could've dragged us further off the beaten path?" The road's a dried-up brook as they rattle painfully uphill, and he mutters that it'll be a miracle if they don't blow a tire. The article leaves newsprint on her fingers; spitting on them delicately, she tries to wipe it off. Not really describing the route, the writer had passed it off as a jaunt through the woods. That poor knitter, she thinks, the one with gnarled hands; hard to imagine her casting on a stitch, before *or* after. Chugging, the whole car shakes. If they make it back with a muffler, Jewel says, they'll be lucky: "Where the hell are we?" Threading a mountainside, round and round, the noise is like stones plopping into a bucket. Knit into each other, the spruce almost but don't quite hide the gully below. "Hope you've got life insurance," he tries to joke.

There's nowhere to turn around, even if they wanted to: nothing but the trail ahead and the view like bumpy indoor/outdoor carpet. Still, all that green offers hope, well, distraction, as does a darning needle flitting through some weeds, its wings flashing. She'll never live this down. But when she apologizes, he tells her to forget it, like he's talking to Robert. Ah, Robert. "It's an adventure, all right?"

Abruptly the trail levels, the bouncing and rattling letting up. There's a clearing: the wreck of an orchard and lilies gone wild, their orange flames beside piled stones. Something shines through the branches: clapboard gleaming almost yellow in the sun, the trail merging with a bald patch of dirt. It's the church, if she can call it a church, wildflowers waving up to its rotting shingles and nearby, gravestones poking between baby spruce. "Eureka." Jewel snorts.

A dollhouse version of St. Columba's, the chapel's steeple has a crooked cross. The reflections of clouds float in the windows, clouds and gently swaying treetops. *Rock a bye baby.* She peels herself from the seat, the hot breeze nudging her. Already Jewel's on his knees inspecting the tailgate, cursing a blue streak. But the breeze douses his words with rustling, the sounds melting into the woods. Opening the trunk, he dumps their bags on the ground. "To top it off?" he rants. "A goddamn leak!" Guilty, guilty as charged: she feels like throwing up her hands. But when a man gets this way, it's best to walk — even when he's your son.

The devil's paintbrush tickles her ankles as she wades up to the door, thistles snagging her slacks. Her knees click, climbing the punky steps. Painted mud brown, the door feels like warm taffy under her palm. She half expects it to be locked, but it gives easily, a horsefly buzzing into the vestibule the size of a coffin. There's a candle stuck to the windowsill. Outside, scowling at the sun, Jewel flings the spare to the ground.

Beside the dusty baptismal font is a woodstove with a jar marked *Donations*, some quarters at the bottom. Drifting forwards, it seems best to tiptoe, her very presence causing a stir, the fly zigzagging overhead. Kneeling in a boxy pew, she stifles a sneeze; everything smells musty. Shabby hymnals rest on the battered piano, faded plastic flowers decorating the altar laid with a grimy cloth, set for Communion. *Happy are those called to the Supper of the Lamb*, the painted words arch over the cracked plaster. *Celebrate the Good News*, too plain and forthright. Curtseying awkwardly, blessing herself the way Mrs. Slauenwhite had, passing graveyards that time on the train, she loiters in the aisle. All this way, and *this* is it?

"Happy are those who can get the hell out of here," Jewel booms behind her. He's in a complete sweat, his shirt unbuttoned; she can see the tip of his scar. "Great news, Ma. The spare's shot — that frigging Bucky, Christ only knows what he did to it." The thing's done like dinner, he says, and he's going to have to walk. No asking if she minds being left; little choice anyway, given her knees. "Sit tight, there's people down there somewhere," he says with more spunk than she feels.

Outside, the breeze is balmy as he shambles off. She needs to pee, never mind how carefully she sipped her water at lunch. There's an outhouse in behind those ratty apple trees crowded by the forest. A two-seater. Spiders have knit webs in the door's crescent moon; people have carved names, dates. Flies swarm over the holes, the skunky smell rising up. Oh, glory, the stink summons the cabin in the Grounds. Plugging her nose, she has to work to shut it out. Wouldn't it be nice to wash her hands.

Pegging the door, she spies something she'd missed, an arrow nailed to a spruce bleeding sap. Just ahead is a mossy path. *Let all who are thirsty drink*, says a sign, its lettering burnt into the wood. Wetness seeps between her toes, but not far in there's a glen with a tiny pool edged with sandstones. *Rest here, and may the Blessed Virgin be upon you*. It figures, the bag with the containers is back at the car, lying on the dirt. Squatting carefully, she peers down at the water. Not a foot deep, murk bubbling from a crack so tiny she has to strain to see it. Pushing up her sleeve, she dips her hand.

The water is shockingly cool, yet lifeless, the rock slimy to the touch. What was she expecting — a fizz, like ginger ale: a burning, tingling? Holy fire, holy *something*.

She should go back for the bottles; Rebecca'd taken pains cleaning them, leaving hardly a trace of bleach. But the breeze stills her; a robin tweets from a branch. Removing her shoes, rolling up her pant legs, she peels off the knee-highs. Veins like tangled yarn under the skin, her shins glare against the grass; her toes with their corns and yellow nails. The wind sighs, gently changing direction, a bit stronger now, riffling her tight curls. Will Jewel have got midway? How long before he finds help? *Be with him*, a prayer leafs through her. He's hardly a hiker — never was one for exercise, none that she knew of anyway. Always that worry about his chest. What if he's lost? At least, for all its ruts and twists, there's just the one trail. *What's the use in worrying?* the robin trills. *It never was worthwhile.*

Cupping her hand, she dips it again, considers taking a taste. But was it fit? Sure, if you're a raccoon, Jewel might've said. *You don't want to get the trots, travelling*: that would be Rebecca. All the same, if she fills the bottles, they'll be set when he returns. Plenty of time, though; the sun has barely crossed the steeple poking above the trees. That image of the arthritic woman fills her, the notion of her dunking her hands. No one had mentioned drinking the water. Tugging her pant legs higher, she rolls them up over her knees. As if she's kneeled in paint, the scars resemble potato prints — like Robert used to do in school — and, after all these years, the colour of a night sky: a deep, vacant blue.

"Star light, star bright," she mutters aloud, splashing each knee, wincing. A murmured blessing — a blessing, perhaps, there isn't another soul around to hear. Squinting, she lets her eyes bleach each scar a gentler blue. *Hail Mary, full of grace; blessed art thou amongst women.*

As the sun tilts behind the little spire, she hobbles out to the car. Her purse is on the seat, where she left it. Digging inside, she finds the Aspirin bottle tucked there at the last minute. She's thirsty now, really thirsty, and famished: how long since lunch? Her toes feel clammy, gritty, the knee highs yanked on too hastily. "Where can he be?" she aims the question at the steep little roof, a turkey-sized bird perched there — an eagle?

Fingers closed around the pill bottle, she ambles purposefully back to the pool. The water clouds and fizzes with crumbs of Aspirin. *Acetylsalicylic acid*, she imagines Rebecca rhyming off, always the expert. An antiseptic? Not likely, but she takes a sip anyway. The water tastes sour, peaty. Tightening the lid, she gives the bottle a shake, feels a stab of worry: Harry. There's a flap of wings: crows. In the bushes squirrels natter. Pocketing the little bottle, to amuse herself she tramps towards the headstones.

Curved, toppled, more lie buried in the grass, tinged orange by the diamond of sun skimming the trees. The names and dates are worn smooth. *Once a thriving community*, she remembers the article saying. Doubling back through the stretching shadows, she re-enters the shabby little sanctuary. Shadows wash the corners, shrouding the altar but for a mote of brilliance. She tries to picture a priest offering Communion, the Host a tiny stone in that brook of light. For a second it's as if she's submerged.

Praying helps pass time. To an explosion of caws outside, she pictures a rash of wheelchairs on TV, pushing towards the grotto. "For everyone who's ailing, not just Harry," she tries to be inclusive, clasping her hands tightly; with the souvenir water in her pocket and her knees bathed, it seems petty not to. But against the image of Harry bedridden, even with time on her hands it's hard maintaining pity, upholding all who need help: Mrs. Slauenwhite's great-granddaughter on the Pill and pot-head son-in-law; somebody else's husband, the one with cancer. Her heart can barely stretch wide enough to channel it all — the needs of the world, the poor and the homeless, the almost homeless, like Miss Van Buskirk and that crazy

Benny, let alone her needs and Harry's and the others'. Lord have mercy, it's enough to make a martyr throw in the towel. And then there's Robert.

At the windows, the sun blazes orange, then red. There's a scuffling, raccoons perhaps, overly hopeful, scrounging for food. *Oh ye of little faith*, the scratching seems to say; and plucking up her nerve, she ventures outside again. Trekking back to the pool, she's thirsty, desperately so, and out of nowhere the awful thought comes to her of miners trapped underground drinking their pee. Dusk has painted the water and trees black, staining her hands and clothes purple, dissolving everything else to blue. Only the wind whistles through the branches, damp and alive and fragrant: nothing yet everything, she thinks, no more, no less. As she kneels there, a sliver of moon crosses her own reflection rippling back, ghostly against the jagged treeline: Christmas trees a forest of tents.

Stumbling back — the darkness a country darkness, pitch now, complete — she feels her way into the vestibule. Loony to be afraid: who or what is there to fear? Pressing her palm over the planked walls, she searches for a switch. But there's only the candle, and as she steps out into the fizzling moonlight, a memory arcs, searing her. Stealing her breath, it lifts and drops her: the slash of time years ago when everything had split apart. A divide of darkness: the instant the floor had let go underfoot, and she had felt herself airborne. *Helena*, the thought pierces her, and out there in the darkness something howls.

As she moves towards the car, it cries out again. But she isn't really hearing it. Suddenly, instantly, she's transported, her knees smooth again, supple. Catching her breath at the foot of the stairs, the sound of crying echoing down to her. There she is, still in her nightie, lolly-gagging as if she has all day. Picking up the milk, inspecting herself in the coat-stand mirror, rubbing her big round belly — and nearly nine o'clock in the morning! *Ship on fire*, the fellow in the downstairs flat had yelled. And upstairs, crying; the little one teething, always teething. Her own breath had fogged the glass. Harry hollering down,

Where are you, dolly? Bracing herself for the stairs, she'd adjusted her smile — Careful, don't show your gums, gums like the felt edging the accordion's keys ... Peeling the child's fingers away, once more she's getting dressed. *London Bridge is falling down. Down down down*: Helena yanking on her itchy stockings, teetering, bawling. In the kitchen, she's splashing water into the pan for eggs. Stoking the fire. Cracking each one and sliding it in, one two three. Those baby fingers climbing. *Hot hot hot!* And Harry yelling from the bedroom, *Where'd you put my —?*

In the blackness, Lucy feels for the handle, yanks open the car door. Light floods the interior; a moth flutters. A match, that's what she needs: a match. Sliding in, shivering, barely noticing her knees, confused, she tugs at the ashtray. Nothing but butts, half of them lipstick-stained.

Jesus, dolly, Harry's voice echoes down the steps and hallways of all those years. *Smell something burning? Lucy — you seen my —?* But she's prying Helena's fingers away, pushing ... *London bridge* on her lips, and ... Not a split second later, no time to pry or slap *or* squeeze — her lips had spread in a scream, a scream that stuck in her throat as the windows blew in, and the ceiling opened, and the blitz of wind ripped her hand from ... Ripped it away so fast, all she saw — God of mercy, of miracles? — was the skillet rocketing upward, the milky spritz of egg. Flying up, and out — pieces of the house tailing her like the wake of a comet — she'd felt herself being sucked skyward. Flying, cartwheeling through space, her body walked then spun like a jack, tossed and dropped. It had all happened faster than sound. A hand sweaty as her own scouring the stairs the day before, the hand that saved her, spinning with her in a vortex.

The air in the car is close, as close as that hand reaching through the stream of metal and glass. Trembling, she opens the glove compartment, claws through it. A spare pack of cigarettes, unopened. Bills for repairs, a book on maintenance, a penlight whose batteries are dead, and no matches, not one. The forest tightens, pressing closer: a vision, long buried, of Christmas trees bent in a blizzard, stretching for blocks; the headless ghosts of nurses, soldiers, weaving between them. The screaming wind: a baby crying ...

Abandoned, weaving back to the chapel, she feels her way inside. The walls are the colour of dirty snow, but, curling inwardly, furled like a bud, she lays herself out in the pew. The worn wood fallen rubble.

If only, the voices mock — a trinity: Harry's, Mama's, and that tiny, childish, barely-formed one, Helena's. *Elinor's? No!* If only she'd been more patient, and good — like Holy Mary? — and with the forgiveness of Job kept those tiny, creeping fingers locked in hers.

Twenty

HEADLIGHTS AND A RACING engine rouse her. Beams swinging in: searchlights illuminating splintery wood and water stains. The shock of voices, Jewel's loud one. "Ma — you still here?" As if she'd hiked or flown away. "Jesus, there you are." His mutterings, as if she'd got lost or something had eaten her. "Saving on power, or what?" he teases as a stranger in a ball cap shines a flashlight. "Holy water musta kept her going, what?"

He hands her a paper cup of coffee, which barely warms her hands. Explaining that it took a dog's age, finding buddy here. "But you're okay, Ma?" Even in the darkness he looks exhausted but relieved. She stays put while they change the tire in the glow of the fellow's headlights, the motor revving. The coffee's weak but sweet, and tastes like more. But now that she's been found she has trouble moving. Wiping his brow, Jewel slips into the pew beside her, as if she means to stay. "Beds are kind of hard, aren't they Ma, and they don't have cable. Let's *go*." But silence has enfolded her like a quilt and she hates to leave it for the wildness outside. Of all things, she asks if he's seen her purse.

"It's not in the car? Oh, right. I forgot," he teases almost feverishly. "You're shopping." Under her touch his wrist feels sticky and hot. Helping her up, he sways over her, his chin jutting in the flashlight's beam. Her hand trembles as she asks for a dollar bill; "Never mind," she thinks aloud, poking it into the bottle.

Their journey back is silent, like falling down a shaft, the bobbing tail lights of the truck ahead their only guide. Rushing in through the window, the chill is laden with an earthy smell. Before long the truck slows, a dog howling at its wheels, and the fellow waves them on to the highway. It's as if she's been on the mountain for weeks. She longs to be home, but it's too late to even think about driving back.

"Damn," Jewel mutters suddenly, remembering Rebecca's bottles, empty. "She'll have my head." Smiling wearily she pats her purse with the Aspirin bottle wrapped in a tissue, as a transport truck shoots past, trailed by a Winnebago towing a car. In the distance a light blinks weakly — a motel backed by the dark mountain. A painted rock welcomes them, and a sign advertising vacancies and dew worms. The café next to the office looks dead except for a TV blinking inside, but before they can drive on, a woman waves them in. The kitchen's closed, but she can make them a sandwich; there's one room made up, a twin. "We'll take it," Jewel says.

The café has fishnets hanging from the ceiling, starfish and a buoy caught in them, the walls covered with rusty tools. Jewel glances around nervously for a phone, saying he'd best check to see how they're making out. Rebecca and Harry. The thought sends a shiver down both her arms. Having strayed from her mind since sunset, it stirs a chilly gnawing. "Everything's copasetic," Jewel announces, sitting down again as the woman brings rubbery cheese on Holsum bread. "Dad's like a pig in poo." Eyeing his sandwich, he crams it in. Lucy takes a long drink of water, which tastes suspiciously like the spring.

"She remembered his pills?"

"Sure. Sure she did."

It's as if they've landed the Apollo: while the terrain is different, their feet are the same. Until it dawns, what a small thing her absence is, and yet huge, having little to do with distance. A feeling of removal, freedom, she'd never dared expect.

The room is clean enough and has two of everything, narrow beds with faded spreads, and lamps that remind Lucy of molten lava.

Despite the ache in her knees, she goes around inspecting things, slipping into the bathroom to put on her nightie. In the long, spotted mirror, the nylon clings to her crinkled thighs, and her knees resemble knots in a tree. She rubs on some of Rebecca's Avon, some "fountain of youth" concoction that smells of cucumber, and despite her weariness lays tissue over the seat before using the loo. She's forgotten her robe, another of Rebecca's gifts, deep mauve and fuzzy — Marryatt written all over it.

Fussing with the broken blinds, Jewel fiddles with the TV but nothing happens. "Imagine, roughing it like that." On the mountain, he must mean. "Like Bucky, and all that 'back to the land' crapola. He could go over to your place any time, Ma, and weed the garden." It's as good as an invitation to mention the money. But underneath her the mattress gives like bread, and all but her memory on the mountain evaporates. She feels almost giddy confined here in this little room, roped in yet free, thinking crazily of the driver in a hot-rod race they'd seen once on TV, pulling ahead to finish first. Glancing at her purse propped there with the Aspirin bottle inside, she's almost dizzy.

The sheets keep sliding off. "How was the bed?" she imagines Rebecca's concerned voice asking, and she longs now for something solid: the dryness of the garden's dirt, or her kitchen floor. Stretching out on his bed, Jewel leaves the light on, saying to kick him if he snores. The last time she's slept anywhere near him a lifetime ago; with a pang she pictures his room when it was still his, his photos, the ones from the war she'd stumbled across. As if there's an urgency, and she needs to grasp his childhood, his youth, and hand it all back. Digging out the Aspirin bottle, she gives it a shake, holding it up to the grimy fixture. Flies inside the shade make dark spots, like spots on an X-ray, spots on a lung. "Do you remember, darling?" she murmurs, choosing her words. The old place, she means, when they'd go for walks. "Up by the Big House, the barn," she prods, but he shrugs, and this dredging of memory, this probing, has nothing to do any longer with what she needs to know.

Propped against the pillow, he downs the dregs of his pop. "Where Babineau and them used to get lumber? Becky might, why?"

Nothing, dear, it's nothing, she says. What she wants to ask is about Miss Van Buskirk, but a second later he's snoring. Rising stiffly, she moves the pop can. Without her glasses, his face looks softer, a bit less craggy; when she squints it's her little boy lying there after being sung to, lullabies that once swung together in a tuneless singsong. Leaning down, she cups his face in her hands, as if he'll wake and pull away. His skin feels clammy under the scrape of beard, as cool yet stale, somehow, as the air in the room. Her heart a jellyfish filling and emptying, she kisses each of his cheeks till his eyes fly open, mortified. "Ma? What are you doing?" An embarrassment — of riches, the notion glides through her as they close again, his arm around her shoulder. Sliding out from under it, folding herself once more between her slippery sheets, she hunkers down. *Now I lay me*, a part of her yawns, an opening. A pinhead of brightness that for years has been distant enough as to not exist. *I pray the Lord my soul to keep. If I should die before I wake, I pray the Lord my soul to take.*

IN THE MORNING JEWEL doesn't stop to shave, going to load the car. For breakfast there's tea and oatcakes — sawdust cakes, he calls them. Across from the motel lies water as smooth and blue as the Holy Mother's robes, with pale hills in the distance, serene. It only feeds her need to get home, but up ahead is a tannery, where Jewel buys a sheepskin. Its edges curl like the hide of that gutted pilot whale she'd seen once with her father, long, long ago, the fleece like blubber. Dad, she thinks as it floods back: her four-year-old hand in his, the creature hanging from a gaff, its entrails steaming on the dock. The best thing for somebody bedridden, to prevent bedsores, Jewel keeps saying. Which reminds her: has Rebecca remembered to turn Harry? But, having made a point of getting down on all fours, inspecting the muffler, huffing and spluttering, now Jewel seems in no hurry to get back, hell-bent on sightseeing. "Is that what I think it is?" He points to something, a bald eagle — or a vulture. Since when was he a birdwatcher?

Gulls do loop-the-loops as they cross to the mainland, the water satiny smooth on one side of the causeway and rough on the other, she makes the mistake of commenting, and Jewel backs up traffic watching for a spot to pull over. If there's a problem with the car, it can't be too important. "Not like we do this all the time," he says. She laughs, but that pain has started in her belly again: worry, like a virus.

Without warning, Jewel veers off onto what must be the scenic route. Next they're winding along a dirt road beside a wharf; she can't hide her jitters. "Will Robert be helping his mom?" It's the first time she's mentioned him. "Harry's not easy to move, you know." Admiring a fish plant, he slows to a crawl. "Don't worry. Becky's got help." But then he coughs. "It's just that, when I called last night? They had a bit of an emergency." A plumbing one, he quickly adds. Harry's waterworks? Oh, Dinah! She tugs at her flattened curls. Reading her mind, perhaps, he says something about the old pipes from the bathroom.

It takes forever to reach the place he promises will connect them with the highway, a town she recognizes. But as they follow the signs, there's a clunk, the racket of metal beating the pavement. Creeping down the tree-lined street the car makes noises like the noon gun, but they make it to a garage. It takes another age to have it looked at; they sit outside watching traffic move past what were once stately homes, now slightly run down, used for businesses. A hairdresser's, where ladies can get their ears pierced — with an ice cube and needle, she wonders, or a fancy little gun? Jewel slouches there, rattling his newspaper, sweating. In a proper snit, he is, all this damned expense and bother. His face red, his breath coming in snorts. He lights a cigarette, but stubs it out. The worry worm inside her gets worse when she recognizes a big grey house down the block; it has to be the same place, though Mrs. Edgehill must be long gone, the lovely leaded panes replaced with sliders. As Jewel wheezes with impatience, it all comes back: that proper woman and the sightless child with her pink ribbon.

At last the mechanic comes out, wearing a greasy cap otherwise like a surgeon's, and says it's ready. The car smells of grease when she gets in, Jewel shuffling off to pay. He's awfully poky; maybe they don't take Chargex? She starts to fret again about how long they've been away, and what's waiting when they get there. What's taking the boy so long? The boy, she catches herself. Jewel. He's being silly, putting up a stink about "highway robbery."

The attendant raps at the window, looking cheesed off, no, alarmed. "You'd better come," his voice is a slur, saying he's not sure what's happened. Inside, Jewel slouches on a chair, his legs splayed, his face drained. The Chargex card's on the floor, and the receipt. His meaty hand rests against his shirt, its damp knit.

She claws at him, claws at his buttons, her choppy breath melting into the sweaty afternoon as someone calls an ambulance. As everything inside her stops, or seems to, the day, the station a heat wave, a greasy stream moving forward without her. In the back of her head, a burning instant, snagged forever. A single raspy breath coming from Jewel: she hears it. No no no. It stops too. The pallor of his skin, the graze of stubble under her sweaty palm, her heart beating through her skin, beating through the pores and creases. Her love. Her boy. One small line, a tiny crease below her baby finger, one of two creases: her babies, her fortune. Her mind falls backwards, refusing, refusing, to lurch forwards into now. The now of his not breathing. Briefly his eyelids flicker. Light! As if this has been a joke, a prank. *Fooled you, Ma.* Like the time ... "Ma," she hears it, and he smiles, yes. A smile from the dark, though, from the past and the not to be. *Ma.* Her mind closes around it, a bell capturing sound, shaped forever around the echo.

No no no, she hears her own whine, a child's, whined into the dampness of his chest, the still-warmth of his cheek. His body slumped there. Somewhere on the wall, a clock twists and judders: five o'clock?

There's a fragrance, grease on cooling skin. Something dribbling from his pant leg to the floor. Gently, a medic presses his stethoscope, tries to find a pulse. Gone. Her treasure, her reason for putting one foot in front of the other, for turning her back on the icy waves of all those years. The howling little face of mercy.

There are channels that have to be gone through, arrangements made. But she's fallen out of time, can't make a phone call. Can't drive. More stubborn than she ever realized, she can't leave her son, can't leave the tiny hospital where they take his body. Finally someone puts her on a bus, and it's on the bus that she feels herself crumble, her heart of granite being ground into sand. A beach, minerals. Salt pouring down her face as the tears come.

The cab driver ferrying her from the bus depot asks what's wrong. No words, no sound. She can't speak, getting out. In the yard, the fence doesn't look any different, the night a thin place as she climbs the steps. Music wafts down to the veranda, and a strange laugh, a little like a donkey's. Jewel nowhere but everywhere, a pressure on her skin, her spirit. *You put one foot in front of the other, that's how you do it, baby boy!* Baby steps: Jewel learning to walk. Who knows how she makes it inside.

Rebecca grins from the landing, her face flushed, beaming. It falls even before she asks. *Where is he?* ringing inside the bell of Lucy's brain. She doesn't have to speak, Rebecca knows something's wrong, crumpling on the stairs. Somehow, somehow, Lucy makes it past her to Harry's room. She's known all along who will be there, helping. Miss Van Beeswax — Elinor — perches on the edge of his bed, her arms spread wide, the Don Noble in mid-jiggle. "Für Elise" is the tune, it comes to Lucy belatedly, a tune she recognizes from before, from Mama playing it on the piano, gloomy, except it's speeded up. Jubilant. Elinor, her own — *Helena* — and the urgency, the recognition she felt on the mountain, as black as coal melting into the cracks and bubbles of concrete, cools like something volcanic, the volcanoes she's seen on TV. And now there is Harry to think of, his weakness, *his* heart. They could be inside a foundry, that wrecked one years ago, with its smoking wall a reminder of death, and in the middle of it, in the middle of her, the hardening blackness around her Jewel.

Never mind that the stranger, the lost and now the found, has come into the house and turned everything upside down. Coming to tidy, at first, then gotten carried away. Cleanliness *is* next to godliness as she looks into Miss Van Buskirk's, Elinor's, eyes and mutely slips past her, curling into Harry. Even as she finds words to tell him — *Gone, gone* — something inside her sprouts, the shoot of a beach pea pushing from sand. *For now I see as through a glass darkly, but then face to face.* Even as the weight of Jewel presses down. *If I have faith to remove mountains, but not love, I am nothing.* And what is love? The heat at her throat is no different from the flashes she'd gone through. The change of life, the change — the changes — of heart.

Miss Van Buskirk *is* an oddball, all right, like Jewel said. Her dress a vision of the jungle as she sets down the 'cordine and moves from the bed. The dusky mountain rushes back, and the steamy garage and her boy slumped there, Lucy's memory of them liquid now, molten: the warmth of Helena's tiny, slipping fingers, and his big rough ones.

"Poor sweet darling," she hears herself murmur into an ear, not Elinor's but Rebecca's. Rebecca's face is wet; her tears taste of hairspray. A flood.

"MISSUS," HELENA-ELINOR-*HELINOR* murmurs, her strange, leathery hands fussing, stroking. She's good at this, has had practice, it seems. Still, there's a coolness to her eyes, an unknowable blue, the skin around them crinkling. Somewhere in the dark, across the Arm, a train rumbles as the woman rubs her back. Rebecca sits there staring, mute. But it's as if little kids are singing in Lucy's head. Tiny ones hardly old enough to talk, yet knowing all the words. *Someone's in the kitchen with Di-nah, someone's in the kitchen I know-woa-woa-woa.*

The tunes slur into one: *London Bwidge is fawing down. Down down down lady-o.*

Helena's hair is clipped back now with a pink plastic butterfly, instead of a rag. The sound Harry makes is terrible, a hound weeping. "There, there, Harry," Helena comforts him in her country drawl. As if they're alone, though, and have known each other for some time — until she moves a chapped hand to her mouth and nervously bites a nail. There's a scar by her thumb, Lucy sees, a tiny crater the shape of a vaccination mark. When Helena asks if they want tea, her voice seems far away, like Robert's used to be inside his cardboard Sputnik when he'd pretend to be a Martian. What she hears is Harry yelling: *Lucy? Something's burning!* and the sound of crying upstairs, her tiny daughter, and herself shouting, *Coming!* The milk in her arms half-froze from sitting out there on the stoop, cream pushing out the top of the bottle, and her thinking how it would taste. The cravings she'd had, pregnant — cream and brown sugar — a wonder she and Jewel both hadn't ended up butterballs. *Put that in your cup and drink it, Harry.* The effort of climbing stairs. *Dolly, when she's not teething, she's scratching!* Helena's chicken pox. *Jesus Murphy, where did those cufflinks go?* The milk on the counter, eggs sliding into a boil. *Find them yourself!* Her own angry voice. *Danger! Hot!* Slap.

Her voice now, when she finds it, is a whisper: "What should I call you?" For she's come unravelled, may as well be a sock off the needles. Through grainy eyes, she spies a clot of paper near Harry's pills. Embarrassed, Elinor — "just call me Elinor" — mutters about the leak and plumbers finding something near the sill, way down in the wall in the basement. A note? Rebecca glances up, little rivers in her makeup, and says nobody could make heads or tails of it.

Harry at last has stopped his sobbing, and Lucy squeezes his hand, squeezes it for dear life. "Harry?" she hears herself, a damp croak. "There's something you should know," as if he needs it spelled out. She looks at Helena, *Elinor*, as she says it, taking in the whole of her as vague as someone on TV when the rabbit ears got bent, slowly fixing the ghost with another face, another voice, a tiny, wordless one. Rebecca sits there empty, all her scheming, the ending she's cooked up, sweet and sour; and yet, a floozy warmth lights her ruined cheeks. Harry doesn't open his eyes; his lips tremble, but he squeezes back. "I know, Lucy. The girls told me." His words knit her together, and as if to celebrate, Elinor lugs the 'cordine onto her lap and wheezes out "Twinkle Twinkle Little Star" ever so softly. A lullaby perhaps.

The stars seem to ache when she flees outside, constellations dancing jigs and reels. The poor invaded moon shining, too, round as the Superball Robert had once that bounced so hard it could destroy a car by hitting it, he'd boasted. The wind is sticky, the grass so wet her toes feel numb as she kneels by the garden. Around her the lilies are done, but the asters are out, early; their tiny blooms mirror the stars — *the heavenly bodies*: Jewel's voice comes back, as if from a science scribbler. Not even a year since Harry's fall, which makes what's happened all the more shocking, unfair. As if troubles can be cancelled, lent and borrowed. Yet she's filled with an urge to kiss the ground, the way someone holy like the Pope might do at an airport, bum to the sky. Except, there's a squeak from the porch.

"You'll catch your death out here, Missus." Elinor's eerie calm snares her.

"How ever did you find us?" she calls out stupidly, knowing it's been Rebecca's doing. Breathing through pins and needles — her poor, poison knees — she takes in the sputtering arc overhead, the fading twinkle: a star for everyone who's walked the planet. One for her and one for Elinor slouching on the step, her uncanny likeness haloed by the kitchen light, and one for Jewel. *In the name of the Father, Son and Holy Ghost*: the words shower down inside her. Rubbing her eyes, wordlessly Elinor slips inside.

The mudroom fills with rosy light as Lucy creeps back in. Moving down the hallway, her feet barely touch wood. In the front room, Elinor's stretched out under a blanket, not asleep but resting her eyes. Lucy has to get a chair to reach the cup; dreadful now if she dropped it. The springs complain as she settles near Elinor's feet, holding it out. *The Lord giveth and the Lord taketh away*, and isn't everything possible in him or her? The shade of a smile on her lips, Elinor balances it in her palm. Seeing this gives Lucy wings; for a moment she's lifted and held, but thinking of Jewel, lands with the hard earth for cushioning, her grief black. "Can you call me *ma*?" The word chafes; she wishes she could hide underneath it.

Elinor smiles into her cup, harbouring secrets? "I had a mother, once. She just never outlived me," she says, and how crazy. As dawn fills the room, Lucy feels as though a wave has broken over them, and drying, tightened her skin. She lets Elinor, nurse, cook and bottle-washer, help her upstairs; watches as Elinor clears off Jewel's old bed, and shoves aside grocery bags full of who knows what — Valley luggage? From the next room, as the light at the window opens to nothing, she hears Harry ask over and over what day it is. A rough, kind hand draws the quilt up to her chin, against memories deep inside her of kerosene, canvas, a nun offering a newborn with flailing limbs. As she dozes, her mind becomes grit. *For every one shall be salted with fire, and every sacrifice shall be salted with salt.*

When she opens her eyes, the light stabs them, her sight blurring once more with grief. But there's something pressing against her, a weight against her hip. Lying there, Robert's curled up in his uniform, that putrid green jacket, shredded jeans and muddy sneakers. The smell of beer — sickness — as he shifts in his sleep. *As if I don't see what you've been up to*, twisting her fingers through his curls, ignoring the dampness on the quilt: drool. Clutched in his hand is an old penknife of his father's, lost, she'd thought. It's folded, the way her stomach feels, gripped again by their loss, a loss that jerks her upright. Gently, she shakes him. "You must pull yourself together, dear." But isn't it what a dad would say — his dad — and certainly not his mother?

ROBERT RETRIEVES THE CAR in time for the funeral, the same day Rebecca receives the hospital's report. Not a thing anyone could have done, nothing that could have been predicted or prevented:

this is what they tell her. A sliver of metal, shrapnel, working its way through a valve — a relic from a wound, a war wound. A ticking time bomb, a secret smaller than a minute. In the flickering light of St. Columba's, Lucy focuses not on the casket or Father Langille or the windows, but on Robert's wrinkled suit in front of her, and the teardrop of bare skin at the back of Rebecca's dress. Glancing at the figure hanging from the cross, the apple on his tree, her tears are vinegar. She cannot look at the stained-glass Mother nearby cradling her jewelled Boy, not even when a mote of sunshine lights the infant's cheeks. *The fruit of thy womb.* "The body and blood of Christ," the priest intones, "who died and suffers now with you." Such wild abandon, such crazy love. *And so we must be fools for him.* "That's right, and I got a shiddle to sell you," says Harry afterwards, reaching up from his wheelchair for Rebecca's hand.

In the basement, the league ladies put out tea and squares, a sweet feast on doilies. They serve and pour, hugging Lucy and murmuring sympathy. One looks like Mrs. Slauenwhite, who must be a thousand years old: her daughter. Their faces blur and she forgets names, yet she is grateful. For everyone there sipping tea like the drinking bird Harry used to have on top of the TV; the thought of it cheers her. Oddly, so does Benny, the sight of him in jaunty plaid, loading up his paper plate on the other side of the room, as grizzled as the old coot who shuffles forward, nudging Harry with his cane. Elinor tries to swivel the chair away, but the man manages to clip Harry on the shoulder. "What a goddamn thing," he says, his jowls shaking. He tips his gaze from Lucy's. "Just a young fella, too. I'm that sorry for youse."

Those monkey eyes, that familiar look; glory, how long since he'd come around hawking anything a person could drag sounds out of? Not much better than Benny. Nice fella, Jewel, he says: "What I knew of him. He was just a kid." Edgar Boutilier, who'd started Harry fiddling; barking up the wrong tree if ever there was a wrong one, back when Harry himself was either hawking things or being in hock, and little she could've done but turn a blind eye.

When Elinor pushes Harry towards a crowd from Black's, an elderly gent surrounded by women, Boutilier limps along too, hovering as Lucy lays her hand on Harry's shoulder. It's as if she's not there. "Guess he seen a lot," Boutilier mutters, "old soldier and all, eh Harry? Buddy?" His gaze shifts, those eyes too bright. "Listen," he says, "I never meant for him to see." That night in the cove, she hears. "That frigging Babineau had it coming. But I never knew the boy was with you. Honest to Christ, I never seen him in the boat." The feeling she has is about the same as when she'd watched the moon perch on a swaying, folded rooftop. But before Harry can speak, a woman — one of Birdie's daughters? — tugs Edgar away, his soles scuffling over painted concrete.

When Robert nudges Harry, "Who *is* that old bastard?" Harry blows his nose, three sharp blasts.

GRIEF IS A DARKNESS where the only sound is an endless foghorn. Though in a dream, somewhere above, in blue, haloed light, Helena laughs. Looking down, Lucy glimpses the baby inside her — the purl of a tiny thumb. Pushing, her body opens. But then he's grown, weaving between rows of lilies, and when she holds out her hand he vanishes, a pile of ashes the wind scatters. Cartwheeling towards the sun, she catches the glint of water, sees clear to the seabed. Broken things: china, ivory stained with algae. Yet, flashing upwards, sprayed with sunlight, are the faces of both children as she'd want them to be.

Work will set you free: that evil slogan from some program they'd watched before Harry's fall. Words arched over a Nazi gate. Had Jewel seen things like that? Best not to wonder, to busy herself instead with what's *here*. Her knitting a lost cause, though, replacing dropped stitches as tedious as reattaching nerves. But there are eggs, lemon for a cake. *Worship with thy lips* and *thy hands*. They live on Elinor's "specialties," casseroles she learned to whip up "when things got bad at home." The tea she makes is weak and Lucy discovers why: tea bags dangle from the clothesline, to be reused. *Waste not want not*: the way she was raised, Elinor admits with some pride, saying how her first word was *helener*. How part of her died when her father did. How her mother got sick and her brother spent more time picking up pickers than picking apples, which was when Elinor had started going out to work — though she'd have been happier just playing piano.

There are so many things Lucy wants to ask, Elinor's life a jigsaw puzzle with most pieces missing. Sometimes she lets things slip: how she'd started her monthly, to everyone's dismay, at one of Mother's teas, blood on the Persian carpet patterned with men on horseback. How a school friend stole her lucky rabbit's foot. Lucy would rather not hear about the brother, the *step*-brother, twenty years older, or how deer ransacked the orchards, or how someone accused Elinor of stealing milk money, which is what drove her from Coltsfoot, her home in the Valley, to the city and eventually to Benny, never mind that he's old enough to be her dad.

The house smells of bleach, everything scrubbed, scoured. Even Harry, his hair newly Brylcreemed. *A little dab'll do you*, Elinor teases. In the dimness of grief, her vacuuming threatens to swallow them, and every last dust mite and mote. Against the cupboards' whiteness, Elinor's hair looks iron-grey, her tan yellow. A tot under an ash pan frozen to the snow: a *pearl inside a cast-iron shell, unharmed.* The thought will always twist Lucy's stomach, and she has to ask, "Was it nice, where you grew up?" But in her mind's eye, anyway, the faces from that faded clipping dissolve, the way rain appears to dissolve a pane of glass. When Elinor picks up the accordion something changes: the pooling of their lives rushes forwards. There's a grace as notes spill over, as clear as the comb of water at the edge of a dam. No looking back. Grace is the peace Lucy makes with what none of them, not even Elinor, can know.

Rebecca arrives just as the cake is done, the first she's been dressed since the funeral. "You're *baking?*" She sounds stunned. Without makeup her face looks smaller, farther away, and all Lucy can think of is Lil — drunken, disorderly Lil. But Rebecca's eyes follow Elinor fixing Harry's lunch, filled with a kindness — affection? — Lil wouldn't've shown anybody in a skirt. As she leans close, her whisper is scratchy, and Lucy's scared she'll cry. But it's not about Jewel, it's something Elinor's confided, how, every year, instead of celebrating her birthday, in December old Mrs. Van Buskirk would order a cake with *Happy Anniversary* on it. "Can you beat that, Ma?" More than Lil ever did for *you*, she's willing to bet, and not just because she needs to excuse that other reluctant mother.

Blinking at the ceiling, Rebecca cocks her head, listening? "You know, Ma, when she first came, she told Benny she was just going out for chigarettesch," she imitates Harry, blinking harder, trying to be funny. She is, too, and Lucy could almost laugh, even when she says Benny depends on Elinor something fierce.

Lucy swallows. "The way Jewel did on you, I guess?" She catches Rebecca's arm before either of them can back away. "You were good to him. I know you were, though I never gave you credit."

Rebecca stares, her voice a bit sarcastic: "Coming from where I did, you mean."

Taking a deep breath, Lucy stares back. "Maybe I blamed you for your mother's antics."

HARRY KEEPS ASKING ABOUT Robert's plans, never mind that everyone's in limbo. After making himself scarce — scarcer than his dad when Lucy used to cook beef tongue — the boy just appears one day, the hall light giving his paleness a glow that makes her reach up and hug him fiercely. Never mind that money; he's so thin, he can't be healthy, she thinks, as he babbles about Sheryl, yes, *yes*, his girlfriend. He can help today, not with painting, but maybe the garden? Wouldn't know a dahlia from a dandelion, she mumbles. But it's now or never for the lilies; the clouds lately remind her of the billowing ones in Westerns. The kind that say, to her anyway, *Get along little doggie, pee or get off the pot.* Not to Robert apparently, oblivious. Threatening rain, and nothing on his feet but holey sneakers. Any luck and it'll hold off, while Elinor's minding Harry. But there's a problem finding tools; they turn the mudroom upside down looking for the trowel. A chance to pop the question, Harry's question, and he says he'll hit Vancouver by Christmas, some park people camp out in.

"In a tent?" she can't help herself. "In December?"

As she gropes through the clutter, he shoves his hand in his pocket, holds something out the way she might a missing sock. Blushing, he presses it into her palm, a little wad of money. Ones, twos and fives; she never was sure of the total. "I never meant to steal it, Gran," he pleads.

Finding the trowel, she swings it, snorting as the sting returns of being so badly let down. "I ought to put you over my knee and smack you one for each buck, Bucky." He looks down, startled. But she's busy tying on her plastic bonnet.

Harry's vests and boxers droop from the clothesline, and what resemble tiny, muddy mermaid's purses. *Waste not, want not,* she imagines Jewel snorting. "'Miss Nuts-and-Bolts,' the old man called her," Robert remarks cattily, asking how long Elinor's sticking around. "Long as someone keeps feedin' her," he mimics his dad.

"As long as she keeps us going," she corrects him, with a sharpness she's not used till now.

Rain plasters his T-shirt to his chest, and she nips back in for the umbrella, then shows him where to dig. The lilies bend in the downpour. On his knees, his eyes on the dirt, he murmurs that he wasn't planning to keep the money for good. "You don't believe me, but it's true," he says, and she knows he's hoping she didn't tell Jewel.

Hogging the umbrella, well, allowing herself the lion's share, she takes her sweet time. "Your dad would've been disappointed. *If* he knew." Stooping, she shields him a little as he tugs up roots, and with unusual gusto hacks them apart. "They're living things," she nudges him, as the rain seeps through her old coat, kept for these chores. Already she's picturing the lilies multiplied, spread around the yard: the lilies of the field, the roots pale and fleshy against the grass, as she hooks her arm through his, directing: There, and *there*. After digging a couple of holes he peers up through his straggly hair.

"Do we have to do this today?" He asks if he can come back tomorrow, or Saturday.

She'd like to cuff him, but his look makes her laugh. "Not if you need the money," she says slyly. "You're hitting the road soon, aren't you?" A worm makes him jump, but he shrugs it off, jamming a fistful of tubers into the ground, rocking slowly backwards.

"Enough of this shit," he mutters, as if he's too smart for her, too smart for the world, "when I hit BC —"

THE HOUSE IS SMALL, with a third person around — she will not say third wheel — the bathroom the only hide-out, with Harry's walker serving as a towel rack. Even this room feels different, the work of younger, brisker hands. They get into debates about Harry's care, Elinor sure he sleeps better without the TV. Sometimes it's like being a guest in her own house, leaving things as spotless as she finds them. A relief when Elinor goes home to Benny. Stumbling upon Elinor's bible, the stain book reclaimed from Rebecca, Lucy reads: S for *Schedule. Hit-or-miss housekeeping results in frazzled nerves,* it says, *ineffective work, wasted time, cross children and unpleasant husbands. Should your schedule hopelessly elude you, do not attempt to catch up with it ... let it come round to you.* Amen, *a-women*: it's hard to argue with such wisdom.

Then one afternoon Rebecca asks about the water. Lucy has to think what she means, the Aspirin bottle a relic in her purse. The cache of empties likely still in the trunk, though Robert dropped off her suitcase and the sheepskin for Harry. A keepsake now: when Harry sits on it in his wheelchair, he says he can feel Jewel's "touch" coming through. The sort of comment that, from him, makes her think his mind's going.

Uncapping it, Lucy wets her fingertips, a little flame starting in her cheeks as she presses them to Harry's slack jaw. *Thy will be done.* Elinor says there's a sucker born every minute, and goes to get his snack. A bunch of hocus-pocus, he slurs, batting the bottle away: "Gwan!" Rebecca sniffs it, saying Lucy could've saved herself the trouble and got some of the stuff blessed by Father Whasisname; they all could've saved themselves the trouble. There's silence, but then Rebecca holds the bottle to Harry's lips. "Be a sport. Pretend it's beer." As he takes a little slurp, she murmurs, "Walk, sinnah!" Like Jewel would've, mimicking the TV preacher they watch sometimes for fun. Lucy's aghast — for Harry's sake. But he sputters, laughing, and through a glint of tears Rebecca chuckles.

"Buncha foolishness," Elinor clucks, returning with a tray. The look Harry gives her is the look a bird would give its mother. "Feelin' anything, buddy?" she rubs his shoulder, then hoisting the accordion onto her lap, squeezes out a Quiet Time number, "What a Friend We Have in Jesus." His clapping shakes the mattress. It's as if one of his old cronies has stepped in for a drink. Elinor grins the way he used to, her mouth wide and straight. Then she pops in his pill — "Open sesame, bud" — giving him some magic water to wash it down. For a second, Lucy can almost picture a finicky gloved hand stroking a child covered in soot: a tar-baby, a tar-toddler. *Dinah won'tcha blow.*

Rebecca sprinkles a bit on Harry's leg. "Git behind me, Satan!" Forgive her: she never did know when to stop. Emptying the dregs into the African violet, Elinor plunks the 'cordine on her dad's lap; wiggling in behind, she works the bellows while he fingers a melody. A gleam lights her face; if Lucy weren't so forgiving, she'd call it cruel. But she tries to imagine a child — with braids, wearing pink? — her little hands tickling the ivories, and she hears herself ask, *Your parents, were they musical?*

"Couldn't carry a tune in a bucket, Missus."

REBECCA'S NOT DOING so hot, so Lucy takes leftover frankfurter casserole. Robert's downstairs entertaining the girlfriend. At least, she hears the TV — *Mod Squad?* — and smells that smell. Washing dishes, she's trying not to think of tiny Jewel mucking around in the sink, when Sheryl slips out. Robert appears, stinking of tobacco; no, that evil weed, she guesses, and it fills her with a fuzzy dread. What can she do? He's too big to threaten or bribe. As he scrabbles through the fridge, his eyes look as though he's been crying. There's a mark on his neck; glory, the girl's a vampire? "What is it?" she prods, but he doesn't make a peep, and she's shot with an image of Jewel in his little bed, and that day in Sister Jerome's office, the day Lucky struck: a dog, God spelt backwards.

"Your dad, he wouldn't want to see you like this." Her voice is as firm as the one she imagines whispering sometimes from the clouds: Jewel's. "If you're going, my darling, *go*. No good hanging around. Heavenly God," she finally blurts. "You mustn't just give up."

"*You* give up," he turns on her. "That God stuff. If God was real, why would he let so much crap come down?"

ELINOR SETS UP THE washbasin, gets Harry's razor and Old Spice, then holds the mirror, telling him to help himself. His hand shakes. It's painful to watch, so Lucy tries to help him. He's got to learn to do it for himself, Elinor insists, and she's right. That doesn't make it any easier, though there's something she's learned from Elinor, that things handle themselves, more or less. Afterwards, Elinor bathes his face. A minister dousing that tiny forehead, Lucy thinks: Helena's christening. How she'd screeched and waved her yellow fists, Harry sneaking off for a beer. *Give her a kiss for me, dolly — she'd best be asleep by the time I get home.*

Lucy's downstairs when there's a shout: "Quick, Missus!" An urging. She's up the stairs in a flash, in time to see Elinor manoeuvring Harry in the chair, practically popping a wheelie. It's like watching Robert alone on the Ferris wheel when there weren't enough spots, and waiting below, she wished she were there, too, in that rinky-dink seat. Harry nestles on his sheepskin cloud. *Let sleeping babes lie*, that advice rushes back, the words of women in that basement, not St. Columba's but the other, earlier one where she'd nursed Jewel and the fissures inside her. A blanket of memories, white as a snowy field and black as tar.

Harry's half out of the chair, almost but not quite standing. She moves quickly, trying to ease him back, till Elinor stops her. His dark green slippers pedal the floor, his face red as he steadies then lifts himself again. Trembling, like a heron testing its wings, then lifting off. Elinor holds out both hands as he shuffles towards her: one foot before the other, baby steps. "C'mon, bud. You can do it!" Arms around each other, they're glued together, those two. "Where there's a will there's a way, eh, Missus?"

Except, Lucy's heart seems to have quit beating, her pulse replaced by a hum, the air in her lungs? There's nothing for it, but to bury her face in the wood of his neck.

"If this doesn't call for a celebration, I dunno what does," Elinor brays.

SOMEBODY'S GOT TO GET Robert up, if Rebecca can't. The kid would sleep forever. "When's he leaving, anyway?" That's Harry. *Don't give up, Ma.* The voice from the clouds is dogged at first, though little by little it loosens its grip. Someone has to keep an eye on Robert, keep him in line. Eighteen, still a baby as far as that goes. The Lord opens a door whenever he, or she, closes a window. There's talk now of Benny kicking the hippies out of his mother's place, him and Elinor moving in. She's even talking about going to sea, cutting Benny's moorings and drifting out — thankfully, not in front of Harry. Maybe wanderlust's contagious.

"Get up!" she hollers, "Get the frig up!" as his grampa would say. It's noon, and she's got something, fifty dollars, in her pocket. A donation, though a kick in the pants might be better deserved. A nudge, it is. He'll need to eat on the road. Worse than ever, he's sluggish and stubborn, glued to his bed. There's a stitch in her neck, as if the ache in her knees has wiggled its way up. Never mind, she flaps the blankets, the first time in ages she's made it past the threshold. The hair above his shorts and his hairy thighs a shock. His eyes squeezing out the world, the world of his room. There are pictures on the wall, greyish snaps taped up, row on row. *Mary, Mary, quite contrary, how does your garden grow?* In one of them, his dad props his foot on a man's back in a field of backs, uniforms, helmets. The look on his tiny face sober, triumphant.

"What the fu —?!" Robert stirs. *Fudge*, he means, half asleep.

Wetting a cloth with icy water, she presses it to his cheek, saying he mustn't waste his day. As he squirms a healthy hum rises up, the one Harry used to give off, so remote it's as if that young Harry never existed, beyond her wanting him to. Mixed in is a smell like freshly-laid carpet. Opening an eye, he glowers, swings out a leg.

"I thought you'd come for a walk, dear." It's if she's asking him to steal a car, but she tells him he could use the air, that it helps people think. Pushing her out, he slams the door. She hears him getting dressed. Not a peep from Rebecca upstairs. "How's Sheryl?" she asks through the wood.

"I dunno," he mumbles sourly, yanking on his jacket.

Sink or swim, the voice carps, the voice of the man in the picture holding bodies captive. Robert grabs some bread, cramming it into his mouth. "The shore?" she elbows him; the top of her shoulder barely reaching his ribs. At least being half-awake, he won't argue, not at first. "Down where the old place used to be, where Grampa and your dad and I ..." Her voice malingers. "What's there now? Not much, I guess." She doesn't mention Ida Trott's or that day he'd kicked the tire, or how the Grounds is the last place she'd have visited once, willingly.

Shrugging, he scuffles along, the day ripened to a pearly grey as they walk in silence. Below the road, the rocks shine dully, the first dabs of red in the trees mirrored on the tide. When he veers off, she keeps up the best she can, following through the woods. The pines have been razed, making way for something. She'd hardly recognize the place, though a queer comfort creeps up from the ground, up through the roots and stones. She could find her way blindfolded.

Rubble from the Big House sinks in a blaze of alder, wood from the barn crisscrossing the swamp. Robert stumps past Ida's inkbottle house as if it were gone, too, though that van is still there, its wind-shield like a spider web in the timid sun. Soundlessly, a jet scores the spreading blueness overhead. Its plume links the clouds, cutting the path, perhaps, that fiery bits of metal once did. Parts of a ship, and souls sprayed like milk and eggs and perfume, invisible as a sliver in the heart, or a baby about to enter the world, leaving behind snug darkness.

It's not so hard, keeping up. Only a bit out of breath, she tugs his sleeve. She needs to show him something, never mind if he's seen it a thousand times. Just ahead, the shank of iron surrounded still by knotweed; like bamboo that might grow in Japan, probably did, in Hiroshima, the stalks dwarf her. The dead blooms barbed as wire.

"Here, darling." Her voice is a murmur, a soft rasp. Somebody's painted the shaft, recently by the looks of it, and it no longer lies on dirt, but on concrete. Pieces of beer bottle glint up, and a plaque: *Mont Blanc's anchor, Dec. 6th, 1917.* His hand leaves his pocket easily when she reaches for it, touches his fingers to the metal. It's cool and pitted, as if the air's eaten it. The money waits in her pocket, but first she hikes her coat to bare both knees. That blue, a prayer.

Dampness seeps between her toes; she can feel her hair frizz as they poke towards shore. The path is slippery and she takes his arm, feeling it tense. "Your father ..." she begins softly, her heart swelling, but he's not listening. His eyes are locked on something out in the water — a shag, maybe, a loon with no mate? Straight as can be she clings to him, shivering in spite of the fallish warmth. The spring of his muscles soothes her, their warmth through that stupid khaki. Suddenly she could weep — with joy, the seedling of it, being here with him. The two of them mismatched but kindred as runaways from the fair. Maybe he feels it too, but just can't speak. Behind some brambles, what look to be bedsprings rust in the grass. The remains of Babineau's cabin, Artie's love-shack.

His elbow presses hers when they finally reach the rocks. The seaweed's laced with junk: things that make her want to look away. As always, though, the water is a magnet, redeeming what's before it, and she can't help scouring the edge with her eye. No better than a crow, a scavenger on the lookout for something shiny and free.

"As if the sea can swallow it all — what's *wrong* with people?" she has to ask, grappling for his hand again, pressing the bills into it. Shamed and afraid, too, because who knows how he'll take it? *Our Lady of bleeding hearts and mustard pickles*, Rebecca called her once, not to her face, but still. Rebecca, their Lady of Avon: as close to a daughter as she can get. A cloud yawns inside her, a mushroom, but his boyish laugh blows it out over the cove. "Gran. What the fu—?" That language alone would make her despair, more than a little Marryatt there, not to mention — but shutting her eyes, she lets the gleam float through her lids. God have mercy, for the sins of the fathers and mothers too, and give us hope, even if it's pinned on things nobody will ever see.

When she looks, Robert's perched on a rock rimmed with weed, waving something. "Shit, Gran! This is kind of frout." Far out, wild, he means: good. It's a bottle, with nothing so quaint as a note inside. A glimmer from her childhood, walking the jetties with her dad. Skidding towards her, Robert holds it out. An antique, the kind milkmen used to deliver, and not even chipped! As she steadies herself, bending close, the stink makes her flinch. A host of creatures are lodged inside, periwinkles and barnacles laced with algae. Home, the way an empty shell shelters a hermit crab.

Already Robert's face shows disappointment, that restlessness creeping in. But as he hauls back, aiming his find towards the drop-off, she catches his wrist. "Wait, it's a souvenir — don't you see?" and he stops. A sullen patience lights his eyes, those eyes so like Jewel's, and almost tenderly, without answering, he wedges it between the rocks.

Acknowledgements

THANKS TO THE KINDRED, family and friends who gave support, especially those who read the novel in its various forms. Thanks, too, to the Canada Council for the Arts for its generous assistance, to Acadia University's Writer-in-Residence program and to Dr. Thomas Raddall Jr. Legions of others helped by sharing knowledge and expertise, whether on the nursing of stroke patients or playing the 'cordine, and thanks to all of them. Humbled by their perseverance, I'm most grateful to the Explosion survivors whose stories have appeared over the years in local newspapers, and in Janet Kitz's recordings of their accounts — I'm indebted to her for her book *Shattered City*. On a lighter note, thanks to Alma Chestnut Moore for the tips in *How to Clean Everything* (New York: Simon and Schuster, 1952). Finally, I thank my boys, my dad, my Aunt Elizabeth and my friends at St. Paul's for their inspiration, Marc Côté for his editorial brilliance, and Don Sedgwick, Shaun Bradley, Jane Buss, and, most of all, Bruce Erskine for being there, and Sheree, Cindy and Dawn Rae for their wisdom and encouragement. Finally, I would like to thank Joy O'Brien for sharing her Edmonds' Grounds photos.